'Margaret Catchpole, you have been found guilty of the crime of horse stealing. You will be taken from this place, back to the prison whence you came, and there to a place of execution, and there to be hanged by the neck until you are dead, and may God have mercy on your soul.'

For love of a sailor, turned smuggler, Margaret Catchpole, a law abiding, religious young woman, found herself condemned to death. Yet, she would live to be transported, for life, to the colony of New South Wales where she became servant, shopkeeper, midwife, heroine and a household name.

This is the story of an illiterate Suffolk maid who became a legend and has left us with one of the few convict accounts of life in the penal colony of New South Wales on the other side of the world.

Aileen Pluker. Born in Victoria, mother of four, with a passion for European and early Australian history. A teacher for over thirty years she took up writing in retirement. She has written two teenaged novels under her maiden name, Patricia Cunningham. Margaret Catchpole is Aileen's second adult novel.

MARGARET CATCHPOLE

AILEEN PLUKER

Cover Image:

View of Sydney, Port Jackson, NSW, taken from the Rocks on the
western side of the Cove, ca. 1803
drawn by John William Lancashire
Call No: DG SV1/60
Dixon Galleries, State Library of New South Wales

ISBN-13: 978-1519200709
ISBN-10: 1519200706

DEDICATION

For Catherine (Kitty) Brownbill

ACKNOWLEDGMENTS

My thanks goes to:
Isabel Storey and Rosemary Rendell for proofreading.
Mary Gudzenovs for publishing assistance.

Cover Image by John Lancashire, used with permission of Dixon Galleries, State Library of New South Wales.

William John Lancashire was sentenced in England on the 6th of April 1796 for seven years. His various occupations were draughtsman and painter. Crimes he committed in Sydney were mainly forgery. The last known record of him was in 1807.

PREFACE

When the Reverend R. Cobbold, a man whose family was closely involved with the life of Margaret Catchpole in England and who had access to many family letters and documents, wrote the story of her life, some thought it a fictitious account of the life of Mary Reiby (Raby) another convict who rose to prominence in the colony of New South Wales. Others claimed that no such person as Margaret Catchpole ever existed and that the Reverend's story was pure fiction.

But Margaret was not a figment of anyone's imagination. Her exploits are well documented in her native Suffolk. Her arrival on the ship *'NILE'* and her death in Richmond are recorded in official documents.

Reverend Cobbold's story contains well-documented evidence, supplied by real people, to substantiate his story, so there is no doubt that his is a true record of her life. If this is so, why then must we doubt his 'happy ending'?

Yet, if Margaret Catchpole became a happy wife and mother, then who is the spinster whose death is recorded in the register at St Peter's Church, Richmond?

This is an attempt to answer that question. It may not have happened this way, but there is no evidence to say that it didn't.

ENGLAND

1773 - 1801

All place names and the names of most of the characters have been taken from Rev. Richard Cobbold's book: *The History of Margaret Catchpole, A Suffolk Girl.*

CHAPTER ONE

Harvest time, and everyone was busy. Young Margaret was sent up to the big farmhouse for the mistress, Mrs Denton, needed extra help. As she hurried along the shady path, bordered with cow parsley, Margaret heard a scream coming from the house. She ran towards the kitchen garden as the shrieks were coming from there. She opened the gate just as Bessy, one of the housemaids, came rushing out, throwing her apron over her face and screaming, 'The Mistress... She's dead! The Mistress is dead!'

Margaret pushed past the distraught woman. Inside she found Mrs Denton lying unconscious on the floor and the other maid, Doris, standing over her, wringing her hands.

'Mistress dear! Oh dear God. Oh please no! Mistress!'

Bessy, following Margaret into the house, began wailing again. 'She's dead! What will we do? She's dead!'

Both servants were hysterical and incapable of rendering any assistance to the prostrate woman. Margaret was years younger than either of them but she immediately took control. She knew what her mother would have done if she were here.

'She's not dead. Stop your blubbering and lend a hand. Bessy, take off her bonnet and loosen her clothes. Doris, fetch some cold water, quickly.'

And miraculously they obeyed her.

Margaret dragged a chair towards the open door. 'Help me get her into the chair, Bessy.'

They struggled to lift their mistress. Though not plump, Mrs Denton was a dead weight. Doris, returning with a pitcher of water, set it on the table and assisted as they dragged and lifted the unconscious woman into the chair. She collapsed like a rag doll. Margaret grabbed the jug and began splashing water liberally to her face and chest, issuing more instructions as she did so.

'Bessy, get some vinegar. Sprinkle it on her lips. Doris, take off her shoes and stockings and start rubbing her feet. Try to get blood to flow back up towards her heart.' Margaret began to do the same with her mistress's arms. Soon the breathing became more normal and the blood began to flow back from the extremities When Margaret was convinced that her patient was recovering she stopped massaging.

'Doris, make some sweet black tea, very sweet. Bessy, you run across to harvest field and get Master. I'll go for Dr Stebbings.'

For the first time Bessy found her voice. 'How are you goin?'

'Never you mind. That's my problem. Just you go and get Master.'

Without another word the thirteen year old raced to the stables, unslipped the knot of the rope that tethered a pony to a rail and, with only a halter in her hands, sprang onto the back of the fiery little Suffolk Punch, dug in her heels, and was up the lane and onto the Ipswich road before Bessy was halfway across the first paddock.

People on the way to Ipswich market were amazed to see a Suffolk pony, speeding along the road, a young girl, skirts billowing and black hair streaming out behind, on its back.

Nothing seemed to check the speed of Margaret and her horse. She passed carts jogging to market and farmers walking along with baskets on their backs. She even passed a young farmer astride a well-bred horse. Astonished at being outpaced by such a common nag he stuck in his spurs and gave chase determined to outpace her. But the little pony, hearing the sound of hooves behind him, redoubled his effort so that Margaret was fairly flying.

It was Market Day in Ipswich and big carts, carrier vans and wagons lined one side, taking up more than half of the road, but the pony did not slacken. For Margaret, her mistress's wellbeing was all that mattered and nothing would be permitted to get in her way. Her urgency transferred itself to others and the people of the town followed them, anxious to know what the calamity was.

Margaret, unaware of anything around her, continued her dash. Not till she reached the doctor's door did she check her steed. Sliding off the horses back, but still clutching the halter, she rang the bell vigorously. By now the street was full of spectators all wanting to know what had transpired, but the child, oblivious of them, rang and rang, impatient until the doctor appeared.

'Oh Sir! Come! Please come and see my mistress. Please come!'

'My dear girl, what is the matter? Calm down and come inside. Tell me what all the fuss is about.'

Margaret, still intent on delivering her message, would have taken the pony in with her had not someone taken the rope. The door was not closed and people crowded into the passage, passing information back to the crowd outside.

'What's she saying?'

'What's the matter?

'Shut up and let me listen.'

'She's from Seven Hills.'

'Has there been accident?'

'It's Mistress Denton. '

'Is she dead?'

'Be quiet so I can hear.'

'The girl revived her.'

'What's the doctor saying?'

'Did she ride all the way from Seven Hills?'

'Yes.'

'Who is she?'

'She's Jonathan Catchpole's daughter.'

'She's Margaret Catchpole.'

'She's no more 'an a babe.'

'Here's the doctor.'

When Margaret emerged with the doctor everybody had some idea of what had happened. When they saw the girl they began clapping and cheering. This confused Margaret and she tried to hide behind the doctor. Dr Stebbings handed her into his gig, which he had had his man bring to the front of the house. The little pony was tied behind.

As they began to move, someone shouted, 'Three cheers for Margaret Catchpole' and the, 'Hip Hurrays' followed them out of town.

Safely away, Margaret turned back in her seat and looked at them. 'Why did they do that?'

'They think you were a very brave girl to ride so far.'

Margaret frowned. 'Well what else was I to do?'

She turned back and faced ahead, silent for some time. 'Doctor, do you think Master will be angry with me for taking pony?'

'I hardly think so Margaret.' replied the doctor.

'Will you tell him there were no other way? Will you beg him to forgive me?'

'I promise I will.'

The doctor smiled and looked anew at this remarkable young girl. He had already heard from her father that, when she set her mind to something, she was very single minded. Today he had seen an example of what the man was talking about. He wondered what her future would be.

Margaret was the fourth child, and second daughter, of Jonathan Catchpole, head ploughman at Denton's farm, and a respected member of the little community around Nacton. Jonathan was proud of all his children, Charles and Robert who worked on the farm with him. Susan who, although sickly, was an accomplished seamstress, and little Edward, for whom he had great hopes.

But he had a special fondness for Margaret. They shared a love of horses. From the time she was small, her job had been to take the lunches to the fields. She had been unafraid of the carthorses and was soon riding on their backs. She tried, when she could escape from her mother's eye, to go to the fields at the end of the day. There she was allowed to ride one of the horses home. He often wished that she had been born a boy for, with her ability with horses, she would have been able to become a groom at some large house, and her future would then be secure.

He was not at all surprised at her feat but, like her, was surprised at the amount of publicity her ride had generated. '

'They say now that the jockeys at Newmarket are talking about your ride,' he teased.

'Well I wish they'd stop. Everywhere I go, people talk. I don't even enjoy riding the horses any more. Why can't they stop?'

Jonathan was genuinely worried. He had noticed that she no longer came near the stables or rode any of the horses home.

'Don't worry, Peggy. People always need somethin' to talk about. They'll soon forget about you as soon as somethin' new happens.'

'Well I hope it happens quick.'

'Tell you what, Love, next week when I go to Ipswich, you can come with me. We'll arrive at a dignified pace in the wagon and you can see if you can find a pretty ribbon for the harvest festival.'

'Oh thank you, Da.' His daughter gave him a hug.

Ipswich, at the head of the Orwell River was, before all else, a port. From ancient times it was the export city for the cloth trade and when that declined it later became the centre of agricultural and manufacturing industries.

Jonathan enjoyed showing the many historic buildings to his delighted daughter. He was not an educated man but he was proud of his East Anglian heritage and knew the important part Ipswich had played in the history of England.

'Now this is Sparrow House though we folk call it The Ancient House. See the symbols on the front - Europe with a sceptre and a horn of plenty, that's because we produce all the best things and are masters of the world. That camel's head is for Asia. Of course you know what this is?' He pointed to a Red Indian head, complete with carved feather head-dress. 'That's for America. How do you like that one with the crocodile? That's for Africa.'

Margaret looked critically at them all. 'I like Africa best. But there's a new one now, isn't there?'

'Yes. Captain Cook found it and claimed it for England,' replied her father proudly.

'It must have been a long way away if nobody had found it before.'

'It's so far away that Lord Sydney wants to send all the bad people there, so they will not do us any harm.'

Margaret shuddered. 'What a terrible place it would be if it was full of bad people.'

But, interesting as the buildings were, Margaret was more interested in the people and the great variety of goods for sale. There were animals and produce stalls all mixed up together higgledy-piggledy. There were sailors and farmers, merchants and fishermen, women in coaches, women walking, children dressed in their best, sitting primly in handsome carriages with their wealthy parents. There were children on the footpath gazing into small, shop windows and urchins on the lookout for business, legal or illegal, anything to help them to survive

They walked down to the harbour to look at the vessels from many lands, vying for space, their masts rocking. Here, at close quarters, were those reckless men whom she had heard so much about, SAILORS. She wanted to see more of them but her father hurried her away, for he did not think them fit company for young girls.

'And don't you go talking to the likes of them when you get older.'

As he hurried her away she took sly looks at these men of the sea. She knew better than to quiz her father about them but later tackled her brother, Charles.

'Why did father say I should not speak to sailors, Charles?'

'Well nice girls don't.'

'Why?'

'Well they lead young women astray and then abandon them.'

'But I don't want to go with them. I just want to hear what one sounds like.'

'It ain't so much how they sounds as what they says.' her brother tried to explain

'Why? What do they say?'

'Don't know exactly but it seems to unsettle the girls, like.'

'Oh,' said Margaret, more curious than ever. 'Then you could come with me so that I could hear one without getting unsettled.'

'Ar' go on with ye□r,' he laughed ruffling her hair. 'There'll be plenty of time for that when you're older.'

'Why?'

'Just wait until you grow a bit and then you'll know.'

This answer was not satisfactory to Margaret but she knew she would get no better. She would just have to wait and keep her wits about her and find out, by herself, what it was that sailors said. But she thought that perhaps Charles was right. She would wait until she was a little older.

What neither Jonathan nor Charles had explained to Margaret was that, as far as the people of East Anglia were concerned, there were three types of men who sailed the seas.

First there were the Naval officers, many of whom came from the best of families and were the heroes of Britain.

Then there were those who sailed the ships. They were the paid weaklings who showed their strength only by leading young maidens away with their tales of far away places. They were shifty and reckless and not reliable like honest farmers.

Last were the smugglers. Smugglers, while they were successful, were brave unhampered thinkers, whose disposition precluded them from knuckling under to the oppressive regulations of an overbearing government. This opinion however changed dramatically if they were caught. Then they were evil villains robbing the country of much needed revenue. Hanging was too good for them.

*　　*　　*

Whether or not Margaret knew the niceties of these distinctions, it was certain that they were furthest from her mind on this day.

For it was Harvest Home. The last corn would be ceremoniously gathered in the field and taken, in royal procession, to the big farmhouse, where the Master, his wife, his children, and his servants would all provide the traditional banquet to the labourers and their families.

Margaret was one of the children who had been commandeered to collect wild flowers to decorate the entrance, the passage, and the great dining room where the festivities would be held. She had set off early, armed with a large wicker basket that her mother had made from supple, stripped willow. She always enjoyed being in the big farmhouse. It was an old building, and rumour had it that King Edward had once supped there, grateful for the owner's good Suffolk ale and delicious Suffolk meat.

She loved the richness of the old oak furniture, and the shiny, silver plate, which always stood on the great sideboard. All were polished to perfection for the big event. It gave Margaret a sense of belonging to another world, yet one in which she did not feel a stranger.

'Do you suppose the King really did have his supper here?' she enquired dreamily of her neighbour, Mrs Cracknell, who was in charge of the decorations.

'I don't know about the king or his supper, but I do know who'll be looking for his lunch. You'll be late in taking lunches to the field if you don't hurry. Ploughmen have to eat as well as kings.'

'I suppose so. But wouldn't it be grand if Farmer George came and sat at this table?'

'Farmer George indeed! Where did you learn such disrespect for your King? Still there are those who do say he knows more about farming than many who does do it. But never you mind. We'll not be seeing him in Suffolk, more's the pity. Now stop your prattling and get on with you.'

Margaret, with one backward glance at all the preparations, left the house, walked quickly through the kitchen garden and made straight for the hedgerow. There was one more ceremony she had to perform, but it was private. As she went swinging along she hummed the harvest song, unconsciously rehearsing for the afternoon chorus, her mind dwelling on the delicious food that would follow the ceremony. Margaret had never known want, but that did not stop her fantasising about the feast to come.

The breeze was soft, and puffed playfully around her face. Her heart was full of the joy of life.

Under the willows and through a shallow stream she went. She reached out and took a willow switch as she came to the other side, scrambled up the bank then headed towards the higher hawthorns in the hedgerow.

Here was what Margaret was seeking. She pressed through the branches and, sure enough, it was still there. Nobody else had found it. Right at the top were fronds of rich, creamy white honeysuckle. They were there every year and Margaret thought of them as her special blooms.

Bigger than the rest, the old vine had twisted its thick stem around the hawthorn and spilled its perfumed blossoms all over the green leaves. It reached its glory at the very top. This was the prize Margaret sought. It was better than all the rest. Each year she watched, from the time its first creamy tips appeared and judged, with practiced eye, its growth towards perfection.

She stood on the hot earth, still peering at the blossom, pleased that no one had already picked it. She stretched towards it but it was too high. She collected a few stones and placed them one on top of the other to make a little platform. She stood on her rickety structure and reached again for the bloom. Her platform was uneven and she began to wobble. She clutched the hawthorn to save herself from falling.

'Oh!' she yelled, licking her hand where a thorn had scratched her.

'Here. I'll get it for you,' said a voice from behind. The voice startled her and she was in serious danger of falling from her platform. Looking down she saw a tall, dark young man. This startled her even more, for she was sure that she knew everybody in the district, at least by sight.

He must be a STRANGER!

A quick thrill, half of fear, half of excitement, passed through her.

He held out his hand to her. She hesitated a moment then took it and jumped down.

'I was trying to get the honeysuckle,' she explained in a matter of fact way.

'I know. I was watching you,' came the laughing reply.

'Then why didn't you help me?' Margaret inquired. She knew that that was what she would have done.

'You looked so funny. I couldn't help watching to see if you would succeed.'

His reply seemed quite logical to her.

'That bunch is much too high for a girl.' The stranger found the scrutiny of this young girl disconcerting and wanted to establish his superiority. 'Do you want me to get it for you?'

Not waiting for her permission he pushed forward and by extending himself to the full he was able to reach the bloom. He snapped the stem, stepped back and presented it to her.

He made a slight bow. 'There you are.'

'Thank you very much,' she replied primly, surprised at her own formality.

'There's another one up there. Do you want me to get that too?'

'I only wanted this . . . ' She stopped short. How could she explain to a total stranger that it was only this bloom that was precious? How could she explain that she felt this same flower bloomed for her, year after year? She had never felt the need to put a rein on her thoughts before; but then she had never spoken to a stranger before. Perhaps, if she knew him better?

She watched as he stretched to get the other bloom. A bird suddenly darted out of the hedgerow. It flashed past his face and straight past Margaret. Startled though she was, she laughed indulgently. But he savagely swiped at the bird with his hat. He came out from the bush without getting the flower. He realised that the girl was looking at him in horror.

'I don't like swifts,' he said, by way of explanation, angry that he felt the need to explain.

'That's not a swift. That's a swallow. It weren't doing any harm. It were only looking for food.'

She could not imagine why the bird had annoyed him. She was going to tell him about the pair that nested each year in the barn, and how she and her brothers observed, without disturbing them, but she felt that the stranger would not be interested.

Margaret gave him a critical look. He's an odd one, she thought to herself. He sounded different. He even looked different. Most of the boys she knew were inclined to be short and stocky and many of them had coarse frizzy hair. He was tall and slim, like a foreigner, with his long, straight black hair. It looked soft and shiny. She thought that she would like to feel it. She blushed slightly at the thought. Truth to tell he had a curious charm, almost a kind of magnetism about him. She wanted to know him better, though she didn't know why. She felt the first stirrings of sexuality. She could not understand the feeling but it was not unpleasant She looked harder, trying to discover what it was that attracted her so.

Those steadfast brown eyes had a strange effect on him. He felt uneasy in the presence of this young girl, but he was adroit at avoiding uncomfortable situations by changing the subject.

'I bet I know who you are. You're Margaret Catchpole, the girl who rode the horse.'

Margaret was annoyed. First because he mentioned the ride but also because he knew her name but she didn't know his.

'Oh, that.' She tossed her head impatiently. 'Well, what's your name then?'

'Will Laud.'

Margaret said nothing. Even his name sounded different. It didn't have a homely sound, like Catchpole or Cracknell or Leader.

Will thought that she did not hear what he had said so, snatching a twig, squatted and began writing his name in the soft earth. He did it with great deliberation. He was very proud of his signature which he had practiced until it was perfect. He hoped the girl would be impressed, and she was. She squatted beside him and watched the stick, mesmerised.

'You can write!' she asked in wonder.

Will sat back on his heels and surveyed his handiwork with pride. 'Of course I can. Can't you? Then you can't read either. I'll show you.' Very carefully he read out his name, his finger tracing each letter as he spoke.

Margaret repeated the action, feeling magic in the grooves in the earth. She sat back and looked at Laud with new respect. Nobody in her family, not even her father, could read and write.

Well pleased with the impression he had made, Laud quickly changed the topic again in case she should ask him to write her name. He was not sure how well he could do it because, apart from his name, he could read and write very little. He had never regarded it as a great accomplishment.

'Well, you are the girl, aren't you?'

'So, what if I am?' Margaret was angry that he had returned to that topic. 'What would you have done? Walked I suppose?'

Laud thought a moment before answering. 'No. I'd have run.'

'Can't you ride a horse?'

She was surprised that he showed no shame to admit it. The boys she knew might not be able to write but they could all ride. Perhaps this stranger was not so special after all.

Unaware of the effect his revelation had made on her, Will went on, 'I don't like horses. They smell.'

'They do not!' Margaret was horrified. 'Well, at least Primrose don't smell. You'd never say that if you knowed her.'

'Is she really your horse?' It was his turn to be impressed now.

'No. It's not my horse. My father is head ploughman on Denton's farm and I'm allowed to ride the horses any time. My favourite is Primrose and she's the best horse in the world.' She felt sure she had regained Primrose's honour. 'What does your father do?'

'He's a ferryman. Down there,' and he pointed towards the river.

'Where, down there?'

'Down the Orwell at Felixtowe. He goes Landguard to Harwich.'

'Do you go with him?' Margaret's eyes shone with new respect for her new friend. He might not be able to ride a horse but he had seen more things than most of the boys she knew.

Laud swelled with pride. 'Of course I do. I help him with his work and I help him build boats. I'm going to be a sailor.'

Margaret stared, wide eyed.

Laud casually took a knife from his belt and picked up a tree root, deftly cut several strokes and presented his work to Margaret. Margaret was amazed to see the grinning face of an elf. It was like magic. No one she knew could have done that. She looked at his hands and noticed they were unlike her brother's large, rough, square ones. His were long, lean and brown.

'I like the sea,' Laud said drawing up his knees and wrapping his hands around them. 'Better than horses. You begin to smell like horses if you're around them all the time.'

Margaret was shocked. Her startled brown eyes searched his face. 'Do I smell like horses?'

Laud bent over her and took her by the shoulders dragging her towards him.

He sniffed her hair. 'No.' he decided. 'You smell of soap.'

Margaret was relieved. Willing to form an affinity with him she went on. 'I like the smell of the sea, but,' and here she had to be truthful, 'I don't like being on it.'

'Well, there you are. I like horses too I suppose, but I don't like being on them. It's all the same.'

Margaret didn't think it was, but she was happy that the little cloud of contention had been cleared from their relationship.

'What kind of smells do you like?'

'Oh, spices and perfumes, sausages and things like that.'

'What kind of spices?'

'The kind you have on buns and Christmas cakes.'

'We don't have spices. They're too dear. Mistress has them in pantry though. Do you have them often?'

'Of course we do.' He was enjoying impressing this

unsophisticated girl, but he was taken by surprise with the next question.

'Where do you get them from?'

There was a slight pause as Laud realised that he had unwittingly put himself in a compromising position. An angry look passed over his features. He had begun speaking to Margaret just to pass the time. He did not think she would be old enough for a little dalliance, but one never knew. Now he found himself within an inch of confessing that he sometimes did favours for smugglers and was suitably rewarded.

'From ships,' he said vaguely, and then, to get off this rather dangerous topic he asked. 'How old are you'

'Thirteen,' Margaret replied. 'Well, thirteen and seven months so I'm really almost fourteen. How old are you?'

'Seventeen,' he stated his age confidently, then caught her eye. 'Well I'm sixteen and five months.'

'That's nearer sixteen than seventeen,' she said giving judgment.

Laud was a little annoyed. 'Well, I'm older than you at any rate.'

Margaret studied him. 'That's true, but I don't think you've got more sense.'

There was a deathly silence. Margaret had only been stating what she felt was a fact. She could see that Laud didn't see it that way. He continued looking at her, a frown on his face. Then, like sunshine after rain, it disappeared as he burst out laughing at her audacity. She was certainly different from most girls he knew.

Margaret waited until the laughter stopped, then got up. 'I'm going home now.'

Laud got up too and grabbed her hand. He had stopped laughing and his face was dark, almost savage. Margaret, unimpressed by this display, wrenched her hand from his grasp and began walking purposefully towards her home.

Will was unused to having females walk out on him. He searched for some parting barb. 'Well, at least I can read.'

'That's true, but I can learn,' she replied with a toss of her head.

He absorbed this statement then laughing, all resentment gone, he hurried after her. He liked her spirit. He caught up and, grabbing her by the wrist, twisted her towards him.

'I like a girl with spirit,' he declared. 'You're the girl for me.'

'Indeed,' she replied coldly. 'And who would trust a sailor?'

A wistful look came into Will's eyes. His anger was gone. 'Who indeed?'

He dropped down on the ground again, drawing her gently with him. For some reason that Margaret could not explain she made no resistance. She was beginning to find the situation most unusual. He sighed deeply again, looking quizzically at her, trying to weigh her up.

'You might.'

Margaret forgot any vexation she had felt towards him. All she felt was a new sensation, an excitement, which stemmed from the fact that this young man seemed to belong to a race apart, and she had discovered him.

'I might,' she answered, after thought, hoping to herself that it might be true. He was good to look at and, in spite of his strangeness, she liked him. She was fascinated by him.

'But you'd have dozens of girls in dozens of places.' She remembered things that she had heard about sailors.

'True,' replied an amused Laud.

'And you'd be unfaithful to me,' she went on, remembering songs she had heard.

'Probably.' He was impressed by her seriousness.

Margaret looked at him intently. 'But would you love them as much as you loved me?'

'No.'

And for some reason Will knew that he was telling the truth.

'Very well then, we can become betrothed.' Margaret wasn't quite sure what the word really meant, but she knew it was the right one to use in this situation. She was quite pleased that things were progressing so satisfactorily.

However, Laud's feelings were of total confusion. What was going on here? He had begun his acquaintance with Margaret out of curiosity - to pass a pleasant hour while waiting for a friend. A little conversation, perhaps gleaning information that he could pass on for gain, perhaps a little kiss and cuddle, but certainly not anything more serious than that.

Now, here was this girl, a mere child, bold as brass, declaring that they were betrothed. Even if it was meant as a joke he wanted no part of it. He stood up and stretched to his full height, intending to give her a piece of his mind, but the steady, brown eyes caused him to pause.

What was this girl about? Her countenance and words bespoke of an innocence of one even younger than her years, yet there was an underlying fire, which belonged to someone much older. He felt a kinship with her. She did not fit her situation any more than he did. Somehow he knew that she suffered from the same strangeness that he did. They were both born out of time, out of place.

They belonged together.

A cloud lifted from his mind. Surely here was his soul mate. Why shouldn't he ally himself with this spirited girl? He laughed and held out his hand.

'Yes. We shall be betrothed. Now we must do something to mark the event.'

'What do people usually do?'

Will thought. 'Let me see . . . I know. They pledge their . . . er . . . fidelity and then exchange tokens.'

'What kind of tokens?' enquired the amazed girl.

'Well, usually a jewel, a ring or something like that.'

They looked at each other and grinned. Neither of them had ever owned a single jewel, but Laud was equal to the task.

'Here,' he said grandly, twisting a button from his jacket. 'You shall have this button as a token of my fidelity.'

Margaret reached up and received the button reverently.

'But what can I give?' Then she looked at the bloom in her hand. 'I know. I'll give you my honeysuckle.'

As graciously as any lady bestowing a favor on her knight she presented Will with the flower, the cause of their meeting.

Just as respectfully, Will accepted it, twisting it around, admiring its colour and perfume.

'That's not the end of the ceremony,' he laughed mischievously 'The bargain has to be sealed with a kiss.'

'Ohh!'

Margaret's mouth formed a perfect circle and her eyes filled with doubt. She felt it was the right thing to do in the circumstances but kissing was something she had had little practice at. It was not an activity often performed in the Catchpole family except towards babies.

Her puzzled look had a strange effect on Will. He had intended giving her a long, loving embrace. But instead delivered a chaste kiss on the forehead.

Margaret stood on tiptoe, indicated for him to lower his head and did the same.

The sincerity of her action quite unmanned him. He had to turn aside and brush away a tear that threatened to fall from his eye.

Margaret missed the moment, her mind on practical things. 'When will I see you again?'

Surprised at the new feeling inside, Will replied seriously. 'When you are older. Then I will come and claim you. You are mine, Margaret Catchpole, and don't you forget it.'

The last words were said aggressively for suddenly he meant it. Margaret was his and he never surrendered willingly anything that was his. He put the honeysuckle in the band of his hat, then put it back on his head.

Satisfied that all the formalities had been performed, Margaret remembered her duties. 'I'll go now. I have to take my father's lunch to the field.'

Laud was shocked that his open declaration had been dismissed so casually. He grabbed her around the waist, drew her towards him and kissed her savagely, crushing her pretty mouth against his teeth. He felt Margaret go limp in his arms and he knew that at that moment he had complete power over her.

He let her go and she stood there dazed.

He turned suddenly and began striding towards the nearby wood. It took him some time to get his emotions under control.

Then he turned and looked back at Margaret who was standing just as he had left her.

He raised his hand in farewell and was delighted to see that the hand she raised was clenched tightly, holding the button as if it was for her very life. Suddenly a surge of joy filled him.

She was his!

He continued on his way, singing a nautical tune, happier than he had ever been in his life.

CHAPTER TWO

Margaret watched until Will had disappeared from sight then, coming out of her daze, she remembered that she still hadn't taken the lunches to the field. She raced across the fields and through the stand of trees.

Anyone seeing her would have thought that she was trying to repeat, on foot, what she had already accomplished on horseback. Her feet had wings and the movement suited exactly the elation she felt as, hair streaming out behind and skirts billowing, she sped towards the cottage.

At another time her arrival, red faced and breathless, would have earned a scolding from her mother, but, thinking she had been detained at the farm house, Elizabeth was pleased that Margaret had made such speed home.

When she arrived late to the field where her father and brothers were working they did not chastise her for her for it. They knew how much there was to be done on festival day. They were going to finish early so that they would be time for everybody to be scrubbed and dressed in their Sunday best for the big occasion.

Margaret sat with them and shared their lunch, talking excitedly about the preparations and food. She waited until they were finished then, with much banter and laughter, they headed for home. Margaret, sitting on Primrose, bent low and whispered her secret in the horse's ear. Primrose pricked up her ears and snorted, as if in reply. Riding home, Margaret sang the harvest song at the top of her voice and her brothers joined in.

Jonathan, watching her, wondered what her reaction would be when given the news that, thanks to Dr Stebbings, a position had been secured for her at Great Bealing. She would be leaving as soon as the harvest was over. It was a great opportunity for her. She would be well trained, which would give her a key to a secure future.

The girl herself did not know that her time at home was over. Elizabeth had decided to tell her after Harvest Home.

Jonathan and his sons headed for the pump to wash away the worst of the soil from their faces and necks before subjecting themselves to a full emersion in a steaming tub. Edward joined his sister in the stable to prepare Primrose, for she had an important part to play in the festival. She was fed, then curried and combed until her chestnut coat and silver mane shone like velvet. Her blinkers had been hung with ribbons and flowers, her mane was dressed into knots with corn stalk fans and her tail was bound in a large knot.

When everything was done Margaret stepped back to survey their work. 'Prim, you look magnificent,' she declared.

The horse stood proudly. A veteran of Harvest Homes, she was completely unfazed by the ordeal ahead. Ribbons, flags, flowers and noisy children running everywhere worried her not one jot. She lowered her head to touch Margaret's outstretched hand. An action performed almost daily, it now caused Margaret to ponder. The hot breath and velvet mouth reminded her of another kiss received earlier in the day.

A shadow of doubt passed over her happiness. Prim's kiss spoke of love and devotion but what of the other one?

She shook herself to dispel this concern. Time enough to worry about it when she was older. For now she would glory in her first experience of romance. Let the future take care of itself. She pressed her lips to Primrose's nose and was conscious of the smell that Laud had spoken about. What was wrong with it? It was the grandest smell in all the world.

She stood back and let Edward take the bridle. He was already dressed and was to take the horse over to Cracknell's cottage. Catherine, the eldest daughter, had been chosen as this year's queen, and it was their responsibility to decorate the cart. Edward would walk the horse taking care not to speed in case she should sweat and spoil the shine.

Margaret watched them clatter over the stones in the stable yard. Then she raised her hands to her nose and sniffed. Yes. They did smell of horse. She hurried to the cottage where she hoped the men folk had finished their ablutions so that she could give time to her own toilet.

Perhaps Mam would let her use some of her violet toilet water.

As she neared the big farm house Margaret could hear people gathering in the field, the shouts of children, the occasional scrape of the fiddlers as the players tuned up and the barking of dogs, for even dogs came to Harvest Home, looking important in polished collars, bespeckled with flowers.

She hurried through the trees, but her mother walked slowly along the path with 'poor Susan' who, for once, was well enough to at least be a spectator at the gathering.

Margaret was flushed with excitement. Though approaching womanhood she was still child enough to take part in childish ceremonies.

She stood for a moment, taking in the scene; the women in their colourful skirts and paisley shawls, their hats bedecked with ribbons, the young men, with hair slicked down and white shirts gleaming in the fading light.

The last of the corn had been reaped and the farm wagons, decorated for the occasion, stood ready. In the centre was a special East Anglia farm cart. The thick timber, elaborately carved, had been polished till it shone. Entwined in the big wheels were stalks of corn and wild flowers. Long fronds of willow, tied with ribbons were draped from the sides. Flags and ribbons decorated the shafts and harness. Primrose stood between the shafts waiting for the ceremony to begin.

Enthroned on the cart was the Corn Baby. Its arms and legs were made of straw and tied with ribbons. A floral crown was on its head and its arms were sheathed in long, flowing, lawn sleeves. Flowers and garlands almost covered it.

Margaret looked at all the preparations and gave a nod of satisfaction.

Everything was as it should be.

The harvest festival preceded Christianity by many centuries but these good Christian people saw no paradox in celebrating this pagan feast. They knew that all good things came from God, as their minister often reminded them, but it was the Corn Baby who would ensure next year's harvest.

Laughing, Margaret joined the group of girls whose duty it was to choose the Harvest Queen, while the boys chose her Special Attendant. Of course everybody knew who the couple would be. The Harvest Queen, having already been chosen, had the privilege of choosing her attendant, often a young man who was courting her. Catherine was already engaged to Peter Ramsey so he was her choice.

Each group circled the chosen one then, taking each by the hand, snaked along to join the other. Depositing the Queen and her Attendant in the centre they formed a circle and danced around them singing The Farmer's Song.

It culminated in the farmer taking a wife, sealing the bargain with a kiss and a reed ring.

As Margaret danced she watched Catherine, beautiful in her flowing white dress, smile at the young man by her side. She sensed the secret understanding that seemed to pass between them.

The gentle kiss bestowed by the attendant did not cause her any anxiety, only a happy contentment that one day this would all be hers. One day soon, she would be Harvest Queen and Will would be her attendant. After all, weren't they already betrothed?

The circle broke and the attendant took his queen's hand and led her towards Jonathan Catchpole, who, as head ploughman, had the privilege to bestow on the Harvest Queen, a garland of wild flowers. Then, taking the bridle, they walked, either side of the horse, in procession with the cart bearing the Corn Baby, towards the far yard. Primrose walked with dignity. This was her moment.

Farmer Denton and his wife were waiting beside a bonfire carefully prepared by some of the labourers. The rest of the assembly lined up behind them singing the harvest song, the men adding their deeper voices to the children's chorus.

> *We have ploughed. We have sown.*
> *We have reaped. We have mown.*
> *We have brought home every load.*
> *Hip Hip Hurray! Harvest Home.*

When the procession reached the bonfire it stopped. The Corn Baby was lifted down and placed on top of the pile. Margaret watched as Catherine performed her special duty, for she was to light the bonfire. She was handed a lighted taper and very carefully she put it to the kindling at the base.

This was the most important moment. Margaret held her breath. She knew that if the fire didn't immediately take, then their offering had been rejected and next year's harvest would be a disaster.

But no such omen was seen that year. The kindling caught and, as the flames spread, a mighty cheer went up from master and man, mistress and maid, farm labourers and nearby villagers.

Then, one and all, they began to dance to the fiddlers' tunes. On this night there was no social bar. The master danced with the maids, his wife danced with the groom, villagers danced with farming folk and everyone rejoiced that another year's labour had been successfully completed.

The part that Margaret liked best followed. Mistress Denton, completely recovered from her recent illness, invited everyone into the big dining room to partake of the food that had been lovingly prepared

Later in the evening, replete with food, Margaret sat back and watched as some of the young men, having consumed large quantities of good Suffolk ale began to lose their reserve. They sang riotous songs, played tricks on their neighbours, and tried their chances with likely lasses. There was nothing in the world she wanted more than this.

Then a shadow passed over her happy thoughts and she gave a little shudder. This was all she wanted, but what about Will?

*   *   *

Margaret planned her happy future that night but with the morning came news that she was to leave her home.

'I don't want to go Mam,' sobbed the young girl

'Margaret, don't you realise the opportunity Dr Stebbins has obtained for you? You must know that for a cottage girl to be employed in a great house is an honour. You will be trained in all manner of skills. You might even be lucky enough to become a lady's maid.'

'Mam I'm grateful to Dr Stebbins for finding me this place, but I don't want to go away from home,' Margaret pleaded.

'Silly goose. Every girl has to leave home sooner or later. That's a woman's lot. You will be permitted to visit us often and we can always send you a message if something important happens.'

'What about Susan? Will I be able to come home if she gets worse?'

'God is good and she may have years yet, but if anything happens I will send for you.'

'Do you promise? I will only go happy if you do.' Then to her sister, 'When you get really sick, Susan I want to come home and nurse you.'

'And so you shall,' promised Susan, trying, for her sister's sake to appear well. 'I want you to go Peggy. It will be good for you. You've learnt everything you can here. You need a bigger world for all your energies.'

Margaret dried her eyes and they talked about her future.

Great Bealing was one of the largest houses in the district. Margaret began to feel that she might enjoy the experience after all. She knew she was a good worker so she had no fears on that score. She would be meeting new people and seeing new sights. With Susan's positive suggestions she began to feel quite happy about this new turn of events.

However, when the day came that she was to leave, all her sorrow returned. She found it very hard to say goodbye, especially to Susan. The two girls embraced once more. Margaret's tears were uncontrollable.

'Hush little sister,' Susan soothed. 'We are all in God's hands. Mind you be a good girl and do your duties well. I want to hear good reports of you. Now dry your eyes and say goodbye to the rest of the family.'

'Only promise me,' Margaret said, trying to stem her tears, 'only promise that, should you get worse, you will make them send for me. I don't want anyone else to nurse you.'

'I have made Da promise that one of the boys will go over once a week and give you a report of all that is going on. When I need you I will send for you. Now smile and make me happy.'

Margaret did the best she could but the kisses and best wishes of parents and brothers brought more tears and she left red eyed and despondent.

Her Uncle Leader had come to take her in his cart. She was silent for the first part of the journey but the good man worked hard to cheer her up. He owned a shop not far from Bealin and knew many of the people who worked there. He told her little anecdotes about them and about her employers, the Southgates.

By the time they turned into the shaded driveway that led to the house she was feeling quite cheerful.

Because of her celebrity, Mr Nicholas Southgate felt he should meet her himself. His wife was a little apprehensive that the new dairymaid's head might be so full of horses that she would not keep her mind on her work. If it had not been for Dr Stebbins strong recommendation she would not have employed her at all.

Nicholas looked at the thin, young girl and wondered that she had had the strength to accomplished such a feat.

'So Margaret, they tell me that you are quite a horse woman.'

'Oh! Please Sir,' Margaret implored. 'Don't mention the ride.

People make such a fuss about it but it was no great thing to do. I beg you not to mention it to anyone in the house.'

Nicholas smiled at this simple request. The child did not seem to realise that her reputation was already known to everyone. However the reply pleased him. She certainly wouldn't be one to seek the limelight.

Margaret began her new life as one of the many servants in the great house. Because she was a dairymaid she held a rather lowly position on the social structure but, to a cottage girl, her new life seemed a wonderful change. She was up with the larks each morning and worked happily, endearing herself to her fellow workers. Though slight in build, she was strong and willing. No duty was too much for her. As a consequence the reputation that had preceded her was enhanced.

During this time she grew to womanhood. Though slimmer than most of her peers she reached her full height of about five foot three. She was not what, at the time, would have been classed as a beauty but her appearance had a striking quality that made her noticeable.

Margaret worked happily at Great Bealing for two years and would have remained had not it been for the dreaded news that poor Susan's condition had deteriorated and Margaret was needed at home to nurse her.

*   *   *

At home, Margaret spent her time tending to her sister's needs, spending hours at her bedside, for Susan was now bedridden. It was then that Margaret wished that she could read so that she could help pass the long hours for her sister. She racked her brain trying to think of incidents from her life at Bearing to amuse Susan.

'Margaret,' Susan enquired one day. 'In all the tales you tell me you never mention any likely young man who took your fancy. Surely there was one? I'm sure you must have attracted many beaus.'

'I didn't give it much thought,' she admitted then added mischievously. 'But then, I am already betrothed.'

'What!' exclaimed Susan in astonishment.

Margaret laughed. 'It was only childish nonsense,' and proceeded to tell the whole story of her meeting with Will. 'I took it very seriously for a time. I even wore his button on a ribbon around my neck. But it was all ages ago. I doubt Will Laud would even remember me now.'

'And you?'

'Oh, I had almost forgotten all about it. I can't really remember what he looks like now.' But this was only a half-truth. There were nights when she would play over in her mind the whole incident and at those times she could remember him very clearly.

*　　*　　*

At the time that Margaret started at Great Bealing, Will Laud had begun his new career also. The day he met Margaret he was on his way to see a Captain Bargood who had offered him a berth. Will first approached his uncle, to whom he had been apprenticed, telling him of the offer that had been made.

'Will lad, if you were my own boy I would wish that you would stick at boat building, but I can see your love is for the sea. From what I have heard you have a natural talent for it. But you must think of your father. Poor Nicholas has been mother and father to you for years. He would not take kindly to you changing his plans for you. I will give you time off to visit him. If you can persuade him, then I will let you go; though sorry I'll be to lose you. However I know, with young people nowadays, if their heart's not in their work they never prosper in it. Now mind you get permission from your Dad.'

Will hurried back to Felixstow. At first Nicholas was angry and disappointed, but he also could see the possibilities that could open up for Will.

'You speak well of this captain, and his offer seems a good

one. However I have made enquires and although, on the whole, his reputation seems good, yet I have heard rumors that he has friends who will help him run a cargo of moonshine now and then. I know that many regard this as a virtue, but Will, it is against the law. I have always brought you up to respect the King's laws and I, myself, am a King's man, carrying letters to the fort.'

Will was shocked at his father's words. 'Father, I have never heard anything of this. Whenever I have been with him I have never seen any suspicious characters.'

A memory of a ruffian he had seen at Ipswich, talking to the captain, flashed into his mind, but he dismissed it.

'Captain Bargood is held in high esteem by everyone. Anyway, no one could ever persuade me to become involved in that work. I am a King's man too and I hope that I can prove to be an honest tar.'

'I hope so. I really hope so.'

'Don't be afraid Father. You have schooled me too well to ever let me disgrace you.'

'Then there is no more to be said. You always had your own mind and I will not stand in your way. I see I cannot persuade you, so I will give you my blessing. Only promise me that you will never become involved in unlawful acts. If you find yourself unintentionally involved, you will leave his service forthwith.'

So Will got his wish. Captain Bargood took him into service on his own vessel and was pleased that he had not been mistaken in the lad. He gave him special attention and cultivated a friendship with the boy, relying on the hope that the loyalty he cultivated would be returned. For he had plans for Will Laud.

Captain Bargood owned seven ships. Four of them, at all times, were engaged in legitimate trade, reporting to customs all cargoes. This was his bread and butter. But the other three were often engaged in more dubious enterprises. It was these which provided the cream.

The business of successful smuggling required a network of

helpers, trustworthy sailors, who knew all the secret estuaries and beaches along the coast, landsmen, who knew their way in the dark about the country as well as sailors knew their seas, traders, who knew how to dispose of the contraband, and spies, who spent their time keeping check on the coast guard and were ready with their secret signals to warn of danger.

Finally there were the farmers and gentry who, though they took no part in the trade themselves never complained when horses or carts were used without permission. They knew that shortly after a keg of Holland gin, a packet of tobacco or some other acceptable trifle would mysteriously appear at their door.

Will loved his work at sea. He sailed to all the ports along the coast and many times to Holland and Portugal, once even to the Ivory Coast. He revelled in the strangeness, the excitement, the danger but most of all the companionship.

It was not long before he realised that what his father had said was true. The good Captain was indeed involved in 'the game' but as Will was never asked to participate he felt he had not broken his promise. Even when called on to assist in a rescue of sailors whose plans had gone awry he saw no inconsistency. He secretly envied them their adventures, for he loved the taste of danger.

Little by little he was being lured into the smuggler's web.

*   *   *

'I'm sure you will be welcome.'

Nicholas was delighted that he would have an opportunity to show off his handsome son. 'But you will have to keep a wary eye on James. Two of his daughters are of marriageable age and the old rogue will be on the look out for a likely catch like you.'

'As a matter of fact it is for the sake of a young lass that I wish to go, but it's not one of the Cracknell girls. I'm interested in Margaret Catchpole.'

'Ah, the girl who rode the horse. You've heard of her?'

'I've more than heard of her. I'm betrothed to her.'

'What!'

'Don't fret Father. It's just some foolish act of childhood. But I wouldn't mind getting a look at my 'beloved' again. Maybe she might be the one for me, after all.'

'Well her family lives on the same farm as James so, if she is not in service, you may see what kind of lady she has grown into. Of course she may already be spoken for.'

'She'd better not have taken up with anyone else without my permission.' Will laughed. But a darker thought belied his smiling countenance. Though he had hardly given her a thought over the years, Margaret was his.

The Catchpoles and the Cracknells were the two families that principally worked the Denton land. Their houses were quite a distance apart. While the Catchpoles lived at the lane leading up to the farmhouse, the Cracknell's cottage was situated near the street on the way to Nactor. Nevertheless the two families were often in each other's cottages. Mrs Cracknell, an enterprising soul, had converted the front room of her cottage into a little shop. She made many of the goods herself and bought others in bulk in Ipswich, then sold them in ones and twos. In this way she provided a service to those who did not have the time to go to town as well as supplementing her husband's income.

Susan Catchpole and Catherine Cracknell had been bosom friends all their lives. Had Susan been well she would have been godmother to Catherine's first child. But she was now bedridden so Margaret was asked to perform the duty.

When the Lauds arrived at the church the ceremony had already commenced so Will had the opportunity to observe Margaret without her being aware of it. He was delighted with what he saw; a slim young woman, of average height with black curls creeping from her bonnet. Her features were delicately shaped with soft, red lips and dark sweeping eyelashes. He could not see, but could imagine the intense, brown eyes of memory that they shaded. She seemed at ease with her duties and her responses were given in a low, melodious voice.

Will felt his heart beat a little faster. She was all that he remembered and more. He stood in the shadows anticipating her reaction when he revealed himself. A shiver of uncertainty ran through him. He knew he had nothing to fear from his appearance; too many women had already assured him of that. But what if, in the years that had passed, she had found another love? He became nervous at the possibility that he may have lost her.

The ceremony over, Nicholas moved towards the group gathered around the font. Will followed him, feeling like an awkward boy again. James proudly began to introduce his relatives.

Margaret had handed the baby back to its mother and turned to be introduced to the stranger when her eyes fell on Will. For one moment she hesitated, in doubt, but the smiling eyes that challenged hers set her heart aflutter. She could feel a blush spreading over her cheeks and she had difficulty breathing.

James, in the process of introduction, realised that there was something strange going on. It was as if some invisible spell held them, eye linked with eye.

Then Will broke the spell.

'Well Margaret, I hope you have kept your promise.'

'Will!' It was all that Margaret could manage.

Nicholas turned to the bewildered Jonathan. 'I believe our children know each other.'

Everybody began to talk at once. Will explained how he had met Margaret and Jonathan remarked on the coincidence.

James, bursting with pride that it was a relative of his who was the one to disturb Margaret's composure, invited everyone to come back to his cottage for the celebration.

The walk was not long but Margaret and Will contrived to fall behind. Everyone else conspired to assist them. When they were a decent distance from the others Will stopped and, taking Margaret's hand, turned her to face him.

'You haven't answered my question yet. Have you remained true to me?'

There was no guile in Margaret's answer. 'Will, I never thought you would still be thinking of me. Yes, I have been true.'

'Margaret, my dearest girl, wherever I travelled, you have always been in my heart. Didn't I say I would be back?'

He drew her close to him and imparted a long, loving kiss on her lips.

Margaret thought she would melt away. She placed her hand on Will's shoulder for support and nestled into his breast. He raised her chin with his fingers and kissed her again, a teasing kiss this time. He felt supremely confident now.

'Ah, Margaret. What a clever fellow I was, to snare you so young, elsewise you would surely have been spoken for by now and I would have had to fight a bloody battle for your hand.'

Margaret, recovering her composure, joined in the banter. 'I see you did become a sailor. Do you remember you boasted that you would have dozens of girls? Is it so Will?'

'Not dozens, but a few, I must confess. But then I was only waiting for you to grow up.'

'And will you break my heart?'

'Never! Now that I have found you again there will never be another woman in my life.'

At that moment Will believed every word he said.

'And now that I am grown?' Margaret enquired, anticipating the answer.

'Well, we'd better do something about it.' Then formally, 'Margaret may I ask your father for your hand?'

'You already have it.' She laughed because he was still holding it. 'But wait a little until they get to know you. Let's hurry and catch up so that they can meet you properly, but I must warn you that people around here have a very low opinion of sailors.'

And holding hands and laughing they ran towards the cottage.

It was arranged that Will would spend the rest of his leave with the Cracknells, but he spent most of his time with the Catchpoles. Will had a natural charm and when he really tried few could resist him. He went out of his way to please each member in turn.

He had a head start with Elizabeth. When she learned that his mother had died early she took him to her heart. He complimented her on her cooking and helped with little jobs like chopping wood and fetching water. He won Edward with his tales of the high seas and his whittling. The other two Catchpole boys enjoyed his stories too, especially Charles, who found farm life boring and longed to see more of the world.

He and Will became great friends. Charles confessed his frustration with his mundane farm life.

'I know what you mean,' Will agreed. 'I felt the same way when I was working for my uncle. I knew it was the sea I wanted and that I would never be happy as a boat builder. Why don't you join me? I'm sure I can get you a berth.'

'No thanks. The sea doesn't hold any appeal for me. It's the army I'm interested in. It's not the uniform. I want to be part of our growing empire, go to strange and exotic places and plant the flag on foreign lands. It fills me with excitement just to think of it.'

'If you really feel that way Charles, then do it. Once you get a desire like that you will never be happy on a farm.'

'You're right. Next time the recruiting officers are in Ipswich I'm going to accept the King's shilling. I'll just go and do it and tell the family afterwards. But keep my secret, Will. If Da' gets a whiff of it he'll talk me out of it, for sure.'

'Don't worry. I don't want to be accused of leading you astray.'

'It was not you. I've been thinking of it for a long time. You have just given me the courage to do it.'
Will tried a different tack with Jonathan. He did not try to impress him but instead, listened patiently as Jonathan explained the problems of farming. He asked questions that gave Jonathan a chance to air his knowledge.

The whole Catchpole family was enthralled with Will. All except one, Susan. He resented the time Margaret spent with her sister, but he tried to entertain her because he knew how much Margaret loved her.

Will soon realised that his best efforts had not impressed Susan. Unused to failure he put it down to jealousy, but that was not an emotion that existed in Susan's generous nature. She knew how much Margaret loved him and tried very hard to like him for her sister's sake. She could not put her finger on the trouble, but she felt that, one way or another, Will would break Margaret's heart. He quite obviously cared for her, but not, she feared, as well as he cared for himself.

By the time Will had to go back to sea it was accepted that Will would become Margaret's husband. It was only a matter of time. On the last evening they were given privacy for their leave taking.

'I know leaving is part of a sailor's life, but Will, I find it so hard.'

'I never have felt less like leaving myself, Peg. Would you have me leave the sea?'

'I would never ask you to do anything against your desire. I suppose it will just be something I will have to get used to.'

'Maybe you won't. If I could get my own ship, and Captain Bargood has hinted that I might, then you can come and live on board with me.'

'No Will. I don't think I'd like that. I love my home and Mother needs me, especially since poor Susan is so ill. Let it go for now. Let's not spend our last night worrying about the future. Let's just enjoy what we have.'

They sat beneath an old, spreading oak tree and kissed as lovers do. Will would have wished his loving could have been more fulfilling but he sensed that Margaret would reject too close an intimacy. He respected this. He was, in fact, proud of it. He might happily frolic with other women but he knew, deep in his heart, that he wanted his wife to come pure and virginal to the altar.

CHAPTER THREE

The next three months were perhaps the happiest of Margaret's life. She kept herself busy helping her mother and caring for Susan. She was content in her love for Will and pleased that the family thought so well of him. Will managed several coastal trips, so his absences were not long.

He was anxious that they take the next step and marry, but the circumstances were not right. Will did not have a house to take her to and she was needed at home while Susan lived. So they had to be content to enjoy the day and dream of the future.

During one visit Will mentioned that he felt Susan did not care for him. This disturbed Margaret, as she wanted everyone to love him as she did. She denied the suggestion but, after he had gone, she confronted her sister.

'Susan, Will feels that you do not like him. Say it is not so.'

'It is not that I do not like him as a person, but I doubt he will make you happy Peg.'

Margaret was surprised and hurt by this answer. 'How can you say such a thing? Will loves me dearly and is always doing things to make me happy. He has good employment and will be able to provide for me. What could you possibly find that is wrong with him?'

'Peggy, I don't want to upset you. It may be only an old maid's premonition, but I fear that life will end sadly for Will Laud. He is too fond of adventure and, please do not be hurt, of himself. He is not as serious as I would like. But then, what would I know about men? I have hardly left this cottage for years and I will never have a love of my own.'

'Dear Susan, don't be sad.' Any anger she had felt about Susan's criticism of Will was gone. What she said was quite true.

There was no sense in denying it. Her beautiful sister would never experience the happiness she now had. She would gladly have traded a little of it to give her sister a chance at real life. But there was nothing she could do except be the best sister she could for Susan while she was still with them.

'I'm not sad Peggy. I have long come to terms with my fate. My only sorrow will be the sadness my leaving will give you all. Let me say one thing and then we will leave the topic forever. I want you to promise me something.'

'Anything,' Margaret cried passionately. 'You know I couldn't deny you anything.'

'Don't be too quick to promise before you know what it is. I want you to promise me that you will not give yourself to Will before you are married.'

'Susan!' Margaret was shocked. 'How could you say such a thing? You know how well our parents have brought us up. I would never do anything to disgrace them.'

'Hush! I dare say every maid thinks that way, but men can be very seductive and love has turned the heads of many. Why else would there be so many songs about abandoned maidens? Will is a man, with a man's wants and he can be very persuasive. There will come a time when he will want you, wed or not, and you, with your loving nature will find it hard to resist.'

She placed her hand on Margaret's arm. 'Don't protest, it's a natural feeling after all, else the human race would have died out long ago. Accept that you are going to face this circumstance. All I ask is that, when the time comes, you think of me and desist.'

Margaret fell to her knees and took her sister's hand.

'I'll gladly promise and I'll keep it no matter what the temptation. But you must believe that it will not be necessary. Will respects me and will restrain himself until our wedding day.'

'Then kiss me to seal the pact and we will say no more.' Margaret realised, as she embraced Susan, how frail she had become. She knew without being told that her sister would soon be gone. This made her all the more determined to keep her promise.

*   *   *

The happy interlude did not last. The first sadness came when Charles fulfilled his dream. Having heard that recruiting was going on in Ipswich, he contrived to go there and sign up. Having made his mark, he had no time to go home and break the news to his parents. Because he could not write and because they could not read he could not let them know the reason for his absence.

His non-return caused great consternation in the family. After three days Jonathan took himself off to Ipswich to find out what had happened to his son. It took him two days to discover that his eldest son was now a member of His Majesty's Army.

Soon after an official letter was sent to Mr Denton who relayed the information that, not only was Charles in the army, but that he was on the high seas on his way to India to help keep that British possession safe from warring factions and from the French.

The next sadness, though expected, nevertheless caused great grieving in the family. Susan began to slip away before their eyes. Margaret and Elisabeth kept constant vigil and the rest of the family went about their duties, but their thoughts were constantly in the sick room.

Susan made her peace with her God and her thoughts turned towards heaven and she assured everyone that she was happy, her only sorrow the grief that her going would give to her family.

One early evening she whispered to Margaret, 'Call the family I fear my time is here.' She raised herself on Margaret's arm while the grieving members of the family took their farewell of her.

'Let me pray for you all,' whispered the dying girl. 'May God bless each of you and keep you from harm.'

She lay back, resting for a time, her gentle breathing the only sign that there was still life. Then she seemed to revive. She became quite agitated. The bedclothes rose and fell with the effort of turning herself half around to face Margaret.

She groaned, with what little power she had left. 'Margaret! Margaret!'

'Hush,' her sister soothed, 'I'm here. I won't leave you. Just hold my hand.'

Susan rested, husbanding what little strength she had to deliver her last warning. Margaret leant close to hear the words from her sisters dying lips.

'Margaret, Will Laud, he will break your heart. Do not let him lead you astray. Never break your promise to me.'

'I never will,' sobbed the distraught girl.

'Bless you, dearest sister,' Susan whispered. Then raising herself again. 'And God bless you all.'

She raised one hand, as if in benediction. Then, with a slight shudder her spirit took flight to eternity.

The family had believed that they were well prepared, but the loss of such a gentle soul left them bereft. Jonathan and Robert, though outwardly composed, found conversation difficult and would pause in mid sentence having forgotten what they were saying. They were glad that work provided them with a routine and something to distract their minds. Edward was still a boy and could give way to grief. He felt no shame in tears. Elizabeth, whose heart was broken at the loss of her beloved daughter, suffered doubly because she had no way of passing on the sad news to her eldest son.

Margaret was outwardly calm and it was to her that most of the duties fell in the first couple of weeks. Her mind, however, was in turmoil because of her sister's last words. One thing she was sure. Only marriage, before her family, would satisfy her. No matter how Will pleaded, that would be the only way she could be his.

*   *   *

Captain Bargood took a lively interest in Will's love affair for he saw in it the possibility of luring him into 'the game'. From discussions with Will he dismissed any idea of the possibility of drawing the Catchpoles into the chain, though he gained important information about carts and horses on the property.

He encouraged Will to talk about his courtship and gave him plenty of advice.

'She sounds like a grand girl, Will, but I think you may find it hard to prise her away from her family.'

'Don't get me wrong,' Will argued, 'she is no Mammy's girl, but she has strong principals and I admire her for them. It's hard courting from afar but I know, in my heart, she is true. Still I worry that, while I am away, someone else might steal her heart.'

'Well, some lassies like a bit of jewelry. It seems to turn their heads a bit. If she were mine I think I might try a little bauble or two. It helps to keep you in their mind when you are away. I have a few trinkets here. Perhaps you would like to choose one that she would like.'

He showed Will several pieces that were part of the valuables to be exchanged for contraband. They were the currency used to buy the smuggled goods as English pounds would be useless outside that country.

Will's eyes settled on a ruby necklace. He imagined how it would look on Margaret's olive skin and reflect in her brown eyes.

'This is a beautiful piece Captain, but I fear it would be beyond my means.'

'You show good judgment boy. It's the pick of the pieces and would fetch a pretty penny.' He watched slyly as Will handled the warm, blood red jewels. 'There is a way you could earn them. There is a small duty I would have you do for me. If you do it I will give you the necklace.'

Will dragged his eyes from the rubies. 'I presume the job has to do with smuggling?'

'Ay, it has. But your part in it will be a sailor's one only. You know the Orwell and all the inlets along it. All I want you to do is to navigate a small ship to a destination I will give you. You will take no part in the transfer. You will not touch the cargo. Only get it safely to the spot and pick up the lads afterwards. There will be no danger to yourself.'

'It's not the danger I fear.' Will bristled. 'It's the disgrace to my father if ever I was found breaking the law. He has great respect for it.'

'I understand boy. I know you are no coward. I admire your principals, working for small gain when you could be making yourself a fortune.'

The wily captain rested a protecting arm on Will's shoulder. If he could only get him to do one job he knew that it would be but a matter of time before he had him.

Will picked up the necklace again and ran it through his fingers, noting them rippling fire from the stones.

'I'll do it Captain, but only this one time. I'll do it for Margaret. She deserves the best, but the good Lord knows I would have to work a year to get something as beautiful as this.'

'Good man,' replied the captain, patting him on the back. He knew, for sure now, how to ensnare Will.

The enterprise was set for a moonless night five days hence. Will was unpleasantly surprised to find that the operation was under the control of the surly figure he had seen with the captain the day in Ipswich when he had begun his life at sea.

He knew, by now, that the man's name was John Luff and that he had a reputation of being an iron fisted, iron hearted desperado who ruled his subordinates without pity and did his best to stamp out any goodness in them.

Luff knew that Captain Bargood had had his eye on Will for some time, for he and the captain had an understanding with each other. He resented Will for his youth and capabilities but knew better than to upset the captain's plans.

Will had no difficulty bringing the ship to its appointed position that was several miles offshore. There they waited anxiously scanning the sea for any coastguard vessels. The craft rode quietly at anchor while they waited for darkness, the wind soughing around furled sails.

When the day had died and darkness came, the ship came to life; sails spread, bellied in the breeze, anchor raised, They slipped silently up the Orwell to a cove half way between Felixtowe and Ipswich. Quick, naked feet. below rolled up trousers, padded purposefully across the decks and powerful men dragged the kegs up from below. These were not landsmen, hired as labourers – amateurs - they were smugglers trained and desperate, many of them deserters from the navy with a price on their heads.

Nearer the coast sails were once again furled and the command came to drop anchor. The vessel rocked in the wind and the small waves, the creaking of the timbers, the occasional puff around the canvas and the straining of the leathers as the men hauled the kegs, were the only sounds to be heard.

Close to midnight, somewhere to the north of their position, came the gleam of a lantern. It shone twice, then there was a long pause of blackness, then the light gleamed brightly, flashed three times, a pause, then the sequence began again.

'Once, twice, pause, one, two, three, then once again. That's it.' Luff nudged Will as if doubting that he had picked up the signal.

'I see it, man,' replied Will impatiently. 'Let's hope no coastguard cutter saw it also.'

'No matey. They won't be round here. Already been fed some information to keep them many miles away from here. We'll not be disturbed tonight.'

On shore the organization was brilliant. Three carts were pulled up and men were gathering seaweed. If questioned, their leader would explain that they were collecting stream weed and marsh weed to be used on the outbuildings and the tap-room floor of a certain tavern.

If questioned, the landlord of that tavern would swear that this was so. A little further along the coast there was another group doing the same thing, ostensibly collecting seaweed, this time, for manure. The gathering of weed would be the explanation for the presence of so many carts and men on the beach, if anyone should ask.

If five minutes to midnight did seem to be an odd time to be gathering such material, there was no law in the land that said one could not collect it at any time one liked. The seaweed would act as a covering for the cargo once it was landed, though a thorough investigation by the coastguard would soon reveal all. It only concealed the smuggled goods from those who preferred to believe that they had seen nothing untoward.

On the cliff top, resting on one knee, was a shepherd leaning on his crook, waiting, patient and silent. His flock was behind him. He had been waiting for over an hour, but he was used to waiting. When the signal was given he would begin driving his flock over the tracks the smugglers had made,

Further up the river, in one of the reaches, in the shadow of the willows that grew up to the water's end, waited a solitary figure. It was his job, when the contraband had been loaded onto the carts, to make contact with Luff and hand over the payment for the goods. All these people, regardless of what they pretended to be doing, were alert, waiting and watching. They were part of one great organization.

The only one missing was the Organiser himself At that precise moment he was having a final drink with one or two local dignitaries, including a clergyman, having consumed an elaborate meal. So well did he choose his men that he had no need to supervise, and should misfortune befall them, he knew that they would not betray him. He paid well, treated them well and they knew that retribution would be swift if anyone should inform against him.

Will revelled in the excitement as he watched the cargo being taken to shore. He wanted to see more, so climbed into the rowing boat with the last load. He loved the silent effort that was going on around him. It was like a well-oiled machine. No unnecessary movement was made, no word was spoken, for everyone knew his part in the plan.

Will's blood raced and his heart beat faster as he contemplated the risk he was taking. When he reached the shore he was surprised to see that some of the carts looked familiar and among the horses he recognised Margaret's favourite Primrose.

Luff was standing, watching Will's reaction. 'The farm was so near it was a pity not to use them.'

'But Catchpole would never consent.'

'What he doesn't know won't hurt him and he'll be well rewarded.'

Will was worried about how the family would react when they found that their horses had been used. Then he reasoned that there was no way that they would know he was here. There was nothing to connect him to the raid. Farmers all over the country were visited by 'the gentlemen' and few of them complained.

'I'm off, up the river to pick up the payment. Want to come?' Luff enquired.

'Might as well see it all,' Will laughed. Then each taking an oar they silently rowed into the stream.

The boat ran into a little inlet and Luff indicated for Will to stop. They sat silently for a moment, then, raising his hands to his lips, Luff proceeded to do a very good imitation of an owl. Out of the shadows stepped a young man who, having satisfied himself that it was Luff, handed over a heavy bag containing gold and jewels, the currency used in these transactions.

When they got back to the cove the transfer was nearly finished. The last cart was being loaded and the rowing boats were being readied to take the sailors back to the ship.
Suddenly a single piercing whistle was heard; the warning signal they did not want to hear. Everybody on the beach stood like statues cast in the act of bending, loading, pushing. All eyes turned towards the direction of the sound and then towards Luff.

It was then that Will realised the value of this man. He may have looked an oafish ruffian but, in a crisis, he was the leader. Calmly he snapped orders and every man jumped to obey.

'Don't worry about those last barrels. Roll them against the cliff, cover them and hope no one discovers them. Get the carts out. Get them beyond the headland. Old Ned will do the rest. Will, get back to the ship and be ready to sail.' Then to the sailors, 'come on you villains. Time to earn your keep. We'll take it to them and give the carts time to get away.'

With cutlasses and pistols drawn they stealthily raced along the beach and up the rise to confront the enemy who were moving silently in formation, hoping to catch the smugglers by surprise.

Will's heart was pounding with fear, with excitement, with anger at Bargood for exposing him to this, with exhilaration at this new experience. Furiously they rowed back to the ship, scrambled over the side, raised the anchor, unfurled the sails and waited. It was still too dark to see, but sound carried. They heard the shouts, the clash of steel, the explosion of pistols and one agonising scream. The skirmish lasted about twenty minutes, then, in the half-light of early dawn Will could just make out figures running towards the sea. Some manned the remaining rowboat while others raced straight into the sea and began swimming furiously towards the ship.

The steady breeze was favourable so Will turned the bow towards the shore. He knew the shoals and steered towards the frantically rowing smugglers. Oars were raised and they scrambled aboard. Will waited only long enough to pick up those he could see swimming towards him then turned to race down the estuary to reach the open sea before anyone was able to notify Harwich or Langer Fort.

It was not till they reached the safety of the open sea that he handed the wheel over to a seaman and went along the deck to enquire from Luff how many had escaped.

*   *   *

'Da! Someone has used the horses. They're covered in sand and mud!'

Jonathan hurried to the stables. 'So they have Rob. We've had visitors and they've used the horses cruelly. Look at Pumpkin. He's been cut on the rump!'

He was angry. No one was allowed to abuse his horses. Now the poor animals, exhausted from their night's use, were scarcely able for a day's work in the field. Jonathan examined each animal in turn, shaking his head over the evidence of abuse.

'Father look! A box of Dutch tobacco!' Rob was ecstatic. He had never seen a whole box of Dutch tobacco in his life.

Jonathan frowned. 'Then it definitely was the gentlemen. They must have been hard pressed, they usually take good care of the horses.'

'But the tobacco? What shall we do with the tobacco?' Robert was excited at the prospects of using or selling the high-grade shag.

'I'll take it to Master. He'll tell me what to do with it and he will need to know what happened to his horses.'

'But it's ours Da'. Why should he have it?'

'Because they're his horses and his carts, and because I don't want anything to do with it.'

'But why should we tell him about it?'

'Because it's the right thing to do. We can't keep this,' holding up the box, 'twouldn't be honest.'

Jonathan and his master discussed the evening's events. 'There's not much we can do about it Jonathan. It might cause more trouble for us to report it.'

'What about this tobacco?'

'Keep it and use it. Don't sell it to anybody. No one needs to know about this.'

'But don't you want it?'

'No I don't. I don't want my name connected with smugglers. With luck this was an emergency. If I do not take their bribe they will probably leave us alone. Best keep an eye out for a while.'

'What if they do come again, Master?'

'Then we will have to do something. Make sure your family doesn't say anything about this. For now we will just wait and see.'

'T'is only Rob who knows and I'll warn him to keep his mouth shut.'

But when he got back Margaret was in the stables, fussing over the horses, particularly Primrose. Jonathan swore his family to secrecy, but of course James Cracknell had to know why the horses were in such a sorry state and he had to tell his wife, so in the end the news spread anyway.

Once again the Catchpoles were the subject of gossip. A number of the village men came around to sample the tobacco, then speculate whether Jonathan had indeed been an innocent party at all.

Margaret, already furious at the way the horses had been used, was angry at the false accusations. She was glad that Will worked for an honest captain and had no reason to be involved in such a trade.

Will was not free to visit Margaret for a while after his adventure. During that time he learnt, from his father, that Susan had died. He was doubly happy that he had taken the risk to get the necklace. There would be no reason now why Margaret would be needed at home so they could make plans for a wedding straight away. The necklace would indeed be a token of their betrothal.

When he did come Margaret found that she had no bad feelings. Susan's words were forgotten and her heart was so full of love for him that she feared it would burst from her chest. He offered sincere condolences for the family's loss and was secretly pleased when, inquiring of Charles, learnt that he had indeed followed his dream. Everyone wanted to hear Will's latest adventures, but he did not mention the greatest of them, which had taken place so close to where they lived.

It was quite late when he was able to be alone with Margaret. After embracing, fondling as lovers do, he became serious. 'Margaret, you have been mine for many years. I think it is high time we talked of marriage. Do you want to marry me?'

'With all my heart, Will. You know I would have married you long since if I had not had a greater commitment.'

'And now that dear Susan is gone there is nothing to stop us?'

'Nothing save where we will live.'

'Then my darling, let us make official the promise we made when we were young Do you remember I said that a betrothal should be sealed with the giving of jewellery?'

'That was just childish talk . . .'

'No it wasn't. Now close your eyes and turn round.'

Margaret did as she was commanded, fiddling excitedly as Will fastened the necklace, then turned her back to face him. The jewels sparkled in the moonlight, just as he knew they would.

'Now open your eyes.'

Margaret opened her eyes, smiled at Will and then, cupping the necklace in her hands, looked at her present.

Will was horrified at her reaction. Instead of the joyous cries he expected, the smile vanished to be replaced by a worrying frown.

'Where did you get these?'

Will realised at once that he had made a big mistake. He would have to brazen it out.

'You don't think they are real, do you?'

'Aren't they?' Margaret asked haltingly.

Will laughed. It was ironic. After risking his life to get her something precious he must pretend that they were worthless.

'What a silly goose you are. Where do you think I would get the money for real rubies? They are just pieces of glass, but very pretty. They come from Italy. They make things so real that only experts can tell the difference. Now tell me you like them.'

'Oh Will, they're beautiful. I have never seen anything so beautiful in my whole life.'

'Then kiss me thanks.'

They duly embraced, but a barrier seemed to have come between them. Margaret's reaction worried him. He realised there were many values that they did not share. He knew he would never be content with the common things that those of his station were content with. He wanted the best, for himself and for Margaret. He would have to change her once they were married.

Margaret felt a nagging worry. She wanted to believe him that the stones were only glass, but she felt in her heart that they were real. And if they were real, what then? Perhaps it was just the recent smuggler's raid that had made her suspicious. Suddenly all the joy had gone out of the meeting, but if she planned to marry Will then she must learn to trust him.

'Will, you must think me a foolish girl to doubt you, but we had a disturbing experience recently. Smugglers borrowed our horses and used them to transport goods. There was a battle on the cliffs and one of the smugglers was killed. Please forgive me, but I must ask this. Can you swear to me that you had nothing to do with those smuggled goods?'

Will smiled quietly to himself. He had never touched the goods so he could swear in good faith. Putting his hand on his heart he began. 'On my honour I swear I did not touch those goods. Shame on you Margaret Catchpole to think so ill of your future husband.'

'Oh Will, I am so sorry. What can you think of me?'

'I think that you are my own precious girl and the sooner you become my wife the sooner you will be rid of these fancies. But tell me, would you still love me if I were a smuggler?'

'I will love you Will, no matter what you are; but I would never marry you. I would never marry any man who did not earn his living honestly.'

Will wondered what she would say if she knew that his 'honest captain' was engaged in the trade, but he kept his peace. He held her close to him but was distracted and they spoke no more of marriage. When they got back to the cottage nothing was said. Margaret held her shawl close to her to hide the necklace.

Will left soon after. As he walked along he deliberated on his problem. He had enjoyed his night of smuggling and had been thinking that he wouldn't mind being involved occasionally. Now he knew how Margaret felt. He contemplated the dull life he might lead as a married man and was not sure it was for him.

So occupied with his thoughts was he that he did not stop at the Cracknells as he had planned but walked through the night until he found himself on the outskirts of Ipswich. He found a place to sleep in a barn then set out bright and early for his appointment with Captain Bargood.

He argued with himself, at one time deciding he would give up the sea altogether rather than become involved in smuggling.

Then he would contemplate the boredom of life on land. The comparison between the predictable, regular life on land with one of excitement and adventure at sea made him want to stay with the life he had. He was not sure that he could give it up, even for Margaret Catchpole. He was still in this state of indecision when he met up with the captain at Felixtowe.

Captain Bargood greeted Will and, after one drink to quench his thirst, led him down to the shore opposite the harbour and the town of Harwich. A short distance from the shore was a small rowing boat, and not far out to sea, rocking gently on the calm waves, was a brig, standing proudly in its new paint. It was this brig that was the subject of the captain's conversation.

'What do you think of her, Will? Note her line, boy.'

'She's a fine vessel Sir. I think, perhaps, that she was built in my Uncle Frederick's yard.'

'That she was, boy. That she was.'

'Then she will be as seaworthy as she is handsome. Only the best comes from his yard.'

'How would you like to command her, Will?' Bargood eyed the young man slyly to observe the reaction to his bait.

Will's face glowed. 'I would be the happiest man in England.'

'Then Will, she could be yours. But of course there would be conditions. You can see she was built for speed and maneuverability. You know by now lad what my main trade is, and this vessel was built for that trade. You did well on that raid and I firmly believe you have the capability to become a great captain.'

He could see doubt clouding the blue eyes.

'It's a fair offer lad, command of a vessel, a vessel whose keel you may have helped to lay, but she is meant for the trade. The decision is yours. You can live as a ferry man like your father or spend your life building ships for other men to sail, or live the life of adventure with mates who will never let you down. I'd be disappointed in you boy, if you chose the former life. I believed you a fellow for adventure or I would never have taken you on at all.'

Will was in an agony of indecision. He knew, in his heart,

what his choice would be, but he thought of his father and Margaret and knew what his answer should be.

'When you took me on Captain you knew I was an honest man. Now you want me to be a smuggler. My father is a Government Servant. How can I bring disgrace on him?'

'Ah, tell me Will, where's the disgrace? Because I do a little bit of free trading does that make me a wicked man?'

'But you would be cheating the government.'

'Cheating the government! Why, Will, everyone from the highest to the lowest will do that if they get a chance; just so long as they think they will not get caught. Who do you think I sell my goods to? Don't be deceived that they do not know where they come from. You think too well of your fellow man.'

'I find that hard to believe.'

'That's because you don't want to. But tell me, who pays more than they have to? Everyone feels they have won if they get something for less. Gentry as well as commoners, aye even the clergy are not immune. I tell you this truly for I deal with them every day. Now, let me put it to you, am I worse than them if I indulge in a little free trade and pay my men well for what they do?'

'You pay them well, but they risk their life and liberty for their pay.'

'So! It's the danger then. I never thought you would be so choosey.' Will winced at the look of open disgust on the face of the man he so admired.

'No stomach for the fight boy? No heart for the risk? Then boy you would be better at the plough. No risk there. No danger. But no adventure either and no reward, working every day from dawn to dusk just to keep body and soul together. Yet for a little risk you could be wealthy. Think what you're throwing away, for if you say nay then we will never sail together again.'

The captain signalled to his boatman, but he had not finished with Will yet. He knew his man and he had a few hooks left still.

'It's the girl, I think, Will. Then go to her. She'll be happy enough to see you unemployed and sick for the sea and all for her sake.'

Will was stung. 'She's a good girl Sir, and she loves me for myself, not for what I've got.'

'I'm sure lad, but love wears thin when money's short. If you really love her then you'd want to provide for her. After a few runs you could have a snug little cottage near this very cove and be as comfortable as you wish. But I can see that rather than risk a few trips you would have her working for some master all her life and getting old before her time. Is that love, Will? If I loved a woman I would want to set her up, mistress of her own home, and living like a queen.'

Bargood could see that Will was weakening so he pretended that the discussion was at an end.

'Goodbye Will. I thought I was a better judge of character. You have disappointed me. Still I will have little trouble finding a new skipper for that lovely craft, not as good a one as you maybe, but one with spirit. Now I have business elsewhere so I bid you goodbye.' And he began to walk towards the incoming boat.

'Wait, Captain. How many voyages need I do before I made enough to do as you say'

'That depends on luck. The quicker the work, the quicker the pay. One year, two perhaps, but for a bright boy like you I would say nearer one.'

'If I said yes, what would be my share?'

'Well there's the main cargo, rum. That's mine. The other goods, snuff, tobacco, cloth. You can barter that for yourself. Only bring my cargo safe home to England. Of the profits you will receive say, one sixth, the first year, one third the second and after that, if you wish to continue we could go equal shares. 'I know your pluck Will, other than that I would not make you such a handsome offer. I know we can both make a good profit from the enterprise. But you must say aye or nay right now. I have a ship to sail and there are others who will quickly take your place.'

'I'm your man, Captain! I'm your man.'

Will's face was flushed and his eyes were shining. In his imagination he was already a successful smuggler, outfoxing the customs men, running the gauntlet to make a fortune and bringing it home to Margaret. As soon as he had made his pile he would quit and they could live like gentry for the rest of their lives.

As Will hurried down to the waiting boat with the captain he saw that the rower was Luff.

'Took your time reelin' him in, Captain,' remarked the surly fellow, looking slyly at Will. He knew of his captain's plans for the young man but, although he agreed that Will was an asset, still he resented him. Luff knew he would never possess the skills necessary to captain a ship but that did not stop him from wanting to command.

Also there was an innate goodness in the young man that rubbed against Luff. He was determined to reduce Will to his level and he would have plenty of opportunity to do it, for he was to be the Mate.

CHAPTER FOUR

Spring came early that year, and it was beautiful. The English countryside was clothed in sunshine, and the Suffolk hedgerows were dancing with flowers. The trees, newly dressed with green, made faint singing noises of welcome in the soft, caressing breezes scented with spring perfumes. The swallows, nesting in the barn eaves, chirpy and sure of tenancy, the sparrows hopping in the fields and darting in and out of the willows, celebrated the return of the sun. It was as if they all wished to contribute their warmth and life to the already warm and lively world. In the gardens the early roses added their proud colour and sweet scent to the clear, crisp air.

Margaret walked often by the streams and ponds, watching the water lilies, listening to the frogs, and felt a part of the rhythm of the earth, She, like the rest of nature, felt the tingling warmth of the sun as it released the world from the grip of the long, uneasy winter.

And like the sun, Margaret shone. She was now certain in her mind that she and Will should soon marry. As captain of a ship he would soon be able to afford a home for her. She thought of the weary, winter months just gone, associating them to the sadnesses in her life - Charles' absence, Susan's death and her doubts about Will. Now, with the spring, she felt a new, brighter beginning and gloried in this happiness.

She believed that Will had spoken truly, and yet she had still not shown the necklace to anyone. She felt this was a small betrayal, but she could not help it. Late at night, when everybody was asleep, she sometimes took it out and admired the warm glow of the stones in the candlelight, but she never wore it, even in the privacy of her room.

Margaret had long since ceased any kind of struggle against

her attraction to Laud. Susan's dying words no longer troubled her. Her love was as much a fact as the rising of the sun and nothing would ever change that. She longed for the time when she and Will would be man and wife. She accepted his long absences because she knew that, as master of the *Alde,* he had to think first of business. It made his infrequent visits all the sweeter. When he could not come he often sent small tokens to her and the family. These were gladly accepted as they showed that, even in foreign places, he thought of her and longed to be with her. Again, she wished that she could read, then Will could have written her messages, and if only she could write then she could send him many loving tidings.

Because they were of little value, the gifts did not trouble her in any way. In fact they reinforced her belief that the rubies were not real. But there were those who began to talk about the frequent visits from sailors, bringing packages.

One evening in late August, when the twilight was shortening and trees were turning red and orange and gold, a stranger knocked at the cottage door.

'Come in,' said Jonathan, and in walked a weather beaten man, who, from his clothes, could have been a ploughman, but whose face spoke of a shrewd, shifty nature. His eyebrows half covered the sockets of his eyes that peered from under them with a wary glance as if checking that all was safe.

Little did Margaret know that this rough looking character would be her nemesis; for it was Luff who, curious to see the girl who had won Will's heart, had volunteered to deliver his package.

Seeing the pitiful trinkets and guessing that Will had concealed his real occupation, he decided, in a round about way, to inform her, and to test the strength of her opposition. He had put together, from his own bonus, a collection of pieces to tempt any wayward heart; silks, shawls, caps, ribbons and gloves, tea, coffee, tobacco and snuff.

'Does one Margaret Catchpole, live here?' he enquired innocently.

'Yes she does,' was Margaret's quick reply. 'I am she. What do you want her for?'

'Oh. It be ye. Then I be commissioned to deliver this parcel into your hands.'

With that he eased a heavy swag of goods from his shoulder and presented it to her.

'Who asked you to deliver it?' Margaret was surprised at the size of the present, though she was almost sure that it was from Will.

'I don't know who he be. I was a'workin' on the marshes at Bawdsay Ferry when this young sailor came up and asked me did I know where Nacton was. When I told him yea, he paid me a small sum and asked me to take this here bundle to a Margaret Catchpole livin' in just such a place as he described to me.'

They all guessed who the sailor was. Margaret asked Robert to carry the swag into the sitting room while the messenger was invited to take a seat in the kitchen and have a drink of ale.

When the parcel was unpacked Margaret's heart sank at the sight of such riches. They could have come from only one source, as they were far too costly to have been honestly procured. With Robert's help she bundled them up again and returned to the kitchen.

'No doubt you found a pretty thing or two to take your fancy.' Luff enquired slyly, observing the effect his goods had had on the girl.

'There is nothing here for me. You may take them back and tell the young man that one pair of gloves, honestly paid for, would have pleased me far more than all these valuables he has sent.'

'Now look 'ere,' cried Luff, with feigned indignation. 'I've lumped that stuff many a mile and I'll not take it back for twice the money. And what's to say the young man won't give me a cracked head for me pains. I don't want to be mixed up in lover's quarrels. I've done me duty and now I'm off.' And with that he hurried quickly from the house.

The rest of the family was mystified at Margaret's outburst, but when the contents of the parcel had been revealed they understood. It was just as they were discussing what to do with the goods that Mrs Cracknell arrived. She had been up to the farm delivering some of her home made candles.

Margaret was all for throwing everything away but her neighbour deplored such waste.

'You cannot be serious, Margaret. However the goods were obtained they are here now. No one in this house has done a thing wrong. These are superior goods. Broken down, I could sell some of them in my shop. As for the others, my husband knows many of the traders, from buying for my shop. He could dispose of them in Ipswich and no questions asked. We, none of us, are so rich that we could not do with a little more money. '

'We want none of that money,' replied Margaret indignantly.

'Speak for yourself,' cried Robert. 'You might want no part of it, though I don't know why, but I'm all for getting something for it.'

'Do what you like, only don't bother me with it,' and Margaret rushed from the house to seek the tree where Will had sworn his innocence. Throwing herself on the ground she wept for the trust that had been betrayed.

Will had sworn on his honour that he had had nothing to do with smugglers. Now she had proof that this was a lie. She also remembered her statement that she would never marry a smuggler. She had meant what she said. Now she was faced with the death of all her dreams of a happy married life with Will. It was worse than the death of her beloved sister. She hardly knew how she would recover from this blow.

Luff, pleased with the reaction to his deception, told Will what he had done and informed him that Margaret seemed quite receptive to the more extravagant presents he had provided.

Will took this as a softening in Margaret's attitude and, wanting to please the lady of his desires, began sending bracelets, combs and laces as well as useful things like tea, coffee, tobacco and snuff. He even sent an ornate, silver tipped pipe, which he thought would give pleasure to Jonathan.

Margaret and the rest of the family would have nothing to do with the goods, but Robert and the resourceful Mrs Cracknell saw to their collection and disposal. Robert often intercepted the parcels before they reached the cottage.

When asked where she had obtained such fine gifts that she now displayed in her tiny window Mrs Cracknell, by inference, suggested that the goods belonged to the Catchpoles, having been provided by Margaret's young man, and that she was only helping the family to pass them on. She omitted to tell them that, apart from Robert, she was the only one making a profit. To the outside world she was but a good friend helping out a neighbour.

There had always been a degree of envy of the Catchpoles, first because of Jonathan's position on the farm and because of the fame of Margaret's mercy dash, so the gossips seised on this information and enlarged on it. One or two would-be suitors spoke disparagingly of Margaret's character, jealous that she had chosen someone from outside the district.

This was the state of things when an incident happened which broke Elizabeth's heart and spirit.

A parcel arrived from India containing a beautiful shawl and, even more wonderful, a letter from Charles. He had taken advantage of his time in the army to learn to read and write.

Mrs Denton was called on to read the letter. She was asked to read it several times until Elizabeth knew every word by heart. She slept with it under her pillow and 'read' it often during the day. Never was a lyric love letter so dear as that letter from her eldest son.

On the next Sunday Elizabeth, dressed in her best, wrapped the shawl around her and proudly entered the church. She heard, with pride, the murmur her entry caused and could hardly wait till the service to end so that she could display the shawl and show the letter her son had written.

However, when she exited the church, her late friends turned from her, then, at a distance, began to express their distaste at her wearing smuggled goods into God's house.

Elizabeth, bewildered, heard snatches of what they were saying, but Margaret, more attuned to the mood of her neighbours, was mortified. She would have liked to remonstrate with them but knew they did not want to hear her explanation. Her mother had been publicly disgraced in the eyes of the parish and it was all her fault. Taking her mother's arm she proceeded up the road, head held high, but weeping inside.

The incident so distressed Elizabeth that she no longer left the house. Her once robust health began to decline.

Robert, now that he had a ready supply of money, began to frequent a near by shanty and often was so drunk that he could not find his way home.

The once strong family was reduced to an older man having to do all the work formally done by three, an ailing wife, a drunken son, a small bewildered boy and a daughter with a broken heart. What once had been a happy, welcoming home became a cold, silent place where few visitors called.

It was to such a household that Will eventually came. Instead of the usual cheery greeting he was offered the casualest of nods. Margaret gazed at him, her brown eyes filled with reproach, and led him from the house.

'Margaret! What's wrong? Has some great misfortune befallen your family?'

'Misfortune indeed. To have such a daughter as I am, to bring ruin to them all.'

'What do you mean? How could you bring misfortune on your family?'

'By giving my love to an untrustworthy vagabond who earns his living by smuggling.' Margaret's anger overcame her misery. Will thought he could see hate in those brown eyes he loved so much but he could think of no reason why she should accuse him.

'What do you mean, a vagabond? Why untrustworthy? And how can what I do have any effect on your family?'

'Those goods you send us. Everyone knows they are smuggled and they think we are in league with you. Will, you swore to me, the night you asked me to marry you, that you were not a smuggler, when all the time you were lying. How could you do such a thing? You knew it would break my heart.'

Will was angry now. He had been called a liar. He sought to justify what he was doing, as he now regarded it at no crime, but rather a service.

'I'm a man of my word, Margaret. When I swore to you that I was not a smuggler it was the truth, for then I wasn't. However, the very next day Captain Bargood offered me command of an excellent ship if I would turn smuggler. If it had just been for myself I never would have done it. I did it for you, Margaret. I did it for us. I wanted us to start life with a little money. I swear, Margaret, I do not mean to stay a smuggler. I am only in it till I can buy a little cottage by the sea. Then I will never be involved again. I have already saved quite a pile. In another year I will give the game away. '

He sounded so sincere Margaret's anger cooled a little. 'Will. Do you think I love you for your money?'

'Then you do still love me?'

'To my sorrow, yes. I told you I would always love you. How could I change? But I hate what you are doing. Why did you send all those things to me when you knew they would be unacceptable.'

'But Luff said you were pleased with what I sent.'

'And who is Luff?'

'The sailor I sent with some goods some time ago. He said he added a few extras to what I had given him and that you were pleased.'

'Then he lied. I think I know the man you mean. He pretended to be a farm hand but I was sure he was from the sea. I fear he wanted to cause you a mischief. '

'You are probably right. He has no love for me, nor I for him, though he is my Mate. He probably thought it a grand trick.'

'Well, his grand trick has near ruined my family. These are evil men you associate with and they will corrupt you.'

'All the more reason for you to marry me and keep me from them. Marry me Margaret. Come away with me. We can sail abroad and marry there. I will work on a foreign ship, and then, in time we can come back.'

'Why can't you marry me here?'

'Sad to say I have become too successful. I am known to the authorities. That is why I have not come sooner. If they knew I was here they might apprehend me.'

Margaret placed her hands on his arm and pleaded. 'Will! Will! Look where your life has taken you. I will not marry you until I can do it in front of my family.'

Will broke her grip. 'Then you don't really love me.'

'I do! I do, with all my heart. But I cannot bring more disgrace on my family. And I would never be happy living in a foreign land.'

Will's flash of anger gave way to sadness. 'Then there is no hope for us.'

'There must be a way. You must leave what you are doing and seek an honest trade. When your name is cleared you can live like any man instead of hiding from the law.'

Margaret was sure she had found a solution but Will shook his head and sighed. 'It seems so easy to you. If only I had you by my side each day I could do it. But on my own I don't know what I would do. If you love me come with me and make an honest man of me.'

'Will, I will love you forever and pray for you each day but I will not go with you.'

'What if I leave you?'

'Then I will have to live a sad, old maid.'

'Margaret, this is madness. Please come with me!' Will begged.

'No I can't.' Margaret was in tears but still strong in her resolve.

'Then you will hear no more of me.'

Margaret sobbed. 'If that is your wish, so be it.'

'It is not my wish but yours.' Will shouted angrily and Margaret felt afraid of such strong emotion.

'No matter what you say you don't really love me.'

He roughly pushed back the restraining arm Margaret reached towards him and stomped off into the night, leaving the sobbing girl behind to weep for all that she had lost.

Margaret believed that life had dealt its final blow but fate had not finished with her yet.

The Catchpole family had become suspect in the community. The gossip of their connection with the smugglers had reached such a state that the Dentons felt it reflected on their own good name. Robert had become almost useless for farm work and Jonathan was unable to do all the work on his own. New hands would have to be found and the cottage was needed for a working family.

Jonathan had to leave the home in which he had been born. Of all the calamities that befell them this was the one that hurt Margaret most.

'Da' how you must curse the day I was born. I have caused you to lose your birthright.'

'Never believe that Peg. It is no fault of yours that you have such a trusting heart. All I wish is that it could have settled on another. But this cottage was not my birthright, as you claim. It belongs to the farm. I cannot fulfill my part of the bargain so I must be replaced.'

Margaret knew that what he said was true but still she resented the Denton's for dismissing a man whose family had served them for generations.

Jonathan moved his ailing wife, his drunken son and his heart broken daughter to a mean little cottage on the edge of town and began earning his living as a day labourer.

His youngest son, for whom he had had such high hopes such a short while ago, was sent to live with his brother in Woodbridge in the hope that the shame would not affect his future.

Shortly after the move, in an inebriated state, Robert fell into the Orwell and was drowned.

So in the space of two years Margaret had lost a beloved sister, a brother, a happy home and all her dreams of love and marriage. She had always tried to be the best person she could but it had not been enough. Those she thought should have known her better, now spoke badly of her, and of her family too. Through no fault of their own they had lost their good name and the respect of their neighbours. It was no wonder that she became morose, getting through each day as best she could with no expectations for the future.

CHAPTER FIVE

As unseen eyes watched, a strong, eight-oared boat rowed steadily towards the shore. It was heavily laden and lurched through the breakers as Laud ran it onto the beach. Figures leapt into the surf and dragged it higher up the beach so that they could unload the cargo on board.

Twice, each man, carrying a bulging sack, struggled up the sand to an appointed spot under the cliff. They sat, resting on the sacks, while one of them scaled the low cliff to check that all was well. Assured that it was safe they hoisted their loads and began their ascent up a narrow gully.

Just as the last man entered, a piercing whistle was heard and a warning shot was fired ahead of them.

'We've been sprung,' Will shouted. 'Run for your lives.' But his order was not needed. Each man dropped his bundle and began running for the safety of the beach. They were not going to be caught in a defile.

However their escape route had been cut off. They had been ambushed. Fourteen customs men confronted them. The smugglers formed a close line, pistols primed and cocked and swords unleashed from their scabbards, but their attackers had spaced themselves to make a harder target as the two groups approached each other.

Two smugglers had already fallen before the two lines met with wild shouts and curses and the clashing of steel.

Will was in the thick of it, more than holding his own, when he felt his balance going as he fell over a rock. As he fell his adversary delivered a savage blow that caught him across the head causing a deep gash.

Fortunately for Will a stray pistol shot hit the coast guard in the shoulder. The man staggered away, taking no further part in the battle. Will fought desperately to remain conscious long enough to crawl back towards the gully, where he remained concealed.

The fight continued for some time and then a sudden yell from the boat crew and a cry for quarter from the remaining smugglers ended the fighting. Some sank to their knees in exhaustion, others fled to left and right along the beach. The coast guard did not pursue them, being content to make prisoners of those who had surrendered

At sunset, Margaret was in the habit of walking along a lane that ran past the small cottage where she now lived with her father and ailing mother. It was the only time of the day when the dark cloud of despair seemed to lift. She breathed more freely and became aware of the gentle light flickering between the trees. She smelt the soil and heard the day birds making preparations for the night. She never wandered far and was always home before the last light disappeared from the sky.

She was nearing the end of her walk when a figure stepped onto the path behind her.

'Margaret Catchpole?'

She remained facing the way she was going. 'Who wants her? If you have a message from Will Laud I don't want to hear it. Go away.'

'Will Laud is dying.'

Turning, Margaret saw Nicholas Laud. The poor man had aged since their last happy meeting. All anger and resentment gone, Margaret hurried up to him and seized his arm.

'Oh, Mr Laud! Say he isn't dying. Please, say it is not so.' Forgotten, in an instant, were all the wrongs she believed Will had done to her and her family. The door she had shut on her feelings for him was thrown wide open. He was dying and he needed her.

'I'm afraid he is, Margaret,' sighed the grieving father. 'He has been sorely wounded and would have died had not one of his men found him and taken him to a little cottage on Walton Cliff. He is so dreadfully wounded and so out of his mind in pain and fever that, even now, I cannot be sure he lives. He calls constantly for you, Margaret, though sometimes he curses you for being unfaithful, but he does not know what he says, so out of his mind is he with pain. Will you come to him?'

Margaret knew immediately that she must go to the side of her lover. Her heart was wrenched with pity for the poor father.

'Oh, yes Sir, I will gladly come. Only let me get a cloak and tell my father.'

She raced back to the cottage. In spite of the dreadful news her heart was alive again. 'He needs me,' it seemed to sing. 'He loves me and he needs me.'

Jonathan was appalled when he heard what Margaret was planning to do.

'How could you? After all he has done to ruin this family? I should have thought you, of all people, would never wish to see him again.'

'Da, he's dying, and he needs me. You know that, in spite of everything, I have never ceased to love him. Perhaps I can nurse him back to life or else help to ease him into eternity, prepare him for a happy death. God's mercy is boundless and I would have him reconciled with his Maker before he dies. Father, please forgive me for I must go to him, but I would prefer to go with your blessing.'

Margaret stared at her father, her brown eyes pleading for understanding. He softened and took his daughter in his arms.

'Peg, you have the grandest heart. If only the good Lord had seen fit to see you give it to a better man. But go, my Darling. Go with my blessing. Go to your lover and may God put into your mouth the words that will change him. Stay as long as you like, then come back to me, my darling child, for to lose you would be a blow from which I could not recover.'

He bent and kissed her head, then watched as his dearest child hurried towards the man who had broken her heart

Margaret and Nicholas arrived at the cottage. Will had fallen into a troubled sleep, convulsive movements and fitful moans revealing the agitated state of his mind. By the feeble light from a storm lantern Margaret gazed on the face she loved, partly covered by a filthy, blood encrusted bandage, his features distorted with pain, lips cracked by fever and white moisture exuding from his closed eyelids.

As she stared at the battle-scarred face Will let out a sudden painful cry. 'Margaret where are you? Why don't you come?' He tossed around then fell back into his fevered sleep

It was all too much for the young woman who collapsed in tears. But soon the shock wore off and the practical side of her nature took over. She spoke firmly to the old crone sitting by an open fire nonchalantly munching on a piece of bread.

'Have you any clean linen? He must be washed and his bandage changed. Fill the kettle and stoke up the fire.'

Molly was inclined to object, but one look at Margaret and she shuffled off to get water from a barrel near the door.

A quick glance informed Margaret that no clean linen would be found. She stepped out of her petticoat and began turning it into bandages. While she waited for the water to boil she found an old tin dish, scoured it, filled it with warm water and began to gently remove the bandage, softening the sticky mess that clung to it.

Underneath lay an angry red gash from hairline to cheek. Black blood oozed from the crust forming over the cut. Margaret tenderly cleaned the wound and sponged Will's face. She dampened his fevered lips and fed him tiny sips of water. Eventually his sleep became more peaceful and he had his first real rest since the fight.

Next morning, Will was lucid for short periods and knew that Margaret was present. While he slept Margaret was busy sweeping and cleaning. She opened the shutters to let in the early spring sunshine. She noticed Old Molly hurrying towards the edge of the cliff. Part way she was met by two dark figures. They engaged in conversation for some time then Molly came hurrying back. Though she could not see them clearly Margaret believed that one of them was Luff. She guessed that they were interested in Will's progress and knew that her fight to keep Will from his former life had begun.

She quickly took charge of the establishment such as it was. Old Molly grumbled but did as she was told. Nicholas came with food and by the second day Will was able to take a little broth. From that time he began to recover, though still experienced severe pain in his head. Because of the loss of blood and the fever that had weakened him, he found he could only walk a few steps without becoming dizzy.

He and Margaret spent some time sitting in the sunny doorway holding hands and talking.

'Margaret, I never believed you would come. I thought at first that you were part of my dreams.'

'Darling Will. I could never turn my back on you.'

'Then you do love me in spite of everything?'

'Surely you know that Will.'

'But still you won't marry me?'

'I will marry you any time when it can be in front of my family. This thing that has happened could be a blessing. You can see now where this life will lead you. Leave it Will and start again.'

'Ah, but you don't understand. I could not stand beside you in a public place now. I am too well known. There is a reward on my head. I know now that you were right. I should never have begun this game. Now there is no hope for me if I live in England.'

Will shook his head and Margaret could see that the worry for his future was causing him pain.

'Don't worry about it now. Get well first and then we'll see. I will pray to God to help us find a way out of our troubles. We can face anything together.'

'Yes. I know that with you by my side I will be safe.'

That evening Old Molly again kept her rendezvous with the smugglers and Margaret knew that she was in a life or death struggle for Will's future.

'Sweet Jesus help him. He is a good man only led astray by evil company. Help me get him away from them. I know he is not evil at heart.'

As if in answer to her prayers Nicholas arrived with news that Will had been declared dead. The guard who had cut him down was sure he had killed him. The fact that his body had not been found was easily explained away. Perhaps some of the smugglers had taken it or perhaps it had been washed out to sea.

The government spies had confirmed this report. Will had not been heard of since the raid and the word was that he had been killed. Will was now a non -person.

'Well lad, this is your chance. They will not be looking for you any more. You can go right away, to Scotland or even to Holland and start a new life under a new name. Later you might even be able to live in Suffolk again.'

Margaret was delighted. 'Oh Will, it is the answer to my prayer.'

'Would you come with me Peg? Would you leave your family and come with me?'

'You know I would. Only let me be wed before we go, with my Mother and Father as witnesses. They would never tell.'

'And I know a parson who will perform the ceremony.' Will laughed. 'He owes me for many a keg of good port.'

The happy lovers sat long into the night making plans. Old Molly listened and next day, while Margaret was out gathering driftwood she quizzed him.

'Thee'll not be serious about this marryin, Will? She's not the one for thee lad. I heard she talking to thee. She'll make ploughboy of thee as soon as look at thee.'

'But she's a good girl Molly and I really love her.'

'Love - pshaw - a good looking fella like thee can find it anywhere and not with one that'll bind thee hand and foot. She's got no spirit Will.'

'There you're wrong Molly. She's got plenty of spirit.'

'But not for adventure, boy. There's good friends waitin' for thee. They be keeping your place. That's what thee need, high adventure and a quick fortune, not stay at home in a little cot and working till the day thou die.'

'Molly, there's a part of me that wants to go, but Margaret won't marry me while I'm a smuggler.'

'And why doest thee need to marry?'

'She won't have me otherwise.'

'Thou meanst thee's never been with lass, Will?' Molly's surprise was genuine and Will blushed at the admission he had made. 'Then thee's not the man I thought thee was.' Molly sneered in disgust. 'All this time and thou haven'st got thy leg over yet. No wonder she has thee by the nose. Why Will, what thou thinks as love might well be unrequited lust. Bed her boy and then thee'll be sure. And, if thou know's how to use that piece between thy legs, thee'll hear no more of this marriage business. She'll want thee then, wed or not.'

'I could never force her Molly.'

'Then marry her if thee must but don't give up the game. Once the deed's done there's nothing she can do about it.'

Will thought long and hard on Molly's words. He really wanted to return to his old life if only he could be sure that he wouldn't lose Margaret.

But he never had to make a decision because word was brought that Elizabeth was very ill and Margaret was needed at home. Will was well on the way to recovery and she had to go. Her love had called her to Will's aid. Now it was love and duty that called her home. She had done all she could, now it was up to a power greater than hers to protect Will from the evil men who would drag him back to a life of crime. She left with a heavy heart, hoping that her dream would come true but fearful of the influences that would be there once she had gone.

Will made promises but, in her heart of hearts, she was almost resigned to the fact that, without her presence, he would go back to his smuggling life.

Margaret nursed her mother for three months but with her family life destroyed Elizabeth's had lost the will to live. On a sunny day in high summer she was laid to rest beside Susan and Robert.

A fortnight later Margaret kissed her father fondly and left to go as servant of all works at Priory Farm. She had given up all hope of marriage to Will. When he had been well enough to leave the cottage she could not accompany him because of her commitment to her mother.

Nicholas brought news that Will had fled to Holland. He had sworn, before he went, that he intended getting legitimate work there but Nicholas doubted his resolve. Although he loved his son, Nicholas urged Margaret to forget him. But she knew that, having given her heart, she could never love another while Will lived. In spite of all the evidence to the contrary she still hoped that one day he would change.

*　　*　　*

Margaret believed that she could make a new life for herself at Priory Farm. Determined to regain her good name, she conducted herself in an exemplary manner and soon gained the respect of her employers and fellow workers.

The Wades had five children, a son, thirteen, already away at school, and four daughters, three of whom were of school age. Because of her reliability, Margaret was soon put in charge of these three girls.

One of her duties was to remain in the classroom with them to ensure that they were not distracted during lessons. While watching, she was expected to do the children's sewing but, so interested did she become in the lessons, that the sewing was often neglected.

Her interest did not go unnoticed by the tutor who reported it to her mistress.

Mrs Wade questioned Margaret. 'Peggy, Miss Crundle says that you are so interested in the children's lessons that you are neglecting your sewing.'

'I'm sorry Mistress, but I catch up at night.'

'I know. I have seen your light burning late at night. I am not chastising you. I am curious about your interest in learning.'

'Forgive me, Mistress, but the dearest wish of my life is to read and write.'

'It's all right. I approve of servants learning, even girls.

Would you like to join the class in the nursery?'

'Oh Mistress! Could I? I would try so hard and I promise not to neglect my other work.'

'Then you shall. Perhaps your enthusiasm will rub off on my daughters, particularly Louise.'

So Margaret joined the class. She found no embarrassment in learning her letters with her youngest charge. She was so grateful that at last her dream of reading and writing was coming true.

When her long day was over she spent her time in her little room practicing her strokes or deciphering the words in her primer.

This new interest, as well as the responsibility she had been given, rekindled her zest for living. Once again her life had a purpose, a future. She put on a little weight, colour came back into her cheeks and her brown eyes shone with interest.

Priory Farm, called for the monastery it had once been, was a large establishment employing many people. All the house servants as well as some of the outdoor workers ate in the large room that had once been the monk's refectory.

When Margaret had first come to work there, little notice was taken of her, but as she began to emerge, like a butterfly from its cocoon, from her despondency, several of the young men began to take notice of her. The fact that she did not respond to their overtures caused resentment in some but in no way dissuaded others.

Among the latter was Jack Ingham, one of several sons of Robert Ingham, a small farmer and miller who lived about eight miles away.

Jack, anxious to turn his hand to farming, had asked for, and obtained permission from his parents to seek employment on a large farm. He had no difficulty getting a position at Priory Farm.

Because of his background and his general good character, he lived in the farmhouse with the Wades. He was also considered quite a scholar.

He was first attracted to Margaret when he learned of her efforts to read and write. This gave him a ready topic of conversation and he and Margaret soon became good friends, the first male friend Margaret had ever had. She was grateful for his friendship. He made no demands on her and she knew she could always rely on him when needed.

Jack's feelings for Margaret were much stronger. The more time he spent with her the more he realised her worth. He knew the story of her past association with Laud but, rather than condemn her, he admired her for her constancy. He refused to believe any slander spoken of her and shielded her from gossip.

Another period of tranquility began for Margaret. It was during this time that her brother, Charles, came on leave to England. He had so changed that even his own father did not, at first, recognize him. The army had discovered that he had a natural ear for languages and quickly mastered different idioms. He came to the attention of Lord Cornwallis himself who employed him as a spy on the Persian border.

Margaret was given permission to spend a few days at the cottage during his short visit. Listening to his stories of daring she remembered the happy days when Will used to entertain the family with stories of his own exploits. She could not help contrasting how each had used his love of adventure. Though both were engaged in dangerous work, Charles had risked his life for king and country while Will risked his life defying them.

Margaret was sure that, had Will's talents been put to another use, he too would have been a hero rather that an outlaw.

She had heard nothing from Will since he had left. She prayed that the silence meant that he was establishing himself in honest trade but experience suggested that he had gone back to his old ways.

Jack had been at the Priory for some time and his father was pressing him to make up his mind about his future. If he really wished to be a farmer then a farm could be bought, or he could take over the management of the mill. There was also another brother in Canada who was urging Jack to join him there.

Before deciding on his future, Jack wanted to test Margaret's feelings towards him. He made several false starts but finally found himself in a position where they would not be disturbed.

'Margaret, you must be aware of my feelings for you. Do you have any feelings for me? Could you see a time when you might want to be my wife?'

Margaret, honest as ever, thought before she replied. She was well aware of the honour Jack was paying her, as they were socially so far apart. She knew what a good person he was and she was very fond of him. Life with Jack would give respectability and comfort. But she could not offer him more than friendship as her heart was already given to another.

'Jack, you are my dearest friend and I would do anything rather than cause you pain but I must confess that my affection has already been given to someone else.'

'Another! You cannot mean that you are going to remain faithful to the memory of Laud forever?'

Margaret hesitated then decided that Jack could be trusted. 'Jack I know I can trust you with this secret. Laud is not dead.'

'Not dead! But everyone says . . . '

'I know what everyone says but, believe me, he was not killed.'

'Then he still lives.' Jack was stunned by this revelation. He sat on a rock, his head in his hands. 'And you still love him Margaret? How can you? How can you go on waiting for him when you know he will only bring you shame and misery?'

Margaret sat beside him and, taking his hands in hers, tried to ease the pain in she could see in his eyes.

'How can I explain to you Jack? When I first knew him, when I first gave him my heart, he was not as he is today. I know another side of him. He has many good qualities. I love him and I pray each day there will come a time when he may change. He may even be doing that right now. I can't give up on him. He needs me, for I know that without me he will never change. But, whatever happens, I know I can never love another while Will lives.'

'Then you would have me wait until his death?'

'No, Jack. You must forget this nonsense. You cannot pin your happiness on the death of another.'

'You call it nonsense that I remain faithful to you? You of all people to say such a thing.'

'Forget me, Jack.'

'I will when you forget Laud.'

'Jack, there's no future in this. You're a young man. You can start a new life.'

'And you're such an old woman, Margaret? Why can't we both start a new life, far away from here, in one of the colonies?'

Margaret thought. Here is another man who loves me and wants to take me away from all that is familiar.

'Jack, you must understand that this is useless. If you wish to leave England so be it, but do not let me be the cause.'

'If I leave it will only be because of you. Margaret. If I cannot have you as my wife I could not bear to live where I might see you. But only tell me this, if you had never met Laud, if he was already dead. Would you have married me then?'

'Jack, you are the kindest person I know. If my heart were free there is no one I would sooner give it to. I am so sorry Jack.'

'Then that will have to do me. I understand Margaret, even though it breaks my heart because I see no happiness for you. If you were going to marry someone worthy then I could accept it. But I can't stand by and watch this happen. I will leave England as soon as I can, but Margaret, I will always love you.'

Margaret was close to tears. 'Ah Jack. I have lost my dearest friend. Will you come to say goodbye before you go?'

'I promise that I will.'

The day before Harvest Home a sailor of foreign appearance approached Margaret as she walked with her charges along the wooded trail that led to a little stream.

'Is dis de Preary Barm?' the sailor asked in broken English.

The girls giggled, but Margaret, her heart beating fast with anticipation, instructed them to continue with their walk while she listened to the stranger.

'This is Priory Farm,' she replied eagerly.

'How far lpwich?'

'Four miles. Where do you come from?'

'Myn heer be born in Hamsterdam. I leaf my Bessel in de harber. Myn heer de capterain did command ma up to Ipwich. He tell me top at Preary Balm to one Margaret Catch-er-poles'

Margaret could scarcely contain her joy. 'I am she. What is your captain's name?'

'E be von Villiam Laud.'

Margaret covered her face with her hands. She had to restrain herself from hugging the messenger. She plied him with questions. How was the captain's health? How long had he been in England?

In his broken English the sailor managed to convey that the captain was well, that he was successfully sailing between Holland and England, that he was doing well in his work and that Margaret should wait by the shore at nine the next evening and look for a small sail boat which would come up the river and run ashore against the creek. The watchword was to be 'Margaret'.

She could hardly find words enough to thank him and found it hard not to burst into song. When she caught up with the girls she made up a story of the man looking for directions. She mimicked his speech so that they laughed together all the way home.

That night, when all were in bed, Margaret knelt and thanked her God that she had remained faithful to Will. She admitted to herself that she had been tempted by Jack's offer.

How dreadful it would have been if she had accepted, and then received Will's message. She felt ashamed of herself that she had doubted him when all the while he had been busy making good.

She realised that the meeting would coincide with this year's Harvest Home just as their first meeting had, so many years ago. She did not know how she would get through the hours until next evening and was happy that the preparations for Harvest Home would keep her so busy that the hours would fly. She prayed that no unforeseen incident would make her late for her rendezvous.

As Margaret, having finished her duties, slipped into the night, a small boat, sails filled with a friendly breeze, skipped along the river. In it were two men, Will, anxious about this meeting with Margaret, whom he had not seen for nearly two years, and John Luff, getting sadistic pleasure at Will's agitation.

Will, with not too much persuasion, had rejoined his old companions and, under the name of Captain Hudson, had become again the scourge of the Coast Guard. He had largely recovered from his wounds though he still suffered from headaches.

Unfortunately for Will, Old Molly had passed on to Luff the information she had learned about the state of his relations with Margaret. Luff had used it to taunt the young man whom he had always resented.

The initial dislike Will had felt towards Luff had grown to hatred. Several times it was only their shipmates who had kept them from each other's throat. Yet they still worked successfully together. Will had allowed Luff's constant ridicule to affect him to such an extent that tonight's journey was a last ditch effort to persuade Margaret to leave with him or at least to finally consummate his claim over her.

There was another boat sailing on the Orwell that night, an old, homemade vessel, a curious patchwork of scrounged timber. The heavy, oft mended canvas was incapable of speed and was soon overtaken by the swifter craft.

The ancient owner of the boat was a well-known character, the cranky old fisherman of the Orwell. He had long ago been nicknamed Robinson Crusoe because of his quaint attire and solitary habits. He was a haunted creature who believed in demons. He protected himself from these evil spirits by festooning himself with charms and uttering constant incantations. He was sometimes capable of rational speech but spent most of his time conversing with the devils that plagued him. Many a night he had sat cowering in his boat while the Prince of Darkness himself taunted him.

But tonight he was happy, for his evil demon had abandoned him. As the two vessels approached Robin saw that his tormentor had taken up position on the main sail of the other boat. As the two vessels drew level Robin cackled with glee and shook his fists at his persecutor. He stood up and peered at the occupants of the other craft.

'What the devil! Who's that?' the gruff voice of Luff demanded.

'Don't worry. It's only old Robinson Crusoe,' Will laughed. 'He's a mad old codger who makes no sense to himself or any one else. Ahoy there, Robin. How's the fishing?'

'Ahoy yourself! I know that voice. It's Will Laud, that's dead. Taking your master for a ride eh? You watch him, Will. He's a slippery customer.'

'What's that bloody fool going on about?' snapped Luff. 'How does he know your name?'

'Pay him no mind. There's no harm in him, though I wish he had not recognised me. Still nobody will take any notice of his ramblings. That's if he remembers himself.'

Robin watched as the little skiff darted along the river. Though afraid himself, he decided to follow, mumbling to himself the while.

'Take care, Will. The black fiend has ye in his eye. There'll be evil abroad tonight and ye have nary a charm to protect thyself.'
On the far bank Margaret waited, her eyes strained from watching. At last she saw the little sail and hurried forward, not waiting for the signal. As the boat grounded in the mud Will leapt over the side and, hurrying up to her, took her in his arms, crushing her to him.

'Peggy! Oh my darling girl.'

He led her quickly away from the prying eyes of Luff, onto a grassy bank where they embraced hungrily. The time apart had been as difficult for Margaret. She could not get enough of kissing and holding, tracing the scar from the sword and kissing it gently.

Though he had not been celibate during their absence, Will was over-whelmed with desire. He explored her face, her hair. She was wearing a light muslin dress and he could feel her body so close, her small breasts, her pounding heart, her slim hips.

As he kissed the much loved face his hands explored places where they had never been before. Margaret made no resistance as his ardor grew. His breathing became shorter and his movements stronger and rougher.

Margaret, sensing how far their love-making had gone, made to resist but realised that Will was past restraint. She felt a moment's fear. He would have her now even if by force. Her own body betrayed her, arching towards him, her arms crushing his head to her breasts.

Will entered her and began a rhythmic movement. A melody to which she could give no name filled her mind and she began to move to its rhythm.

Margaret's response took Will by surprise and he climaxed long before he meant to. He collapsed on top of her utterly spent.

Margaret, her melody stopped abruptly, felt a vague disappointment. As Will lay on top of her she pondered the enormity of what had just happened. She remembered her long ago talk with Susan and marvelled that her sister, who had so little experience of life, could have been so knowing. Now she understood those songs about betrayed maidens.

But she was not one of them. Will loved her. He would never desert her. Soon they would be man and wife, in law as now in deed.

Will rolled off her and lay, gazing at the starry sly. He never, in all his experience, had known a love making like this. It was what he had been searching for all his life. Now he knew that he and Margaret must be together always. This thought brought him back to the reason for the tryst.

He stood, brushed himself down and gave his hand to Margaret, pulling her to her feet. She rearranged her clothes, shy now to look at her lover.

'Margaret! My dearest Margaret! You must come away with me now.'

A warning fear ran through her body.

'What do you mean Will?'

'My ship is anchored in the bay. The boat is on the bank. We must hurry, before any one comes.'

'Will, you can't mean for me to go with you this minute, without any notice to anyone. Where would I go?'

'You will come with me to Holland. We will get married there.'

'Oh no Will! I can't just leave without saying goodbye to my father and I must tell my mistress. She will need to find someone to take care of the children. Will, I don't want to be married in Holland. I want to be married in the presence of what family I have left.'

Will could not believe what he was hearing. 'What is this nonsense Margaret? It was all right before, but now you are already mine. You must come. Quickly!'

Will was getting anxious and he was annoyed at Margaret for being so stubborn. He pulled her towards the boat.

Margaret, shocked, resisted. 'Would you force me against my will?'

'Yes, my girl. You are mine now and I will force you if I have to.'

Without realising they had raised their voices. The ever vigilant Luff, already worried about the time they had been there, heard them and called out.

'Hurry man. We can't stay here all night arguing. Just grab her. Hit her if she won't come.'

At the sound of Luff's voice Margaret stepped back, horrified. She would know that voice anywhere.

'Will! Oh Will! You have gone back to your old life and that evil man.'

Will was angry that she should criticize him. 'Well. What if I have? You were stupid if you thought I would become a puny farm boy that you could order around. You've got a real man here Margaret and you'd better get used to it.'

'Oh no I won't, Will Laud. I will never go with you.' Margaret made to run but Will caught her in a couple of strides. She knew now that he really meant to abduct her and her fear gave her strength. Though slight, she was strong. She resisted him with all her might

'Hurry Laud,' Luff shouted. 'I'm not waiting around to be picked up by the guard.'

'Then come and help me.'

As Luff jumped over the side of the boat and sloshed towards the shore, Margaret knew that she was lost. She began screaming,

'Help! Oh help! Is there nobody there to help me? I'm being kidnapped! Help!'

CHAPTER SIX

Jack had made known his decision to join his brother in Canada. Tonight was to be his last Harvest Home. He had hoped to say his goodbyes to Margaret but she was so busy serving food and drink he had had no opportunity to speak to her. He had no heart for the festivities and, as soon as he felt he had fulfilled his obligations, he slipped out, intending to sleep the night at his parent's home.

The still, dark evening suited his contemplative mood. He listened to the night noises, identifying them and committing them to memory for the years ahead.

A human voice, and then another, disturbed his reverie. A third, angry voice added urgency to the discourse. He could now distinguish three voices, two male and one female.

Should he ignore them and mind his own business or should he investigate? A scream, and then a cry for help, decided him. He raced towards the shore and in the pale light from the stars he could just distinguish two men trying to drag a woman towards the water. Though she was putting up a spirited defense it was obvious that the contest was unequal. As he watched, the stouter figure grabbed the woman and threw her, like a sack of potatoes, over his shoulder. Jack got a glimpse of petticoat and thrashing legs.

Arming himself with a strong breakwater stake he tore from the sand, Jack leapt from a small bluff and rushed towards the struggling couple. He swung the stake above his head and delivered a forceful blow at the man's hamstrings. They both fell to the ground and the woman was thrown over and over to come to rest in the muddy water at the side of the Orwell.

Luff, taken completely by surprise, was momentarily stunned but Jack went on the attack and turned to face his other adversary whose attention was on the woman struggling from the water. A misdirected swipe warned Will who turned, drawing his sword. Jack parried the blow with his stake. The two men, shaping up like cavaliers, began the uneven duel .

Though young and athletic Jack was at a disadvantage against the seasoned fighter, but the outcome was put beyond doubt when Luff, regaining his feet, joined in the fight. Jack had worked himself back against the bank, desperately fending off the heavy steel.

With all attention on the skirmish, nobody noticed the tall, gaunt figure striding along the beach. Above the clangs and grunts of the struggle, nobody heard the jingle of the dangling charms as Robinson Crusoe, armed with a long fisherman's pike, joined in the fray. Although normally the most peaceful of beings, Robin, once roused, could fight with deadly determination.

Together he and Jack began to force the two smugglers towards their boat. Realising that they were not going to overcome their adversaries quickly, Will and Luff strove to disengage. Luff drew his pistol and fired in the general direction of their attackers. The shot imbedded itself in Jack's shoulder spinning him around. Luff gave the boat a shove to refloat it while Will took deliberate aim.

With a cry of agony Jack sank to the ground. Unnerved by the pistol shots, Robin, like some biblical patriarch, followed the boat into the water, waving the pike in the air, muttering curses against the foul fiend. He shook his staff at the departing vessel.

'The foul fiend goes with thee. He will consume thee yet.'

Margaret, realising she was free, struggled to the shore, climbed the bank and ran, as fast as her sodden clothes and muddy boots would let her, back to Priory Farm.

Her sudden, dishevelled appearance in the midst of the revelry caused instant attention.

'Hurry! Oh hurry! There's murder happening on the shore.'

As if to prove her statement a pistol shot was heard, quickly followed by another. Tankards were dropped and tables overturned as everyone raced towards the door.

The sound of shots filled Margaret with dread. Who had fired them? Had anyone been hit? Was it Will or her rescuer? Fearful of the outcome she raced back again and was one of the first to arrive.

Recognising the prone figure as Jack, she sank down beside him. He was covered in blood from his shoulder wound. His more serious wound only became evident as they tried to move him.

Margaret, distraught, sobbed, 'Jack! Oh dear Jack. Have they killed you?'

The gamekeeper pushed her aside and feeling beneath Jack's shirt felt a heart beat 'He's not dead. We must get help at once. You men, carry him back to the farm. Gently, he's bleeding freely and in great pain.'

Several men formed a double line and then, lifting him as gently as they could, carried him back to the house and the remains of the revelry.

While Jack was being carried carefully to the farm, Margaret again raced ahead of them. All attention was on the procession so, though exhausted, she slipped up to her room, got out of her sodden clothes, and returned to the kitchen in time to assist her mistress who had taken charge.

Margaret was the first to respond to the command for hot water. She flinched as Mistress Southgate removed Jack's jacket and gently bathed the worst of the blood away. She feverishly tore a cotton sheet into strips and folded them into swabs for her mistress to pack around the wound.

The surgeon had been sent for so, as soon as bleeding had been staunched, Jack was moved to a small room where a bed had been prepared.

When she realised that Jack was not going to die, Margaret's thoughts turned to Will. Had he also been wounded? Had he been the one who fired the shots? She desperately wanted to know what had happened but did not want to draw attention to her part in the proceedings.

She tried to shut out the events that had taken place, but

could not throw off the anguish and disappointment felt at the dreadful end to what was to have been her happiest night.

In the kitchen everybody wanted to know what had happened down by the river. Unnoticed at first, Robinson Crusoe had entered and sat on a hob near the fire mumbling to himself. The foreman of the field became aware of the ancient fisherman and wondered if he had seen anything on the riverbank, and if he was coherent enough to recall it.

'Tell me Robin, were you there?'

A gleam of recognition came into the old man's eyes. 'Robin were there,' he chuckled to himself. 'Robin were there and he sees the foul fiend. He told' em to take care.'

He had everyone's attention now.

'Did you see the shooting, Robin?'

'Who fired the gun, man?'

'Who's the foul fiend?'

Robin, ignoring most of the questions, settled on the one that was most important to him.

'The foul fiend be the Devil himself. Left off tormenting poor Robin and settled on their boat. I knowed he would be up to his foul mischief. Always making trouble but he don't get away with it with Robin. Not while I got my spells. See this,' and he held up one of his talismans, a piece of perforated bone. His eyes had glazed over again and he was back in his own tortured world. 'They be a mighty powerful spell, bone of an abandoned maid, died of grief. Thee be afraid of this,' and he cackled madly as he held up the bone to an invisible foe. 'Thee can't touch Robin when he point this at thee.'

His eyes cleared again, 'But narry a charm did they have. I knowed there would be evil. I warned poor Will, but the devil was in him. I had to drive him back.'

His audience had diminished but a few were still attending.

'What did he say about Will? Will who, Robin?'

But Robin had gone back to his mumbling, his hands formed gestures to ward off the evil ones.

'Do you think he knows what he's saying?'

'Did he say there was more than one?'

'Will. Will who? Anyone know who he's on about?'

'He's raving again. Take no mind, it's probably just one of his phantoms.'

'Wait a minute. Wasn't Margaret Catchpole there? Why was she there?'

This new evidence added to the conundrum.

'Margaret and Will Laud. Could it be Laud?'

'Not unless he's come back from the dead to join Robin's ghosts. He's dead as a door nail. I know the man what killed him.'

'Yes, but they never found the body, did they. What if he wasn't killed after all?'

Everyone had something to add to the discussion now. If Will Laud was alive then Margaret's presence made sense. But still, what was Jack doing there? Was he a rival for Margaret's affections? They plied Robin with questions and ale but his lucid moment had gone.

Margaret, unaware of the discussions going on, entered the kitchen. She was immediately plied with questions and accusations.

She looked around to deflect the conversation. Not knowing of Robin's part in the fight she turned on him asking, 'What are you doing here Robin? Did you see the fight?'

Robin's eyes cleared and he grinned back at her.

'Did you see it? I seed thee, long before the fight, waiting by the shore.'

Margaret, shocked, turned to face a sea of accusations but was lucky that at that moment her mistress called for assistance.

As she left Robin chuckled. 'There's a clever girl for you boys. Who would have her as a wife?'

'Ask Joe,' said one sly fellow

'What about Jack? They seemed awful friendly. She must have had a tryst with him. But whose his rival?'

'That foul fiend, Robin? Was he Jack's rival?'

'Nay, though the black fiend was in him. Back from the dead he was, and tried to claim his girl and take her back with him.'

'Back from the dead! Who are you talking about you old

fool?' The head fieldsman, who had been paying scant attention, felt that there was something to be learned in the old man's rambling after all.

'Why, Will Laud of course, back from Hell this long time, looking well and hearty.' The old fisherman rose rattling his charms. 'The foul fiend has brought him back to do his bidding. Many a time I've seen him in the mist. I wished the fiend would let him go before he gave the poor lad that fearful blow. I offered him a charm.'

Once again Robin was off with his signs and incantations. They knew they would get no more from him for a while but they already had enough to argue on for the rest of the night. Never had there been such an exciting Harvest Home.

Margaret requested that she be permitted to assist the surgeon as he worked to extract the bullet and clean Jack's wounds. Knowing her reliability Mistress Southgate readily agreed. The two women prepared the room and the patient for the operation.

When the surgeon arrived the full extent of Jack's wounds was revealed. One ball had hit the upper arm, breaking it. Then it had passed between the scapula and clavicle. It could be felt lying in the external portion of the shoulder muscle. It would be relatively easy to retrieve. The problem lay in removing the particles of clothing that had been carried into the wound.

The other wound was more serious. The shot that had been fired by Laud had pierced through the long dorsal muscle and the ball lay directly against the bone. It was this that was causing Jack agonising pain.

At this point he was fully conscious so he was given a large glass of whisky and steeled himself for the ordeal. He had not spoken but looking around him and, seeing Margaret, he gave a deep sigh.

The operation took time and Jack moaned in pain, sweating profusely. Mercifully he finally sank into unconsciousness.

The surgeon was Margaret's old friend Dr Stebbins. When he had finally finished he turned his attention to her. Though efficient when helping, at other times she stood shivering as if she had experienced some great shock.

Knowing her mettle he was sure that it had not been caused because of having assisted at the operation, painful as it had been. Something greater was troubling her and he was determined to get to the bottom of it.

'Would you like to partake of a little food, Doctor?' Mistress Southgate enquired when the surgery was at last complete. 'It is late and you have a long ride home.'

'I had already supped before I was called, thank you. If I could have a little nutmeg in brandy and water and a liberal slice of your harvest cake that will suffice. But first, if you will permit, I would speak with your servant, Margaret. We are old friends and I feel she may be in need of medical advice. May I see her in a private room.'

Margaret was present during this conversation but made no effort to interrupt, only looked to her mistress for instructions.

They were shown into the parlour and Margaret stood before the man she had always regarded as a friend. She remembered her first encounter with him and the tender way he had cared for poor Susan during her long illness. The memory of her dear sister, the doctor's kindness and the happiness she had known in those days was too much for her. She was quite overcome and would have fainted had not Dr Stebbins taken her by the hand and led her to a settle.

'I do not like the look of your complexion, Margaret. Let me feel your pulse.' He listened for a short while and felt her brow.

'Your pulse is quick and you have some fever.'

'Thank you sir, but I will be better tomorrow. I am sorry sir for all that has happened. I am the cause of it all.' The pent up emotions had reached breaking point. Like a bursting dam the tears splashed down her cheeks and for some time she was incapable of speech

Dr Stebbins, knowing that tears were often the best medicine, let her cry herself out. When the shaking had stopped and the storm of tears had been reduced to a misty rain he took out a white linen handkerchief, wiped the sodden cheeks then gave it to her to blow.

'Why did you say it was all your fault, Margaret?' he asked.

'Because if I had not been there nothing would have happened.'

'And why were you there?' the doctor probed gently.

Margaret hung her head. 'I was there to meet somebody,' then, looking earnestly into his eyes, 'but please, I cannot tell you who it was.'

'Then you saw it all Margaret. You saw who fired the shot.'

'No, Doctor! No I didn't. I swear I was gone when the shot was fired. I only wish I knew who fired it.'

Dr Stebbins did not doubt the truth of her statement.

'There, there. I believe you. Jack will be able to tell us later. Just tell me the whole story as you know it.'

Margaret told him everything, excluding Will's name. When she had finished he suggested that she tell her employers. Though afraid, Margaret could see that it was the right thing to do. Her repentance was so sincere that her mistress forgave her, only extracting a promise that she would never do such a thing again.

Happier than she had felt for some hours, Margaret went to her room to spend the night in fretful sleep, in her mind seeking answers to two questions, was Will hurt and who had fired the shots. She dreaded the morning when she would again have to face questions from her fellow workers.

CHAPTER SEVEN

Doctor Stebbins had decided that it would be unwise to move Jack for a few days and suggested that if Margaret could be spared she would make an excellent nurse. Mistress Southgate was only too happy to agree. Though accepting Margaret's remorse she was nevertheless anxious about her continuing to be in charge of her daughters. This would give her a chance to replace Margaret without seeming to punish her.

Margaret was most willing to act as nurse as she felt responsible for Jack's injury. It also kept her away from the prying questions in the kitchen. She was hoping that Jack would be able to tell her what had happened and on the second day Margaret judged that Jack was well enough to speak with her.

'Jack. I am so sorry that all this has happened to you.'

'I'm sure that with you to help, Margaret, I will get well all the sooner.'

'It is the least I can do seeing I was the cause of all this.'

'What do you mean? What have you to do with it?' Jack asked

Margaret was surprised. 'Did you not know? I was the woman you rescued.'

'You!' Jack was so surprised at this news that he tried to sit up. The effort caused him pain. He sank back, his face almost as white as the pillow. Margaret fussed over him, bathing his brow with a little water and vinegar. She was afraid that her news had set his recovery back but in a short time he was well enough to continue.

'Margaret. I had no idea it was you. I only knew that a woman was in distress. I'm now doubly glad that I intervened.'

A sudden thought occurred to Jack and his eyes clouded. 'Margaret, was one of the men Will Laud?' he enquired tentatively.

'Yes Jack, it was Will, but I beg you to keep that secret.'

'You know that I will, but please, Margaret, will you tell me what it was all about?'

Margaret composed herself. She was ashamed of what she was about to confess but if anyone should be told the whole truth it was Jack.

'The day before Harvest Home, Will sent me a message to meet him by the shore. The message was delivered by a man from Holland and I was sure that Will had made good his promise to change his life.' She looked earnestly into Jack's eyes. 'You must believe me, Jack. I had heard nothing from him for two years. I was so happy to get his message, but I would not have gone if I had known he was still a smuggler.'

Jack nodded encouragingly. He knew how hard it was for her to tell her story.

'It was a happy reunion but then he wanted me to leave with him.'

'And you didn't want to go?' enquired Jack hopefully.

'I was more than ready to go with him, but not to run away without telling anyone. We were arguing about it when Luff called out. Then I knew the truth, that Will had not changed his trade. There was no way that I would go then.'

Tears formed in Margaret's eyes. Now it was she who needed time to compose herself,

'But surely Laud would not have taken you against your wishes?'

Margaret hung her head and whispered 'I'm afraid, Jack, that he would have if you had not intervened. He has changed since I last saw him.'

'This Luff. Was he the man who grabbed you?'

'That was he.' She replied between clenched teeth. 'The most evil man I know. It is he who has turned Will into the man he now is.'

Jack had another opinion but he knew better than to express it. He knew that the disclosure was hard for her. He noted that she had still not condemned Will himself. To turn her mind from the distressful confession he asked, 'Did I dream it or was there a strange creature in a long garb all covered with bones and bells who came to help me?'

Margaret caught her breath. That explained Robin's involvement in the proceedings.

'That was Robinson Crusoe. Have you not seen him around? I did not know, but it must have been him'

'He was magnificent. Without him I would have been cut down for sure. He saved my life.'

'And you saved mine Jack, for I had resolved to throw myself into the sea sooner than join those men.'

Again they sat in silence, each contemplating what might have been. Finally Margaret asked the question that was troubling her.

'Jack, who fired the shots?'

Jack paused before answering. He knew his answer was of vital importance to Margaret. 'I must say truthfully that I do not know. Each of them fired their pistols but which one fired at me I cannot tell.'

Margaret sighed. She knew that Jack would not lie to her. She would never know now, not unless she asked Robin, but could he be relied on? Perhaps it was better to remain in doubt.

Mr Ingham, Jack's father, visited him twice before Dr Stebbing declared him well enough to be moved. On the second visit Jack confided to his father his fondness for Margaret.

'But Jack, how could you? Not only is she a ploughman's daughter but it is said she has connections with smugglers.'

'Father, you do her an injustice. A more honest person you could not meet. She may be a cottage girl but she is intelligent and hard working. She can read and write and has an enquiring mind. She can turn her hand to all manner of work and has more common sense than anyone I know. I have loved her for more than a year and I have vowed that only she will be my wife.'

The father, realising that Jack's devotion was not just an infatuation, brought on by the tender care he was receiving, said no more, but he was determined that Margaret Catchpole would never become his daughter-in-law.

When Jack was well enough to be moved his fellow labourers constructed a device for carrying him. A frame was constructed and, on a fine October day, twelve undertook the task. They managed to place him and his bed onto the frame. It had shoulder pieces, and in this way he was conveyed to his home, his mother supervising operations. Jack's father remained behind, and asked Mrs Southgate if he could have a few words with Margaret to thank her for the care she had given his son.

So, once again Margaret was summoned to the sitting room to talk to an older gentleman.

'My dear, Jack's mother and I are grateful to you for the careful nursing of my son,' the old man began.

'Oh sir, do not thank me. It was no hardship and Jack has been my good friend for some time.' Margaret was confused in front of this kindly man.

'Your good friend,' he repeated softly. 'And are you also his good friend?'

'Oh yes sir. I hope so.' Margaret replied earnestly.

'You seem a sensible girl and I'm sure it will not embarrass you to have me tell you that my son has a great fondness for you. Being a sensible girl, I'm sure you will realise how unsuitable a match between you two would be. My son is an educated gentleman and, whatever he chooses to do, has a great future ahead of him. Do not take this amiss, my dear, but for a young man like my son, a wife such as you, with your reputation, would be a disaster. It would destroy any opportunity he has to advance himself.'

Margaret's eyes widened with distress. She could not believe what she was hearing. Here again was someone of a higher standing than herself, judging her, not by the deeds, but by her reputation.

'Dear Miss Catchpole, I am not trying to insult you. I have the highest regard for you personally, but, as a good friend, you can see that my son's infatuation with you must cease.'

Margaret swallowed her shock and anger and, retained her

dignity, replying civilly, 'I can assure you, sir, that you have no fear of me taking an advantage of your son's feelings for me. I have ever held no more than friendly feelings for Jack but for your sake I will not speak to him again.'

Watching the departing cavalcade Margaret gave a deep sigh. Now that Jack was gone she could not hide herself away. She knew that she was in for an unpleasant time.

Margaret's fears were soon realised. Released from the sick room she found that she had been replaced as the children's maid. She no longer had close contact with the family and had to surrender her single room next to the nursery to share one of the maids' rooms in the attic. She resented her demotion and felt she had been shabbily treated by her Mistress. Her duties were now in the kitchen where she became the butt of everyone's jeers and gossip. She accepted this as punishment for her part in the happenings on the river, but could not understand why no one stood up for her.

'Ho Peggy,' leered Joe Simpsoll, one of her rejected suitors. 'Been wandering to the shore again lately?'

'No joy in that,' teased another of the men. 'Will Laud won't show his face around here again. You'll have to make do with an honest ploughboy. That's if anyone of them would have thee.'

'I would no mind a quick dip behind the barn if you feel the need Peg,' cackled an old, weather beaten cow herder.

Though Margaret had not confessed that Will was still alive, it was generally assumed that he had been present during the fight. Some were not convinced that he was alive which added mystery to the adventure.

The women were no better. They delighted in spreading rumours about the capture of smugglers. Bella, the girl who shared a room with Margaret was very superstitious. She was convinced that Margaret was consorting with spirits and burned candles night and day to keep them away from her. She also searched through Margaret's belongings looking for proof of her suspicions. She gained some notoriety by telling of strange noises and conversations that were supposed to come from Margaret's side of the room in the dead of night.

Margaret, determined not to sink into the melancholia she had known before Will's injury, kept her sanity by taking on more than her share of the work, happy if she could fall into her bed at night, too tired to think. But even though her hands were kept busy, her mind wandered in the mire of misery, wondering what her future would be.

A few weeks after he had left, a letter came from Jack, full of hope and good wishes. He informed her that, as soon as he was well enough, he would come to visit her.

'. . . *now that you know what an evil heart Laud has, I'm sure he will no longer have any hold on you. I would hopefully renew my wish to make you my own. I welcome all that I have gone through if it will gain me the prize I value above all others*'

Margaret read the letter over again, weeping bitterly and wishing she could turn back time. If only she had never met Will, if only she hadn't given herself to him, if only she had not given her promise to Jack's father. Jack had opened his heart to her even though he knew of her rendezvous with Will. She would not break her promise but she did not want to hurt him. How would he interpret her silence? If only she could explain.

She looked at the paper she was holding. She could read his message. Why couldn't she write a message back? Writing was not talking so she would not be breaking her promise, but did she know enough words to tell him what was in her heart? This would be the first letter she had ever written. Could she really do it? She decided that she would at least try.

Having decided to try, she set about the practicalities. Where could she get pen and paper now that she no longer had access to the classroom?

Eventually she decided to take the problem to her Mistress. That good lady was most impressed with Margaret's resolve to keep her promise to Mr Ingham and offered to write the letter for her but Margaret declined. She wanted to explain in her own words, be they be ever so inadequate. It was sufficient that she was given pen and paper.

After several false starts she began to try and break her ties with Jack without hurting him.

My derest frend Jack,

My hart is ful as I rite this I was very hapy to here that you ar recovring so wel God is good to di rect the shot into your sholder and not into a vitle spot hop you will regan the ful us of yor arm

My der frend, the Honor you giv me in arskin me to be yor Wif will be my gratest tresure and it braks my hart but i canot acksept such a sincer proposl but all that has hapened has not distroid my promis to Will or leson the hop that some day somwere i will be the agent of his Chang i canor abandon him Jack i am his only hop
Plese Forgiv me Jack forget me and start a New life

From Your Derest frend

Margaret Catchpole

Margaret persisted, ignoring the taunts and jeers of her fellow workers, continuing to work at Priory Farm. She remembered that, years ago, her father had said that people forget when something new happens, but for now she was still the main topic of gossip.

She did not complain until one day she discovered Bella searching through her possessions. She was already suspicious of Bella and had kept her eye on her. Noticing that she was not at her usual place of work, she slipped up to her room to find Bella on her knees, in the process of opening the pouch that contained, among other things, the necklace Will had given her.

Her anger, long suppressed, exploded. 'How dare you. How dare you touch my things.' She caught Bella by the hair dragging her to the ground'

The girl was taken completely by surprise. ' Ooh! Help! Murder! Help!'

Bella's screams were heard all over the house. Many of the staff ran towards the source but, fortunately for Margaret, Mistress Southgate was in the vicinity. She hurried up the narrow stairs, ordering everybody out while she investigated.

'What is going on here?' she demanded

Bella was still too shocked to give a coherent account, but

Margaret had regained her composure. 'I found Bella going through my things.' She held up the pouch as proof

Mistress Southgate assumed that the motive was theft. 'Bella, you deceitful girl, I will not have a thief in my house.'

The frightened girl tried to defend herself. 'I wasn't stealing her stuff. Don't want anything to do with her stuff.'

'Then what were you doing with this pouch?'

Bella was struck dumb. How could she explain to her mistress that she was looking for proof that Margaret was consorting with the Devil?

'She wasn't stealing, Mistress. It was just mischief. Ever since the incident when Jack was shot she has been spreading rumours about me.'

'They not be rumours Mistress. She entertains the devil here at night.' Bella was getting her courage back. She was sure the mistress would dismiss Margaret.

'Bella! Stop that nonsense at once. Had I known you believed such superstition I would never have employed you at all. Go and pack your case at once.'

'It's not her fault, Mistress,' Margaret explained. 'They're all at it in the kitchen. They get pleasure in tormenting me with all manner of accusations. Bella is but repeating what she hears. Don't punish her for it.'

The good woman was shocked that such things were going on under her roof. She would have sacked Bella if it had not been for Margaret's intersession. She summoned all the kitchen staff and warned them that all such persecution must cease.

Her warning gave many food for thought and the more active tormenting ceased, but a more insidious form of persecution began. Bella showed no gratitude for Margaret's intervention. She was seen as the victim of the event and her standing in the kitchen went up a notch. Any little tit-bit that she had to tell was eagerly listened to and repeated.

Margaret stood alone, doing her work in silence. She often wondered if anything could be worse that the misery she now felt. She had heard nothing about Will.

She knew that the gossip was nothing but malicious rumour.

If there were any real news, her fellow workers would have been only too glad to tell her. She longed to know if Will was well, but dreaded the thought that he might try to make contact with her.

Such were the circumstances when a small package arrived. Walking into the kitchen the messenger informed. 'Package for one, Margaret Catchpole.'

Margaret, suspicious, moved slowly to take it but Bella was faster. She grabbed it and held it high.

'A present from her smuggler lover. Let's see what treasure he has sent.'

Everyone crowded around the long table as Bella ripped off the covering to reveal a small bible!

There was a deathly silence as Margaret, with dignity, moved forward with outstretched hand to receive the book from the shame-faced Bella. Not a word was spoken as Margaret walked out of the kitchen and up to her room. It was only then that she really looked at the book. Just inside was a short message.

I am leaving England. I will not see you again but I will always love you - May God bless you and bring you happiness. from your dearest friend Jack.

Margaret sat on her bed still holding the bible. She had already promised that she would never see Jack again but here was proof. Now she would she never, even accidently, see her dear friend. He was leaving England and he would never be back. He was going to a place that she knew nothing about. She would not even be able to imagine that he was walking beside some familiar river or climbing an English hill. He was going so far away that he might as well be dead. The two men she most cared for in all the world were banished from her life, one because of love of her and the other because of love of adventure.

She imagined herself, growing old, with never the chance to be wife and mother. She would end up a lonely, old spinster, alone and unloved. She lowered the guard on her emotions that she had kept in check for so long and cried out all her agony, anger and loneliness. When she had cried herself out she wiped her eyes, got out her valise, packed her possessions and went to find her mistress.

'Dear Mistress, I can no longer work here. I have no criticism of yourself, nor the master but I suffer so much from the taunts and even the looks of those who work here that I am miserable day and night. I wish to go home to my father's house.'

'My poor Margaret,' Mistress Southgate sighed, shaking her head at this unfortunate girl who had brought so much misery upon herself. 'I am so sorry that this could happen under my roof but I cannot command my servants how to think. I will be sorry to see you go for you are most excellent worker. Would it help if I wrote you a character?'

'Oh Mistress, that is so good of you. I am a poor girl and will always have to earn my keep. A letter from you will surely help as I wish to find employment where I am not known.'

With the consolation that her employers, at least, held her in some regard Margaret left Priory Farm to return, once more, to the reduced state in which her father now lived.

CHAPTER EIGHT

Margaret knew that she would have to find work so took her problems to the one man she knew she could rely on, Dr Stebbins. He knew her whole history and yet he had never judged her harshly.

'I need to change my life, Sir, I am a good worker and I want to be useful, but I can't put up with all the sneers and gossip. I need to get employment far from Nacton. Please can you help me?'

The old gentleman smiled encouragingly. 'My dear, you know I would always help you if I could. However the only person who can really help you is yourself. Can you give up all association with your smuggling friend?'

'Oh Sir, how can I answer such a question?'

'You must, if you want my help. Can you promise me that you will never see Will Laud again. I know that it was Laud who tried to abduct you. Promise me that.'

'Doctor, I cannot make that promise, for I still believe that there will come a time when he will want to change and then I must be there to help him. But I will promise that I will not seek him out and I will have nothing to do with him unless I have proof that he has changed.'

Dr Stebbins sighed. He wanted to help this girl for he saw much good in her and realised that this would be as big a concession as she would make.

'That will have to be good enough for me, Margaret, though I must tell you that I think your faith in him will never be fulfilled. Still, no one can foretell the future and stranger things have happened.'

The good doctor shook his head in wonder at the girl's

fidelity. 'I think I can help you. A good friend of mine, a lady who is mistress of Cliff, on the banks of the Orwell, has written, asking for my help in finding a suitable servant. Do you think I can trust you not to disappoint me?'

Margaret felt like a drowning person who had been thrown a life-line.

'Yes, yes, Dr Stebbing. I am willing to do any work and I promise that I will never disgrace you.'

The kind doctor smiled at the sincerity of her answer. In many ways she had not changed from the earnest child he had first encountered so many years ago He wondered what her future would have been if she had never encountered Laud

'I will write a letter immediately and if she has not already employed another I am sure you will be suitable for her. One last thing, Margaret. If you are planning to leave your old life behind, I think it would be as well to tell all to your new mistress in case she should, in future, hear gossip and think the less of you.'

'Oh Sir, how can I tell anyone but you?'

'You know you must, if you want to have a future. There is no way that your employer will not hear of your past, sooner or later. Let her hear the truth from you rather than some fabrication from others.'

Margaret thought over this advice for a few moments. It would mean telling things of which she was ashamed. Would this new prospective employer use it as a reason not to employ her or would she judge her more honest for her telling. In the end, she knew that it was good advice.

'You are right, Sir. But will she employ me when I have told her everything?'

'That's a chance you will have to take, Margaret but, if I know anything of Elizabeth Cobbold, I know she is a fair minded woman and will recognize that you will be a valuable addition to her establishment.

Elizabeth was John Cobbold's second wife. He had already had twelve children by his first marriage and Elizabeth had presented him with two more by the time Margaret joined the household.

Margaret's time was to be spent assisting in the nursery and the kitchen. Her greatest joy was that she would again be working with children so she quickly became content, if not actually happy, in her situation. The children were a constant joy to her. She delighted in the morning lessons in the schoolroom, over which Mrs Cobbold presided, because they enabled her to continue the learning that had commenced at the Priory.

The afternoon walks were another source of pleasure. Cliff was set in a spacious park and the surrounding countryside of dells and river were a never-ending font of enjoyment to her as well as to the children. These walks had another fascination for Margaret.

Along with her many other interests, Mrs Cobbold was quite a well informed botanist. She felt it important to pass this interest onto the children, particularly the girls. During these afternoon walks they were expected to collect specimens, which they would later identify, press and when dried, enter into a book and label with their common and botanical names.

Margaret enjoyed learning the long Latin names for flowers she had known all her life by their common names. In fact she was sometimes able to add local names to many flowers.

She began a book of her own. Having always been a keen observer of nature, she found this new knowledge added to her interest. Walks were never dull.

One afternoon, during the walk, Masters, George and Fredrick became engrossed in listening to the sound of a rat that they had chased into a hole under the foundations of a building where workmen had been making alterations.

'Peggy, come and listen,' they called to her. 'Come and listen. You can hear the rat chewing as clear as clear.'

Margaret, fearful that the rat might appear and bite one of them, hurried forward, the other children trailing behind. She listened at the hole and quickly recognised the sound for what it was. She grabbed each boy by an arm and pulled them to their feet.

'Come away! Quickly! The wall is crumbling,' she called in terror. The boys, sensing the urgency in her voice scrambled to safety. They were only a few yards away when the whole thing came crashing down just where the boys had been listening.

They watched in awe then threw their arms around Margaret, thanking her for saving them. On reaching the house they raced to tell their mother of their miraculous escape. This incident earned the undying love and gratitude of the family and from that time Margaret was treated more as a colleague than a servant.

The Orwell was a pleasant place in summer but in the winter it became a sportsman's paradise. Millions of black coot darkened the water and duck, mallard, diver, bar goose and even wild swans were seen in great numbers.

One of the Cobbold boys, Roland, was particularly addicted to shooting. Though only twelve, he was a good shot and usually brought home a brace of duck and mallard whenever he went out.

At four o'clock one winter's afternoon he set off with gun and oars towards the boathouse, intending to go up the channel to get some birds. He took no notice of the darkening clouds. His sisters, Harriet and Sophie, saw him but he made them promise not to tell anyone where he had gone.

In a large household it was hard to keep track of individual members all the time, so Roland's absence was not noticed until teatime. This was the one time of the day when all but the youngest members assembled. John Cobbold came from his private rooms to take his seat at the head of the table. He cast an affectionate eye over his brood, ready to give his blessing before they began consuming the great pile of toast and bread and butter. His smile turned to a frown when he noticed an empty place.

'Where is Roland?' he enquired.

Harriet and Sophie began to titter nervously.

John looked at them sternly. 'Do you know where Roland is?'

Both girls looked apprehensively at each other.

'What tricks are you two up to?' their father demanded.

'Do you know where Roland is?' his wife inquired sweetly of the girls. 'You must not play games at this time. Tell your Papa where Roland is.'

Sophie hung her head and Harriet blubbered. 'But we cannot.'

'Cannot,' their father roared. He loved his children but he had little patience with their nonsense. 'And pray, madam, why not?'

'Because,' whispered Sophie, 'we promised not to.'

Exasperated John Cobbold rose from his chair.

'Sophie, Harriet,' Elizabeth intervened, 'it is good to keep promises but not from your parents. Now answer Papa truthfully.'

'We saw him going down to the boat house,' Harriet declared.

'He had his gun and some oars,' Sophie added. Released from her promise she was happy to supply details. 'He told us not to tell you as he was only going to be gone for an hour.'

'What!' cried their father, his tone turning quickly to concern. 'When was this?'

'Just before the big clock rang three.'

'But that was two hours ago.' Elizabeth Cobbold, her usual composure gone, hurried to her husband's side. 'Oh John. You don't think he would have taken to the river in weather like this?'

'Knowing Roland, I fear he would.' John Cobbold strode towards the hall. 'Parkinson, get lanterns, rope, every available man. Get them down to the boathouse. Dear God, if he is on the river on a night like this he is lost.'

In no time the house was all bustle as lanterns were lit. The brew-house men were summoned and two strong fellows hurried to launch the skiff. While they began their search along the channel others went along the shore calling and flashing lanterns. Among the searchers was Margaret, as desperate as if she were herself the mother of the child. She had thrown a cloak over her head and, in spite of a command to stay back, had followed her master to lend a hand if needed.

It was a desperate situation. The tide was running out fast and a piercing sleet, a forerunner of snowstorms, was falling. The two groups communicated for a time but then the boatmen's cries could no longer be heard. Those on the bank walked for miles flashing their lanterns, calling, then listening for any reply but only the sound of the wind could be heard.

John Cobbold had lived all his life on the river and knew its dangers. He was steadily coming to the conclusion that his son could not have survived such a night.

He held up his hand. 'It's no good. If he were alive we would have found him by now. It is useless to continue.'

'Oh, don't give up, Sir! Not yet.' Margaret pleaded. 'Let us go a little further. Roland is a resourceful boy and he knows the river well. Let us go a little further. We cannot go home yet.'

They had gone no more than a hundred yards when, a short distance away, they saw a figure sheltering under some trees.

'Who goes there?' John Cobbold shouted.

'Who wants to know?' came a gruff reply.

Margaret's heart pounded. There could be no doubt. She would recognize that voice anywhere.

'Will? It is you?'

'Margaret!' came the astonished reply. 'What are you doing out on a night like this?'

'Mr Cobbold has lost his son. Please help us in the search.' There was no time to speculate on this surprise meeting.

'My son is missing on the riv□er,' Cobbold explained. 'Did you come this way?'

'I did sir. I came up the river as far as I could but the ice floes were so troublesome that I decided to come ashore and walk to Ipswich. If there had been a boat along the way I would have seen it.'

Just then they could hear voices calling from the water.

'Ahoy! Ahoy!' Laud called.

An answering voice called across the river. 'We have found the boat but it is empty.'

'Then my son surely is lost,' sobbed the distraught father.

'Maybe not, Sir,' Laud argued. 'If the boy knows the river he would have known this point. Maybe he abandoned the boat and tried walking along the channel to reach this hard ground.'

'But he had no mud splashes. He would never have made it,' reasoned the heart broken father.

While the men were discussing these possibilities Margaret had been searching the shore.

'Sir! Look! What is that dark shape?'

'It is only one of the buoys that the boats tie up to,' explained Cobbold.

'No,' replied Laud. 'There are no buoys along this part of the river.'

'Then what is it?' Margaret persisted.

'I don't know, but I'll soon find out.' Without more ado Laud, throwing off his coat, stepped into the river and began to investigate. Soon he was lying full length, crawling over the soft mud to avoid being sucked under.

The watchers on the bank took heart as they saw him quicken his pace until he reached the shape.

Frantically he called to them. 'It's him all right. Margaret, you were right. It's him.'

Cheers went up from the bank as Laud hoisted the boy on his back, put the boy's arms around his neck and tied them with his handkerchief. Then he began the slow trip back through the mud. When he reached the bank, anxious hands helped him ashore.

The boy was stiff and lifeless. He was completely covered in mud, his legs hanging uselessly like two muddy logs. A sigh went up from those around.

'Don't give up hope,' Laud shouted. 'He's just frozen stiff but I've seen men recover from worse. We must get him to warmth and shelter as quickly as possible.'

Will supervised the construction of a makeshift stretcher from a hurdle lying on the bank. He covered it with his own jacket and Mr Cobbold's greatcoat. Margaret covered the body with her cloak. Then they set off at a steady pace.

Margaret, filled with a new energy, raced ahead to get help to prepare the household, but the news had already reached Cliff. One of the searchers had raced back to Cliff as soon as he could see that Will had the boy. Mrs Cobbold immediately organised servants to help the searchers. They were already coming towards Margaret, carrying blankets and brandy in case the boy should be in need of them. They took over from the near exhausted rescuers. Margaret continued on to the house to be sure there was plenty of hot water when they arrived.

A fire was lit in the sick room and the bath and the salt to rub his limbs were ready by the time they carried the limp form into the house. He was stripped of all his sodden, muddy clothes and two servants began to administer first aid. They worked on the seemingly lifeless body for some time without seeing any noticeable change. Someone had already hurried to bring the doctor.

When Dr Stebbins arrived he quickly took over. First he opened a vein and was encouraged when the smallest of drops of blood appeared. He ordered the boy to be put into a tepid bath then, by degrees hot water was added. The drops of blood came a little faster. Soon he could detect a gentle pulsating of the heart. A few drops of brandy were forced into Roland's lips, which had been colourless, but slowly began to redden. At last the chest began to heave. The anxious watchers relaxed.

Roland was alive!

As soon as Margaret was sure that the boy was out of danger she went to speak with Will and learn how he had appeared at such an opportune time. She was sure, in her own mind, that he had been sent by God, but she wished to learn how this miracle had occurred.

In the kitchen he was the hero of the hour. Mr Cobbold had already given orders that he was to be offered the hospitality of the house. A generous supply of his finest ale was provided. When Margaret entered the whole assembly was seated around a well-spread table in front of a blazing fire and Will was asked over and over to explain all that had happened on the banks of the Orwell that night. They plied him with questions about his part in the rescue. Will was suitably modest but everyone knew that it was his actions that had saved the young master.

She stood at the door, her heart swelling with pride to see Will so well received by her fellow workers. She gazed fondly on her lover then noticed, for the first time, what he was wearing. The worst of the mud had been scraped from his trousers but they were still stained a dun colour, his jacket was drying on a rail above the fire but it was still obvious that he was wearing the uniform of the King's navy.

'Oh Will!' she spoke in awe. 'You have become a real sailor.'

Grinning, Will stood, held out his arms and turned around, displaying his new appearance.

'Do you think it suits me?'

Margaret's eyes feasted on him; his black hair hanging in a long man-of-war pig tail; his black beard adding strength to his broad open face; the very archetype of a weather beaten tar.

'But how - why are you here?' she asked, still only half believing what stood before her.

'The 'why' is easy. To see you. I approached your father. When he was sure that I had changed my ways he told me where you were. He said he did not know if he was doing the right thing but he believed you loved me still and that your only hope of happiness was with me.'

Margaret forgot that there was anyone else in the room. 'It's true Will. I will never love anyone but you.'

Her declaration brought cheers from all in the room. It was only then that she became aware that a room full of workers was listening to her declaration of love. She covered her face in embarrassment but Will took her hands in his.

'Come, sit over here and I will tell you the 'how'. It takes a little more explaining.' They retired to a bench against a far wall and the rest of the company gave them the privacy they sought. They sat in the shadowy corner, facing each other and holding hands as Will began his story.

'Not long after you last saw me, and please forgive me for my stupid actions,' he squeezed her hands, 'I was seised by a press gang. I was bound to serve His Majesty's navy for three years aboard the *Briton*. Such was the need of ships to fight the French that I was offered a free pardon if I served my time honestly. I was a great catch.

'Fortunately my captain, who is a grand fellow, recognised my worth and gave me recognition and responsibility. He is so pleased with me that, being in this area, he has permitted me to visit you, but I must join the ship in Ipswich in the morning.'

'And Will,' whispered the girl, hardly daring to break the magic of the moment. 'Do you find the life of a sailor satisfies you?'

Will squeezed her hands again and gazed earnestly into her steady brown eyes.

'If your question is 'will I go back to the old game,' then I can assure you, my love, the answer is no. I have seen through the excitement and adventure to the cruel and squalid side of that life. I have fallen out with Bargood and could not spend another day on a ship with Luff

'Though I cursed it when I was first press ganged, I have come to realise that it was the best thing that had ever happened to me. I believe that it was your prayers that led me into their hands. Now I am a free man. I can get all the adventure I want while serving my country. I may never make the fortune I dreamed of, but I have steady pay and we get a percentage of the prize money for the ships we capture. I already have a small sum waiting for me. Who knows I may have enough to buy myself a small ship and become an honest trader.

'So you see, my darling girl, I may yet become the fellow I promised to be all those years ago. If you still want this foolish rogue, I will marry you, in front of your family at the Nacton church as soon as my time is up?'

Margaret was dizzy with happiness. It was as if all the things that had happened since that first day when he had entered her father's house had been wiped away.

'Dearest Will, I feel as if my heart will burst. It makes all that went before worthwhile. I shall pray for your safety every day and I know that the good God, who has been watching over you, will keep you safe until that time comes.'

The two lovers sat together in the darkened corner, lit only by the flickering flames from the fire, sometimes speaking quietly, at other times being content just to sit and glory in each other's presence.

Eventually it was time for the household to retire. Having kissed Margaret in spite of her embarrassment, in front of others, he went to the bed that had been prepared for him.

Margaret begged to be allowed to stay in the sick room to watch the sleeping boy. She knew she would not be able to sleep, her mind being too full of hope and plans. Just to be under the same roof as Will was the greatest gift she could imagine. She had been faithful for five years, sometimes despairing that she would ever become Will's wife, but now, in her twenty first year, it seemed that at last the waiting had not been in vain. She did not feel that it was tempting fate to indulge in dreams of a family wedding and a happy future.

Very early next morning, refreshed by a good night's sleep and a hearty breakfast, Will took a tender farewell of Margaret and set out with a song in his heart, confident that he was facing a wonderful future.

CHAPTER NINE

The weather of the night when Roland was rescued was a precursor of one of the severest winters ever known in England. Blizzards raged, rivers and lakes froze over and communities were cut off for long periods.

It was hard for everyone but for the poor it was a disaster. Without fuel for their meager fires many of the poorest froze to death. The undernourished soon became victim to bronchitis, pneumonia and other winter ailments

Those better off felt it their duty to assist the famishing poor. There were established, in different parts of Ipswich, distribution centres for soup, coal and blankets. The Mistress of Cliff was one of the leaders in these charitable efforts. Not only did she supervise the collection of needed goods, but in the kitchens of her house, the staff was busy cooking nourishing soups and stews to assist the destitute.

In the middle of all this activity the family cook became seriously ill. Because she was so reliable and had had experience in the kitchen at the Priory, Margaret was relieved of her nursery duties to become cook. In an establishment as large as Mr Cobbold's the cook was a person of utmost importance. Though she had domestics under her, she was responsible for the preparation and presentation of dinner for the parlor, the kitchen and the nursery, as well as hot suppers for the whole house. During this crisis she also had to supervise the cooking for the poor.

All this meant that Margaret, at only twenty-one, was now head of all the domestic staff with a considerable increase in salary that she looked on as nothing less than a fortune. She was conscious of the responsibility that had been given her and cheerfully worked all the hours available to her. She shared the general distress felt for the destitute and not only supervised scrupulously the distribution of food to them, but also took great care that every economy was practiced in the kitchen.

With food in short supply she felt it a sin that there should be waste. She also proved to have a natural ability to work with others. There had never been such harmony below stairs. Her talents became even more obvious to her mistress and that good lady, remembering Margaret's story, felt it her duty to see that the young woman should have a better life than to waste it on a smuggler.

Mrs Cobbold had never been informed that it was Will Laud who had rescued her son, nor that he was now a member of the Royal Navy.

Margaret. unaware of this omission, assumed that Will was held in as much esteem in the parlor, as in the kitchen. Her calm, orderly running of downstairs activities and her sympathetic handling of problems endeared her to the staff. She was respected throughout the household and little acts of charity meant that her good name reached far beyond the gates of Cliff.

The long winter dragged on but finally the gales ceased, the snow began to melt and the little green spears of snowdrops and crocus peeped above the ground. By May all the fruit trees were in bloom and small birds were busy in the garden seeking food for their young.

In the garden at Cliff was a deep pool with tufted sloping sides, so steep that the gardener had to descend to the water by means of a flight of steps. Two stately weeping willows overhung the pool, dipping their branches into the water.

On the first day of June, Margaret was in the kitchen garden selecting herbs, when she heard a wild shriek and the distressed sounds of children. She ran down the path to see a group of children standing at the edge of the pool screaming and pointing. The nursemaid was paralyzed with fright. Master Henry was shouting and thrashing about helplessly in the water but his efforts were forcing him towards the middle of the pond.

Margaret, taking in the scene at a glance, was galvanised into action.

'Children, get back and stand beside that tree. Edith, run to the stables and get help. Go girl! I'll take over here.'

The nursemaid, relieved of responsibility, lifted up her petticoats and raced to carry out the order. Realising that help might not come quickly enough, Margaret climbed up one of the willows, creeping along the strongest of the branches, which overhung the water, as far as she could go towards the terrified child.

'Henry love. It's Peggy here, I'll save you. Don't be afraid. Just try to stay still and do as I say.'

She grasped a handful of hanging branches in her right hand and, swinging herself over the pond, stretched out her left hand and grabbed the child by the collar of his jacket, using all her strength to pull him out of the water and towards her.

'Don't fret, Master Henry. I've got you. Keep still! Don't struggle. Help is coming. Just stay still and trust Peggy.'

The gardener and coachman came hurrying up, carrying a rope and ladder. The ladder was let down from the arm of the tree, the upper stave resting against its branches. The gardener climbed down a few rungs until Margaret was able to pass the boy to him. When the boy was safe, she told them to throw her the rope so that she could let go of the branches and be towed through the water to the shore.

So, for the third time Margaret had saved one of the Cobbold children. The parents were so indebted to her that there was no request they would not grant and Mrs Cobbold pondered again how she could help this exceptional young woman.

A few days later news reached England of the 'Glorious First of June' victory over the French. There was general celebration and nowhere more so than in Ipswich, for many locals had fought in the battle. Soon news reached Margaret that Will Laud had taken part in the battle and had covered himself with glory. In fact he had been chosen to be one of the crews to bring the prize ships home to Portsmouth. She was assured, by those who knew, that he would be granted shore leave when his work was completed.

However, Will remained in Portsmouth until he could get a share in the prize money and his discharge. She waited impatiently for his arrival. For the first time in her association with Laud she could believe that they would have a future together. At long last the fear and shame were gone. Her faith in him had been justified. If his leave was long enough they could even get married without waiting.

But as the weeks went by her anticipation turned to anxiety. Other sailors had returned, but not Will. She began to fear that his love was not as true as hers and now that he had a successful future he had forgotten her. Seeking news of him, she began to visit the public houses hoping to hear word of when her lover would return.

The news of Margaret's visits reached the ears of Elizabeth Cobbold. She had a general concern for all the servants and a particular interest in Margaret. She believed her to be a cut above most of her other employees and she also felt a great debt of gratitude for the services Margaret had rendered the family. She looked on Margaret almost as a friend and, as she would for any friend that she felt was in danger of losing her good reputation, she decided to speak plainly to her. She had assumed that Margaret's visits to public houses had been to seek the company of sailors of whom Elizabeth did not have a very high opinion.

Calling Margaret into the parlor she got straight to the point. 'Margaret, I have been hearing reports of you visiting some of the more unsavory places in the town. I do not suspect you of any wrong doing, but other people do not know you as well as I do. If you are not careful you will be getting a name for yourself. A young woman in your position has only her good name to recommend her. It is her most precious possession and must be guarded at all times.'

Elizabeth, confused by the changing expressions in Margaret's face, thought to explain herself clearly. 'You confessed to me, when you first came, how news of your friendship with undesirables had led you to leave your last employment. In this establishment you are highly regarded by all but, I am sad to say, it does not take much to have the staff gossiping about you, and you will find yourself in the same position again.

'Margaret, as your employer, and as someone who has great regard for you, I am telling you, you must cease these visits to public houses.'

Margaret was absolutely stunned by what her mistress had said. She knew she was doing no wrong and to be falsely accused of inappropriate behavior was so unfair in her eyes that she was speechless.

Had she been able to talk with her Mistress, had she been able to explain, no doubt the good lady would have listened, advised and even sought news of Will herself. But Margaret had no words. All she could think was that the Mistress was accusing her of loose morals. She stood before Elizabeth, her head lowered as if accepting the reprimand.

Elizabeth waited for some response but, when none was forthcoming, she dismissed the girl.

The criticism by her beloved mistress had a devastating effect on Margaret. Adding to all her worries about Will's whereabouts, she now had the feeling that she was no longer appreciated. This time she was being accused of things she had never done. Once again someone who should have known her better was judging her wrongly. They were all the same at heart, she thought. They feign friendship, then dismiss you out of hand. I do not trust any of them. If that is the way they treat me, I will not try to please them as I did before.

Gone was the cheerful, ever willing servant. Now she resented any request made of her. She became sullen and taciturn. She did her work as efficiently as ever but became critical of others. Also she became niggardly. Though the meals in the dining room were above criticism, the generous portions that always meant there was plenty left over for the kitchen staff, disappeared.

Staff meals were adequate but hardly generous. Worried that she might be accused of pilfering she became suspicious of everyone. All stores were carefully checked and accounted for, as if she suspected them of trying to rob their master. All the good will she had accumulated began to dissolve. The happy kitchen was no more. Margaret's mood set a cloud of gloom over everything.

Elizabeth Cobbold unaware of the effect of her helpful advice, could not understand why Margaret had become less than communicative. 'I do not understand Margaret these days,' she remarked to her husband. 'I asked if she was unwell, but she said there was nothing the matter. Would you believe, John, she was quite rude to me.'

'I noticed she is not her usual, cheery self about the place. Look Elizabeth, if she is going to become insolent then she must be dismissed.'

'John, you know I could never do that. Not after all she has done for the family. No, I am sure there is a problem, but I can't help her if she will not help herself. If she rejects my offer of help there is nothing I can do.'

She gave up trying to engage Margaret in ordinary conversation. Theirs was now a strictly mistress, servant relationship. Had Margaret still had access to the children, her attitude may have thawed, but as it was she spent her spare time nursing her grudges, wallowing in her own misery.

One of the sailors whom she had got to know was Bert Fallow. He had been wounded while serving with Will on the *Briton* and Margaret had met him many times at the tavern. He was happy to tell her stories of Will in exchange for a drink or two.

Missing the pints she used to buy him, he came to visit her at Cliff. Soon he became a regular visitor and though there was nary a slice of bread spare for the staff, Margaret could always find cold cuts and pieces of pie to serve Bert as she plied him with questions about the latest nautical news and begged yet again for the story of Will's gallant actions on the 'Glorious First'.

Bert, nothing if not generous, spread the news among his sailor friends that a warm hearth and a good meal was always available in the kitchen at Cliffs.

This steady stream of visitors did not go unnoticed among the staff, already resentful of Margaret's austerity. It was eventually reported to the Mistress. Because of the breakdown of communication between mistress and maid, Elizabeth did not convey her wishes personally but rather sent a message, via the housekeeper, that sailors were not to be welcomed in the kitchen of the great house.

If the directive to keep away from taverns had upset Margaret, this second command, delivered by a fellow servant infuriated her. For the first time she began to remember the services both she and Will had done the Cobbolds. She believed they owed her a debt of gratitude and she was angry at her treatment.

In a rebellious mood, she was sitting by the fire a few evenings later when a knock came at the back door.

'Go and see who that is,' she commanded Nora, the youngest of the kitchen maids, who was busy at the sink, scrubbing pots.

Nora dried her hands on her apron and casting a malicious look at Margaret's back proceeded to find out who was knocking. A minute later she was back.

'It's a sailor, wants to see you Peggy,' Nora reported, a smirk on her face. She had heard of the ban and was anxious to see what Margaret would do.

Without rising from her seat Margaret replied in a raised, angry voice, 'Tell the fellow to go about his business. I have nothing to say to sailors. Tell him to be off.'

Nora moved back towards the door but there was no need to deliver the message for it had been spoken with the intent of being heard by the visitor.

'I heard,' the sailor told the girl. 'I'm going. Only give her this,' and he handed her a sprig of honeysuckle.

When Margaret saw it she gave an agonising scream. 'Will! Oh Will! Come back!' She jumped to her feet, shod only in slippers and, without a shawl, raced into the night, calling again and again for her lover. But he had fled.

All night she searched the streets and lanes her hair blowing wildly about her face and her dress becoming wet and splattered, for a steady rain had made the roads muddy. She looked like one demented and people turned away from her.

Towards morning, exhausted, she stumbled back to the house and collapsed, semi-conscious on the kitchen floor.

The housekeeper, remembering the many kindnesses Margaret had done for her before her present melancholy state had made her so unpopular, took pity on the girl and helped her to her room, removed her sodden clothes and put her to bed, slipping a hot brick between the sheets to warm her frozen feet.

In the morning, having heard of her plight, Elizabeth Cobbold came to her room to ascertain the cause of her distress. Margaret, much recovered, rounded on her Mistress.

'You ask what is the matter? You, who caused me to send my Will away. Where will he go now? It is all your fault. You, who I thought my friend. You have taken away my one chance to a happy life.'

Elizabeth was taken aback. She had never been spoken to like this before She could not understand why Margaret thought her the cause of all her trouble, but hearing Will's name, she remembered the story that Margaret had told her when first she came.

'If it's Will Laud you speak of, then it is a good thing that he has gone. He brings you nothing but trouble.'

'How could you say that?' Margaret screamed at her, 'when he was the one who saved Master Roland. When he has turned King's man and is a hero. How can you condemn him now?' She dissolved into uncontrollable tears.

'What do you mean? Laud who was the sailor who saved Roland? Why didn't you tell me?'

But Margaret was beyond answering her mistress, All the anger, resentment, disappointment and heartache that had built up during the last few weeks burst forth in floods of tears, She was incoherent for some time. Eventually the storm subsided and the exhausted girl fell into a deep sleep.

Margaret's tirade could not be ignored and yet Elizabeth was a just woman and, as she mulled over the situation, she could understand better Margaret's side of things. She decided on what she felt was the best solution. When Margaret awoke she was summoned to the Parlor. She stood, head erect, expecting dismissal but refusing to show any sign of repentance.

'Margaret,' Elizabeth began. 'You do realise that your behavior was totally unacceptable. However I realise that I did not know the full story. Had I known that it was Laud who bravely rescued Roland I would have felt differently about him. And what is this about him joining the Royal Navy?'

Margaret was more than willing to defend Will's honor. 'He is now a King's man. He has been pardoned his former crimes and fought so bravely against the French that he was rewarded. I have been waiting for his homecoming. That is why I have become familiar with sailors. They sometimes brought me news of Will.'

'And it was Will who came last night?'

'It was.' Tears began to form in Margaret's eyes. 'He came at last, and I sent him away, not knowing who it was. By the time I did, he had gone. And now I do not know where he is or what he is doing. If he thinks I have abandoned him I know he will go back to those evil men. I have driven him away.' Margaret glared at her mistress and shouted, 'It was all your fault.' Then she dissolved into tears once more. Elizabeth waited until the girl had control of herself.

'Margaret, I am truly sorry that this has happened. I take some responsibility but you are the one who has really caused all this to happen. If only you had told me, when I first spoke to you about your visits to public houses, all this could have been avoided. Still it is done. We must now discuss the present situation. I do not think that it would be wise for you to resume your duties at present. You must go home for a time. Later, if you feel that you can again work happily at Cliffs, then come and see me.'

'Then I shall leave,' Margaret replied defiantly.

Elizabeth tried, one more time. 'Margaret, I am truly sorry to send you away at this time. But there is nothing else for it. That does not mean that I think any the less of you. I wish to retain your friendship. Keep in contact with me and we will discuss your reinstatement later.'

Margaret, a little mollified, agreed. She left Cliff and returned, yet once more, to her father's house.

CHAPTER TEN

Matthew now lived in a 'one up one downer' near the commercial centre of Ipswich. Though he still earned part of his living as a day labourer, he often obtained work in the market and on the wharves. It broke Margaret's heart to see her father, once a respected man, now reduced to peddling his labour where he could.

'Da, I'm so sorry that I have brought you to this.'

'Na lass. It's not so bad. I enjoy the variety. Farming was fine but it's very predictable. Here I never know from one day to the next where I'll be. And I tell you truly, I have a little aside for when I can no longer work. This house is cheap and my needs are few. It's you I worry about. Such a good worker you are, but do you have any prospects? I'll not talk about your Will, but what is to be your future, girl? Do you intend to live an old maid? If you do you must get yourself a position where you will be cared for.'

'Da, I know my obsession with Will has cost us all. Now, when it all would have had a happy ending, I cannot find him. And because he thinks I have abandoned him he will probably turn to crime again.'

'Peg, you are not his keeper. You cannot be responsible for the path another takes. Each man makes his own decisions. If Laud intends changing his life he will do it whether you are with him or not. He is, in the finish, his own man and you would not have him otherwise.'

'What you say is true, Da but I hate the thought that he may think ill of me.'

'That's as it may, but what of you? How do you intend to live?'

'I will have to work. Mrs Cobbold has promised that I could return to Cliff and I probably will, when I feel I can forgive her. I know she did not deliberately do it, but she was the cause of me sending Will away and I can't forget that yet.'

'Do you have any money saved?'

'A little, but it won't last me long. I do have one other thing that I think is valuable but I don't know what to do with it.'

Margaret showed the necklace to her father and explained where she had got it. She insisted that Will had come by it legally, else she would never have kept it.

Jonathan took the necklace in his hands, held it up to the light and felt its weight.

'I know little about jewellery, Peg but it looks real to me. Why do you keep it? You know you will never wear anything as fine as this. Better you sell it and use the money. I think you should take it to your uncle. He knows more about these things. He will see you get the best price and he will not be talking about it. Anyway it's time you went to visit Edward. You were so fond of him when he was young. He must be quite a lad by now. I hear good reports about his scholarship. I always wanted him to get an education, so he, at least, is fulfilling my hope.'

Margaret paid a three-day visit to Woodbridge with Edward. Her Uncle Leader, recognising that the necklace was indeed valuable, found a buyer and deposited the one hundred and fifty pounds he got for it in a bank account that Margaret could draw on if she needed to, but he recommended that she find employment rather than live on her capital.

He would have found work for her in Woodbridge but she wanted to remain near Ipswich where it was more likely that she might gain news of Will. The one bright outcome of the trip was that, as Edward had learnt to read and write, they promised to write to each other. Edward's learning was much in advance of Margaret's but he was proud of his sister for having advanced herself without having been to school.

Back in Ipswich she again began to frequent taverns, hoping to learn news of Will. She was much wiser now and was not taken in by those she met. She learnt to sift the facts from the fiction.

One of the men she met was not a sailor, but had known Will since they both were boys.

His name was John Cook. He worked with horses, so he and Margaret had a common interest. He assured her that he had never been involved in smuggling, but was willing to admit that he had sometimes procured horses for 'the gentlemen'. He had seen Will after Margaret had sent him away.

'I can't deny he was sore upset, Margaret. But he had more pressing problems. He had finally fallen out with Luff who vowed to kill him if ever he got the chance. Will had his prize money on him and Luff was after him to steal his money. So you see he did not have time to stay and sort out his problem with you.'

'Then you don't think that he will have taken up with the smugglers then?'

'When I last saw him he had no intention of going back. He was planning to use his prize to buy a boat and start trading on his own. He had planned a future for you both aboard his boat.'

Margaret felt again the twists of fate that seemed to be keeping them apart. 'Oh, why is our life together so beset with difficulties? Can we never have a chance for happiness?' and she put her head down and cried piteously.

'There now girl, don't take it too hard,' soothed Cook, embarrassed by her display. Then a thought came to him as to how he could profit from the situation.

'Tell you what. I'm between jobs at the moment. What do you say to me making a few inquiries around the ports. Someone's sure to know some news of Will.'

Margaret's tears ceased and she grasped his hands, her eyes shining with expectation 'Oh would you, John? I'd be that grateful. I'd go myself but I don't know where to start. Just you find out where he is and I will go there immediately. If only I can speak to him I know we can sort things out.'

'Trouble is,' explained Cook slyly. 'I'm a bit short of the readies at present. I'd need a bit for travel and something for accommodation and food.' He gazed innocently at Margaret.

She was about to offer all her money, but an inner voice whispered caution. 'I have a little money I could offer you, but it would not last more than a week.'

Cook was a bit disappointed, as he had had an idea that she might have more. Still he decided to make the best of what he could get. Even a small amount could grow at the racetrack

A few days later a message came from Cliff asking her if she was ready to return. Had she not already made the arrangement with Cook, she would have gone back, for truth to tell she missed her work at Cliff. But now she could not leave. She wanted to be free to leave if there was any news of Will.

On the day she was next to meet Cook, she encountered her old friend, the housekeeper, who informed her that someone else had been appointed to her old position. This news renewed the resentment she felt for her old mistress. She was still angry and indignant when she met with Cook. The wily man let her talk hoping that it would be to his advantage.

'I worked with them three years and the mistress herself often praised me for my service. I have saved the children time out of time and, though I did not do it with hope of reward, still I expected their gratitude. She always said she was my friend, but now she treats me like this.'

'She probably wants you to come begging to be taken back.'

'That I never will, even if I starve,' replied the defiant Margaret.

Cook could see his plan getting better and better.

'Well, at least I have some good news.'

'John, are you telling me you have seen Will?'

'Not exactly seen him, but I have news of him.'

Margaret could not contain herself. 'Tell me. Tell me. Is he well? Has he bought his boat? Where is he?'

'Wooh! One question at a time. He is in London but the news is not all good. He did catch up with Luff and they had a fight. Will was wounded, but not too seriously. However, he incurred some debts while he was sick and the people who looked after him won't let him go until they are paid.'

Margaret had gone through a series of emotions during this

revelation. When she learnt that it was just a case of money she was greatly relieved.

'But I have money. I can pay his debt. How much is it?'

Cook paused, trying to come up with an amount that would be beyond her resources. 'It's a large amount. Nigh on 100 pounds.'

Margaret smiled. She had more than that amount. 'I will be able to get that much.'

Cook looked at her with new respect and wished he had gone higher. His original plan had not included money. Now he could make a double killing.

'That's marvelous. You get it and I will take it to him straight away.'

Margaret felt a twinge of caution. 'No I do not have it in cash. It is deposited in a bank and only I can get it.'

'Well, you can do that.'

'I can, but how do I know these people will do what they promise. Better I get a note from the bank and they cannot cash it unless I am satisfied.'

Cook began to realise that he was not dealing with an ignorant maid. Still a note might yet be useful and if his plan did misfire then he would not be implicated.

'Then you organise what you have to and I will find out just where Will is. I think he is in London. Have you thought how you would get there when I find out where he is?'

'I suppose I could go by coach.'

'That's expensive, and why should you pay it? I think the Cobbolds owe you a trip. You're a good rider. What about borrowing one of their horses?'

Margaret looked a bit doubtful but Cook played on her feeling of unfair treatment.

'Why shouldn't you? They've treated you badly. If it wasn't for them, you and Will would be happily wed by this. It's not as if you are going to steal it, although I wouldn't blame you if you did. You wouldn't be much punished anyway, seeing you're a woman. A man maybe, but have the authorities ever charged a woman with horse stealing? I don't think so. But it wouldn't be stealing.

It's only borrowing. Who's to know it's you anyway? The horse is missing for a couple of days and then it turns up again. Nobody would find out.'

Margaret mulled over these words. She did feel that the Cobbolds owed her something, and it was their fault that Will was in the predicament that he was. She made her decision.

'All right, I'll do it.'

Cook sat back, satisfied with the result. Now all he needed was to finalize his plans.

'Brave girl. I can see why Will loves you. Now while I am doing my investigating there is one or two things you need to do. Get yourself some men's clothes for it would be too noticeable for a girl to be seen riding through the night. Get your money, or whatever it is and meet me tomorrow night at eleven. We will work out our final plans then.'

Both left satisfied, Cook because his plan was working, and Margaret because she felt that at last she was doing something to bring her closer to Will.

The next evening when they met, Margaret confessed that she had only been able to get a man's top hat and a pair of boots. She was beginning to wish that she had not agreed to the arrangement but Cook, sensing her change of mood, decided to sweeten the bait.

'I have sent a message, by a good friend, to tell Will you are coming. I have written him a letter explaining why you sent him away. He has been told to expect you.

'Where are we to meet?' Margaret was all enthusiasm now.

'The meet is arranged at the Dog and Bone in Lambert, but it is a dangerous place, full of thieves and villains. So I have arranged for a friend to meet you at Chelmsford market tomorrow morning. He will go with you and see that all is safe.'

'Oh John. You are so good. We will be forever grateful.'

'It is my pleasure to help,' he replied gallantly. He was very pleased with himself for coming up with such a clever plan

'But what to do about my clothes?'

'You can take some from the stable. Dinny Wade keeps his

stable dress in the far manger. I have been with him when he has changed so that he does not have to go into the loft. He has lately returned from Mrs Prody's and will be sleeping. His riding clothes will be in the manger and he will be well tucked up. He'll not miss them till morning. By then you will be nearly in London.'

It all sounded so easy. Margaret took the lantern and found the clothes just where Cook said they would be. As thrills of excitement ran through her, she dressed in the groom's clothes. They were a little loose on her but the length was right. She rolled up her own clothes and buried them deep in the feed bin.

She hurried back into the yard to help Cook who had gone to catch and saddle a horse that was there. But Cook was having trouble catching him. They both tried, to no avail, and the horse was so stirred up that they were in danger of being discovered.

'It's no good,' Cook finally declared. 'We must take one from the stables.'

'But they are carriage horses. I daren't mount one of them.'

Cook stood back and surveyed her in the moonlight.

'Margaret Catchpole! Not dare to ride a horse! I cannot believe it. Where's that courage that Will loves you for? Are you going to desert him now? What will he think when he waits in vain for you? I swear I will write to him and tell him you refused to help.'

Faced with the dual rebuke of having her courage challenged and of letting Will down, Margaret agreed to Cook's plan. Together they entered the stables where the horses slept. Cook knew which would be his choice. Though Rochford was a fine animal he would probable be too fiery to be saddled by a stranger, but Crop was a fine strawberry roan, known for his placid nature.

Neither horse was troubled by Margaret's entrance for they were used to seeing her around the stables but when Cook entered Rochford rose up and snorted.

Margaret, terrified that the groom would wake, spoke to them in soothing tones. She had to hold Crop's head and pat his neck while her companion saddled and bridled him. She spread straw over the floor and tied straw around his feet so that no noise would be made in the stable yard as he was led out.

He quivered as Cook helped Margaret to mount then walked quietly out of the gate and onto the Woolbridge road. She felt her spirits rise at the prospects of a long ride and a happy meeting at the end of it. Cook gave her final instructions.

'Now Margaret this is the plan. You must head for Chelmsford market. There you will be met by one, Henry Pike. He will be looking out for you. You can rest there and then continue your journey to London. Should you by any chance miss Henry, head to the Red Bull in Aldgate and wait for him there. He will take you to the Dog and Bone where your man will be waiting. Never fear, Henry will want a little for his trouble, but make sure he does not demand too much. You can take that up with him but do not let him take you for an ignorant cottage girl. Now be off with you and may God speed your way.'

Crop's spirit was up and so was Margaret's. As she felt the horse move under her she resolved that nothing would come between her and Will this time.

Three miles on the Ipswich side of Colchester they passed the coach from London. The driver hailed what he thought was a groom, but neither horse nor rider took the slightest notice of him, so obsessed were they in the journey.

The coachman rubbed his chin. One didn't pass many travellers at three o'clock in the morning. It was unusual to be ignored in this fashion.

He turned to look at them but they were already fast disappearing into the misty darkness. The rider was totally unfamiliar to him but he knew the horse.

'That's John Cobbold's horse,' he said to the man beside him.

'Whoever it is they're in a great hurry,' was the sleepy reply.

The driver prided himself on keeping abreast with all that was going on. He felt it was part of his job to pass on anything of interest that happened.

'Why would anyone be racing to Colchester at this time of night? I wonder if there is an emergency? I think I'll call on Mr Cobbold when I reach Ipswich.'

But Margaret did not stop at Colchester. She flew down the hill, along Castle Street, past the square old castle, romantic in the moonlight, and out of the town again.

Several miles further on she patted Crop on the neck and began to slow him down, but the horse would have none of it.

Margaret bent down and whispered to him. 'We must stop now. We have a long way to go and you need food and water. '

Ahead was a small inn. She felt uncomfortable in her men's clothes. This would be her first test. She thought of changing horses if one was available but Crop seemed fresh and it would mean explaining afterwards that she had taken the horse. Better to see if she could get it back to Ipswich without being recognised. Also Crop was a friend.

She tumbled off Crop's neck and, giving instructions to the ostler, strode into the little parlour. There was a light burning, and a man, half-asleep, lolled over the counter. He was not expecting casual customers. He was waiting for a coach. He looked up, bored as she came in.

'Brandy and water, cheese and biscuits for me,' she demanded briskly as she turned her head, looking backwards towards the door as she spoke, then took a seat in a dark corner of the room.

She paid for the food when it was brought but said nothing. The man saw nothing strange about her, just another moody customer passing through.

All the time Margaret nibbled at her biscuit and drank her brandy she watched the ostler outside by the light of his lantern. He rubbed the horse down and gave it water and oats. When he was done she strode out of the inn, tossed a coin to the man, grabbed the reigns and sprang into the saddle. The ostler was too sleepy to take much notice of her.

Crop, as if sensing the urgency of the situation was glad to be back on the road again. Margaret gave him his head. On through the night they galloped. She did not slow the pace again until they reached Chelmsford.

She clattered into the sleeping town but the market square was deserted. She walked around the square peering up adjoining streets but no one was to be seen hurrying along to keep an appointment.

She stood, undecided, for about fifteen minutes. Perhaps Henry Pike had already left. Perhaps she should not have taken a break at the inn. She walked around the deserted square one more time, then, seeing the signpost to London, made her decision. She would continue to London and Aldgate. Her guide would probably already be there. If not she would find Will on her own.

Some two hours later Henry Pike wandered down to the square expecting to meet a young groom enquiring for him. He intended taking him to an inn, slipping him a draught and, after relieving him of the bank notice, take the horse and proceed to London, there to sell it. But he did not know of Margaret's riding ability. John Cook's plan had gone awry.

The stage-coachman, after he had passed Margaret, kept telling himself that he would go at once to Cobbold's place to tell him how he had seen his horse galloping towards Colchester. He was mightily interested in the reason for it but, by the time he reached the place, he felt he might be making a fool of himself, so instead gave his information to the postmaster.

This man, who knew most everything that went on, felt there might be reason for alarm, and sent a messenger to Cobbold's house to inform him that one of his horses had been seen galloping at break neck speed along the London road.

The house was quickly raised and, on inspecting the stables, John Cobbold quickly realised that one of his prize horses had been stolen. From that moment a sense of urgency set in. The groom raced to the home of the constable and raised him from his bed.

Wasting no time they all hurried to the home of Bush, the bookseller. This man lived above his shop and, when he had got over the surprise of being so rudely summoned from his bed, was soon printing a set of handbills to be ready for the morning coach to London.

They read:

Twenty Guineas Reward

Whereas, last night, or this morning May 24th a fine, strawberry roan, grey gelding CROP was stolen out of the stables of John Cobbold Esq. of Ipswich, together with a new saddle and bridle. Whoever shall have information of this robbery, so as to lead to the recovery of the horse, or the conviction of the offender, shalt be rewarded at the hands of the owner

Ipswich May 24th 1779

John took some of these posters and sent his man post haste in chase of the villain. The first stop was Colchester, but there was no evidence that the horse and rider had stopped there. Leaving behind one of the posters, he set out again along the London Road, seeking information along the way. Inquiring at every tollgate they passed through, they followed the progress of the ride. They nearly were sent on the wrong track at Chelmsford but fortunately a gentleman, listening to their enquirers informed them that he had seen the pair at about seven o'clock heading in the direction of London.

This information seemed to confirm that London was the destination. No more time was wasted on enquires, the chase was on to London.

As for Margaret and Crop, both horse and rider had tired long ago, regained their second wind, then tired again with a weariness that was hard to shake off. What kept them going was sheer determination and courage. Margaret encouraged the horse when he showed signs of faltering and the response from the horse encouraged her when she would have wavered.

It was nine o'clock when they approached London. They had covered the distance from Ipswich to London in nine hours!

There was a turnpike at Whitechapel. At each side of the road were small, square, two-storied houses with their tall rounded doors, two four-barred timber gates obstructing the roadway, and in the centre, a huge standard carrying three lights on iron brackets.

Impatiently, her heart pounding, Margaret joined the dusty line of redcoats, wagons, market carts and private carriages and waited her turn. She heard those ahead shouting their destination and receiving directions if needed. When her turn came she summoned her gruffest voice and shouted 'Aldgate.' The squat little gatekeeper, two days growth on his chin, passed her through and nodded vaguely down the street. She did not dare to ask more detailed directions so, stroking Crop's neck, she rode on.

At another time Margaret would have had a grand old time gawking at the motley collection of humanity that thronged the streets, at the variety of vehicles and the impressive buildings. But her mind was on one thing, finding Will as soon as possible. She felt less conspicuous in her borrowed clothes, here. There was such an array of fashion that she melted into the crowd. Crop, however was another matter and many a discerning glance was cast at the horse.

Margaret had slackened her break-neck dash, first, because the press of traffic would not permit it and secondly because she needed to seek directions. Fortunately her destination lay on a direct route and she could easily follow directions when given.

Just when she felt that she had indeed lost her way, she saw, ahead of her a sign depicting a bull's head, and underneath the words. THE RED BULL

Margaret took a deep breath. Apart from the worry of losing her way, she had enjoyed her entry into London, but now she was to face her greatest test. It was now daylight, and if she were to make contact with Pike, she would have to make inquiries where all could see her. She would just have to bluff it out.

She rode quietly into the yard, called for an ostler, dismounted, smoothed her costume and gave instructions casually, as if she were a real groom.

'Rub the horse down well, and get him cool and comfortable. Give him some water and see you do it well.'

She went into the bar, ordered breakfast and sat, pretending to read a newspaper but all the while keeping an eye on the goings on in the yard. As far as she could ascertain no one had come enquiring for her.

How was she to make contact with a man that she had never seen? If Cook had chosen this place for a meet, Margaret reasoned, then perhaps Ned Pike was known here. She walked casually, up to the ostler and watched as he went about his business.

'Have you rode far, young man?' he enquired.

'No. Just from Chemlsford. I was expecting to meet someone there but seem to have missed him.'

'And what would his name be?'

'One, Ned Pike. I have some business with him.'

The ostler gave her a scrutinising look that made her feel uncomfortable.

'Then you be planning to sell your horse?'

Margaret was taken aback. For the first time she wondered if Cook had been entirely honest with her but dismissed the thought. The ostler had obviously assumed she was a groom so, having started on the fantasy, she had to go on with it.

'That depends.'

'How much is he offering?' The ostler, alert for business, paused in his work.

Margaret, having started on this charade, could think of no other way out so she made a quick calculation. 'He has offered eighty, but the deal is far from settled. My master is coming up this evening. He's not even certain that he will sell the animal, for he's a beauty.'

'Aye, that he is. Your master must know that Pike is only a go between. He will sell him again at a profit. I know a gent that might be interested who would raise the bid.'

'Well, that's as maybe. It doesn't seem that the man is here and I have other errands to do. If he turns up would you tell him I have been here and have gone to the Dog and Bone to see a mutual friend. Could you direct me to it?'

'It's quite a way. Will you ride the horse?'

'No. He has gone far enough and I would welcome a walk. Is

it hard to find?'

'No. It's on the main road, but it's not the best of neighbourhoods. You will have to keep your wits about you.'

'Oh, I'm used to taking care of myself. We have lots of taverns where I come from.'

'The Dog and Bone is no tavern, but the customers are sharp. A country boy like you needst be awake for hustlers and con men, not to mention pick pockets. Take a care.'

'Thanks for the advice. Could you stable Crop and I'll be back when I can.'

'Crop. Now there's a name. Comes from this new fangled idea of cropping the ears, no doubt. Don't hold with it myself.'

The man would have gone on talking but Margaret was impatient to be off. She was worried that the longer she stood talking to him the more the chances she would give herself away. As soon he had given her directions she set off.

Now that she was walking she could take more notice of her surroundings. She tried not to gawk like a country bumpkin, but the sights amazed her. At last she came to the long mass of buildings that had been described to her and crossed the Thames on the bridge called Westminster.

She could sense a change as soon as she crossed the river. People were less well dressed and seemed to move in a more furtive manner. There were smaller streets and lanes leading off the main thoroughfare. She was glad that she did not have to venture into them.

Margaret was used to walking, but she was already tired from the long ride and was relieved when she saw the Dog and Bone sign with its signature picture. She walked through an archway, crossed the small courtyard then entered the bar, her feet scraping on the sawdust on the floor.

The room was dark and seemed to be occupied mostly by old men sitting in pew-like seats. Self-consciously she walked the length of the room but there was no sign of Will.

Perhaps she was too early.

She found a seat in a dark corner, out of sight of the other customers but commanding a view of the door where she hoped Will would soon enter. The barman had noticed her entrance and, when she made no movement towards the bar, observed where she sat and soon came up to her.

'W'ot's yours?' he enquired.

Margaret, taken aback by his sudden appearance was momentarily nonplussed then, recovering, ordered the first thing that came into her head. 'Oh . . . brandy and biscuits I suppose . . . Yes brandy and water . . . and cheese and biscuits.' She didn't want anything but realised that she could not stay here without ordering something.

The man brought them to her. She paid and sat there drinking brandy and water very slowly, nibbling at the biscuits and cheese to make them last. She had no idea how long she would have to wait.

Her entrance had been noted by some of the customers, several of whom strolled past, eyeing her appraisingly as they replenished their glasses. She was thankful for her male garb, but she was to learn, before the day was out, that not only women were solicited in the city.

She became deadly afraid, gazing down at the floor, not game to make eye contact with anyone. The bar tender visited her regularly and she was obliged to repeat her order. Her request for tea was scoffed at and so she requested a jug of water and proceeded to dilute the brandy again and again.

She waited, hope rising each time a new customer entered, only to be dashed when it was not Will. The moment's doubt she had felt this morning returned but she tried to dismiss it. Cook had said that Will would be here and so she waited. It was now getting on in the afternoon and, remembering the long walk back, she eventually had to give up her vigil. She decided that she could never repeat the journey in daylight so eventually summoned a cab to take her back to the Red Bull.

While Margaret was learning the ways of London, Peters, Mr Cobbold's man, having sent a message back to Ipswich informing his master of the information he had been given, proceeded post haste to London. He entered by the same gate as Margaret, then began to inquire at all the livery stables on his way. He felt sure that the thief intended to sell the horse as quickly as possible so headed for Yard and Parkes, horse wholesalers, as the most likely place to dispose of a horse quickly.

By coincidence, the ostler from the Red Bull, when his shift was over had proceeded to the same place. He had a relative there who was willing to pay for information about the availability of saleable horses.

Peters, having had the advantage of two changes of horses, arrived at Yard and Parks soon after three p.m. while the ostler and his relation were still discussing a likely offer for the horse. As soon they were shown the poster the ostler, who could not himself read, but listened intently as it was read out, recognised that this was the self same horse that he has been speaking of.

'Crop. It must be the one. That's what he called him.'

'Good,' exclaimed Peters. 'Where is the animal now?'

'It's in the stables at the Bull. Seemed a bit tuckered out. Restin' quietly he is.'

'And well he may be,' replied Peters, 'having been ridden all the way from Ipswich like the devil was after him. Now, the man who stole him, tell me about him.'

'More like a boy he was, voice not long broken I'd say, and from Suffolk, I guessed from the start. Should have knowd there was something fishy when Ned Pike's name was mentioned.'

'Yes, yes. But the youth, where is he? Is he coming back for the horse?'

'He went off on business before mid-day. Said he'd be back to talk about the horse later. Expected Pike to turn up, but he hadn't, before I left.'

'Then the sooner we get back the better. I will make sure it is the right horse and then go to the magistrate for a warrant. You must keep him there until I can get a constable.'

'I'll come too,' suggested the relative. He had seen the reward sign and was hoping to share in the proceeds. 'I'll pretend to be a buyer and keep him busy until you come.'

They all hurried back and Peters quickly identified Crop. He went off to organise the warrant while the other two waited for Margaret's return.

As she sat in the cab she tried to make sense of her day. She had been so sure that she would find Will, but now she didn't know. Perhaps she had been too impatient. She should have waited in Chelmsford for Pike. Now she was alone in London with only the Dog and Bone as a clue to Will's whereabouts. She was unwilling to go back there without an escort. But where was Pike?

She would have to wait at the Red Bull until he came, but her money was fast running out. As well, she knew that by now Crop would have been missed. They would already be searching for him. She would never be able to ride him back without being caught, and then what would happen?

Perhaps she should take up the offer of the ostler. If she sold Crop she would have the money to get home. Then she could go and tell Mr Cobbold what had happened and pay him back. If only she had thought the whole thing through. She should have taken the coach.

Still undecided what to do, she reached the yard and was immediately confronted by the ostler and his relative.

'This here's the man I was telling you about. Wants to buy your horse and willin' to pay more than Pike.'

'Just a minute,' interrupted the other man, 'I warrant he's a good looking horse but I need to know a bit more about him 'fore I part with my money.'

'What's wrong with him?' Margaret demanded.

'That's for me to find out. Who's his owner?'

Margaret was exhausted from lack of sleep and dizzy from the brandy she had been forced to drink. In this muddled state she found that lies were coming easier and easier.

'John Cook of Ipswich.'

'Never heard of him. Still I don't know many up that way. You do have his permission to sell him?'

'Ye . . . es.' Margaret replied doubtfully. She had not even thought through her idea of selling the horse and now it all seemed to be getting taken out of her hands. She was weary from her long, long day. All she wanted to do was rest. She knew that things had gone terribly wrong but did not know how to get out of the situation.

'He's a fine looking horse and there's no denying, but I need to know how he moves,' the pretend buyer continued. 'Would you mind if we put on the saddle and you take him for a ride?'

How could she refuse?

The saddle and bridle were brought out and Crop came out of the stable. He was fresh and ready to trot all the way back to Ipswich. Margaret mounted, so weary now that she could hardly drag herself up, but Crop seemed to understand. They went out of the stable yard and Margaret galloped a short way then turned the horse in and out as she was directed.

Unbeknownst to her, the constable and Peters were watching, the former anxious to make the arrest, and the latter trying to recognize the groom in the fading light.

Receiving a prearranged signal, the dealer told Margaret that he had seen enough and instructed her to head back into the yard. She dismounted gratefully and stood beside the horse leaning on him for support. If this did not all end soon she knew she would fall.

'I'm satisfied. A price of eighty pounds was mentioned, but I'm willing to up that. How does ninety guineas sound?'

Weary beyond caring Margaret replied. 'That will do.'

The dealer, reaching into his pocket, asked, 'You said this horse comes from Ipswich?'

'I did.'

'When did he leave there?'

'Yesterday.' Margaret's answers were automatic. Her brain could no longer function clearly.

'Did you bring him?'

'Yes. I told you that.'

'No, you didn't,' interrupted the ostler. 'You said you rode him from Clemsford.'

'And so I did; and from Ipswich too.'

'Did you say your master's name was John Cook?'

'Yes. Yes.' Margaret knew that there was something wrong but she was beyond caring

'Are you sure that this horse does not belong to John Cobbold?' He shoved a handbill in front of her face. 'Look at this, young man.'

Margaret looked and saw her late master's name. Her last vestige of courage left her. She felt the earth slipping sideways and gave up the struggle to stay upright. She swooned and would have fallen had not the constable, who had moved closer to hear more clearly, the damning conversation, caught her by the jacket.

Peters hurrying behind looked fully into the face of this thieving villain and fell back in horror.

'God in heaven,' he cried. 'It's not a man at all! It's a woman! It can't be and yet it is! It's Margaret Catchpole!'

CHAPTER ELEVEN

As soon as the first message had arrived Mr Cobbold had left Ipswich to drive to London in his carriage. He was especially proud of Crop and anxious that no harm come to him.

Along the road he was intercepted by another messenger telling him that the horse had been found. Satisfied, he proceeded at a more leisurely pace and did not arrive until after eight, where he was greeted by Peters with the news that the horse thief was none other than Margaret.

This news threw him into confusion. He knew Margaret so well he was sure there was a legitimate explanation for all that had gone on. He went immediately to the London Police Office to enquire where she was and explain that there had been a mistake.

The Magistrate was a frustrated, over-worked servant of the law. He had a small, inadequate force of men trying to keep the peace in the heart of the metropolis, and had just congratulated himself that one case had been so successfully concluded. The horse was found and the villain apprehended in the very act of selling it. He was less than interested in the story this East Anglian brewer was telling him.

He might be an important man in that strange place but he was small fry here. He sat impassively while Cobbold related his tale of Margaret's loyalty, honesty and her bravery in saving his children, twiddling with his quill and wondering when he could get back to work. What was the man on about?

'So you see sir there must have been some mistake,' Cobbold reasoned. 'Thank goodness it's all over. I'll take the horse and the girl back with me and there will be no more said.'

He stopped speaking and looked expectantly at the

Magistrate. Only then did he realise that he had been doing all the talking. The Magistrate sat there, silent. It was the silence that stopped him, the kind of silence when you expect the other person to say something, and they don't.

They regarded each other with a fixed gaze. Neither said anything for a moment then Cobbold got to his feet. He walked towards the other man and repeated in an artificially jolly voice, 'I was saying . . . thank heavens it's all over.'

Still the Magistrate said nothing. 'It is over, isn't it?' Cobbold insisted urgently.

'No,' said the Magistrate with finality, drawing an entry book towards him. 'She has been charged with the theft of a horse.'

He drew a line under the first two words in his book

MARGARET CATCHPOLE, this day, in the county of Middlesex. 'I am probably in possession of more facts relating to the law than you are.'

Cobbold went on staring at him. 'But I have my horse back.'

'It doesn't alter the fact that she stole it.'

'She took it, yes. But she hasn't stolen it. I have my horse back. How can it be stolen?'

The Magistrate sighed. 'It has been stolen, and recovered.' Then he paused. 'This woman took your horse from Ipswich and brought it to London. Is that right?'

'Yes.'

'Yet you say she didn't steal it?'

'If you knew Margaret Catchpole you'd know she had no intention of stealing it,' the brewer said impatiently. 'She is a very impulsive girl, but she must have had a good reason.'

'I seem to have heard similar stories from many a horse thief before.'

Cobbold tapped the desk. 'But the horse is mine. Surely I can do with him what I please?'

The official looked at Cobbold and then down at his book. He drew a line under the word 'stealing'. He put down his pen. 'Are you saying then that this woman had your permission to take this animal?'

'Yes. Yes. That's what I mean. She had my permission.'

The Magistrate went on wearily. 'I didn't have that impression earlier. Then your story was that this Margaret Catchpole, with your permission, took the horse from your stables and rode it to London?'

'Yes. That's right,' agreed Cobbold eagerly.

'Why?'

'Why? . . . I don't know.'

'Then why did you give the girl permission?'

'The girl's thoughts and reasons are not a chargeable offence, surely? As far as I can reason she has broken no law. Now, will you please understand that she took the horse with my knowledge and permission.'

'I see.' The Magistrate picked up a piece of paper that was lying face down on his desk.

Cobbold, thinking that he had made his point, pressed home his advantage. 'And now, may I take the girl home? My wife will be worrying about what is happening.'

'Just one moment,' said the Magistrate, a half smile playing on his lips. 'If the girl had your permission, why did you have these printed?' He turned the paper over.

There in bold print were the words *stolen out of the stables of JOHN COBBOLD Esq.*

'Did you have this printed?' demanded the official. 'I mean, did you personally request that it should be done? Or did one of your servants arrange that it should be done, without your knowledge?'

John swallowed. 'No . . . No. I gave permission for them to be printed.'

'Then you must have forgotten that you gave the girl permission,' suggested the magistrate.

Cobbold knew he was grasping at straws but he replied lamely. 'Yes . . . Yes, that's it. I forgot.'

The official turned his gaze back to the book in front of him and said wearily. 'And you forgot that you gave her permission to sell it?'

He sat back in his chair and joined his hands in front of his ample stomach

'No, Mr Cobbold. I admire your loyalty to a servant who has saved the lives of your children. I can even forgive you your untruthfulness in trying to save the girl but I think, even if you had given permission, which I doubt, that you knew she intended to sell it.'

He turned the book around and handed the quill to Cobbold. 'Sign here if you will'

The magistrate pointed to a line in the entry book.

John was still digesting the news about the selling of the horse. 'Sign what?'

'That you have preferred charges against Margaret Catchpole of the county of Suffolk for stealing your property and conspiring to . . .'

'I'll be damned if I will!' Cobbold was aghast. 'Do you know what you're asking me to do?'

'I have already told you that my knowledge of the law is greater than yours.'

'I'll see you in hell first,' said the Ipswich man, throwing the quill on the desk.

'No doubt you'd like to, and there are many who share your feelings,' replied the official, almost sadly. 'Trying to keep the law is not easy and not guaranteed to win many friends. I will do what I can for the girl, and your witness will help when she comes to trial, but there has been an epidemic of horse stealing. You know that, as well as I do. It is rife throughout the country. It is my duty, and yours too, to see that the offenders are caught, and charged. In no other way can we stamp out this widespread vice, which I am grieved to admit to you, is so great in larger cities that it terrifies the law abiding mind.' He paused and then continued seriously. 'I am not exaggerating Mr Cobbold.'

'Then you can find someone else to make an example of. Margaret is a simple girl and no criminal. '

'I regret your attitude sir.'

'My attitude is my own. Whose horse is it anyway?' Cobbold demanded. 'Yours or mine?'

'And whose law is it, eh? Neither yours nor mine Sir? It is the law of the land and I am sworn to uphold it. I think I would like to speak to this paragon of virtue of yours. Perhaps you will see things in a different light then.'

He shouted for the prisoner, Margaret Catchpole, to be brought from the cell she was being held in.

Cobbold paced the floor and the Magistrate continued writing in his book, neither man looking at the other until Margaret was brought in.

She was a sorry sight, still dressed in her man's attire, which was sadly in disarray, her long, black, curly hair lying across her shoulders and her face stained with tears. She truly looked the gypsy she had sometimes been called. She was still in a state of shock and had been brought in from a dark cell, so could not focus for a few moments.

When she saw her old employer she would have swooned again had he not hurried to her side and supported her.

'Don't worry, my dear,' said the brewer, trying to bring some comfort to the wretched girl. 'We'll have you home soon.'

'I'm so sorry Master,' she sobbed clinging to him. 'I'm so sorry that I took Crop. I should have asked you . . . I just didn't think.'

Cobbold swung around to the man at the desk, who raised his eyebrows 'So?'

Margaret went on, 'I had to come to London.'

'Why?' enquired her former master, gently.

The Magistrate stood up from his desk and moved around to hear her answer.

'Why?' Cobbold asked again.

Margaret looked anxiously from one man to the other. How could she explain without compromising Will. During the time since her capture only one coherent thought had settled in her brain. She must not involve Will. She had broken the law, even though she had not meant to, but she could not explain it all without embroiling him.

Margaret's lips set in a determined line. Cobbold knew that expression. He glanced at the Magistrate who was still doing nothing, only listening and watching the girl.

John knew that Margaret was not going to answer. He

wished he had not asked the question. He pressed on bravely. 'Well, we'll be going home now.'

Margaret looked up, surprised.

'Wait,' the Magistrate raised his hand. Margaret watched it mesmerised. 'Mr Cobbold tells me,' he began 'that he gave you permission to take the horse. Is that the truth?'

Margaret flashed a look of gratitude to the brewer, but she had already decided that no more lies would be told.

'No. That is not true. I think my master is only trying to help me. I took the horse while he was asleep, though I am sure he would have given permission had I asked. I know now I should have asked.'

Mr Cobbold attempted to interpose himself between the Magistrate and the girl, but she twisted around and faced him. 'I'll have to tell the truth Mr Cobbolt, and face the consequences, whatever they are.'

The two men looked at each other. Who was going to tell her what they might be?

'Why did you come to London?' the Magistrate enquired

Margaret thought desperately. What reason could she give? What reason that did not involve Will?

The Magistrate was beginning to feel that the interview was becoming embarrassingly inconclusive, so he went back to his book and took up the quill again.

'Why did you come to London!' he thundered

Margaret did not answer.

'No? Then I must tell you what the charge is. That you stole Mr Cobbold's horse and brought it to London and tried to sell it.'

'None of this makes any sense,' Cobbold protested. 'There must be someone else involved. Margaret, did someone else tell you to take the horse?'

Margaret knew that they would not give up. The easiest way to protect Will was to invent an imaginary character. 'Yes,' she said desperately, 'Yes, that's what happened. A man came and suggested I should take the horse ... and ride it to Colchester. He said he would take it from there ... and ... and sell it.'

Cobbolt clearly did not believe the story. 'And what was this man's name?'

Margaret thought desperately. She was beginning to guess that everything had been an elaborate hoax. The person she blamed was the man who should have met her in Chemlsford.

'Pike. Nick Pike.'

The magistrate noted this. He put down his quill with an air of finality. 'Very well,' he said. 'We will prepare a confession along those lines and you can make your sign.'

'We will do nothing of the kind,' stated Cobbold, still coming to grips with Margaret's revelation, which he was sure had been fabricated.

'No?' said the other man, and then to Margaret. 'Mr Cobbold prefers the story that he gave you permission to take the horse. You and I know that it is not true. You don't deny that you tried to sell the horse?'

'No . . . but,' Margaret could hardly explain the circumstances to herself, let alone explain what her motives had been when she presented Crop to the buyer.

'Very well,' the magistrate continued ignoring her hesitation. 'Very well. There's nothing more to be said. Except that if Mr Cobbold persists in his story you will be forever branded as someone who betrayed his trust; someone to whom he loaned his horse, and you, who should have been grateful, could do no better than to sell it and run away with the money.' He was leaning over his desk shouting the last few words at her.

'No! Oh no! I would never do that,' cried Margaret passionately. 'I would never run away. I would have told Mr Cobbold. I wouldn't have done that.'

'No, I didn't think you would,' said the official calmly. He picked up the pen again and handed it to the brewer.

'Will you sign this charge sheet please? You heard what the girl said.' Then looking at Margaret, 'Mr Cobbold has no alternative, has he, seeing that you would prefer the truth, knowing that any other course would be cowardly?'

There was an awful pause.

'Well,' pressed the Magistrate, 'that's true. Isn't it?'

'Yes,' whispered Margaret.

The official tapped the quill and handed it to Cobbold. The Ipswich man, with another look at Margaret, savagely signed his name. He threw down the pen and, turning his back on the man at the desk, took Margaret's hand.

'Be brave, Margaret. We are not finished yet. I will take this up with a higher authority.' Then he strode from the room leaving Margaret, staring horrified at his retreating back, fully aware now of the seriousness of her plight.

Soon after Margaret was bundled into a cab. Still hardly able to credit the misfortunes that had befallen her, she asked,' Where am I going?'

The oaf-like, cunning guard, in whose care she had been placed, leered back at her. 'Newgate,' and laughed as she cowered back in her seat.

Even a country girl from Suffolk had heard of the dangers and depravity of that place. She almost regretted the noble stand she had taken. Perhaps it would have been better to be branded an ungrateful coward than to endure such a place.

She had little time to contemplate her fate for, as soon as she arrived, she was bundled out of the cab, the guard taking the occasion to indulge in a little intimate pawing and a whispered message.

'A girl like you shouldn't fare too bad, if you know what I mean? There's some that would pay well for a favour from a pretty girl like you. Just you give Jemmy the wink and I'll see youse right.'

Margaret drew back from his grasp but the sight she saw nearly had her falling back into his arms. The gloating, excited crowd at the gate had parted at the sight of the guard, and in front of her she saw two lifeless figures swinging on the gibbet, feet dangling helplessly, heads awry.

'We 'ang's 'em here now. The toffs at Tyburn don't like the look of the gibbet round their neighbourhood. Says it made the place untidy. Still it makes our lives easier. No need for transport now, and it keeps the rest of the villains in line. Would ya like a closer look?'

Margaret knew he was taunting her, but she did not have the will to meet his challenge. She shook her head and withdrew as far as she could inside herself.

Jemmy chuckled to himself and calculated just how long it would take to break this one.

But Margaret was made of sterner stuff than he had imagined.

As soon as he knew where she had been taken, Mr Cobbolt sent clothes and a reassuring message. Dressed again in female attire Margaret regained her composure.

She had plenty of time to review the events leading up to her arrest. She was sure now that she had been set up. It was pretty obvious to her that Cook and Pike had been in league and had intended taking Crop from her under some pretext. She had spoilt their plan by not waiting at Chelmsford so all the rest had been her own doing.

If only she had not gone along with the suggestion of selling the horse, then Mr Cobbolt could have saved her. Searching her mind she could not deny that she may have been tempted to take the money. So she was guilty. She must take her punishment.

She took note of those around her. Her companions in the stinking cells, both men and women were thieves, cut throats, prostitutes; the decaying remnants of what had once been people like herself, decent and clean, alive and aware of the beauty of the world around them, capable of loving and being loved. Now they loved nothing except the food they so ravenously slobbered and gulped, when they could get it, their only desire, the next meal. There was no room in their lives for tender thoughts or feelings. Staying alive was all they thought of. When they lost that thought they quickly succumbed to the diseases around them.

What frightened her most about these people was that she knew they represented what she herself might be forced to become if she was left in this fetid hell hole for long. She prayed constantly that her old employer would find a way to get her out.

John Cobbold began a tireless campaign to have Margaret tried in her own county. Ipswich prison was one of the few reformed prisons in England. Its inmates had a bed and mattress, sometimes even a cell to themselves. Elizabeth, his wife was a constant visitor, not only to Mr Rippon, the governor, but also to the inmates themselves. She brought them comforts and Scripture tracts and had become the confidant of many.

She would be able to keep in contact with Margaret and make her prison life as comfortable as possible. Also the people knew Margaret. She had gained a reputation, not only for her famous ride, but also for the kindness she had shown during the terrible winter of '94/95. He planned to awaken public opinion to her plight and to the fact that he had been forced into pressing charges.

Finally, after eleven long weeks Margaret was transferred to Ipswich and her trial was set for the Assizes on August 9th 1797.

Margaret was grateful for her transfer and, as soon as she had had a visit from her old mistress, all the bitterness was forgotten. She recognised Elizabeth as her true friend and confessed to her the full circumstances of her escapade. Her mistress spent no time in recriminations but encouraged Margaret to put her trust in the Almighty and to use the time in reading and needlework.

If it had not been for the lack of freedom, and the disappointment that Laud had made no effort to contact her, in spite of the fact that her plight had become common knowledge, Margaret would have been happy. At least she was at peace. She had forgiven all those who had done her harm, real or imaginary and, fortified by the good wishes of many of the townsfolk and the forgiveness of her father and the Cobbolds, she awaited her punishment.

Shortly before her trial was to take place, Margaret, having made her peace with God, with the help of the chaplain, spoke with her good friend.

'Dearest Mistress, I thank you and Master for the care and concern you have shown me. Now I know how you really feel about me, I would wish to live, if only to prove your trust in me. I have but one sorrow now, and that is that Will has made no effort to contact me. This means that he thinks ill of me. I would that I could be found innocent so that he, hearing of it, would think well of me again.'

'Margaret, how can you still hold love in your heart for a man who has abandoned you?'

'Three times Will has broken my heart and three times I have forgiven him. Even now, when I fear he no longer loves me, my thoughts still turn to him. If I should suffer the punishment due to me, and after you should see him, will you tell him that I remained true to him to the end.'

Elizabeth Cobbold was amazed at the depth of affection this girl felt for such a man. In her heart she was sure that if ever she should encounter Laud she would have many other things to say but, for Margaret's sake, she resolved to deliver the message.

'Margaret, do not give up hope. You have many friends who will speak well of you and if you would plead not guilty then my husband is sure that he can gain your freedom.'

'But I can't plead not guilty, under oath, when I am. I wish, with all my heart I could, but I cannot lie before God.'

'Then we must rely on the mercy of the judges. Surely your story will touch the sternest heart.'

'So my future lies with God and I will await it patiently.'

Mrs Cobbold was so touched by Margaret's simple faith that it was she who was reduced to tears and Margaret became the comforter.

Margaret was also visited by her father who, though sad to see his beloved daughter in such danger, understood and was proud of her decision to plead guilty,

'I know Peggy, that you are the most honest of creatures. Your standing trial for the crime of stealing is but a strange twist of fate. Though I would give my life to save you from this, I know that you could never lie. It will be mercy alone that will save you.' The old man, whose life seemed to have become one long litany of misfortune, bent his head, and father and daughter cried for all things lost. It was the one time when Margaret lost her hard won composure.

The Assizes for the county were held twice yearly at Bury St Edmond. Though they had a serious origin they were also a social event. Dinners, balls and race meetings were all held during this time, taking advantage of the assembly of so many important people.

The trials, themselves, were a colourful affair, with the Lord Chief Baron Macdonald, High Sheriff Mr Justice Heath and High Sheriff Chalonor Archdeckne Esq. of Glevening Hall, with his chaplain, and a full bench of county and borough magistrates, all resplendent in their official robes.

On the day the trials were to begin the judges entered the town. The trumpets sounded, and the bells rang as the carriages arrived for divine service at St James Church then processed to the courthouse, followed by a noisy rabble, excited rather than chastened by witnessing the carriage of justice.

Margaret and three other prisoners had been transferred to the court earlier in the day and waited in cells at the side of the building. Two cases were held before hers and justice, in the form of lengthy sentences, was dispensed,

While waiting for the next case to begin the Lord Chief Baron glanced over the charge sheet. The horror of an offence that so affected his class infuriated him.

'A horse thief I see,' he remarked to his neighbour, the High Sheriff. 'A heinous crime, if I ever heard one. Man's horse not safe in its own paddock. Got to be stamped out.'

He was even more appalled when he saw Margaret's name. 'Good God! It's a woman! What is this peaceful country coming to when women resort to such crimes? A weak, snivelling slattern I'll be bound. Throwing her self on our mercy or else one of those bold, athletic creatures who hardly know what sex they are. Hanging not good enough for them.'

When Margaret's name was called a hush fell over the crowd. Even the members of the bench felt the change of atmosphere. Something important was about to happen.

Lord Chief Baron Macdonald raised his eyes, really surveyed the courtroom for the first time and was surprised at the appearance of the prisoner at the bar.

Margaret was dressed in a plain blue cotton gown. She stood, head lowered, apparently engaged in prayer, neither wretched nor arrogant. She raised her eyes and looked once around the room, hoping, even at this stage, to see the one beloved face. Then, satisfied he was not there, she gave her full attention to the gentlemen on the bench, especially the Lord Chief Baron.

Those steady brown eyes had an unsettling effect on him and he glanced again at the charge sheet, cleared his throat and began.

'Prisoner at the bar, you stand committed, upon your own confession, before two justices of the county of Middlesex of having, on the night of the 23rd. of May this year, stolen from the stables of your late master, John Cobbold Esq., a strawberry roan-grey coach gelding, of having ridden it from Ipswich to London that night; and being in the act of selling that same horse on the following day in the yard of the Red Bull Inn, Aldgate. For this offence you now stand before the court. Prisoner at the bar, how do you plead, guilty or not guilty?'

Margaret looked directly at the judge. 'Guilty, My Lord.'

'Prisoner at the bar,' resumed the judge, 'though you have made this confession, you are at liberty to retract it and to plead 'not guilty' if you so wish. Your plea of guilty will gain you no favours in the sentence to follow. Consider your answer.'

Margaret replied in a steady voice, 'I cannot plead not guilty, My Lord.'

'Why ever not?' demanded the judge.

'Because I know I am guilty.'

This was too much for the judge. He had thrown her a lifeline and she had rejected it. This was no ordinary prisoner, and he began to feel uncomfortable about the sentence he would have to give unless some mitigating circumstance could be found.

'Prisoner at the bar, it gives me no pleasure to address one of your sex in such a situation, I cannot judge the motives for you committing this crime, for there is no mitigating evidence in your statement. The punishment for the crime to which you have pleaded guilty is death. Have you nothing to say why I should not pass this sentence? Is there no one here to speak for this girl?'

There was a stir in the court as several people rose to approach the bar. Margaret raised her hand to indicate that she wished to speak,

'Prisoner at the bar,' said the Chief Baron. 'I am quite ready to hear what you have to say.'

'My lord, I have nothing to say in my own defense because I am guilty. All I want everyone to understand that the fault is mine and mine alone. A more honest and upright father than the one I had could not be found. He taught me right from wrong and it is no fault of his that I am here. My former master and mistress were the kindest a girl could have, and I ask them to forgive me for betraying their trust so shabbily. They have already forgiven me, but I wished to express my regret publicly. I have but one request. If you, in your mercy, should wish to save me by sending me out of the country for life, then I would ask you didn't, for I would sooner die among my friends than live in a foreign land without them.'

Her speech had an immediate effect upon those present in court. Some wept quietly and even strangers who had come to the court for entertainment wished that she be pardoned. Scribes who wrote comments upon trials began scribbling furiously. This was news that would be of interest further afield than Suffolk. This was worthy of national note. Those of a literary bent were already composing ballads.

The judge looked at her with a mixture of astonishment and pity. 'Is there nobody who can speak of her former character?'

Mr Cobbold, her accuser, pushed his way forward.

'My Lord. I am the plaintiff. I must tell you that it was the magistrate in London who bound me over to prosecute the accused. He compelled me to adopt this course. If it had been up to me I would have dismissed all charges and taken her back into my employ, for a better servant I never had.'

Then he gave an account of Margaret's virtues, her honesty,

industry, loyalty and the bravery she had shown in saving the lives of his children.

Next Dr Stebbins gave an account of her early life, touching on her first notable ride, and stating that, should she be freed, he would give her a place in his house for as long as she wanted.

Letters were also submitted from her other two former employers and from her Uncle Leader. By the time all the submissions had been read the entire courtroom could only wonder why such a paragon of virtue should end up in such a place.

The members of the bar were similarly affected. They conferred among themselves for some time. If only the girl had pleaded not guilty then they would not have hesitated in releasing her. It was obvious that she was not a criminal, that, whatever her reasons for taking the horse, she was the most law abiding of citizens.

But the law was the law. What else could they do?

The length of deliberation gave hope to those who watched. The desire for acquittal was strong in the body of the court. The judges felt it, and feared what effect a guilty verdict might bring.

At last the Chief Baron turned around and fixed Margaret with a steadfast stare. The court was instantly silent. When he had their full attention he slowly picked up the black cap and raised it to his head. A terrible moan went up from the body of the court. Most of the women wept and some fainted and had to be removed.

An absolute silence fell on the court as he raised his voice and began his address. 'Prisoner at the bar, I have listened intently to all you, and those around you, have had to say. From it all I have been assured that you are no simpleton who did not know what you were doing. In fact I have never met a prisoner who had a better understanding of right and wrong. This makes your crime so much worse. In spite of the affection you have been show, by all around you, you have knowingly and willingly broken the law of his gracious Majesty. You have betrayed the trust of all who have regard for you. You have given no mitigating reason for your actions.

'The representations that have been submitted will be forwarded to the King, who alone has the power to grant mercy, but it would be cruel of me to offer you hope. The crime of which you stand guilty is so prevalent at this time that only by making examples can it be stamped out. Therefore there is no alternative for me but to carry out the law, which I have sworn to uphold.

'Margaret Catchpole, you have been found guilty of the crime of horse stealing. You will be taken from this place, back to the prison whence you came, and thence to a place of execution, and there to be hanged by the neck until you are dead, and may God have mercy on your soul.'

At these words another groan came from those present and many could be heard sobbing loudly. The only one seemingly unaffected was Margaret herself. She curtsied to him and walked steadily as she was escorted back to the cells.

CHAPTER TWELVE

While Margaret waited quietly in her cell, resigned to her fate and preparing herself as best she could for the ordeal ahead, there was feverish activity going on among her friends, particularly John Cobbold. He reported his progress to Dr Stebbins.

'I have seen Chief Justice Macdonald personally. I informed him that I would be willing to plead Margaret's case before His Majesty, if that was necessary. I have presented again our testimonials, along with those of others of standing in the community that were not available during the trial. He was most impressed with Margaret and has promised to plead her cause in London.

'I would say we have a good chance of getting her sentence commuted. I cannot allow myself to believe … that this dreadful sentence will be carried out.'

'If it is … carried out, will it be soon?'

'Very soon, I should think, but it is unthinkable that such a … a fine young girl …' He could not go on.

'One doesn't realise the harshness of our laws,' mused the doctor, 'until it touches one personally. It really is an outrageous sentence. If she had killed someone I could understand; but just for stealing a horse!'

It was Cobbold himself who brought the news to Margaret. She was already in the condemned cell when he hurried to the prison.

She heard the key in the heavy door and turned from the window where she spent most of her time. She could see nothing through its bars, except a small patch of watery, blue sky, but it was the nearest thing to freedom that she could find in these cold, grey walls.

Cobbold was surprised to see her so calm. 'I've brought great news,' he cried, reaching out and taking her hands in his. 'Your sentence has been commuted.'

'Commuted?' she asked, puzzled.

'Yes, by the King! I have just this minute heard the news.'

Margaret looked at him as though she scarcely understood what he was saying. 'You are really kind . . . I appreciate . . . so much . . . everything you have done for me.' She sank onto a bench. 'Forgive me for not seeming to be grateful or excited but I feel . . . unable to . . . believe it.'

Cobbold sat too. 'I know. It must be hard. I must confess I have found it hard to believe any of this. It has been like a very bad nightmare.'

She smiled at him wanly. 'Unfortunately, I'm afraid it has all been too true. I've learnt to accept that in the last few weeks. I have had to face death and try and prepare myself for it . . . and now you say I'm not going to die. I can't feel anything.'

'I understand. It is the shock. You have been so brave.'

They both sat quietly and then it seemed that the news was at last penetrating her consciousness. 'My father will be pleased. You say my sentence has been commuted? To what?'

Cobbold shifted his feet uneasily and looked at the floor. 'To seven years transportation.'

He heard the intake of breath and the colour that was returning to her cheeks faded.

'But that is good. They are way behind in transportations. They won't get to you for years, three at least. And by that time you will be free. The Lord Baron himself said that if you behave yourself you will be able to earn a reduction of sentence. He seemed to think that you would be out in three years.'

With this news, the restraint that she had practiced for so long snapped. She laughed, she cried, she clapped her hands and danced around. Cobbold, caught up in the moment, took her hands and danced with her.

She was free. What was three years? She would now be allowed to join the general prison population. She would be able to go into the prison yard. She would be given work; that would help to pass the time. She could allow herself to feel again.

Margaret quickly adapted to prison life. She knew she had been given a second chance at life by those who loved her. She would not betray their trust. She would become a model prisoner, do anything asked of her and be free again before the sentence of transportation could be carried out. As each day dawned the possibility faded further and further from her mind.

Though she did not have actual freedom she was free to walk around the prison and talk to whomever she wished. Her many skills, gained through employment, were quickly put to use. Her diligence and reliability were recognised and before the year was out she was put in charge of the laundry. She never played favorites or abused her position so she was popular with the other women. Mr Rippon found that she had a calming influence on the more rebellious of them. Only the most depraved did not respond to her.

She believed she had been given another life

Margaret, as she listened to the stories of others, found that most were not dissimilar from her own. Most of the women were good at heart and had been led astray, often by lovers. She began to counsel them, particularly the young girls, explaining to them that they could start a new life if only they broke from their old companions and their ways.

But even as she gave this advice she wondered if she would follow it herself. If Will came back into her life, would she forgive him? If he beckoned, would she follow?

By the beginning of her third year everybody in the prison was sure that she would soon be released. Her friends were always positive, and Mr Rippon was already joking that she would have to start training another woman to take her place. Mrs Cobbold had told her that, when she was released, she could have her old job, if she wished to come back to Cliff. Margaret went about her work singing quietly to herself She even made herself a calendar so that she could cross off the days.

And then, one afternoon, in the drying yard, as she was taking sheets from the line she heard a voice; one that she instantly recognised, calling softly, 'Margaret. Margaret Catchpole.'

She stopped, holding her breath, then turned to left and right trying to locate the sound.

Ipswich prison held both men and women, separated by a twenty-foot high brick wall. But in one place there was a gate. The bars were close together but it was possible to see a person on the other side. Being near this gate was forbidden but some of the women risked it, particularly if they had friends on the other side.

Margaret turned towards the gate and there he was, with the same arrogant stance and cheeky grin.

'Will!' She could hardly say the word. 'Will, what are you doing here?'

'Well, it wasn't my idea to come,' he laughed. 'I had been living honestly for some time, bought myself a boat and begun legitimate trading, but after I heard what you had done I thought, what's the use?' He laughed. 'But I forgive you.'

Margaret felt her hackles rise. 'You forgive me! How dare you! Forgive me for what?' She was so agitated that she raised her voice, risking discovery. Luckily the guards on both sides were busy somewhere else.

'What for? For going off with Ned Pike of course. But as I said, I forgive you.'

'Ned Pike?' Margaret quizzed, genuinely amazed. She only just remembered the name. 'I have never seen Ned Pike in all my life.'

Will was confused, 'But John Cook said . . . '

'John Cook!' Margaret was so furious she wished she could climb over the fence and give Will a slap. 'John Cook was the cause of all my trouble. He tricked me into taking the horse.'

'Tricked you! How?'

'He told me that you were in London and in need of help. I

went to London to save you.'

Will was stunned by this revelation. 'But John told me . . . '

'And John Cook is such an honest friend? You would trust someone like that before you would trust me? I thought you knew me better, Will Laud.'

'I thought so too, but when you sent me away and said you wanted nothing more to do with sailors, I thought you had finished with me.'

'Then John Cook didn't tell you what really happened. He told me he had.'

'Then it seems that he has been an enemy to both of us.'

'He told me that you could not stay because Luff was looking for you.'

'That was true enough, and he found me. Ambushed me and I am lucky to live to tell the tale. But he will never harm anyone again. He was caught and hanged nearly a year ago, and nobody mourned his going. Rumor has it that he was set up by Bargood, himself. Luff and a few cronies were doing a little moonlighting on their own, using Bargood's currency. He was not only evil but stupid as well. I wish, before God, I had never met him.'

A shout from one of the guards brought this conversation to an abrupt halt.

'Hurry Margaret. I won't be much punished just for looking. Meet me soon.'

Margaret hurried away, part covered by a sheet. The guard peered through the bars then turned back to Will. 'Nothin' to interest you there, Laud. You can't get to those women and they'd not be worth it even if you could. Scum of the earth they be.'

Margaret had no difficulty finding excuses to be near the gate and Will managed to speak with her on several occasions. They caught up on each other's past history and Will confessed that he had gone back to smuggling more in defiance than anything else. But he had not joined a gang. He only smuggled small quantities of goods and sold them to acquaintance he had known in the old days. Captain Bargood had approached him but he had turned him down. He did not want to be part of any cutthroat crew again.

'I think, because I would not join him he set me up. It was obvious that the coast guard was waiting for me. I only had a small quantity of rum and because of my record in the war they only confiscated my boat and gave me a twelve month's sentence.'

'That's no great time, Will. I will be out soon and I will be waiting for you.'

'There was more. I also got a one hundred pound fine, which must be paid before I can be released. So it might as well have been ten years. How am I going to get that kind of money when they have taken everything from me?'

Margaret could not believe what she was hearing. Surely it was God's intervention. The necklace that had first caused her to question Will's honesty would now be the means of saving him. She would be able to help him.

'Will, I can help you. The reason why I went to London in the first place was to bring money to you. Remember the 'fake' necklace you gave me? I sold it for one hundred and fifty pounds. I can get the money for you and we will still have a little over.'

Will could not believe his luck. 'Margaret, you are my guardian angel. I wish I could jump over this fence to hug you.'

'Oh Will. Could it be that at long last all our troubles will be over? As soon as I get out I will get the money and I will wait until your time is up.'

'The ruby necklace! What a stroke of fate. It got me into all this trouble in the first place. Now it is going to be my salvation.'

Margaret contacted her uncle and, swearing him to secrecy, arranged that the money be paid to Mr Rippon on behalf of the prisoner. Will would be free as soon as the year was up.

Not long after this encounter, application was made to the Secretary of State for Margaret's parole. So sure was Mr Rippon, that he told Margaret to prepare herself for her imminent release. However, the prejudice against her crime, that had first caused the sentence of death, was still alive. Horse stealing was almost a daily occurrence so the prospect of her release was not so bright.

Mr Cobbold, who had been the conveyer of such good tidings three years before, was called upon again to deliver the verdict. Her sentence was not to be shortened. She was to serve the full seven years.

Margaret sat, as one stunned, after the first words had been given. Four more years with the high probability of transportation during that time.

She had tried so hard. She had done everything that was asked of her. Will was to be soon released, but she would remain in prison, or worse, be sent to the other side of the world.

She sat so still, digesting these thoughts, that John Cobbold became afraid. He called for assistance but no attention or comfort could draw her from her lifeless state.

She spoke to no one and refused to eat. It was as if the spirit that had so long sustained her was finally broken. Nobody knew what she was thinking but all knew that she was suffering.

Mrs Cobbold took on the responsibility of rescuing her from the despondency into which she had sunk. She visited Margaret every day. She talked to her, prayed for her, sometimes she just sat with her.

Slowly Margaret came back to life. She began to eat and she went about her work in a mechanical way. But still she spoke to no one.

When Will spied her through the bars he hurried up to get her attention.

'Margaret! Where have you been? I have waited for you daily. I thought perhaps you had already been released.'

She did not look his way but spoke for the first time in nearly a fortnight. 'Released indeed. No such luck for Margaret Catchpole, Horse Thief. She must serve her full sentence and be transported to New South Wales.'

'What are you talking about, Margaret? What about your pardon?'

'No pardon for her. Will may go free, but she is to rot in

prison.' The despair in her voice frightened him.

'No, Margaret. No! If I am free. I'll find a way to free you too. Even if I have to scale the prison walls and take you.'

And in this idle statement, spoken without thought, a plan began to grow in Will's mind. He took every opportunity to observe the routine of the prison, its walls and the *chevaux-de-frize*, metal spikes set in a revolving cylinder to prevent anyone climbing over should they, by any chance, reach the top.

Margaret was hanging clothes on the clothes-horses when she heard Will's voice.

'Those frames would make a good ladder.'

'Why would I need a ladder?' she quizzed, recognising the voice without turning.

'To climb over the wall, of course.' he replied cheerily.

'What madness is this? Are you trying to taunt me Will? The walls are twenty feet high. And supposing I could climb up them, how could I get over the revolving spikes.'

'Now that's a question I can answer. All it needs is courage. Do you have the courage, Margaret my love?'

'I have as much courage as the next one, but I still don't understand.'

'If you look, near the outside wall, up close by the adjoining wall, you will notice that a spike is missing. Must have rusted away, but who would worry? The gap is still narrow, but someone as slim as you might manage to squeeze through. Think about it, Margaret. I will be free soon. If once you can get beyond the wall I will arrange everything after. We can get a boat to the Continent and then begin the life we have always planned. We will be penniless, but we will have each other.'

Margaret 's mind could hardly contain these new ideas - to be free- to be with Will! It was all she had ever wanted. Was this crazy plan possible? But what did it matter? Be it ever so far fetched, it was a possibility.

'I'll do it, Will. I'll take note of everything and make a plan.'

Over the time remaining before Will was to be released, they made their plans. Among the interesting facts he had gleaned was that the assizes would be on soon after his release. The governor would be away for seven days. They planned the escape for this time, as discipline was often lax when Mr Rippon was not there. Will would make the plans for getting them out of England and wait outside the walls each night, hoping that Margaret could carry out her side of the plan.

Margaret sat, in silence, at the head of the long sewing table with the other prisoners. She was thinking. The other women, chattering among themselves, left her to her own thoughts.

Stitch, stitch, stitch went her fingers. Was it worth it? Can I do it, went her thoughts? She found herself looking up through the barred windows. Beyond the top pane she could see the huge copper cylinder, spiked with cruel, mocking iron.

Her thoughts drifted to Will, released three days now. He may have been all the things that others said about him, but he was still the only one she loved, and now she had another reason to love him. His flight of fancy had turned into a plan and now she had hope - hope for a future - hope of freedom!

Her eyes went back to the spikes. Her fingers stopped stitching. She wondered how many times she had looked at those spikes; how many times she had visualised crawling through them. Was it really possible?

She shuddered, imagining what would happen if she failed, her mangled body revolving round and round then finally falling to the ground. Would she be dead or would she still be suffering the agony of those iron teeth?

She gave herself a shake to bring her mind back to reality. She must stop or she would lose her nerve.

She had made up her mind to try. There were many more problems to solve and plans to make. The spikes were just one more hurdle. If she spent all her time thinking about them she would neglect the rest and never even reach them.

Still distracted, she resumed sewing but in her mind she was sewing not patches on thick unbleached sheets but a pair of sailor trousers for herself. Will was going to get her a sailor's jacket. If she could make the trousers it would complete the disguise. She could organise the material easily enough, but how to cut them out. She put out her hand to take the scissors, which were chained to the table. She cut the patch and her mind went to the garden. The gardening shears! They were sharp and she had access to them.

One problem solved.

Her mind was on the plans for the escape and her usually neat sewing became sloppy and crooked. She let out a sudden cry of pain. In her preoccupation she had pricked her finger and broken the needle. She looked at the blood and thought again of the thing she most feared. Glancing again at the window she noticed how the cylinder rocked slightly in the breeze.

How easily it moves, she thought with a shudder.
She leant forward to find another needle and take more thread. The cotton came to the prison in large, rounded spools and one was allotted to every four prisoners. The spool was just outside her reach and the woman next along flicked it towards her with her finger. It rolled, stopped, and rocked slightly in front of her.

Margaret's hand stopped in mid-air as she put it out to take the cotton. It rocked just like the cylinder on the wall!

The spool stopped rocking and Margaret, fascinated, stuck her broken needle into it.

'Want another needle Dearie?' enquired the woman next to her.

'Yes, yes,' replied Margaret, still looking at the needle sticking out of the reel.

The guard passed her a packet with four needles. 'And I want three back,' he said.

She selected one slowly, taking a long time to thread it. She glanced around to assure herself that nobody was looking.

Still fascinated she stuck the other three needles into the cylindrical bundle of thread beside the broken needle, in a pattern similar to that of the spikes on the wall.

Watching it carefully she rocked it back and forward. She put her right hand over the spool for a moment. With her palm over it, she rocked it again. Then smiling she continued her work.

It could be done!

When Margaret went to bed that night she had three lengths of thread, a new needle and the broken one which still had its eye, and a very clear picture of how she could squeeze through the spiked, rolling cylinder with one broken spike.

Next day she 'borrowed' the garden shears. As one of its improvements, Ipswich prison allowed its prisoners sheets, confident that they could not be used to escape as the cell windows overlooked the prison yard.

That night, after the guard had locked her in her cell, she cut out a pair of sailor's trousers from her own bed linen and for the next two nights sewed feverishly until they were finished. She had only one more difficulty to overcome. How could she avoid being locked into her cell?

Then this last problem was solved. Rose, the occupant of the next cell died and her cell was left unlocked until such time as another prisoner was sent to fill it. The last vestige of fear or scruples disappeared from Margaret's mind when she saw the eight prisoners hustled into the cart that would take them to Bury St Edmond to be tried. She had seven days in which to make her escape.

She did not doubt for a moment that Will would be waiting for her. But even if he wasn't she had the taste of freedom in her mouth and nothing would stay her now. She would not try the first night, as everyone would still be on alert. Best wait till the second or third day when they would be more relaxed.

On the night of March 28th 1800, the guard came down the stone passage to turn the key in the locks. He peered into Margaret's cell and saw a figure already curled up on her bunk. He smiled. Model prisoner, pleasant, decent. What a pity that they were not all like her. He ticked her off the list.

'Margaret Catchpole?'

'Yes,' came the muffled reply.

He turned the key, locking the great door and proceeded to

move on to the next cell.

Margaret, hidden in Rose's cell next door, heard him continue down the corridor, calling names and locking doors. Her heart was beating so loudly she could hear it as clearly as his footsteps. She had been afraid that he would not be satisfied with the 'yes' she had called through the cell wall. Her whole plan had depended on it. Apparently he had had no suspicion.'

She crouched for the longest time on that bed where Rose had died. She heard the hours strike in the nearby church ... Ten o'clock ... Eleven ...

The time between eleven and twelve was so long that she was beginning to fear she had not heard it strike. She could not believe that an hour could take so long.

At last, at long last, she heard the chimes!

She sat there shivering until the final stroke had reverberated and drifted away into the distance. Then she opened the cell door. To Margaret's strained ears it made a dreadful clatter; in fact, well oiled and well cared for, it made almost no noise at all.

She crept along the passageway. If she were caught it would be all up with her. She would never be able to give a plausible explanation of her presence with a pair of white trousers under her prison dress.

Once she had accepted that the die was cast her fear left her. She set about getting out of prison as wholeheartedly as she did everything else. There were no doubts, no qualms now; only a certain surprise, surprise that this adventure was happening to her. There was no thought of going back, nothing now but a determination to get away from the prison.

Along the passageway she came to the great door that guarded the cells. It was open, as she had expected it to be. The guards believed that the cell doors were sufficient and seldom locked it. She breathed a sigh of relief. Had it been locked it would have taken a charge of gunpowder to open without a key.

Out into the garden she crept.

She had suggested to one of the guards that they leave the clothes horses out in the drying yard, as they were heavy and would be needed next day. To her dismay, someone had put them back. The door to the drying room was locked and anyway there was no way she could have lifted them by herself.

Instead of despairing she looked around to find something else she could use to elevate her sufficiently to be able to throw a rope over one of the spikes.

The garden frames! Could she lift one? They were used to cover the young plants, and the awnings that were usually placed over them in summer had been removed. She tried her strength and found that she could lift one leg. She lifted the frame out of the ground and dragged it to the wall and set it up endways directly under the broken spike. It reached a little more than half way up the wall. She then went and took the linen clothes line off the posts and made a noose at one end of it. She took the longest prop she could find and placed the noose over the horn of it.

She mounted the frame with the help of the prop and, standing on it she lifted the line up and passed it over the cylinder and onto one of the spikes. She pulled it tight, tested it, then, offering a little prayer, she began the ascent.

She drew herself up to the top of the wall. She laid her body directly over the broken spike, one hand grasping the shoulder of iron, to steady it, then pulled until she had all of the line and let it fall over the other side.

Now came the final test of her courage. She could climb back and take her chances of getting back to the cells undetected. She took a deep, deep breath. It was now or never. Taking hold of the rope she bent her body forward and the cylinder revolved, sending her heel-over -head onto the other side of the prison wall.

She came to a stop with a terrible jerk. She was glad of the darkness so that she could not see the distance to the bottom.

Her hands began to slip on the rope!

She gripped it tighter but they slipped again. She gave a cry of pain as the line cut cruelly into her palm. The ache in her shoulder sockets and arms made her want to scream. She slithered the next few feet, her mind blacked out with pain and fear, but she clung to the rope desperately, automatically.

Overcoming her panic she gritted her teeth and with a sob, steadied herself against the wall, and descended bit by bit, She was taken by surprise when her feet touched ground. She fell, no longer able to control her legs.

She heard a movement and felt someone touch her shoulder. She stifled a scream.

'It's me,' Laud whispered handing her up just as the clock in the tower struck one. He put his arm around her, kissing her, trying to sooth her shaking.

'Don't be afraid, darling. You're safe. You've been my brave girl and you've done it!'

Margaret sobbed into his shoulder and held out her bleeding palms. He kissed each in turn then began to lead her away.

'We must hurry. I've got the rest of the uniform for you.'

He led her gently towards the Woodbridge road. In one of the deserted lanes they stopped while Margaret donned the jacket, the pigtail and the hat of a sailor of His Majesty's Navy. She rolled up her prison clothes and hid them in a clump of bushes. They emerged onto the roadway once more. Will had donned his naval garb and they went on their way, a tall matelot and his smaller mate.

CHAPTER THIRTEEN

Will had planned well and surprise was on their side. Because he was not sure when, or if, Margaret would make her breakout, his plans had had to be flexible. He had organised a cutter to take them across the Channel. As soon as the escape was a reality he would send a message and the ship would wait, off shore, at a prearranged spot.

The uncertainty about the date meant the he could do nothing about the two-day delay between the escape and the crossing. This would be the time of greatest danger. They would have to find somewhere safe to hide.

He finally decided that they would spend the time with an aunt who lived in a cottage a few miles from Aldham. His mother's sister, she had always been fond of her wayward nephew. She had never judged him during his smuggling years and was happy to help him now. Will was sure that nobody knew of the contact he had made with Margaret while they were in prison so there would be no reason to connect them and come looking for him at his aunts. It would be a safe place to hide. The only danger would be getting there and returning to the coast.

Margaret was exhausted by the time they reached the cottage. She had had no sleep and the physical and mental energy needed to accomplish the escape had completely drained her.

The good lady dispensed with the celebratory meal she had planned. Instead she led the girl to her own bed, which she had vacated for them. Margaret collapsed into the snowy white sheets and slept the day through. It was nearly sun set when she emerged happy and rested to greet her hostess and Will.

The meal, though unpretentious, was festive. Margaret christened it her wedding tea. She and Will held hands and kissed often during the meal. Will's aunt excused herself and retired to the small room at the back of the cottage as Will led Margaret to their nuptial bed.

'As soon as we reach Holland we will be married,' Will promised.

'Why wait, Will? Let us make our vows to each other now - here. They will be no less binding because we are the only witnesses.'

And so, by candlelight, Will and Margaret pledged their lives. No vows, taken in the greatest of cathedrals, or before the largest of congregations, were ever more sincere than those taken in the small cottage bedroom.

This time there was no need for force, no hasty coupling. They gloried in each other's bodies, in turn passionate or gentle. At last Margaret felt she understood this greatest of mysteries. She did not know such happiness existed and regretted all the wasted years.

Nothing had turned out the way she had dreamed it would, but she was Will's wife and that was all that mattered.

Margaret's absence was first discovered, just before dawn, by a guard when he went into the garden. He saw the frames against the wall and immediately raised the alarm.

The first thought was to account for the male prisoners. When these all checked out they began a roll call among the women.

Margaret's cell door was still locked but when it was opened there was nobody inside. The turnkey was called. His list was produced. Her name had been ticked off. He had heard her call her name. He was sure of that. Obviously the bedclothes had been arranged to deceive him but he was sure she had answered.

How could she have done this if she was not there? Yet how could she have got out and locked the cell behind her?

Suspicion immediately fell on the turnkey despite his protests. He was taken into custody until further investigations could be carried out.

In spite of the garden frame, and later the discovery of the linen rope hanging from the wall, nobody seriously believed that the culprit could have escaped that way. It was only a ruse to put them off the scent. She must still be hiding somewhere inside. An intensive search of the prison and its grounds began.

Mr Rippon was immediately sent for, and any former affection he may have held for Margaret quickly evaporated when he was informed that, as governor of the prison, he was bound, under penalty of five hundred pounds, to answer for the escape of the prisoner.

The news of the escape soon became common knowledge and people flocked to the gaol to look at the high walls and cruel spikes and wonder again at this latest escapade of Margaret Catchpole.

The general consensus was that nobody, least of all a woman, could have scaled those walls. Even if she had managed to climb to the top there was only one way from there.

'The only possible way is to go over head first.' explained one expert in the crowd. 'Nobody, not even Margaret, would do that.'

As soon as he arrived back Mr Rippon, having left his most reliable man to continue the search inside, began looking for clues outside. He, for one, did not doubt that, however impossible it seemed, Margaret could be capable of doing it. It was imperative that he should recapture her. Apart from the financial penalty, he would also have to stand trial and prove that he had had nothing to do with her escape.

The Cobbolds were contacted in case they had any information. In the course of conversation Will Laud's name came up. Rippon immediately remembered the prisoner who so lately had paid his fine and left the prison.

'Laud! Of course! Why didn't I think of it? He's a sailor. He would have many contacts with ship. They will have headed to the coast.'

A watch was immediately organised along the coast from a good deal south of Felixstowe to the border of Norfolk, and beyond.

If Laud were to be apprehended, along with the girl, there were many now only too willing to help with the capture.

Coastguards, revenue men and aggrieved smugglers alike joined the hunt.

But it was Rippon himself, accompanied by two of his men, who finally found the right trail. In spite of the delays, both intentional and unavoidable at the beginning of the chase, Margaret and Laud were still not out of England when Rippon stumbled on his first clue.

He came upon Robinson Crusoe wooing the fish from his waterlogged boat. Covered with amulets and trinkets, mumbling his chants, he sat there, eyes staring and wild. It was not one of his lucid moments. Yet Rippon knew that nothing moved on the river without those crazy eyes seeing it.

Rippon stopped his two men. 'Wait here.' He walked down to the water and called softy to the old man. 'Good fishing to you.'

Robin looked up at him angrily. 'Go away. You disturb my fish.' He made a dive at nothing then turned to Rippon aggrieved. 'See now. That were a demon. They've come back now.'

He stepped into the water and came back to the bank dragging his line behind him in one hand and, opening the other to show Rippon. 'See.'

Rippon knew that the only way to get any sense out of the old man was to humor him.

'Yes. But it looks like a good demon. It may bring you fish.'

Robin looked at him suspiciously then sat on the grass. 'And what would you know.'

'Nothing,' said Rippon sitting down beside him.

'As I thought,' said the old man, winding up his line.

Rippon put out his hand to detain him. 'Don't go,' he said.

'And why not? It would seem that this part of the river is overcrowded.' He dived at another demon and continued winding up his line.

The governor sighed. Perhaps he might get something. 'Have you seen anyone else today?'

The old man took no notice so he repeated. 'Has anyone else been this way?'

'Some dozens of people, I should think. Some dozen people.'

He paused, looking at Rippon meaningly. 'Dozens, plus two.' And then, 'they disturb my fish.'

Rippon phrased his next question carefully. 'Ah, but was there anyone unusual?'

'Who knows what's unusual?' He looked at the other man, a gleam of knowing in his eye. 'Usual, unusual who's to decide?'

Rippon felt sure that the old man knew something, but how to find out what it was? He signalled his men to fall behind and prepared to take his time humoring the old fisheman.

'That sounds like one of Robinson Crusoe's theories,' he laughed ruefully.

'Course it's all nonsense,' Robin agreed then continued angrily, 'I knows what I see, same as any other man. And if I sees more than most, who can say that I don't sees it?'

'Exactly,' replied Rippon agreeably. Perhaps he was wasting his time, but one never knew.

Robinson Crusoe began unwinding his line again.

'The demons hath gone. I think I'll stay. You can stay too, if you be quiet.'

Rippon nodded. The fisherman baited his hook quietly and let the line fall into the water. He sat motionless for a few moments and then addressed the governor.

'I will tell ye a secret.' He cast his eyes around, making sure they could not be overheard. 'Often I see things. You agree?'

Rippon nodded, not wanting to break the spell.

'Today I see him again and I'm afeard.' The old man shuddered and rested his head on the other man's shoulder. 'I saw him before, when he came after the maid. Fighting and shooting it was then.' He covered his face and shook himself back and forth. Rippon was afraid the moment was gone.

'But what does he want this time?' He breathed the question.

It had an instant effect on the old man. He sat upright looking to left and right.

'What does he want, he and his shadow? I don't know! I don't know. But Will Laud never comes back from the dead without causing trouble. Maybe he comes for old Robin this time.'

He was dreadfully distressed. He wound himself into a ball

and began his incantations.

Rippon was galvanised by the name. He believed that Robin had seen Laud. If he was careful he might get information as to which way he had gone. He patted the agonised fishermen gently, and by degrees he uncoiled and looked around.

'Tell me about the spirit,' Rippon asked quietly, suppressing his excitement. 'Tell me where he went and I will see he doesn't harm you.'

'You can do that?' The tortured eyes sought his face looking for truth.

'Yes, I can.'

'And his shadow too?'

'Certainly, his shadow. They will never trouble you again. Just tell me which way they went.'

The old man sat staring into space, describing the scene as he saw it. 'He come, with the sun behind him.' He pointed across the bank to the other side of the river. 'He come across the water.' His hand moved up and down demonstrating the bobbing of the little boat. 'He pulls in there and he and his shadow gets out and . . .' Here he paused again. Rippon could see the cloud of insanity invading his eyes.

'Try Robin. Try and tell me which way they went.'

Robin made one more effort. He stood up and, like a biblical prophet, pointed towards an inlet some two hundred yards away.

Rippon patted the old man on the back. 'Well done, Robin.' He signalled to one of his men. 'Take care of him. Take him to Ipswich and get him some food. Send a message to the coastguard to meet me at Shingle Street.'

Between the ocean and the river there lay a strip of land, so narrow it could scarcely be called coastline at all, hardly land, hardly beach, mainly shingle. This part of the sea-washed Suffolk coast was called Shingle Street.

Margaret and Laud had remained at his aunt's cottage until he received the message that the ship would send its boat for them at dusk that day. They left the safety of the cottage and made their way to Shingle Street. They sat, sheltering themselves as best they could, from the cold breeze that blew across this wasteland. Will reached for Margaret's hands. 'Your hands are cold,' he said, rubbing them between his own.

'Brrr,' she shivered and pulling the sailor's reefer jacket closer to her. 'I have known better days for sitting on the beach.'

He laughed and pulled her further leeward around a small mound of shingles and coarse sand whipped up by the wind. It provided little shelter.

His sailor's eyes saw the sail before hers. He watched it for a moment to make sure.

'Look!' he said, 'there's the ship!'

Margaret peered where he pointed. 'I can only see waves. White clouds, white waves, white gulls. Every one looked like a sail one moment, but none of them the next.'

'It's her, all right!' He strained his eyes, searching the sea, wondering if the small boat could possibly reach them or get close enough to the shore in such a heavy sea.

'And there's the boat!' he cried, pointing, then realised that Margaret was not sharing in his excitement. He looked and saw that she was turned, not seaward, but towards the land. She stiffened as her suspicions were confirmed and Will just had time for a glimpse of two men before they dropped to the ground. There was no cover, no trees or shingle mounds in the desolate landscape. They were plainly visible to the two men Margaret had spied.

'It's Rippon,' Margaret whispered.

Will looked again towards the ocean. The small boat was nearer but it was battling the waves. Landward, the two figures were crawling towards them on their bellies. His hand went to his pistol.

'No!' cried Margaret.

'Peggy, listen to me,' he said quietly, earnestly. 'We are fighting for our lives now. It could be them or us. I want you to do exactly what tell you. If anything happens to me make for the boat . . . Please don't argue. I want you to understand and obey.

There are only two of them. I have been in worse situations and got away, but I was on my own then. You must promise to trust me. Then I can concentrate on getting us away.' He grabbed her arm fiercely. 'Promise!'

He pushed her further around the little mound, almost useless as a shield against the men wriggling towards them.

He lifted his pistol, waiting. 'Get behind me. Keep your eyes on the boat.' He had not taken his eyes off the men. 'Get behind me,' he said more forcefully when she did not move. 'When I give the signal, run for the boat.'

'You must know I won't leave you.'

'And you must know that you have to obey me if we are to have any chance. I know what I'm doing. Just you do as I say and we'll see what happens. But, as you love me do as I say.'

He sounded brusque and business like, but his hand, still clasping hers, gave her a reassuring squeeze.

Rippon checked his pistol, and slid a few more feet forward. 'Laud. We are both armed,' he shouted into the wind. 'And we intend to shoot. Make no mistake. I command you to surrender Margaret Catchpole to us.'

'Can you hear me?' Will shouted back.

'Yes,' replied the prison governor.

'Then you can go to hell.' He laughed, then to Margaret, 'how far off is the boat?'

'Just outside the bar.'

'We must wait a little longer,' he told her. He shouted towards the two men still lying on the ground, but stationary now. 'Who are you?' Anything to gain a little more time.

'Officers of His Majesty's prison,' called Rippon, 'I have no interest in you. You are free to go, but you must surrender Margaret to us for I am determined to retake my prisoner.'

Will roared with genuine laughter. 'You mean you'd like to but you must take me first,' and he pointed his pistol directly at the prone man.

'You've had your chance, Laud,' came back Rippon's voice. 'There are two of us. Do you want to be shot?'

'No,' roared Laud throwing out the challenge. 'Do you?'

There was a silence for a moment, then Margaret whispered, 'The boat is still now. It's as close as he can come, I think.'

Laud patted her hand in acknowledgment. 'Rippon,' he shouted. 'I'll make a bargain with you.'

'I'll make no bargains with you,' yelled the gaoler. 'You're under arrest.'

'But you haven't caught me yet.' Will sounded as if he was enjoying the situation. Then to Margaret, 'When I stand, stand behind me. Run if I tell you. Otherwise stay behind.'

'Will, you can't mean . . . '

'Do as I tell you! He commanded. He rose on one knee.

Rippon's finger tightened on the trigger but so did Laud's.

'Don't be foolish.' Rippon shouted. 'I have you covered. We both have.'

'I can't cover both of you,' Will replied, 'but you can sweat on which one I'm about to shoot daylight into, while I bargain with you. The girl goes free . . . and you can have me.'

Margaret clutched as his sleeve. He pushed her back with his elbow.

Rippon, tense, shouted back. 'No one goes free.'

'The girl goes free . . . or one of you dies.'

'We've both got you covered, don't forget. We could shoot you now out of hand.'

'Try,' shouted Laud and raised himself onto his other knee.

'Laud,' Rippon was pleading. 'Don't make a dash for it. Please.'

'Then the girl goes free?'

'No!'

'Then we shoot it out?'

'But you can't win.'

Margaret tugged at the edge of his jacket. 'Will, we can't win. You know that. Do you think I want to see you shot?'

'I'm not done yet if only you will do as I say.' He rose to his feet and stood in full view of the two men. Margaret did the same. He pushed her roughly behind him and began slowly backing towards the boat, his eyes on the two men who rose too.

'The fool,' muttered Rippon, 'the bloody fool.'

'What should I do, Sir?' inquired his man.

Rippon hesitated. 'Wait,' he commanded.

The sailor in the boat sat, tensely, pulling on his oars, trying to hold the small craft still in the boiling sea, and watching the drama being enacted on the shingles.

Laud walked slowly, relentlessly backwards, Margaret behind him. They had almost reached the water's edge.

Rippon raised his pistol and took careful aim. His finger hesitated on the trigger. It is not easy to shoot a man in cold blood. He took a quick look at his man.

'Shoot for his legs,' he began, but all this had happened in the split second it had taken Laud to see Rippon move to cover him more accurately.

The next second three shots rang out, three bullets whistled, projected by three taunt fingers, which had moved without any real thought from their owners.

A cry of pain came from Rippon's man as he gazed in horror at his shattered hand. Laud stumbled, put out his hand to try to steady himself, then fell to his knees.

'Oh, my God!' cried Rippon. 'His bullet upset my aim. I didn't mean to shoot at all . . . I must have seen him fire and I fired too.'

Margaret, clutching at Laud's coat, fell with him. Will raised himself slightly, telling her to go.

'No' she sobbed. 'No. I'm not leaving you'

Laud painfully raised his hand and signaled to the boatman. The sailor understood. He lifted his oars and began to struggle once more through the churning ocean.

Laud sank back and closed his eyes. Margaret sat and put her arms around him.

Rippon's arm barred his man's way as he made a move towards Laud. 'Leave them alone. They're not going anywhere.'

Laud opened his eyes and turned them on the grieving girl.

'Pity,' he whispered. 'Such a pity.' Margaret clasped his hand to her breast and held him tight.

'Pity . . . .that you ever met me,' he said.

She stroked his hair, tears running down her cheeks, blurring his face.

'Don't be sad.' He moved painfully, taking her hand. 'I have been . . . close to death . . . before. Always before . . . I was . . . afraid. I've never told anyone before . . . Do you love me . . . in spite of everything? . . . Do you love me? . . . still?'

'Still.' It was all she could say amid her tears.

Will sighed, a small smile playing on his lips, and closed his eyes.

Margaret closed her eyes too and saw, not the body slipping into eternity, but the young Laud giving her a honeysuckle branch, smiling, laughing, full of the joy of life.

She clasped him tighter still as if to warm him back to life.

She knew, before she opened her eyes, that he was dead. But when does life begin or end? As long as she lived, he would live too, for in her mind he would never die.

While he waited, Rippon attended to his man. The damage was not as serious as expected at first sight. The man would lose one finger, but that was small damage when one considered what it could have been. Rippon had a fleeting thought that Laud was only shooting to disarm the man, but he shrugged it away. Enough to know that he had killed a man who had fired his pistol.

In the receding light he saw figures moving towards them.

'Ah. Here comes the trusty coastguard. You'd best go to them and inform them what has happened before they shoot us by mistake. Tell them that we have one prisoner and one body. They had best find transport.'

The man headed back towards the coastguard and Rippon walked down to Margaret who still sat nursing Will's body in her lap.

'Come, Margaret. It's time now. The guards are coming.'

Margaret raised her tear-stained face and the look of hate in those brown eyes was like a blow.

'Do not reproach me. I did not want to shoot him.'

'But you did.'

'He fired first and I returned it. I have only done my duty.'

'Then you must be very proud of yourself. You have killed an innocent man and captured a poor fugitive female. What a noble warrior. I'm sure you will be suitably rewarded.'

'Forgive me Margaret, but he left me no other way. I never wished to bring you grief '

'Yet you have. You had two pistols. Why couldn't one of you have fired at me so that I could lie with my love, my poor, poor Will.'

She burst into new floods of tears.

When the coast guard arrived they would have cheered and boasted that an old enemy had fallen, but they were moved by her grief and respectfully left the two alone until a commandeered post-chaise arrived. Margaret was placed in it along with the body of Laud and they were taken immediately to Ipswich.

News of her capture had already spread and people gathered to see this girl that even the walls of lpswich Gaol could not hold. They crowded round the prison gate and when the party arrived a great cheer went up, but it was not in celebration of the capture.

Someone in the crowd shouted, 'Three cheers for Margaret Catchpole, and the 'hip hurrays' followed her into the prison, just as they had followed her many years ago as she left lpswich in Dr Stebbin's gig.

Margaret was once more confined within the dark walls. She was kept in almost solitary confinement. A hastily convened gathering was called of several magistrates. The nature of the offence was then explained to her. She was completely taken by surprise that, in attempting to escape, she had incurred the death penalty, and moreover that anyone else could have incurred punishment for her deed.

'Nobody else was involved in my escape,' she assured them.

'But this cannot be true,' one of the magistrates insisted. 'You could not have done this on your own. How did you escape from your cell?'

'I was never in it. I answered the call from the next cell which was open.'

This had to be demonstrated before they would believe her.

'But you are not trying to convince us that someone didn't open the prison gates? In spite of the trappings, you cannot expect us to believe that you went over the wall?'

Again Margaret's explanation was not enough. They had to go into the yard and inspect the broken spike before they would believe. They shook their heads in wonder as they surveyed the wicked spikes and contemplated the drop on the other side.

Her evidence was enough to exonerate Mr Rippon from any accusation of negligence and the turnkey was released.

After that Margaret was left in peace to reflect on her unhappy lot and mourn the death of her lover. She was given no work to do, nor allowed any visitors, except the prison chaplain, until the courts were ready to try her for a second time.

CHAPTER FOURTEEN

When Margaret was tried again it was by the same judge who had been on the bench when first she appeared. Chief Baron Macdonald sat, his mouth set in a firm, hard line. He felt personally affronted. He had pleaded for this girl and she had repaid him shabbily.

He knew all about her this time; knew how he had been deceived by her demeanor, her words, her pretension of being an upright citizen. He remembered how he had been struck last time at her grasp of right and wrong. If ever a prisoner knew what she was doing, this one did. She had knowingly and willingly thrown the mercy he had granted her back in his face.

There would be no second chance. He would have no scruples about the death penalty this time. In fact he would be glad to award it.

Margaret was dressed, as before, in a plain, blue calico dress. She appeared pale and thin, but free from all nervousness. There was a calmness of deportment. She did not look around the court anxiously, as she had done before. She knew, this time, that the face she longed to see would not be there.

She was quite indifferent to the public gaze. With downcast eyes she did not notice the piercing glare of the judge, though people in the body of the court had seen it, and were amazed that she did not quail.

The indictment was read out by the clerk of the court and she was asked, 'How say you, prisoner at the bar, are you guilty or not guilty?'

Margaret raised her head and her dark eyes rested on the judge.

'Guilty, My Lord.'

The court was hushed as the judge began his address.

'I cannot address you, prisoner at the bar, as I once did, since I now believe that you are hardened in your iniquity. I pitied you at the time for your youth, but now I know that, though young in years, you are a criminal of the worst kind. I believed then that, given a chance, you would develop into an estimable character; but now, as I look on you, I see a person dangerous to the morals of others.

'You have been shown, in the past, the mercy of this court. Your case has been pleaded by prominent citizens, similarly deceived. His Majesty, himself, was moved by your case. Yet you have dismissed all that charity and have dared to break out of your prison. I had fully intended to have you discharged from the Ipswich gaol at the next assizes, depending on the good report of your progress last year, being confirmed. Imagine my surprise when told of your escape.

'You have, I am told, been the cause of one man's death and you might have involved others in your guilt. The turnkey at the gaol might well now be serving a sentence in complicity in helping a prisoner escape. Your governor, who has been a good friend and has given glowing reports of your progress, could well have suffered a heavy fine. You very nearly succeeded in your escape and then these innocent men would have suffered. It is to the credit of that man that he so involved himself in your recapture. The magistrates of this county owe him a debt of gratitude. It is thanks to him that you are not still at large.

'I will not waste words upon a person such as you, an ungrateful wretch who has no humility, no remorse. What could you possibly have to say to justify your actions? You may say whatever you like. It cannot do you any good and will not mitigate your sentence in any way.'

He looked at, her defying her to answer. 'Prisoner at the bar, do you have anything to say?'

But Margaret was beyond intimidation. 'Yes, My Lord, I do. I fully expected that your worship would condemn me severely, but I did not think I would be condemned without mercy. You say I am a hardened criminal. I have committed but two offences; one for which I pleaded guilty, but the second I did not know to be a crime at all, until told afterwards. I could not understand why it should be considered a crime to seek one's freedom. But it has now been explained to me. I did not understand the consequences of my actions.

'I would like to apologize to my gaolers for the stress I have put them under. I was never treated anything but fairly while I was in their care. I have forgiven my governor for exercising his duty as he did. The fault was mine.

'In your address you referred to your intention of pardoning me at the next assizes. To express this at such a time is a cruel punishment. I would go so far as to say it is a falsehood. At the last assizes your lordship received a testimonial, signed by all the magistrates who visited the gaol, and recommending my release on account of my exemplary character. Even you gave me hope at the time of my original imprisonment. Yet you denied me, on a whim, putting me in a position where I risked transportation.

'If you were going to pardon me, why did you not do it then, or at least state your intentions? It was your decision, then, that was the cause of all the trouble. You cannot imagine the despair when freedom is promised and then denied. It is your fault that I escaped and that a good man is now dead. You have the power of death over me and I welcome your verdict for there is nothing left in life for me now. I soon will meet a greater judge and he will see into my heart and know how guilty I really am. One day you and I will stand before that judge and we will see then, who is the guilty one.'

By the time Margaret had finished Chief Baron Macdonald could hardly contain himself at the bar. He wanted to respond but could not trust himself to control his composure. Red faced and puffing fire he snatched the black cloth and rammed it on his head.

'Margaret Catchpole, you have been found guilty of the crime of absconding from His Majesty's Prison. You will be taken from this place, back to the prison whence you came, and hence to a place of execution and there be hanged by the neck until you are dead . . . and . . . may God have . . . have mercy on your soul.'

These last words were forced from his lips but he was not

ready for what came next.

Looking at him steadily, she straightened herself and replied, 'Oh, He will.'

If the Chief Baron thought that he would rest easy after his verdict, he was wrong. The girl's face haunted him, and, now that he had regained his composure, her words had such a ring of truth that they would not stop going around in his head.

He was sure, in his mind that the verdict had been correct, but her arguments persuaded him that justice had not been done. He had never before lost a night's sleep over a judgment he had made, but now this ignorant cottage girl had made him question the very law he had sworn to uphold.

Very early in the morning he gave up all pretence of sleep and sent for a copy of the court proceedings. This time he read, with growing amazement, the account of Margaret's escape. How could she have done it? Could the desire for freedom be such that a young woman would risk such a horrifying death? Where did she find the courage?

As soon as he regarded the hour to be respectable, he ordered his carriage to go to the prison and see for himself.

Mr Rippon was surprised and worried when he saw the Chief Baron's coach and was astonished at his request. The great man walked in the yard, asked to be shown the garden frame and had the gaoler explain again and again how the escape was carried out.

'Amazing, . . . amazing,' he kept saying, looking up at the spikes and shaking his head. He stood, balancing on his toes, hands behind his back, ruminating for some time.

'Such spirit . . . such courage . . . Damn it man, I'll not be the one to snuff out such courage. Don't say anything of my visit. You will hear from me soon,' and he was gone.

Rippon said nothing of the visit but was not surprised when, a few days later, an official letter from the court arrived.

He read it quickly then hurried towards the cell where Margaret was being held. She had made her peace with him and he was a daily visitor since her return. He stopped short of the cell, remembering what Margaret had said at her first trial about being sent away from England. He turned back and sent a message to fetch Mrs Cobbold as quickly as possible. Then he proceeded to Margaret's cell.

He was happy with the news he was bringing, but he wasn't sure that Margaret would receive it in the same spirit.

'Margaret, I've brought you good news,' he began quickly. 'Your sentence has been commuted.'

'Commuted?' She felt that she was visiting the past. She asked the same question again. 'Commuted to what?'

Rippon wished he did not have to answer. 'To transportation.'

'For how long?' she queried flatly.

'For life,' replied the poor man wishing he had left the telling to some one else.

'I see.' Then she tried to rouse herself. 'I'm sorry. I do appreciate everything you have done. You have been very kind.'

'No, you don't understand. It was the Chief Baron himself who changed his mind. He admired your courage.'

'More likely he doesn't want me on his conscience. But if he remembers me next time, when he has to sentence a poor wretch, then that will be something.' This was the only response Margaret gave to the news that she would not be executed. To her, transportation was an even worse fate.

Mrs Cobbold appeared soon after and Margaret poured out to her all the sorrow she had not been able to tell in front of the governor.

'What have I to live for? I was content to die here among familiar places, but now even my bones will rest in some foreign land. I know I should be grateful, but I'm just too tired to care.'

The two women, mistress and maid, sat together then, and on many subsequent days. With the help and understanding of the good lady, Margaret became resigned to her future. She expected nothing from it, but she was reconciled. They talked often of religion and in time Margaret found some consolation in prayer.

Jonathan Catchpole came to visit his daughter for the last time. His troubles had worn him down. He looked like an old, old man though he was only in his late fifties.

Margaret fell into his arms and sobbed, 'Oh Da,' how can you forgive me? It would have been better had you never had a second daughter.'

'No, no, lass. With all our troubles I would never wish that. You have always been my pride and nothing you have done has ever changed my mind. I could wish that you had never met Laud, for that was the only mistake you made, but there must have been some good in him for you to love him so.'

'Oh, there was. I know that there was much good, if only life had led him in a different direction. Da, he died trying to save me. He gave his life for me! Does that not show his nobility?' The tear filled eyes pleaded for a kind word for her lover.

'Yes, Peg. He was a hero at the end and his love for you was as constant as your own. Life often leads us by strange byways. But it's all over now and you must look to your own life. Don't grieve that you have to leave home. You will always live in the hearts of all who knew you. And who knows what the future may hold.' The old man squeezed her hands trying to enthuse life into his precious daughter.

'I do not think of the future. I have nothing to look forward to. I will live each day as it comes. Mrs Cobbold has helped me to see that my life is in God's hands. I will accept whatever He has in store for me.'

Jonathan saw the resignation in her eyes. There was little life in them. Perhaps, for now, it was best. But he knew his daughter. He was sure that her indomitable spirit would rise again in time.

Mrs Cobbold brought a large wicker chest containing things that she felt might be useful in a new land. She had consulted several friends and chosen carefully. There was summer and winter cloth, sturdy shoes and bonnets. She had packed foods such as tea and coffee, spices and preserves. There were also things dear to a woman's heart, needles, thimbles, netting needles and pins, knitting needles, thread, a bolt of Indian cotton, course thread, scissors and knives.

As a special gift she packed combs for Margaret's hair. A friend sent writing paper and several pencils and a few books. Her aunt sent toilet water and soap. The chest would be put on board when she sailed and given to her when she arrived. They all prayed that she would be sent to a place where she could use these gifts, for they had heard some horrifying stories of things that went on in the convict settlement.

On her last visit Mrs Cobbold offered to give Margaret her own bible, but she declined. 'I already have my own. It was given to me by the dearest friend I ever had. If there is one thing I can be thankful for, it is that he will never know the disgrace that has befallen me.'

As if the authorities felt it was tempting fate to allow Margaret to remain in England, they set about dispatching her to New South Wales with as little delay as possible. At the end of May 1801 she was taken to Portsmouth and sent on board the *Nile*.

Margaret was fortunate. The *Nile* was one of three, new ships that had not had time to begin to rot, or accumulate filth. There had been such a great outcry against the inhumanities practiced on the hulks and convict transports that a completely new set of regulations had been drafted before the departure of these three vessels. The captains had particular orders to provide scrapers for the decks and to see that the prisoners had clean berths.

After the first few days at sea Margaret found that she enjoyed ship life. She felt close to Will and found she could understand his love of the sea. The voyage was good for her physically and mentally. In spite of herself she began to hope. She no longer felt that there was nothing left to live for, and began to look forward, with curiosity and expectation to her new life.

The *Nile* arrived in the colony of New South Wales on December 14th, 1801, over seven months after leaving Portsmouth, with the extraordinary record of having not lost one life on the voyage, and the unusual report that all 200 female prisoners were in good health.

AUSTRALIA

All but historical names are fictional

CHAPTER ONE

The convicts were allowed on deck as the *Nile* sailed through the heads. The North Head rose, like a rampart, against the mighty ocean. The South Head was lower with a sweep of sand, backed by a dense growth of dark, green trees. To Margaret's mind they were like two arms encircling the sparkling blue harbour that was her destination. A sense of awe seemed to overtake everyone, even the noisiest among them becoming silent. There was nothing to see but an indented expanse of white tipped, blue water, the waves breaking against rocky cliffs or hustling up sandy beaches. The land surrounding the harbour seemed to rise, layer on layer, as if to imitate the waves. But here there was no movement. It stood silent, detached, no majestic peaks, no splashes of emerald green or tropical flowers, just a relentless, unchanging grey-green; nothing to relieve the eye except to return to the blues of sea and sky.

The cannon was fired to announce their arrival and an acknowledging puff of smoke came from the shore battery. At least the settlement knew they were there though, from this distance, no habitation was visible. A light breeze puffed the sails and the *Nile* sailed slowly and majestically towards Sydney Cove.

The first sight to break the monotony was the masts of ships, then, as they drew closer, a line of dilapidated warehouses. Two windmills were etched against the sky and soon they could discern small buildings struggling haphazardly towards the low hills.

'Surely this can't be Sydney Town?' Margaret whispered to a neighbour.

'Don't look like many people live there,' she whispered back.

'Look, there's a boat rowing out to meet us,' someone shouted. There was a surge towards the rail but the marines quickly forced the women back into line. Still, they could see the small boat being rowed furiously towards them. The rowers were unkempt men, stripped to the waist, but seated each end was a soldier holding a muskets and in the bow, an officer resplendent in scarlet uniform.

When the boat drew level with the ship this officer stood and shouted to a member of the crew, 'Prepare to be boarded as soon as you anchor. The Governor is anxious to inspect your ship.' These words galvanised everyone into action. The marines hustled the women below with instructions to make themselves and their quarters presentable. The crew set about ensuring that everything was ship shape. They knew that the Governor, as a sailor, would soon detect anything out of place.

At last the anchor chain was dropped and the ship came to rest, rocking gently on the waves. Hardly had this happened than a larger, grander boat containing eight oarsmen and three dignitaries left the wharf. It was soon visible to the waiting women, now standing in three straight lines, dressed in what passed for their finery.

'That must be 'im,' a woman near Margaret speculated softly, and they all stretched their necks, the better to get their first glimpse of this being who was the King's representative in this, their new prison. He held their future in his hands.

A tall, plumpish man in navy blue, braided jacket, immaculate white breeches and a three cornered hat perched on his greying locks sat, leaning forward, impatient to come aboard.

When the boat reached the side of the *Nile*, he grabbed the rope ladder that had been hastily lowered and energetically scrambled up the side. Governor King may have been out of condition and subject to gout but, when filled with enthusiasm, such things were forgotten.

'He's anxious to see if his recommendations have been carried out,' a sailor near Margaret explained to anyone who was interested. 'He should be pleased with us. '

Captain Sumpter called the crew to attention and welcomed

aboard the most important person in the colony. He knew he had nothing to fear from this visit, but still kept a wary eye on the women.

King spoke, first with the Captain, and then with the ship's doctor, nodding his head and gleaming at their reports.

'Not one death for the whole voyage.' The Governor chortled, rubbing his hands together. Then he began to inspect the women, pausing now and then to ask a question. The women answered with smiles and a little bob. Even the most truculent among them wanted to make a good impression. They had heard how good behaviour could make all the difference to their sentence and, at least at the beginning, they all wanted to make a fresh start.

Pleased with the prisoners, the Governor now turned to an inspection of the ship. He almost skipped as he went below decks, emerging a little later grinning like a boy. The ship was everything he could have asked for. If only every batch of convicts could arrive in such a healthy state, then the work of building the colony could be accomplished so much more easily. He was already planning, in his mind, the favourable report he would send home, something that happened so rarely. He gave his customary speech with real enthusiasm, impressing on the prisoners the advantages that could be theirs if only they would forego their evil habits and obey their masters.

He remembered something he had promised to do for Mrs King. He walked back to Captain Sumpter and they spoke earnestly together for a few moments. The doctor was called to join them as the three cast glances towards the women who stood patiently, trying to look straight ahead as they had been instructed.

From the looks cast in her direction Margaret had a feeling that they were talking about her. The discussion was concluded successfully for the Governor gave another nod of satisfaction, returned the salute of the captain and began to descend the ladder to his boat.

As they went below decks Margaret played the scene over in her mind. Had she imagined it or had they been talking about her? If they had indeed been discussing her, what did it mean? She had tried so hard during the voyage to follow her mistresses' advice. She knew she had been a model prisoner. Was she going to get her reward or did fate still have a surprise for her?

Margaret had seen, at first hand, how many of the women had become 'sea wives' to the sailors during the voyage. She had been approached, herself. When she refused the offer, professing that she was recently widowed and still mourning the death of her man, her position had been respected. After all there were ninety-six women and only twenty four sailors so there was no need to squabble.

Her celibacy enhanced her standing among women and sailors alike. She was no competition to the women, and the men enjoyed the company of an articulate and self-possessed female. One older sailor, Scobie, had been to New South Wales three times and had had time to observe most of the customs of this strange new society. He had become her authority on the life that awaited her ashore.

He had explained how all convict women were regarded as prostitutes by the citizens and that the lucky ones sought a patron for their own protection. Margaret was determined that this fate would not be hers. She had been with Will, if only fleetingly, and no other man would take his place. Still she wondered how long her determination would last when faced with a situation where her life depended on her acquiescence.

That evening she consulted Scobie about her suspicion.

'I'm sure Captain Sumpter and the Governor were talking about me. Is that good or bad?'

'Well, you didn't get into no trouble durin' the trip so it can't be bad. Perhaps 'is nibs is lookin' for a maid.'

'Would that be a good thing?'

'The best. You'd be treated fairly and your good behaviour would be noted. It could lead to a remittance, even a pardon.'

'Scobie, could that be possible? I'm a lifer.' Against her will Margaret could feel herself beginning to hope.

'Possible, but not probable. He's most likely enquirin' for a friend. But even that's good. No one would ill-treat you if the Governor chose you. No, my girl, I think you've started on a good foot. At least you'll be spared bein' on the stores. It's a degradin' experience. People treated like cattle. Still there doesn't seem no other way. And bein' picked up is usually better 'an workin' for the government. Only the dregs finish up there. The Officers has first choice, then the common soldiers and the free settlers and last the emancipists. The Government has to put up with what's left. For men it's road and bridge buildin' and for women it's the Female Factory workin' the flax. The place is so overcrowded and run by the toughest women I've ever met. No place for the faint hearted, that place. No place for anybody, really. No, Margaret me friend, you'll be lucky if you're spared that place.'

Early morning brought a flurry of activity on the *Nile*. In spite of their uncertain future, the convicts could not help a feeling of excitement. Come what may, their futures would be decided by what happened in the next day or two. The women brushed and mended, twisted their hair into curls, pinched their cheeks to give a healthy glow and tightened their stays to produce an alluring figure, anything to create a good impression. They had all been well schooled in the activities that would soon take place.

When the first boats arrived the women were assembled on deck, there to be inspected for possible employment. Nine women, along with their children, whose husbands were already in the colony were spared the ordeal. They would be given a ticket-of-leave and a grant of fifty acres as soon as they landed. If they and their spouses behaved themselves they could have a bright future.

Margaret proceeded to line up with the rest, but when the Captain came on deck he called her to one side.

'You don't have to line up. You have already been spoken for.'

Margaret's heart beat a little faster. 'What am I to do, Sir?'

'I don't know. The Governor just wanted a well-behaved woman who could cook. You fitted the description. He was enquiring for a friend. You're off to a good start. If you continue your good behaviour you should do well.'

She felt a moment's annoyance at this reminder to 'behave herself.' As if she had been a hardened criminal. However the feeling was quickly overcome by hopes for the future. Treated fairly, she felt sure she could prosper in this new land. Perhaps, one day she could obtain a full pardon and return to England. It was only her love of Will that had led her from the paths of righteousness. Now that he was dead she was in full control of her own future. She explored this thought as she watched the selection process going on.

Every woman was putting a great deal of effort into presenting herself as a suitable candidate for employment. They stood, trying not to stare around them at the brilliant blue sea and the ragged settlement. Their eyes were on Captain Sumpter, who held papers containing their particulars and barked questions at them in his official voice - name, trade, cause of conviction.

From the questions asked Margaret soon realised that she had the qualifications prised among the colonists. She was still relatively young at twenty eight, healthy, used to hard work, could cook, sew, read and had held a position of authority in a large establishment. She could command respect in this colony. Her back became a little straighter, she held her head a little higher. She recognised her worth. She would have no reason to be subservient here. She would be a good servant but no one would be her master.

As the selection process continued those chosen left the ranks to go to the side of the ship and take a more pragmatic look at their new home. Those left in the thinning ranks lost a little of their presence though they still tried desperately to attract attention as each boatload of prospective employers came aboard. From the looks of some of them Margaret felt that the Woman's Factory could hardly be a worse alternative.

Having learnt their fate, the women went below decks to pack up their belongings, ready for disembarking next day. They would be taken to the wharf, there to be collected by their future employers. For the ones who had not been chosen there would be other chances in the next couple of days. Only then would they be taken by boat up the river to Parramatta.

The last night on the *Nile* was a sad affair. Though many of the prisoners and sailors drank heavily, it was more a wake than a farewell party. Romantic attachments were ended and friendships, forged during the months at sea, receded into the background. Suddenly they realised the security of the ship was to be replaced by an unknown future. The bravest of the women, even those who were soon to be reunited with their husbands, were fearful for what it would bring.

Margaret was surprised to realise the affection she now held for these women with whom she had once believed she had nothing in common. She imagined the contempt that the Margaret of old would have felt for them. If prison had taught her one thing, it was compassion for humanity in general and women in particular. She found a quiet corner and said a prayer of thanks for all the good people who had crossed her path, and mercy for those women who would soon offend again. There's not a really wicked person among them, she thought, but some are very weak

Next morning the women were ferried ashore in groups of twenty. They were a solemn group as they left the *Nile,* particularly those who were still suffering from the evening's carousing, but once ashore the mood changed. A crowd had gathered on the wharf shouting names and calling for news from England. In the noisy confusion and excitement of landing there was something of a party atmosphere. Discipline was relaxed as the women discovered friends or relations in the crowd or responded to questions about their district. Suddenly they were important. They were a link with home. They were caught up in the mood as they realised that their ordeal at sea was ended. They had survived the perilous oceans and had landed safely on this land, which was not so strange when they could hear accents from their hometown or see faces that they recognised.

When all the women were ashore they were mustered in the prison yard, attended by the Captain, the Doctor and the Superintendent of Convicts. Because Governor King had already inspected them informally, that duty was now performed by Colonel Paterson. He walked slowly between the long lines, enquiring whether they wished to make a complaint about their treatment at sea, then paused to give them a final address in which he too exhorted them to obey their masters and hinted at rewards that could follow good behaviour. When all the formalities were finished the disposal of the women began.

First to be released were the married women who were given their ticket-of-leave, the deeds to fifty acres of land and were reunited with their waiting husbands. Then, one by one, the other names were called out and the women were released into the custody of their masters or their agents.

Margaret waited anxiously, for she had not been told anything about her future. When her name was called a youth stepped forward. He could not have been more than thirteen or fourteen.

'I'm to pick 'er up for Mrs 'umphris,' he informed the Superintendent who looked at his list, ticked off her name, and proceeded onto the next one.

'Where is my basket?' Margaret enquired. She had not seen it since boarding the ship in London.

'They'll drop it off when it's unloaded,' the boy assured her.

'But how will they know where to send it?'

'Everyone knows Mrs 'umphris. Everybody knows the Asylum,' he laughed. 'Now hop on back of cart. I've got to get them supplies back.'

Margaret was so stunned by his reply that she sat obediently on the back of the open cart, swinging her legs, taking little notice of her surroundings. The word Asylum reverberated in her mind. Had she come all this way to cook for crazy people?

At first Margaret sat, dispirited, on the back of the tray dangling her legs over the edge, taking no notice of her surroundings, but soon, as the cart bumped and rocked over the uneven road she began to look back at the view she was passing.

The area around the docks was busy, pedestrians dodging horses and vehicles whose owners cursed them. She did not see any of the convicts in leg irons that she had been led to believe she would, but there were a number of scarlet-coated soldiers. Both men and women were dressed in drab workaday clothes but they looked healthy and well fed.

The houses were mostly little more than whitewashed huts with thatched roofs. Further away from the docks there were more substantial wooden houses. They were nearly all one storey but had glazed windows and shingle roofs. They were single buildings, each separated by white picket fences, but did not stand uniformly facing the road, which looked as if it had been so constructed as to take the easiest path, rather than conform to any regularity.

Suddenly the sight of a black man, totally naked, arrested her attention. He walked purposely along the road, taking no interest in the people or vehicles around him. His nakedness shocked her, as she had never seen a totally naked man before. She shut her eyes, but curiosity got the better of her scruples and, as he was in her line of vision for some time, she began to observe him closely. He was very black, not particularly tall, with matted, black hair. His face was marked with white lines and he carried a long spear and a small shield.

Had she come upon him when alone she would have been terrified but, seeing the lack of interest shown by people walking by calmed her fears. Knowing that she was safe from observation she stared intently at this alien figure. He had heavy browed eyes, wide nostrils and bewhiskered mouth. This abundance of unruly hair added to his fierce appearance. His arms and chest seemed to be marked with raised mounds, like healed welts from deep cuts. He had quite a pronounced belly but his thighs and calves looked strong and sinewy. He was showing no effort from walking even though it was up hill.

Margaret blushed as she peeped at his private parts but there was little to see. Nature had provided a black bush that partly covered them. As he slowly slipped behind her vision from the cart she was relieved that her first encounter with a native Indian had been from such a safe vantage point. He was so strange, so not of her world, that she pushed his image to the back of her mind until she could feel more familiar with this new land that was to become her home.

The pony pulled the cart through the narrow crooked streets and over a rickety bridge. She became aware of several substantial buildings as well as a number of sheds with a sign saying Government Workshops. They came to a halt in front of a high stone fence on which was printed a large sign, Orphan School Asylum.

She wanted to burst out laughing. She had always associated the word asylum with lunatics but of course it really meant a place of refuge. She was to be a cook at a school for orphans!

'Open gate so I can drive cart in,' the youth ordered. She was so relieved that she jumped down obediently and struggled to open the heavy iron gates.

'I'm gunna' take cart to store house. Just go to front door, ring and tell 'em who you are,' directed the boy as he shook the reins and the pony trotted down a lane.

Margaret began to walk up the drive and was pleasantly surprised at the edifice that greeted her. It was an elegant, sand stone, two-storied building with a wide veranda. It would not have been out of place in fashionable London. It was set in an immaculately kept garden containing poplar and elm trees, shrubs and garden beds ablaze with cornflowers, daisies, wallflowers and foxgloves. In the centre was a small, grassed area with a statue of a young girl holding a shell as a birdbath.

She clapped her hands with joy. She could recognize every flower. True they were blooming at the wrong time of the year, but they were surviving in this summer heat as if to welcome her. She would have liked to wander through this delightful place but, gripping her valise tightly, walked up the two steps to the veranda, pulled the string at the front door and heard a bell ring somewhere inside. She waited for a few moments and was just contemplating pulling the string again when she heard shuffling feet coming towards her. The door was opened by a young girl dressed in black, her hair pulled back into tight well-disciplined pigtails.

'What do ya'want?' she demanded in a belligerent tone.

It surprised Margaret as she was expecting a more subservient enquiry.

'I'm Margaret Catchpole,' she replied with dignity. 'I have been employed as cook.'

'Oh. You're the new convict. Hope you're a better cook that the last one. Wait 'ere and I'll tell Mrs 'umphris you're 'ere.' She disappeared into the dim interior of the passage leaving Margaret wondering.

Her voice, she thought, not quite cockney but not quite the King's English either - and so loud and gruff. She hoped that not everyone spoke that way.

The girl came back and led her to a door, knocked then retreated.

'Come in,' a polite voice commanded. Margaret opened the door on a pleasing sitting room with large windows whose shades had been drawn against the bright sun. It gave the room an eerie golden glow. She stopped just inside the door to observe a young, slightly plump lady with a pleasing smile who sat in an easy chair, a London journal on her lap.

'Come in, please. I believe that you are the new cook.' She gave Margaret a cursory look. 'Do you think you are capable of cooking for sixty children, a staff of eight, myself and my husband when he is at home?'

'Oh yes, Ma'am', Margaret replied confidently.

'You have had experience of cooking for large numbers?'

'Yes, Ma'am. I have cooked in two large establishments.' She drew the references given by her former mistresses from her bag and handed them proudly to Mrs Humphris who stood, and moved towards one of the windows where the light was better. She read the one from Priory Farm carefully then gave a little squeal of delight when she opened the second and glanced at the letterhead.

'La, I know this lady. In fact there is a remote connection between us. The man she married, John Cobbold, he had a number of children didn't he?'

'Twelve, Ma'am.' Margaret was so overcome at the mention of her former mistress' name that she wished she could sit down.

'And Elizabeth has been blessed with children of her own?'

'She had three when I left, Ma'am and, if God is good, by now there should be four.'

'Sixteen children, just fancy, and poor Humphris and I with not one between us.' Margaret could hear the sorrow in her voice, but she continued in a tone of deliberate gaiety, 'and now we have sixty.' She gave a little laugh. 'God works in mysterious ways, or so we are told.

'You will find things different in New South Wales, Margaret. First no one calls me Ma'am, it's Mrs Humphris. Uncouth, I know, but the free people of Sydney refuse to use the old world terms and as our orphans are free they seem to have acquired the same habits. In a country where most of the population are convicts you would expect more respect. Instead, once they become free, they regard themselves as equals. And in many ways they are. My neighbour Mr Underwood, who owns that beautiful mansion that you may have noticed, was himself once a convict. Now he is one of the wealthiest persons in New South Wales. Of course there are those who would never accept him socially, but I believe, like dear Governor King, that a man should be judged by what he is rather than what he has been. What do you think?'

Margaret was left speechless by the easy way that her new mistress spoke with her, even asking her opinion. Mrs Humphris was obviously a gentlewoman, but her freedom with a servant, let alone a convict one, was beyond Margaret's understanding.

'I think so too,' she replied, though she hardly knew the question.

The lady glanced again at the letter in her hand. 'Elizabeth Cobbold, imagine that. I cannot remember the family connection but I do remember hearing about her many achievements. A cultivated lady, it was said, who entertained some of the most talented men in England and also ran her large establishment most efficiently, not at all like me. My husband says I'd be hopeless running a house in England, but here it scarcely matters. What passes for society, apart from one or two, would hardly be accepted in the better houses there.

'But, if you have been trained by Elizabeth, you will know how things are done. You will have to help me Margaret so that when Mr Humphris gets back he will find me a model of propriety. Our Dear Benefactor has done a champion job in choosing you.'

'The Governor has been most kind.' Margaret felt she was expected to respond.

'No, no. I was speaking of another gentleman, a colonist who has been so generous to this establishment and of great assistance to me personally. He is very fond of children, but alas, has none of his own. He is of a farming background and has been most successful since he came here. He is wealthy enough not to be beholden to the political cliques here, unlike poor Humphris, who, ever loyal to His Majesty's representatives, has often suffered for his loyalty. However he has great faith that Governor King will be able to establish proper authority.'

Margaret's blank expression prompted Mrs, Humphris to realise that she had no understanding of the subject.

'Oh la, I'm prattling on again, as Humphris would say. I must try to be more businesslike now that I have such a big responsibility. You see, the Orphanage has only been open a few months and I am still learning. It was all right when my husband was here, but he has had to go back to England on government business and will be gone a year or so. Our Dear Benefactor has been such a great help, but now he will be busy himself on his new property on the Nepean. It is not even settled yet but he is planning to build a mansion there as well as developing the land, so he will have little time for my poor orphans and me. It was well that he found someone as reliable as you.'

'But it was the Governor who picked me,' a puzzled Margaret replied.

Mrs Humphris corrected her. 'It was the Governor who procured you because Dear John asked Mrs King to find a cook for me. The last one we had was a total disaster. She was drunk most of the time. It's a wonder we weren't all poisoned. Now I must stop talking and introduce you to your work.'

She walked across to a velvet rope near the fireplace and gave it a pull. A bell tinkled somewhere in the building and soon the girl who had answered the front door appeared again.

'Pearl, let Mrs Weatherstone know that I will be in the classroom shortly. Tell the maids to gather there too. Old Minnie will be glad to be relieved of her duties.' Then, turning to Margaret as the girl went to deliver the message, 'Minnie is really our nursemaid for the little ones, but she took over the cooking when I dismissed that dreadful woman.'

Margaret felt it would not be out of place to ask what had happened to her.

'Oh, she was sent back to the factory at Paramatta. She will be among her own there. Now come along and I will show you the kitchen. Bring your valise and I'll show you where you sleep.'

Margaret was bustled across a breezeway to a cluster of buildings, the largest of which was the kitchen, a long room containing an iron range and a large, open fireplace, recessed into a chimney place that filled an end wall. On one side-wall were benches containing pots, pans and crockery bowls. In the centre was a big, rectangular, wooden table. In many ways it was not dissimilar to an English kitchen. She felt she would be able to work here. A door at the other end opened onto a large storeroom filled with boxes, jars and sacks. Margaret was used to large storerooms but she was surprised to see the amount of food stored here. She expressed her surprise.

'We have had famine years in the colony,' Mrs Humphris explained. 'So, in the good years we store as much as we can against the hard times.'

'But there is so much land. Surely there would always be food?'

'Unfortunately this is a cruel country, my dear. In good years it is a regular cornucopia, but with floods and droughts and fires we breathe a sigh of relief whenever the harvest is in.' She continued her lecture in a philosophical tone. 'We have not had to fight for this land. We needed no armies to occupy this colony, but the land itself does not surrender easily. Just when we feel we know all its tricks another disaster comes to plague us. This is not a soft land, like England.'

Margaret was amazed anew at the familiarity of her mistress. She felt no offence would be taken if she asked a personal question.

'Do you miss England greatly?'

'No, no,' she laughed. 'I love it here. I'm happy to forgo all the comforts I had at home for the freedom I have here. I dread the day when dear Humphris will be recalled. But I must confess that I am in the minority among the ladies of New South Wales. They long for England, but I think many of them may change their minds when they do go home.'

While this conversation was going on, Margaret was shown into another building across a breezeway from the kitchen that was to be her room. It was bare and functional but it was the largest space that she had ever called her own and, after the confines of the *Nile*, it was like a palace. She was given no time to survey her domain as she was hustled off to the classroom.

It was in the main building at the other end from Mrs Humphris' rooms. It was wide and long with windows facing the veranda. There were benches, three spinning wheels with bundles of wool beside them and a long sewing table, which reminded Margaret of the one at Ipswich jail. Children of varying ages, all neatly dressed in black were engaged in a variety of activities. Five young children sat in a circle around an older girl who was teaching them prayers.

All the classes seemed to be under the control of one woman, introduced as Mrs Weatherstone, with the help of some of the older orphans. This teacher was obviously a disciplinarian as her instruction to stand and greet Mrs Humphris was immediately obeyed. Margaret's introduction was greeted with the same respect, but she detected several side-glances and smothered sniggers. Though the routine was obviously strict, the spirit of the students seemed not to have been broken. This pleased

Margaret in a strange way. She liked the slight defiance she saw. It suited the mood that had been growing in her ever since she landed in this country.

'Now change your clothes and you can begin preparing the evening meal,' Mrs Humphris commanded in an offhand manner.

'But what food do you want?' Margaret had never been given such curt and hasty orders.

'Anything, anything at all as long as it is appetising and there is plenty of it. Go out into the yard and ask Jimmy, that's the lad who brought you, to take you into the meat room and you can make a selection, and tell him to get some wood. Everything else is in the store room somewhere.'

How different from her former employers, she thought. No instructions from upstairs, no consulting recipies. It seemed that she was to be in charge of the menu as well as the cooking. Though slightly bewildered, Margaret felt no resentment at being thrown straight into work. After all that was what she was here for. As she spent the next hours cutting, peeling and sweating in the heat of the room she planned how she would run her kitchen. It was obvious that there would not be any interference. It would be her domain and she could run it as she pleased.

Margaret soon adjusted to her new life. Though there was plenty to do it was not overly arduous. In fact she found she had much more free time than she had had in England. Cooking and housekeeping were skills that girls were expected to acquire so there were always several pairs of hands to assist.

But she found that, though they were physically in the kitchen, most of them were not there willingly. It was obvious that, though they knew little about preparing and cooking food, they were unwilling to learn. They regarded kitchen duties as just another imposition placed on them by those in authority.

Because Margaret was a convict and they were free, they resented taking orders from her. She found their attitude hard to understand and spent a few frustrating days trying to bring order into her domain. One evening, after a particularly trying day, she thought back on her days at Priory and Cliff.

Why were they so well run? Was it the Cook or the Housekeeper who was responsible? She finally realised that the chain of command was underpinned by the mistress herself.

She spoke to Mrs Humphris. 'At Home the order of an establishment is the Lady's responsibility. They control their staff by loyalty to the house, along with reward of wages and a threat of dismissal. Though the mistress does not directly administer reward or punishment, the senior staff has her sanction and backing. If these girls are to respect this order of command, you must give them clear advice.'

Mrs Humphris sighed, 'You're correct, of course Margaret,' then with conviction, 'I must try to establish myself as Mistress and I certainly have a reward to offer. The Governor, in the interests of encouraging good behaviour, had ordered that any girl who graduates from here and marries a respectable citizen will be given one hundred acres of land for farming. This will make our girls desirable wives. I must remind the girls of this.'

She called together the senior girls and explained matters to them.

'I hope you all know that to graduate from the Asylum and to earn your entitlements you must be proficient in cooking. However, I know that many of you do not enjoy kitchen duties, so, only those who wish to, will do it. Those who do must be obedient to Miss Catchpole. She is a highly skilled cook and housekeeper and will give you excellent training. She has my full confidence and anyone she dismisses will not be allowed back into the kitchen until her attitude changes.

'If you wish to learn cooking skills please put your name or mark on this paper. You will be chosen in order of application.'

There was a buzz of hostility among the girls but soon one and then another decided that they would work for Margaret. Soon there was a scramble to get a name on the list rather than to miss out.

Away from the girls Mrs Humphris relaxed and gave a little laugh. 'How did I do, Margaret? Did I have the sound of authority?'

'You did wonderfully, Mrs Humphris. You gave them a choice and a reward. You have also established my own authority. It's up to me now.'

The first students were keen and soon working in the kitchen began to be regarded as a privilege and a much sought after position. They realised that Margaret was a fair boss who neither praised nor blamed without cause. Currying favour, a trick that many had learned during their years of surviving on the streets of Sydney Town, did not help here, and those who complained of unfair treatment got no support from the other girls. They began to respect Margaret and also to learn that command, fairly given, was not always a bad thing.

Margaret enjoyed her work and became a surrogate mother to some of the girls who, trusting her, confided in her their hopes and dreams as well as their daily experiences. It was from them that she learnt the harsh reality of life beyond the asylum walls. They spoke matter-of-factly about such cruelty and degradation that she blessed again the good spirits who had led her to this place.

If she had doubted the girl's descriptions she had only to look from the upstairs windows to see the reality of convict life; chain gangs clanging and tramping off to work each morning; men and women being dragged to imprisonment in the jail further up the street, accompanied by the jeers and taunts of passers by; and at night the lurid and blasphemous cries of men and women who found solace from their misery in the raw spirits that flowed like rivers in this godforsaken corner of the globe.

Margaret's name was a constant source of amusement, which she felt undermined her authority so she insisted that she be known as Cook. This had been the practice in the houses in which she had worked. The girls were amused, but willing to change. However the name quickly changed to Cookie. Margaret did not object to her new name. She realised that, in fact, it was a sign that they accepted her.

CHAPTER TWO

'And You, the least in our society, totally dependent on the grace of God and the good will of Christian citizens, do you ever contemplate the ruin and depravity from which you have been rescued?' The Reverend Samuel Marsden paused in his tirade to catch his breath and wipe away the spittle from his mouth.

Margaret, sitting to one side, cast a glance at the rows of black clad girls, ranging in age from three to fourteen. They sat ramrod straight to forestall criticism, but the dull glazed eyes suggested that they had mentally withdrawn from the plethora of words being thrown at them.

'You were nothing in this community. You were abandoned souls left to become the Devil's instrument. Members of a degraded sex, your instincts would have led you into Satin's web. But these good citizens,' he waved his arms to take in the wider congregation, 'these Christian souls, have reached into the depth of their compassion to provide you with a rope, a ladder, that you might rise out of the pit of Hell to which you were destined and have given you a chance to climb the golden staircase into Paradise.'

He went on to exhort them to take advantage of the wonderful gifts being offered them but Margaret heard no more, for she had joined the girls in wandering, in their minds, to more pleasant pastures.

She was back again in the little church at Necton, sitting beside her parents, brothers and sister, listening to the gentle voice of their pastor telling them of the mercy of God available to all, and of the Gentle Jesus who gave his life for their salvation. Could this be the same God, this great Jehovah of Marsden's sermon? She sighed and wished herself back in that soft gentle country, away from this harsh, barbaric land where even the minister of God had no pity.

After service, the girls were marched back to the Asylum. No speaking was permitted but still a couple of the older girls, with signs and nods, managed to make contact with men loitering nearby.

Having changed from their Sunday best, the girls, clad in their work-a-day black cotton, began the various activities considered suitable for Sunday. Extra hands were needed in the kitchen where a special meal was being prepared for a group of benefactors, including the Reverend Marsden and his wife. This was the first meal Margaret was to cook for outsiders She used all the skills learnt in England to produce food of which Mrs Humphris could be proud, a hearty vegetable soup, freshly caught baked snapper, roasted pork with three vegetables -and for dessert plum pudding or a refreshing fruit salad of peaches, apricots and apples, both served with custard. There were tarts and cakes to be served as afters. Because of the presence of the Reverend Marsden, fruit juices were served instead of wine but one of the girls remarked knowingly, 'He didn't get that nose drinkin' juice.'

Having been carefully schooled by Margaret, four girls acted as waitresses, performing creditably. When the guests had finally departed, Mrs Humphris came into the kitchen to compliment the girls on their performance, then spoke to Margaret.

'La Margaret, you performed wonders. I'm sure I am the envy of every house in Sydney. The Reverend was so impressed with the gravy that his plate was fairly swimming in it. He mopped it up with your delicious bread and could hardly restrain himself from smacking his lips and demanding more. I declare he would rather have had another serving of gravy and bread than the excellent duff. Not that he refused a second serve of that. He could hardly drag himself from the table. I pity the drubbing his cook will get when he gets home. I wouldn't be surprised if he don't send her down here for lessons.'

She gave a look of mock shame. 'There I go gossiping again. I know he is a man of God and worked tirelessly to establish this orphanage but he does little to extend Christian charity to those he considers belong to the lower classes. He believes all unmarried women are, or have the potential to be, harlots. Unfortunately many of the males in the community are of similar mind. But I did not come to talk of such things. I have good news for you, Margaret. A large wicker basket has arrived for you.'

Margaret had been so busy establishing herself that she had almost forgotten her basket. She clapped her hands together and beamed. 'It has come at last. Oh, it's the basket I bought with me from England. I had almost given up hope of ever receiving it.'

'Then you must come and check its contents at once. The girls can finish here and then they can have the rest of the day to themselves.' There were cheers all round and a bustle of activity as Margaret left to claim her treasures.

Mrs Humphris sat on an occasional chair, satisfying her curiosity, as Margaret unpacked one treasure after another. She took out a bolt of cotton and sat back on her heels. 'Now I will be able to make a cool dress for working in the kitchen. My other dress is unsuitable for this summer heat.'

Mrs Humphris exclaimed, 'Margaret, how clever you are. Not only are you the best of cooks but you can sew too! My dear Mama taught me to sew but it was petit point and the like. If I had to make my own clothes I would have to wrap myself in the cloth.

'I'm afraid I am ill equipped for a life in the wilderness. My dear Papa was a gentle man, dedicated to his parish. He paid little attention to the education of his daughters. I suppose it was Mama's duty but, to be honest, she was, at times, a little vague. That's why I never learnt to run a household. We only had three servants and things were rather lax. It never worried us but when I stayed with relatives I could recognize the difference. Still, ours was a happy home. Perhaps that was more important.'

'Oh, yes, Mrs Humphris, a happy family is the greatest blessing. I lived in such, until disaster befell us. I mourn for those times more than anything else in the world. You must miss your family dearly.'

'There is only my sister left now and she lives here, though I see her rarely. When my dashing Humphris won my heart, he lured my sister and her husband here as well. She had never been of robust health and they thought that the climate would be good for her. But she keeps having children, which hardly gives her a chance to recover. Is it not strange that I, so strong and robust, cannot have children while my sickly sister cannot stop?'

'How many children does she have?'

'She has six and they are as sickly as herself. My poor brother-in -law has a good property on the Hawkesbury but he is constantly rushing for a doctor to tend to his wife or children.'

During this conversation Margaret continued unpacking her precious goods. Near the bottom she came upon her botany journal. When she opened it and studied the many specimens so lovingly preserved, with common and botanical names, dictated by her former Mistress, memories flooded her mind and she was close to tears. She held up the book.

'See. My dear Mistress, Mrs Cobbold, taught me this. She had a great love and knowledge of growing things and imparted it to her daughters and to me. How I wish I knew somebody here who could help me gather specimens to send to her.'

'There are botanists here, Margaret. If my husband were here he would know of one. When our Dear Benefactor comes to visit I must ask if he could help.'

The two women spoke easily with each other, more like friends than mistress and maid, while Margaret sorted nostalgically through her treasures. But unbeknowns to them, two of the girls, Pearl and Gracy, took advantage of the holiday to absent themselves and went over the wall, answering a nod and wink appointment made earlier in the day. They were creatures of the streets, having existed there for several years before their recruitment into the Orphanage. While they appreciated the shelter and regular meals it offered, they missed the challenges, the excitement and the mateship of life in the narrow lanes and shanties of Sydney Town.

They were not missed until everybody was assembled for the evening meal. Mrs Humphris was very worried. Although it was not the first time girls had climbed over the fence, it was the first time she knew of it. Mrs Weatherstone was for sending a message to the Military and to the Reverend Marsden.

'I don't think so. At least not yet,' Mrs Humphris reasoned. 'Quite possibly the Military won't be interested seeing they are orphans, but if they do find them they will be arrested and charged with absconding. Goodness knows what the punishment will be.'

'Whipping would be a good punishment for them,' snorted Mrs Weatherstone. 'They will certainly lose their entitlement.'

'We shall see,' cautioned Mrs Humphris, who thought that no crime warranted a whipping. 'Let us give them time to come back of their own accord.'

It was close to midnight when two tipsy, black figures slipped over the wall sushing and giggling as they tried to creep into the building, The sudden confrontation by Mesdames Humphris and Weatherstone, far from intimidating them, reduced them to a giggling mess of arms and legs as they collapsed onto the floor.

Margaret, who had stayed awake listening for their return, heard the noises and joined the other ladies. She was amazed that they showed no fear.

Next morning the girls, wearing their most penitent expressions, listened passively as Mrs Humphris chastised them for their activities, pointing out the consequences of such behaviour, and accorded them their punishment

'To help you realise the magnitude of your crime, you will scrub and disinfect all the outhouses and Tessy, whose unpleasant duty this usually is, will oversee your work. I will inspect it later and the competence of your work will determine what I am to do with you.'

The girls wrinkled their noses and Pearl was tempted to revolt, but a look from Mrs Weatherstone made her realise that she was getting off lightly. As they left to collect buckets, scrubbing brushes and tar pots, Mrs Weatherstone voiced her misgivings.

'I still feel, Mrs Humphris, that the girl's behaviour should be reported, at least to the Reverend Marsden. He is, after all, the spiritual director of these girls. He needs to know what evil exists among them.'

Mrs Humphris composed herself, the better to deliver the appropriate message that would appease this woman. The Reverend was the last person she wanted to discipline the girls. His punishments were too well known.

'Mrs Weatherstone, I understand your misgivings and I can assure you that any further lapse will bring on the severest punishment. But we are, after all, a place of redemption. These girls are the Lost Sheep that the Bible speaks of and we must not only go out into the highways and byways to find them, but, like the Good Shepherd, we must carry them home to the safety of the fold. They have spent their young lives with the most depraved of humans in this penal place and they have been with us such a short time. Let us give them one more chance to reform.'

Her appeal to the mercies of Christ mollified Mrs Weatherstone a little, but she still had to assert her authority. 'What you say may be true, but think of the influence they will have on the others, particularly the younger girls. I refuse to take the responsibility of allowing them to corrupt the rest of our charges. I will not have them in the classroom.'

Margaret, by way of her friendship with Mrs Humphris, was present during this exchange. 'If I may make a suggestion,' she interrupted politely, 'I really need some permanent help in the kitchen if I am to cook the meals and instruct the students.

'If these two girls could be put in my care, I promise to supervise them strictly. And seeing they are of an advanced age and have a leaning to the world outside, I think cooking would be an admirable skill to acquire. I could also teach them practical sewing that would stand them in good stead in the future.'

This suggestion pleased Mrs Weatherstone She felt her opposition had been dealt with. 'I wish you well with them, Cook, but they are both stubborn and wilful. You will find them difficult, but I agree that they need to learn practical skills as higher learning will be of no use to them whatsoever.'

CHAPTER THREE

So, a month after she had arrived and herself still a convict, Margaret was responsible for the disciplining and training of two hostile girls. Many were the trials she went through but even the girls could see the sense of what she was trying to teach them. Caring for them gave her a sense of purpose and a feeling that life still held promise.

The duties at the Asylum were not arduous and now that she had two permanent helpers, Margaret found she had time to spare. She had always been a keen walker and the confines of the sea voyage had sorely tried her. She longed to cover the miles, keeping her own company. Because there seemed to be little restraint to her freedom, she longed to explore her new home.

One day she approached her mistress. 'Excuse me, Mrs Humphris, but I have a request to make.'

'Margaret, you have only to ask and if it is in my power I know how I ever got on without you.'

Margaret accepted this compliment, marvelling anew at the informality. 'Now that I have Pearl and Gracy with me I find I have a lot of time on my hands. Tea is served strictly at five and then I have little to do. I am very fond of walking and, as there are still a couple of hours of daylight left, I was hoping I could spend perhaps an hour out of the Asylum.'

'Of course you can. Though you are a convict there is no restraint on your movements, so long as you have your employer's permission and do not go beyond your boundary. I suppose you would like to explore Sydney Town?'

'Perhaps, and the countryside. I am anxious to explore the plants that grow here. I know my late Mistress would be greatly interested.'

'Then you must take your constitutional as soon as tea is

served. Really, I should follow your example. I am finding it hard to fit into some of my dresses but, alas, I have never been a great enthusiast for perambulating. Dear Humphris calls me lazybones but truly I would sooner read a book.'

Margaret breathed a sigh of relief. She would never have objected if her mistress had wished to join her, but valued her solitude.

So, from that time she took her solitary walks. Though there was no long twilight like at home, she could comfortably walk for at least an hour. She visited the more inhabited areas at first but soon found it more pleasant following little tracks that bordered the coastline. She would stand and watch the endless waves moving in and out from the shore and picture, in imagination, them travelling all the way across the oceans to wash up on the shores of England. For a short time she was not a convict but free again.

But it was only a dream and one evening she had a rude awakening. Not far from the Orphanage she had noticed a solitary young woman sitting at an easel, oblivious to the world as she tried to replicate the scene before her. Margaret was surprised to see that there was no accompanying gentleman in attendance.

Later as she was on her return journey she heard cries for help. It was the woman. She had a sudden picture in her mind of the time Will had tried to kidnap her and remembered the terror she had felt. She picked up a large stone and hurried towards the screaming. A rough character was trying to drag the woman into the surrounding bushes but she was putting up a courageous struggle.

'Leave her alone,' she shouted, brandishing the stone. 'Leave her alone or I will hit you on the head with this rock.'

'You reckon you could do that? A puny little thing like you? I could smash you with one hand.'

'Maybe, but you would have to let her go to do it and she could run for help.'

The girl had stopped struggling. The man thought over his

options. 'What is it to you what I do? Who are you anyway?'

'I'm Margaret Catchpole,' she replied.

'Well, Margaret Catchpole, you'll be hearin' from me. One dark night when you least expect it.' Then he released the woman and ran towards the covering trees because he could hear someone approaching.

An older gentleman and a youth hurried towards the two women.

'Papa,' the young girl cried and, hurrying towards them, threw herself into his arms of the man and sobbed, 'there was this horrible man . . . '

'There, see what I told you, Gerald, you should not have left Alice alone,' the gentleman scolded, then to the girl. 'Are you hurt, my darling?'

'She wasn't doing anything but sitting there and I got bored,' the youth grumbled but nobody was listening.

'No Papa,' Alice replied, wiping her tears. 'This brave, good lady saved me. The man was trying to drag me away and she threatened him with a stone. She was so brave Papa. We must invite her to dinner.'

The gentleman looked at Margaret for the first time. He saw a small, black haired woman in a sombre, grey dress and shawl. She looked incapable of defending herself, let alone the ruffian his daughter described.

'Madam, I am indeed in your debt. Please accept my undying gratitude. My daughter is precious to me beyond all measure.' He held out his hand. 'William Grantham.'

Margaret made a little bob but did not take the outstretched hand.

'Papa, ask her to dinner,' the young woman persisted.

'Of course, Mrs . . . ?'

'Miss Catchpole, Margaret Catchpole.'

'Delighted to meet you, Miss Cat . . . did you say Margaret Catchpole?'

Margaret saw the sudden change of expression. Evidently her name was known even in this corner of the world. She could see the conflict of emotions going on in his mind. He was grateful to her, but to invite a convict to his table?

She raised her head and looked directly at him.

'Thank you, Sir, for your kind invitation, but I am too busy in my employment at the Orphan Asylum. But if I might be bold enough to express an opinion, you should take better care of your daughter.' She walked, straight backed, away from the group as they stood speechless watching after her. She held her head high, never once turning around, holding to herself the anguish of the unspoken rejection.

She was a convict and nobody was ever going to forget it.

'Bloomin' iron pots,' Pearl grumbled. 'They're just gunna' get dirty again. Don't know why She 'as to be so fussy.'

'Because it makes the food taste betta and ya don't finish up with the runs,' Gracy informed her as they scrubbed together.

'Seems this cookin's more scrubbin' than anythin' else. When's She gunna let me make a puddin'?'

'When ya stew's good enough,' replied Gracy.

Though they grumbled, both girls enjoyed their work with Margaret. She was strict, but not in the way of Mrs Weatherstone and she didn't preach religion at them all the time. They wondered about Margaret. She didn't fit the mould of most convicts they knew. Her speech was more refined. She seemed to know a lot about the ways of the gentry, yet seemed to be content with her lot.

'Who cares wot a stew tastes like anyway. Food's food, aint it?'

'Well, ya 'usband will appreciate it betta' if it tastes betta.'

Pearl tossed her head. 'Usbands, 'uh. The man I marry better not complain. I'll be the one who owns the land and if 'e's a ticket-of-leaver I'll be responsible for 'im too. He'd better not complain.'

'But if you luv him,' persisted Gracy.

'Luv. You're a great one to talk about luv. Look where it's got ya? Jest because a man says 'e looves ya don't mean 'e's gunna treat ya right. You've gotta 'ave the whip 'and. That's why I stay away from them soljers. Give me a convict any time.'

Margaret had been casually listening to this conversation. She had heard Pearl's views on marriage before. But this time she noticed the wistful look on Gracy's face. Something was troubling the girl. She had lost her cheeky cheerfulness and often stared into space, her mind far away. She would need keeping an eye on.

A few days later Margaret came upon Gracy in the storeroom weeping piteously. Margaret enfolded her in her arms and let the tears have full reign. When the sobbing had subsided she held her at arm's length and enquires gently. 'What's the matter, Gracy?'

The girl wiped the back of her hand across a snotty nose and looked into Margaret's steady brown eyes. They gave her the confidence to confess.

'Oh, Cookie, I'm that scared. I'm in so much trouble and I don't know what t'do.'

'Gracy, whatever your problems are there must be a solution. Sometimes you need someone else to help. Could you tell me about it?'

'I'm gunna to 'ave a baby,' the poor girl blurted out. 'I'm in the family way and I don't know 'ow t' get rid of it.'

Margaret was shocked, both by the news and the solution, but she went on calmly. 'Do you want to get rid of it?'

'No. I'd luv to have a little baby of me own but I can't. They'll take it from me and lock me up.'

'What about the father? Do you know who he is?'

'Yes, I do. But 'e wont 'elp me. 'E's a soljer and don't want to know me now I'm stuffed up.' She began to cry again. 'Says, 'ow does 'e know it's 'is? Could be anybody's, 'e says. But it's not and 'e knows it. 'E's been the only one. It was 'is idea that I come to the orphanage. Said 'e'd marry me when I got me land. Now 'e don't want anyfin' to do with me. What's gunna happen to me Cookie?' She clung to Margaret and cried again.

Margaret knew the enormity of the problem. Not only would Gracy be dismissed from the orphanage, she would be imprisoned for having a child out of wedlock. Samuel Marsden would see to that. It was one of his solutions to the number of illegitimate children being born in the colony. Many a bigamous marriage had taken place to save a girl from such a fate.

She thought, before replying, a plan forming in her mind.

'Gracy, I know you are afraid but we must tell Mrs Humphris.'

'No! No! Cookie. Don't tell 'er,' the poor girl wailed. 'Don't tell' er. She'll throw me out or report me to Old Marsden. Please! Please!'

'Gracy! Listen to me. I know Mrs Humphris better than you. She is a good woman and your friend. She will help. She is as kind as my old Mistress. If only I had gone to her with my troubles I would not be here now. Trust me, Gracy, and trust her. Now dry your eyes and tell me, does anyone else know?'

'Only Pearl. That's why we went over the fence that day. I told 'er and she said we 'ad to confront 'im. When 'e denied me I was that upset. That's why we got so drunk. I just wanted to forget what' e said.'

'Is Pearl a good friend? Will she keep your secret?'

'Yeah. We've been mates for a long time. She won't tell.'

'Then we have a chance. But first we must tell Mrs Humphris.'

Before approaching Mrs Humphris, Margaret had a private talk with Pearl, impressing on her the need for secrecy as her plan depended on keeping Gracy's secret.

'Ya don't 'ave ta tell me, Cookie,' Pearl assured her. 'I know the danger she'll be in. We knows 'ow ta keep a secret in the streets when it's one of our own. Gracy's problims are safe with me. What ya think ya can do ta 'elp her?'

'I must keep that a secret too, until I know that it can be done. Pearl, keep an eye on Gracy for now. She is going to need you in the months ahead.'

'Right ya are. You're oright, Cookie.'

Margaret felt a glow of pride at this endorsement. She knew that praise was never given easily in this colony. The next job was to break the news to Mrs Humphris but it was not until the following afternoon that she could get an opportunity to speak to that lady without fear of interruption.

'Excuse me, Mrs Humphris, could I have a private word with you?'

'Of course, Margaret. Come in. You do look serious. I hope nothing is wrong. You have been such a success. It's not the two girls, is it? They haven't been giving you any trouble I hope?'

'No, Mrs Humphris. I am very pleased with them. They are willing learners, but it is about one of them that I wish to speak. I'm afraid I have to inform you that Gracy is pregnant.'

'Pregnant!' Her hand went to her cheek and she sank into a nearby chair. 'Pregnant? When? How? I suppose this is the result of her night out. But it is too soon, surely. Is she sure?'

'She's about three months gone.'

'Three months! But that means she must have been out before.' This news shocked Mrs Humphris almost as much as the original announcement. She felt personally betrayed.

'That is so, but I feel you must hear her story before you pass judgement,' Margaret replied and proceeded to tell Gracy's story.

At the end Mrs Humphris' hurt turned to anger. 'How dare he! She was only a child. Now he's going to abandon her! I won't have it! I'll report him to Colonel Paterson. I'll even go to the Governor. He will not get away with it! I will see that he faces up to his responsibilities. I will demand justice!'

She had risen and started stomping around the room as she spoke, thumping a fist into a cupped hand to emphasize her statements,

'Justice is an indefinite thing, Mrs Humphris. There is one justice for the rich and another for the poor; one justice for men and one for women. Do you think that even someone as fair minded as Governor King will take the word of a 'street Arab', as Mrs Weatherstone calls them, against the word of a member of the New South Wales Corp, a woman's word against a man's? No. But with your help we can do what women have ever done since time began. We must close ranks and give what assistance we can.'

'You're right, of course.' The moment of anger had passed and Isobelle Humphris sank back onto a chair. 'But what can we do? Reverend Marsden and his pious ladies will crucify her. She will be thrown out, of course, and probably be publicly whipped. Oh, Margaret! What will become of the baby?' Childless herself, her heart went out to this unborn babe. ' Is there nothing we can do to help?' She held out her hands appealing to Margaret for advice.

'I do have a plan,' Margaret replied calmly, 'but it will require careful arranging, absolute secrecy and could bring censure on yourself if it fails.'

'Don't worry about me. I have Dear Humphris at my back to support me. I love this position but, if I lose it, that won't be the end of my world. It is worth risking it to save Gracy. But we won't fail. I know. I have complete faith in you. Only tell me what to do.'

Her face shone with evangelical zeal. Margaret was amazed that this woman could hold her, a convicted criminal, in such high regard.

'If we can keep Gracy away from the prying eyes of Mrs Weatherstone and the more knowing of the girls, nobody need know that she is pregnant.'

'But the baby? What do we do when it comes?' Mrs Humphris pleaded.

'That is where you come in. If l can keep the baby hidden for a couple of days we can place it on the doorstep, as if someone from outside had left it there. After all, we are an orphanage.'

'Yes! yes! La, what a lovely plan Margaret. Then I can adopt it and I can ask Gracy to be its nursemaid. It's just like Moses in the Bible. I discover it and make it my ward then Gracy, like Miriam, will care for it. She will be able to feed it and everything. This is a wondrous plan. How clever you are. What would I have done without you?'

Margaret thought, she's like a child herself. She believes, because she wants to, that I have only to come up with a plan and it will happen. She has led a very sheltered life.

'There is still one problem. I am worried about Gracy in the dormitory. The girls are very aware about such things and someone might notice the change in her figure. She could also go into labour during the night.'

'Then she must be moved now. Where can we put her?'

'There's a large drying room adjacent to my room. It could easily be converted. But what excuse could you give for moving her, and Pearl too, if possible.'

Mrs Humphris furrowed her pretty brow for a second or too, then broke out into a peal of laughter.

'I have it! La, I am becoming such a devious person. Poor Humphris will have to take care when he gets back. Go and start preparing the room. And on your way out get whoever is on messenger duty to tell Mrs Weatherstone that I wish to speak to her as soon as possible.'

Laughing to herself, she composed her features for her confrontation with the teacher.

When that lady arrived, her mistress was sitting, hands folded, her face a picture of concentration.

'Come in, Mrs Weatherstone. Take a seat. I have an important matter to discuss with you.' She looked earnestly into the other woman's eyes.

'Mrs Weatherstone, ever since that terrible night when Pearl and Gracy were missing I have been thinking about what you said, 'Evil amongst us." I still feel I was right in extending mercy to those lost souls, but you were right too in excluding them from the classroom. What has been worrying me is that they are still with the older girls in the dormitory at night. You know the dark is the Devil's time of day.'

Mrs Weatherstone's bosom heaved with pleasure. She forgave her employer for overriding her pronouncement. She was about to express a polite, 'I told you so' but Mrs Humphris hadn't finished.

'I have been looking around and noticed that there is a large drying room near cook's room that is hardly ever used. I know it has no windows but it has good ventilation and the lack of exits would help cook in her supervision of them. Mrs Weatherstone, I want your honest opinion. As a forgiving Christian, am I doing right placing the girls in this room away from their friends?'

Mrs Weatherstone's cup was full. Short of dismissing them altogether she could think of no better punishment. 'Oh, yes, Mrs Humphris. I think you are wholly justified. In fact I think you have tempered Christian charity with prudence. I heartily endorse your decision.'

So the first part of Margaret's plan had succeeded. Now with careful supervision and a bit of luck it could all be accomplished.

CHAPTER FOUR

The next month passed without incident though Margaret had one moment of panic when Mrs Weatherstone came to her.

'Cook, I think there is something you ought to know about Gracy.'

'What's wrong with her?' Margaret demanded, trying to hide her fear.

'She's putting on weight. I think she's stealing food.'

Margaret breathed a sigh of relief. 'Is that all? No, she's not stealing. I think, before she came here, she must have suffered a lot from hunger. Now she can't bear to see food wasted so eats all the leftovers and scraps. I haven't said anything to her yet, but, now that you have brought it to my attention, I must admit she is getting rather fat.'

Mrs Weatherstone scolded, 'Fat children are rarely healthy. You must put a stop to it.'

'Oh, I will.' Margaret looked suitably repentant. 'I will watch her from now on. She is really a very lazy girl and a little exercise wouldn't do her any harm either. I will make her join me in my evening walks.'

'Just so long as she doesn't try to run away.'

'I don't think she'll do that. I think she really understands how lucky she was not to be reported last time. She is truly frightened about being punished.'

'Good.' Mrs Weatherstone was pleased to hear that Gracy had been suitably cowed. 'And what about Pearl? Do you intend taking her too?'

'Definitely not. You were right about that girl. I wouldn't trust her out of the grounds for a minute.'

Mrs Weatherstone was delighted that her opinion of the girl was shared. She was almost smiling as she walked away.

Margaret was smiling too. She had been worried about the confining nature of Gracy's life. It had always been known in the village that walking was good for pregnant women. Now she could take her walking in the evening, without worry of anyone asking why. She meant what she said about Pearl too. The girl was trying hard to behave herself for Gracy's sake but a glimpse of the outside world after dark might be too much of a temptation.

The girls were jealous of Margaret's freedom so Gracy jumped at the chance when Margaret suggested she accompany her on her walks. However her elation soon changed to protest when she learnt their destination.

'Why waste ya time walkin' in the bush. There's no fun there, least you're meetin' a fella. I wan'ta see sights, meet people. I'm sick t' death of seein' the same faces day an' night. I wanna talk t' real people.'

'This walk is not for your entertainment, Gracy. It's for the good of your health and that of the baby,' Margaret scolded. 'You want a nice, easy birth, don't you?

'But why cant we 'ave a nice walk in the town. There ain't no difference.'

'You know that that world is full of temptation. You've got to stay away for the baby's sake.'

'Bloomin' baby. It's nuffin but a nuisance,' she grumbled as she trotted along beside Margaret. 'Can't ya slow down a bit?'

'No,' Margaret replied firmly. 'This is a walk, not a stroll. It's meant to firm up your muscles and keep your weight down. You don't want Mrs Weatherstone to guess your secret, do you?'

'Blimy, no.' Gracy picked up her speed and Margaret heard no more complaints.

Back at the Orphanage the girl was able to console her disgruntled friend. 'Ya not missin' anyfing. We just walk through the bloomin' bush, look at the sea then walk 'ome. Dead borin' girl, dead borin'. I dunno why she does it. She'll never meet a fella' that way.'

But in a few days Gracy began to look forward to her daily walk and resented the times when the weather curtailed it. She had no idea what a sacrifice it was for Margaret to give up her hour of solitude as she chattered away.

'Cookie, Mrs Humphris wants ya in the par-lar. She gave me this for ya.' The small girl, duty messenger for the day, handed Margaret a neatly folded piece of white paper. Margaret dismissed the girl then opened it.

Margaret, I have a visitor I wish you to meet. Take off your apron and cap and bring your journal.

Mystified by the message, Margaret hastened to obey it. Getting her journal from her room she hurried to the parlour, brushing back her curls and smoothing her skirt as she went.

Her tap on the door was answered by an invitation to enter.

As she came into the room both her mistress and a fresh faced young man, stood.

'Ah, there you are, Margaret. Here is someone I wish to introduce you to. This is Mr Philip Crawley. He is lately arrived from England, an acquaintance of Dear Humphris, but best of all, he is a botanist.'

The young man came forward, extending his hand. Margaret made a respectful bow but did not extend her hand in return.

Unaware of any embarrassment, Mrs Humphris continued, 'Margaret is our cook, Mr Crawley, but much more than that. La, she has so many talents I don't know where to begin. But the one we are interested in today is botany. Show Mr Crawley your journal, Margaret.'

The poor woman blushed and Mr Crawley too, was nonplussed. He was unused to being introduced to cooks, but he was a gentleman and extended his hand to take the book Margaret was holding. However, when he had turned a few pages his attitude changed and he looked at her properly for the first time. Though now twenty-eight, Margaret still had the slim figure and black curling hair that had first attracted Will, but it was the intensity in her brown eyes that held him. A cook she might be, and embarrassed at the situation she found herself in, but she was proud of her work and challenged him to degrade it.

'This is good, very good,' he pronounced looking anew at her work. 'Your labelling is correct and the plants and flowers faithfully reproduced. Where did you learn this?'

'At the hands of my mistress, Elizabeth Cobbold,' she declared proudly.

'Ah, Elizabeth Cobbold! I have heard of that lady. Amongst her other pursuits she is well known as a keen botanist. You were indeed fortunate to have such a fine tutor.'

Isobelle Humphris stood back, pleased that the first meeting between this personable young man and her prodigy, Margaret, was going so well.

'Mr Crawley, Margaret has a desire to learn about this antipodean's flora so that she can send specimens back to her former mistress. Do you think you could help her?'

Faced with such a request from his hostess, and noting the pleasantness of the pupil, Philip Crawley did not think it would be such an unpleasant proposition.

'Yes, of course, Mrs Humphris. I would be delighted to be of service. At present I am only a student of this landscape myself but I would be happy to share my knowledge. If I should be lucky enough to discover a new species you will both be the first to know.'

Philip Cowley became a familiar visitor to the Asylum. Though he always called on Isobelle first, he spent most of his time with Margaret, showing her the specimens he had gathered, discussing their biological names and telling her of the uses that the Aboriginals made of them.

She was particularly interested in the anecdotal information about their medical properties.

'And do these really work?' she enquired

'Some of the white people who have used them think they do, but there has been no real research done.'

'Perhaps this is something you could do.'

'It would be an interesting study and could be useful as people move further from the main settlements, but I don't think it would have much practical application where proper medicine is available.'

'Yet, at home, country folk have their own remedies.'

'And only some of them work,' Philip laughed. 'However there is one tree that must surely be useful, the Eucalyptus. There are many varieties of it, but all have such an aromatic smell I am sure they must be of value. I think I will make them my special study.'

Conversations such as this cemented their friendship. Soon Phillip was confiding to Margaret his thoughts and aspirations and soon forgot that she was, in fact, only a servant.

Margaret hungrily absorbed all the information he gave her. She worked tirelessly, pressing the specimens, recording their botanical identification and representing them faithfully in the journal Mrs Cobbolt had given her before she left England. It was a labour of love. Working on her journal, Margaret imagined scenes back in England and the joy her work would bring to her former mistress. For a short time she could imagine herself back among those she loved, walking the gentle lanes of Sussex, watching the changing seasons.

She longed for the variety of weather, even the sleet and snow of winter. Although the heat of summer was gone there was little evidence in this strange, monotonous land that autumn was creeping into winter. The days were shorter and some mornings there was evidence of frost on the cleared fields but the dramatic colours of England were only echoed in the trees of the Orphanage garden.

Outside, the native trees and the distant hills retained their same dull olive green. The brown grass of summer, however, had gone and a velvet green covered the cleared ground for, in this place, the grasses grew in winter.

Margaret noted the progress of the year more by the developing girth of Gracy's waist. The girl was about six months pregnant and even Margaret's sewing could not hide it. Every morning her stomach was bound, to hide the tell tale bulge. They tried to keep her out of public gaze as much as possible. Sunday service was the most difficult time. They carefully positioned her as far from Mrs Weatherstons's prying eyes as they could.

Margaret's other worry was knowing when the girl would go into labour. If only Gracy could be more definite about when she became pregnant. She was so ignorant that she had not connected menstruation with her condition, but Pearl, who was much more worldly, was sure it had been late November. This gave them about three more months. But would it be at the beginning or the end of August? Only time would tell.

Pearl and Gracy got great amusement from Margaret's friendship with Crawley.

'Is ya boyfriend comin' this week, Cookie?' Pearl enquired.

'He's not my boyfriend in the way you mean, Pearl. He's just a friend who happens to be a male,' Margaret explained.

'Yeah, yeah,' Pearl teased. 'Wish I 'ad a wealthy, 'andsome, male friend. 'E wouldn't remain just a 'friend' fa long.'

Margaret had become used to the interest they showed in her private life. It no longer annoyed her. In a way it was just like the gossip in the big houses, but at least here things were spoken of openly.

'What I'd like ta' know is what do youse talk about all the time.' Gracy had no conception of a relationship with men outside of intimacy.

'Mr Crawley is a respected botanist who is teaching me about the flora of New South Wales.'

'Wot's flora?' Pearl enquired.

'Plants and trees and things,' Margaret enlightened her.

'Cor, ya mean ya spend all ya time talkin' about flowers!' Pearl was stunned. 'Don't ya even do a little smoochin'?'

'Don't sound very promisin',' Gracy advised. 'Do ya think 'e really wants ta marry ya?'

'No I don't,' Margaret assured them. 'You forget, I am a convict.'

'Don't mean a thing 'ere. Lots of swells live wif convicts. Some even marry 'em, proper like, in a church and everyfin', Pearl assured her. 'Ya ought ta set ya' cap at'im. 'E'd be a good catch.'

'Yeah, why don't ya 'ave a go, Cookie?' Gracy coaxed.

'Well,' Margaret laughed, 'a lady has to wait until she's asked.'

'That's oright then, Cookie. You're not a lady. You're a convict so it's oright for ya to ask 'im.'

Margaret knew that Pearl's remark was meant jokingly but it gave her food for thought. She liked Philip. He reminded her of her dear friend Jack. He was well educated and kind and seemed to be developing a fondness for her, as Jack had done. She had a feeling that with a little encouragement he might declare his love for her and then, what would she do? In this land, where men far outnumbered women, it was expedient to have a male protector. But did she have feelings for him such that she could spend the rest of her life with him? And even if he married her would he be willing to take her back to England as his wife? For she still hoped that, one day, she would get her pardon.

Part of her wanted to know the answers, but she remembered how a declaration of love had been the end of her friendship with Jack. She didn't want to lose Philip's friendship too. So she decided that she would do nothing. She would neither encourage nor discourage him. She would leave things to develop by themselves.

Crawley had also been wrestling with his feelings for Margaret. He found she was constantly on his mind. Had she been a member of colonial society, he knew he would be courting her by now, but could he really have a relationship with a servant?

If he did declare his feelings, would they be reciprocated? He was planning to begin his first expedition to the mountains at the beginning of July and, wanting to leave his mind free to concentrate on his work, decided to speak of his problem with Mrs Humphris. That lady was delighted that Margaret had found favour in his eyes.

'La, Mr Crawley, this is wonderful news. You could not find a better companion in all the colony than Miss Catchpole. I'm sure she's ripe to be wooed and won. She is such a good person and

I'm sure she will soon get her ticket-of-leave . . . '

'What do you mean, ticket-of-leave? Surely you are not telling me that she is a convict?' cried Crawley, aghast at the news.

'Of course. Did you not know?' Then, noting the look of horror on his face, 'but surely that makes no difference to how you feel about her? She is still the same, dear person.'

Philip Crawley drew himself up in a formal stance. 'I believe, Madam, that you have been in the colony too long. I bid you good day,' and with a slight bow he took his leave.

Isobelle Humphris was shocked that such an amiable young man could hold such prejudiced views, but then, she reasoned, he is no more than a product of his class. Her next thought was for Margaret who would wonder why Crawley was no longer calling. Isobelle wanted to protect her from the hurt that would follow so, to forestall any questions she went, herself, to the kitchen.

A scene of domesticity and industry greeted her. Pearl was cutting fat from some mutton chops, Gracy sat cutting up vegetables and Margaret was rolling out pastry. They all turned as she entered, wondering what disaster had brought her to the kitchen.

'Cook,' she began in an impersonal, authoritarian voice, 'Mr Crawley has just paid me a visit. He is about to leave on his expedition and came to say his goodbyes. I knew you were busy so offered to convey his message to you.'

'Thank you, Mrs Humphris,' Margaret replied automatically. She was surprised and hurt by the curt message, and that she had been given no chance to say goodby.

She had believed that Mrs Humphris regarded her as more than a servant, yet now she was being treated as if she had no rights at all. At heart, all the gentry are alike, she thought, as old hurts, real and imaginary, that she had suffered, resurfaced. She had been a fool to think that things would ever be different.

When Mrs Humphris had left the two girls were not backward in expressing their opinions.

'She'd got a cheek. She could've called for ya. We'd 'ave covered for ya.' Gracy declared indignantly

'I think she's mean. Maybe she's jealous. I'd go an' ave it out with 'er.' Pearl was angry that Margaret, whom she grudgingly admitted was a good sort, had been treated so shabbily.

Margaret swallowed her hurt. 'It doesn't matter. He may not have wanted to see me anyway. Now stop gossiping and get on with your work or dinner will be late.'

The two girls knew better than to argue when Margaret was 'in one of her moods'. They left her to her thoughts. She was surprised to realise that, along with the hurt from Isobelle's words, there was also a sadness that she would not be seeing Philip Crawley. It was something stronger than just missing a few pleasant visits. Perhaps she had real feelings for him after all. Now she might never know.

August came at last with a promise of warmer days but Gracy, though quite rotund, showed no signs of dropping her bundle. Every morning Pearl and Margaret would quiz her to see if she had noticed any change, any feeling that might indicate that the great event was imminent, but nothing was happening.

Gracy was her usual cheerful self. 'You'se are worryin' enough. I'm just gettin on wif becomin' a muver,' she would joke.

The relations between Margaret and Mrs Humphris were still cool but, as co-conspirators, they had to communicate on a personal level.

'The thing I'm most worried about is the noise that goes with childbirth,' Margaret informed her.

'Why, Margaret? Surely a baby's cry cannot be so loud?'

'It's not the baby I'm worried about. It's Gracy. Having a baby is not without its pain and women make strange, animal noises without knowing it, even well bred ladies. Gracy is not used to restraint and I worry how we can muffle her sounds.'

'La, Margaret, I have a lot to learn. I thought you just went to bed and the baby came. No wonder child-bearing takes so much out of my sister. How do you know all about this? Have you delivered many babies?'

'I have assisted at several births, but always there has been a midwife or a doctor in attendance. This will be the first time I will be doing it on my own. I pray that nothing goes wrong.' A worried frown showed just how apprehensive Margaret was.

'But what if it does?' Isobelle was beginning to realise the enormity of the undertaking. 'Then we must get help and hope the secret can be kept. A doctor would be best as they are bound to keep medical secrets. I shall have to make the acquaintance of one of them, perhaps William Redfern. He is a former convict and is also spoken of as honest and competent. I could, perhaps sound him out about becoming the Orphanage doctor. No one has been appointed yet, but we will surely need one sooner or later. He could examine all the girls to check on their general health. I'm sure even the Reverend will not object to that.

'As to the problem of the noise, I will think on it and hopefully come up with a solution.'

Margaret's attitude began to thaw as she noted Mrs Humphris' enthusiasm for the task. She is not an unfeeling woman, Margaret thought. It's just that she doesn't always understand the feelings of others.
A few days later Margaret was sent for. Mrs Humphris' eyes sparkled with pleasure as she recounted her latest plans.

'I have met Mr Redfern, and quite a refined person he seems. He was happy with my suggestion that he examines the girls. He remarked that the Currency children seem much healthier than their parents. I'm sure he would come if we needed him.

'Now to my other plan. As long as Gracy has her baby during the day it will work. As soon as I know it is coming I will get Jimmy and his father to organise the cart and you must provide lots of food for a picnic. I will come up with a reason for having a day out. I only hope it does not choose to come on a Sunday as we would not be able to get away so easily. It really is very exciting, isn't it?'

Margaret found it hard to share her mistress's enthusiasm. She realised that this lady, so gently bred had no idea of the hazards of childbirth; that Gracy's future and that of her baby were in the hands of God alone. She offered a silent prayer that he would look with kindness on this poor, unfortunate outcast and make her labour simple and short.

The days of August passed and still Isobelle's grand plan had not been tested. She went over and over it, perfecting every little detail, but still the baby showed no sign of arrival. In moments of impatience she even wondered if there really was a baby or whether it was a subterfuge thought up by the girl to annoy her. By the end of the month Margaret and Pearl had given up asking Gracy how she felt. Margaret had prepared picnic food twice, but there was only so long that one could keep prepared food in this climate. The girls were getting a regular diet of party fare. If this kept up she would be running out of ingredients.

On the morning of the 31st Margaret and her girls were busy in the early morning preparing the breakfast before the duty girls came in to help. Pearl was stirring a large pot of porridge and Gracy was mixing a batter for a Toad in the Hole for Mrs Humphris' and the teacher's breakfast. The two ladies always breakfasted together discussing the day's activities while they ate.

'Ouch!' Gracy moaned placing a hand on the small of her back.

'What is it?' Margaret was instantly alert.

'It's nuffin, just a pain in me back, but it comes and goes. I must'f slept crooked. Woke me up, it did.'

'Oh Gracy, you're in labour. It's happening at last.' In her delight Margaret cupped the girls cheeks in her hands.

Gracy's eyes grew large. 'Do ya fink so? Don't feel like I expected. When will it come?'

'That's the big question dear. It could be in a few hours or it may take all day. But you're a brave girl and Pearl and I will be with you all the time.'

Even the unflappable Pearl was caught up in the excitement. 'Cor, girl, you're gunna be a Mum. Does that make me a aunty?' and she threw her arms around her friend.

'Right,' said Margaret bringing them back to the task in hand. 'The plan begins. You were clever to start so early in the day, gives us plenty of time.

'Gracy, you get on with the batter. Pearl, go and knock on Mrs Humphris' door. Say to her, 'Cook wants to know what she has planned for lunch.' Don't say anything else. She will know what the message means. '

'Real spy stuff,' Pearl grinned, hurrying to deliver the message.

Isobelle understood immediately and played her part to perfection. When breakfast had been served she announced to Mrs Weatherstone, 'It is such a lovely day, Mrs Weatherstone that I declare a holiday. We will take everyone on a picnic. Minnie can take the little ones in the cart with the food, and the rest of us can go for a long, lovely walk up past the Governor's house to that delightful area overlooking the Harbour. We will have lots of things to eat and the girls can play games like Drop the Hankie. It will be great fun. I think we should bring the maids too. We will need them to help mind the girls and I'm sure they would enjoy a day out.'

Mrs Weatherstone's features darkened. She did not like disruption to her routine and was even less happy about the long walk ahead.

'Do you intend to include Miss Catchpole in your plans?' she replied sarcastically. 'She is very fond of walking. Perhaps I could stay back and prepare the evening meal.'

'No, no. I have no intention of including Gracy and Pearl in our outing and I feel they still need Cook's supervision in the kitchen. No, while we're away I want Cook and the girls to prepare a wonderful meal. We will all be so hungry when we return. And also, Dear Mrs Weatherstone, I will need you to explain anything we might come across that will improve the girl's minds. You are so much more knowledgeable than I am.'

The good lady was not taken in by Isobelle's flattery, but could think of no suitable response.

'Will it not be fun, Mrs Weatherstone? We can say we are celebrating the end of Winter or heralding in Spring. I'm so excited. I'll go and give Cook my orders straight away. Finish your breakfast, my dear, then hurry the children and the maids. I want to be out of the house by ten o'clock.'

Mrs Weatherstone gave a withering glare at the retreating back, but there was nothing she could do. Mrs Humphris was usually such an easy mistress but when she got an idea into her head there was no stopping her.

By midday Gracy's labour was well advanced. Pearl and Margaret took turns sitting with her, encouraging her and ignoring the curses she levelled at her soljer, themselves and life in general. Between contractions she lay, passively contemplating her future.

About four in the afternoon, Minnie and the little ones arrived home. Gracy could not be left so Pearl went to attend them.

'Don't worry Cook, Pearl.' Minnie assured her. The little darlin's are worn out. They won't want any tea. All they need is a hot drink. They've run around and ate themselves silly all day. They'll be asleep before their heads hit the pillow tonight,' Minnie informed her.

'When will the others be home?' Pearl asked anxiously.

'They'll be at least an hour. I hope they hurry. There's a storm approaching.'

As Pearl was busy making the hot drinks a deafening clap of thunder sounded, followed almost immediately by pounding rain.

'Oh Lord!' Minnie cried, 'Mrs Humphris and the girls will be caught in the midst of this. I best get these little ones to bed as quick as I can and come and help you. There'll be bedlam when they return.'

'I'll go and tell Cookie,' shouted Pearl above the noise of the storm. She ran out and splashed her way to the drying room.

'Cookie, they'll be 'ome in a 'our, Minnie's gettin' the kids to bed, it's rainin' buckets, 'as the baby come?' she burst out in one breath.

'It's almost here. Sit behind Gracy and let her lean against you. I wish we had a birthing stool.'

Gracy moaned as she felt another contraction coming.

'Come on, Gracy,' Margaret coaxed her. 'It's nearly over. Take a deep breath and push with all your might. No one's going to hear you above this storm.'

Gracy pushed, shouting, 'I can't. I can't,' until the crown of the head appeared. She collapsed back against Pearl. 'I can't do no more. I don't want no baby.'

'Yes you can,' Margaret encouraged. 'Next one will do it.'

'Can't stop now, girl,' Pearl advised, terrified at the suffering her friend was going through.

'Take a deep breath and push,' Margaret instructed.

Nature would have its way whether the poor girl wanted it or not. With the next pain Gracy was sure she had split in half. Her scream went unheard as an almighty clap of thunder rent the air.

'It's coming! It's coming!' Margaret encouraged.

'Ooh, blimy,' whispered Pearl as she watched something round and dark and bloody force itself between Gracy's legs.

The girl lay back, panting. 'Is it over yet?'

'Just one more time and it will be. You've done so well.' There were tears in Margaret's eyes as she checked that the neck was clear.

Gracy felt the next contraction and braced herself for it, but as soon as she began to push she felt the body of the baby slither out in one long motion.

'It's 'ere Gracy! It's 'ere,' Pearl cheered, tears running down her cheeks. She was totally overwhelmed by the miracle happening before her.

Gracy collapsed back again, a serene expression on her face. 'Me baby! Me baby!'

Margaret expertly cut the umbilical cord, gathered up the little body, wrapped it in a soft cloth and placed it in Gracy's waiting arms.

'Congratulations, Gracy. You have a baby boy.'

Watching the two girls fussing and cooing over the little bundle of life, Margaret experienced a sudden, overwhelming jealousy as her empty womb ached with desire. Why hadn't her brief coupling with Will produced a child?

This emotion was quickly smothered by the knowledge that, had such an event happened, the baby would have been born in prison or on a convict ship. It would have had forever the stigma of a convict mother. It was better she had not conceived.

But, oh, how she wished it could have been.

She pulled herself together, gave Pearl instructions to take care of Gracy and the baby then headed to the kitchen to be ready when Mrs Humphris and the girls arrived.

CHAPTER FIVE

Gracy hurried back to the kitchen door.

'It's all clear Pearl. There's nobody around. You've got five minutes to get out the front an' ring the bell.'

Because of Pearl's athleticism and native cunning Margaret had chosen her to take the baby to the front of the house and leave it on the veranda. If anyone could pull it off without being caught it would be Pearl.

Mrs Weatherstone had caught a chill from her day out and had spent the next two in bed. This had given the conspirators a little more time. But today she was to resume her duties so they could not risk hiding the baby any longer.

Mrs Weatherstone, a creature of habit, always arrived at the foot of the stairs at 7.30 a.m. exactly. Mrs Humphris wanted the teacher to be present when the baby was found, hence the need for precision timing.

Gracy gave the sleeping child a quick kiss as Pearl left. 'Do ya think it'll work, Cookie?' queried the anxious mother. 'I'll just die if it don't. I'll kill meself afore I lets 'em take me baby'.

'Sush,' Margaret comforted. 'Everything is going to go perfectly. Now pull yourself together. You have a part to play in our plan too, don't forget.' In spite of her reassuring order Margaret was tense, waiting for the bell to ring.

In another part of the building Mrs Humphris waited also, playing over in her mind the scene she imagined would soon take place. She stood, like an actress waiting in the wings, for her signal to enter.

Mrs Weatherstone descended the staircase then stopped, as usual, to check her pocket watch against the large clock that stood at the foot of the stairs.

The bell sounded suddenly, not the ring from the usual discrete pull of the rope but a loud, incessant clanging from an urgent tugging. The sudden ringing quite unnerved the woman, so recently recovered from illness. She lost her usual composure and staggered back against the baluster as girls rushed from the upstairs dormitory and began peering over the balcony, voices raised in enquiry.

Simultaneously Mrs Humphris, her hair still unbraided, appeared from her quarters and Margaret and Gracy hurried in from the kitchen as the last of the dongs echoed along the passage.

The threat of pandemonium revived Mrs Weatherstone's sense of order.

'Silence,' she commanded, and the swell of enquiring voices dropped to a whisper.

Isobelle Humphris picked up her cue. In her best 'helpless female' voice she hurried forward, clutching her throat. 'Oh, Mrs Weatherstone! What do you think can have happened? Goodness, the bell fairly frightened me out of my wits. Do you think there is some disaster? Who do you think is at the door?'

'It's no good standing here speculating, Mrs Humphris. Someone must answer it.'

'Yes. Yes. Of course.' Still dithering, as if afraid to let what was outside into the house, Isobelle raised her head to the anxious faces that peered down at her. 'Who is on messenger duty today?' she enquired.

A fair-haired girl about ten tentatively raised her hand. Encouraged by the other girls, she reluctantly descended the stairs.

'It's me, Mrs Humphris.'

'Well then girl, do your duty,' Mrs Weatherstone directed. Now that she had recovered from the shock of the bell, she was ready, mentally and physically, to confront and deal with whatever emergency waited beyond the door.

The young girl walked slowly towards the door, conscious of all the eyes upon her. Most of the other girls followed her down, anxious now to be part of whatever drama lay beyond the door. She unbolted the lock, lifted the latch and gingerly opened the door, ready to close it again if danger threatened to invade the house. When no one tried to force their way in she opened it wide and stepped outside, looking to left and right. She was just about to inform those inside that there was nobody there when she noticed the little white bundle.

Cautiously she bent and picked it up, then opened the white cotton sheet. She gasped in astonishment at the little, pink face inside.

'It's a baby,' she declared, in wonder. A babble of questions greeted her news. Mrs Humphris pushed through the press of girls and gently took the infant from the dazed girl.

'So it is,' she cooed. 'Oh, Mrs Weatherstone, look, it's a tiny babe.' She did not have to fake the tender tone in her voice. She felt a maternal glow flood her being. This was the child she had longed for all these years.

'A foundling,' Mrs Weatherstone declared, pushing forward to take control. 'We will have to inform Reverend Marsden at once. He will know what to do. We can't have fallen women depositing their offspring on our doorstep.'

'But we are an orphanage. It is our job to take in unwanted children, surely?'

'Not ones who just get dumped on our doorstep. We need to know who they are, and anyway, the mother must be found and punished. If one gets away with it, we will have babies on our doorstep every day. It's quite impossible. We have no facilities for babies.'

Mrs Humphris tightened her hold on the baby, 'Then we should have. Isn't it better to take them in as babies and care for them properly, rather than have them neglected for several years and then try to undo the damage?'

'I mean, we have no means of caring for this baby.' Mrs Weatherstone was beginning to fear she was losing the battle. She knew all about the maudlin desires of childless women. She would have to find stronger arguments. 'We have no nursery and, how would we feed it? You can't give new babies porridge, you know.'

She drew herself up to full height, sure that her arguments had solved the argument. If she had not been so well bred she would have folded her arms and said 'so there'. Mrs Humphris was warming to the game. She knew she still had several trumps to play.

'I'm sure we can solve such simple problems. Many new born babes survive without a mother.'

'As a matter of fact,' Margaret interrupted from the back of the group. 'I have assisted in caring for two babies whose mothers died in childbirth. It's not all that difficult.' Feeling the sting of Mrs, Weatherstone's glare, she moved through the crowd towards the two women, closely followed by Gracy.

Not to be bested, Mrs Weatherstone moved closer to the baby and began unwrapping it. She gave a cry of triumph. 'This baby can't stay here. It's a boy.'

'What difference does that make?' Isobelle demanded, in genuine surprise.

'This is a girl's orphanage Madam! We can't have boys here.'

Isobelle could hardly contain the laughter that was welling up inside her. 'La, Mrs Weatherstone. You are not suggesting that this wee mite is going to corrupt the morals of our girls?'

The woman stepped back, defeated. Even she could admit to the absurdity of her objection.

The baby boy, who until that moment had remained impassive, decided to make his presence felt. Screwing up his tiny face and clenching his tiny fists he let out a loud squeal for such a small creature. A collective sigh went up from the onlookers.

Mrs Humphris clutched him to her heart. He nuzzled into her empty breasts, snuffling, looking for the warm milk to which he had become accustomed. She felt such an overwhelming flow of maternal protection that she was resolved, come what may, to defend this child with her life.

'Mrs Weatherstone,' she began, her voice ringing with sincerity, 'God has not seen fit to provide me with a child of my own. Now this tiny, defenceless creature has come into my life. I do not care where he came from. I am going to claim him and bring him up as my own. He will become my ward and he will be mine in everything except birth.'

Mrs Weatherstone was shocked by this declaration. 'But, Mrs Humphris, you cannot mean what you are saying. Your husband isn't even here to permit you.'

'He may not be here but he knows my mind and I know his. I cannot do this thing without his permission but I will write to him today. I know he will be delighted to grant my wish. We have sometime talked of adoption but usually within the family. Now God has sent this foundling to me and I will not fail him. Darling Humphris will agree, I know. The baby will stay with me until his return, when we will legally adopt him and give him the Humphris name. In fact, here and now, I will give him his first name.'

She gazed at the puckered face getting ready to protest his lack of nourishment. He reminded her of an angry, old man. 'I think I shall call him Frederick. Yes, Frederick.' She touched his tiny cheek with her finger. 'Do you like your name, Frederick?'

Obviously he did, for he stopped his protest as his mouth sought the finger, hoping for sustenance there.

Mrs Weatherstone knew she was defeated but she tried, one last time. 'I do not think you realise the magnitude of the task you have set yourself. You know nothing about caring for babies.'

'But I can learn,' replied the triumphant Isobelle, 'and I will not be short of nursemaids. I'm sure one of the older girls would like the job.'

Gracy had been watching the proceedings, in turn anxious and envious, as Isobelle fought for her baby. The suggestion of help was hardly uttered before she pushed forward. 'I will, Mrs Humphris. I will. I'll do it. I love babies and I'm sure I'll do a good job. Please let me try. Please.'

Her plea had come so quickly and so earnestly that Mrs Humphris knew that nobody would think it strange that she was chosen. 'Of course, Gracy. You can become Frederick's nursemaid. Cook has told me you are a reformed character. I'm sure she can spare you from your duties. You will need to be a full time nursemaid until he is a little older. Then you can combine your duties. We must find somewhere for him to sleep and then you must go to Cook and learn what foods to give him.'

Mrs Weatherstone, having lost the battle, looked again at her watch. 'We have wasted twenty minutes of the day already. We must make it up or we will be behind all day. Girls, go straight to the refectory.' Then, challenging Margaret. 'I hope breakfast is ready Cook.' She marched off, head held high, ready to begin another day of trying to make silk purses from sows' ears.

CHAPTER SIX

The storm that heralded Frederick's birth was followed by a fortnight of rain before September put on its spring mantle. Sunlight shone through the dull olive green to seek out the young leaves. Splashes of russet gave life to the bush, wattle added its brilliant yellow to the scene. Like paints from an artist's palette, colour lifted the oppressive sameness of the surrounding hills and brought joyful hope to homesick settlers.

In the Orphanage garden, so loving planted by the young Lieutenant for his doomed English bride, the full beauty of an English spring gave nostalgic pleasure to those who had come from the other side of the world, and delight to the native born.

Frederick thrived on Isobelle's love and Gracy's milk. He was the pampered favourite of everyone. Even Mrs Weatherstone, after initial antagonism, seemed to warm to this bundle of humanity. She marvelled at his growth on the daily formula of arrowroot made by Margaret, not knowing that its sustenance reached the boy, not by bottle, but from his mother's breast.

One sunny afternoon, as Isobelle was sitting on the wide veranda supervising as Fredrick slept, a familiar figure came through the iron gates. It was Philip, back from his first excursion into the mountain barriers that had already been christened 'Blue' because of their hazy colour.

Isobelle was a little surprised to see him after his curt departure a few months before, but she greeted him affably.

'Philip, how pleasant to see you. I hear your journey went well?'

'Mrs Humphris.' He bowed slightly, taking her extended hand. 'Your servant, Ma'am. Yes, my expedition went well, though I must report I have been no more successful than any one else in finding a path across the mountains. Botanically speaking though, it was a great success.'

'We will be looking forward to your report when it is published. You do intend to publish?'

'Of course.' He paused, obviously uncomfortable about what he wished to say next. 'Mrs Humphris, I must apologise for my churlish behaviour when last we met.'

'Don't think about it Philip. I have long since dismissed it from my mind. I understand your prejudice, though I was suprised to find it in one so fair minded.'

Philip took a deep breath, fearing the answer to his next question. 'Mrs Humphris, excuse me, but did you convey anything of our conversation to Miss Catchpole?'

'La, Mr Crowley, how could you think so little of me? I would never do anything to hurt Margaret's feelings.'

'Forgive me.' Philip breathed a sigh of relief. 'I should have known. Mrs Humphris, I had time to reflect while I was away and I realised that someone of Miss Catchpole's calibre would not be capable of committing an evil act. I suppose that circumstances could make criminals of us all.'

'That is so Philip. If l, myself, were to be held accountable for some of my actions I might well be found guilty by our present laws.' She smiled as she thought of her conspiracy in Frederick's birth. 'But let us speak of happier things. Let me introduce you to my ward, Frederick.' She indicated the sleeping baby. 'He was a foundling, left on our doorstep. I have taken the responsibility of caring for him and if Dear Humphris agrees when he returns, we will adopt him as our own.'

Isobelle beamed as Philip made suitable comments about the sleeping child. Then he brought the conversation back to the topic closest to his heart.

'Mrs Humphris, do you think I could renew my acquaintance with Miss Catchpole?'

'I'm sure that would be acceptable. If you suggest a time I will consult her and see that she is free.'

'Nothing in my life had prepared me for it, Margaret.' Philip tried to describe what he had seen. 'The mountains, themselves, defy description. It is as if some giant child had picked up the land and twisted and crumpled it until no one crease leads to another. There seems to be no rhyme or reason to the gullies and the hills. Streams run in all directions and there seems no main waterway to follow. But the most frightening thing is the sameness. You enter an area of small and large trees and look around. Nothing is notable. Trees, fallen trunks, an undergrowth of bark and leaves, shadows and dampness. Move on and what do you find? The same trees and shadows. Another place, but the same ghostly scene, a mirror image of the one before, a changeless recurring dream.

'Margaret, I'm not a coward but I must tell you I was terrified that I would take two steps beyond the known, for I am sure I would never have found my way back.'

She listened, enthralled, to Philip's description of his expedition. Her heart beat faster as she looked towards the distant mountains and longed to see for herself what Philip was describing.

'The natives, the black men. Did you encounter any?' she enquired.

'Nary a one, though sometimes I heard them calling to one another in a strange echoing call. I think they were watching me, but made no effort to interfere. They were probably wondering what a strange white man was doing stumbling through their land, making marks on trees and recording things in books. They have no concept of our sciences and I suspect we have no idea of theirs.'

'So you think they do have learning?'

'Not as we know it, written down and taught in schools. But they must have a mine of knowledge to live so successfully in such a hostile place.'

'Oh Philip, I would love to see these places.' Margaret clasped her hands together, her brown eyes shining.

'If only you could ride I could take you to the foothills and back in a day.'

'But I can!' Margaret cried excitedly. 'In fact it is because of my riding ability that I am here. If you can get me a horse I am sure Mrs Humphris will grant me a day's absence.'

Isobelle was only too delighted and a few days later she waved them off on their expedition.

Margaret could hardly contain her excitement. Just to feel the horse moving under her brought back so many memories. She wanted to dig her heels in and give herself over to the wild exhilaration of landscape flying past her and the wind against her face, but she proceeded sedately beside Philip.

They rode up the Parramatta road until it became a track. The air was crisper and the heady aromatic smells of the bush filled her with a feeling of euphoria. Nothing in England had been anything like this. She glanced at Philip as he turned his head and smiled at her. A surge of happiness and gratitude filled her and her face glowed. She was so fond of him, but did she love him?

When they reached the foothills they dismounted near a grassy bank, tethered the horses, and wandered into the bush. Philip took on the role of teacher, explaining the different flora in the area. Margaret could have wandered forever but Philip was careful not to stray too far. Margaret had packed a picnic lunch and they eventually returned to the grove beside a trickling stream and ate, hardly speaking, soaking up the silence, which was broken periodically by the flutter of wings and the screech of parrots as they flitted in and out among the trees.

Philip turned to her. 'Margaret, I must speak with you. Every moment I was in the forest you were with me. I spoke to you in my mind, sometimes out loud. I wanted you to see what I was seeing, feel what I was feeling.'

He sat upright and took her hand. 'Margaret, I love you and I want you to be my wife.'

She drew in a deep breath. In part she had expected this declaration but still it was a surprise. She thought she knew what she would say, but still she hesitated.

'Philip, you do me a great honour and I cannot deny I have feelings for you, but before I give my answer there are things that must be said. First, you must know that I have already loved another man, that I regard our union as a marriage, even though it was not official. He is now dead, but will always be first in my heart.'

Philip felt a moment's jealousy. He wanted to be her only love. But he was realistic. 'I never expected that such a wonderful woman as you would have lived without love, Margaret, and I would never wish to replace him in your heart. AII I ask is that you make room for me too.'

'You also realise that I am a convict,' Margaret continued. 'You may love me, but could you love me enough to bear the shame of a convict wife?'

'My dearest, I do not care about your past. I know you for what you are, decent and caring, and I would be proud to have you by my side. I would not want to associate with anyone who would not accept you.'

Margaret persisted. 'I believe you would stand by me in this country but what about in England? I am quite well known there. Would you be willing to introduce your convict wife to your friends, to your family?'

Margaret saw the shadow of doubt in his eyes as he struggled with this new possibility. She reached up and touched his cheek.

'Don't say anything now. Your pause tells me that you have doubts. I once lost my dearest friend when he declared his love for me. I do not want that to happen again. Let us just remain loving friends for now. When you can accept me without any doubt, ask me again, but do not abandon me. '

To break the tension she rose, ran to her horse and, mounting it, turned its head towards the track, dug in her heels and gave herself over wholly to the glory of speed. Five minutes later she pulled up, turned the horse around, and trotted sedately back to Philip who stood where she had left him.

He was surprised and filled with admiration at her horsemanship. 'I see I need not have worried about whether you could handle a horse.'

'How foolish of you,' she laughed. 'Didn't you know I was

sent to Australia for horse stealing?'

When Margaret arrived back at the orphanage she was summoned to Mrs Humphris' sitting room.

'Do tell me Margaret, how did your day go?' The lady asked, her eyes sparkling with expectation.

'It was a lovely day Mrs Humphris. Thank you so much for permitting me to go. I never realised the variety of trees in the forest. They all look alike from this distance, and the ferns in the gullies . . . '

'Yes. Yes,' interrupted an impatient Isobelle, 'but did anything special happen?

'Oh! Mrs Humphris, yes. I have not ridden a horse for five years. I thought it would no longer hold any great pleasure for me, but as soon as I felt the movement it all came back. I'm afraid I quite forgot myself and went galloping off along the track, rather surprising Mr Crawley, but I couldn't help myself.' Her eyes shone as she relived the experience.

'La, Margaret, I had hoped you would have more exciting news than that.' The deflated expression on Isobelle's face showed her disappointment, but then she brightened again.

'Well, I have exciting news. While you were away our Dear Benefactor called. He complimented me on your cakes and was captivated with Darling Frederick, but most of all,' and here she clapped her hands and clutched them to her breast, 'he had an invitation for me to attend a special dinner at Government House to be held for Mr Bass who has lately returned with pigs from the Friendly Islands. He is an interesting man and a great explorer. I'm sure the conversation will be instructive. It has been so sad that I cannot attend official functions while Dear Humphris is away. I haven't dined at Government House for eighteen months. But John would be a suitable partner as he is such a close friend of Humphris. He is calling for me shortly, so you must help me choose a suitable dress.'

Margaret would much sooner have retired to her room as she was beginning to feel weary from her day out, but she tried to join in with Isobelle's enthusiasm. She felt much sympathy for her mistress who so sorely missed the excitement of a social life. How willingly women sacrifice themselves for the sake of their husband's careers, Margaret thought, as she watched Isobelle taking one dress, then another, holding it up and asking for an opinion.

After helping her mistress, Margaret willingly accepted Pearl's offer to supervise the serving of the evening meal. She made a quick ablution then sank gratefully into her mattress. She was surprised to find she no longer had the supple bones of youth and knew that, come tomorrow, she would be stiff from her ride.

Because of her weariness she missed seeing John Ingham as he escorted a radiant Isobelle to his carriage.

CHAPTER SEVEN

1803 brought many changes to the Girl's Asylum, first among them being the return of 'Dear Humphris', loyal servant of the crown and husband of Isobelle. He had been absent for almost eighteen months on business for Governor King. His presence, as the only male in a female establishment, seemed to have an affect on everyone.

The girls became more respectful, Mrs Weatherstone deferred to the 'Master' as she had never done to the Mistress. Even Pearl made every effort to encounter him at every turn.

'It's not that I actually fancy 'im,' she explained to Margaret. 'It's just that it's been so long since I've seen a real man, apart from Jimmy and his Dad. I just want ta' see if I'm still attractive.'

But his greatest effect was on Mrs Humphris. Margaret could not believe that a woman, whom she had grown to respect, could so quickly become a twittering, witless maid, hanging on his every word, her moods adjusting to his slightest whim.

What was it about men, she mused, that makes women submerge their own ability to please their husbands? Margaret thought about the mistresses she had worked under. Only her beloved Mistress, Mrs Cobbold, had been a person in her own right, rather than as the wife of some man. Margaret felt annoyed with Isobelle that she had, so quickly, reverted to the role of the 'little wife'. Was this the real woman or was she just playing a role to please her husband?

One thing that did please Margaret was Gregory's ready acceptance of little Frederick. Whether to please his wife or out of a desire to have an heir, he made no objection to the adoption and seemed to enjoy the child during the little free time he had when he was not engaged on government business.

Isobelle, much to her delight, was now a frequent visitor to

Government House, for informal dinners as well as for grand occasions. Gregory Humphris, a long time friend of Governor King, was shocked at the deterioration he found in his friend.

King, who had come to the office with such high hopes, was being sucked into the same vortex that had swallowed Hunter. Most of the officers of the New South Wales Coup and the wealthy landowners, saw him as an impediment to their growing wealth. He had taken measures to curb the monopoly they held on food and liquor and had limited the number of convicts they could employ. They could draw supplies from the Government Stores for two convicts only. The rest they would have to provide for themselves.

The Governor had known that he would face opposition and had been prepared for confrontation, but it was the passive insubordination and rumour campaigns that undermined his confidence. Derogatory verses, lampooning him, were passed around and often appeared mysteriously among his papers. King was a proud man and such diatribes drove him into a frenzy. But there was nothing he could do about them. He did not know who was responsible and complaining only drew attention to them and made him appear foolish. He began to suspect the most innocent of remarks.

The colony was also being swamped with Irish convicts, many of them arriving without papers to explain their crime or sentence. Some had never faced a trial at all. Others, sent out for political crimes, were educated men who had to be released into the community. King suspected them of continuing the fight against Britain in the colony.

The Governor became fearful as rumours of rebellion spread. Besieged on all sides, he leant heavily on the few he felt he could trust, so it was not long before Humphris was again travelling on government business trying to build up a dossier on these troublesome people

The comings and goings of the Master had implications for the inhabitants of the Orphanage. Margaret had to adjust to the two sides of Isobelle's nature, the one when she was the willing vassal of her lord and master, the other when she resumed the role of Mistress of the Orphanage.

With Gracy busy with baby Frederick, Margaret began to take a greater interest in Pearl. She had turned fifteen, which meant she had only one more year at the Orphanage. The effect of her good behaviour during her friend's pregnancy had turned a rebellious child into a competent young woman. She had become an excellent cook and found that she liked the work. Margaret was proud of her and was sorry that she would soon have to leave. She worried how Pearl would keep out of trouble in the outside world and tried to equip her for future employment.

'Pearl, you must realise that, as a well-trained housekeeper, you will be a prize in any establishment. If you can only curb your wilfulness you will get good employment, and with your entitlement you will be a good catch for any man. Don't sell yourself short. You are a valuable asset to the community.'

Pearl pulled a face. 'Me, a asset, who'd a thought?' Though she had made a joke of it, Margaret knew she had taken the words to heart.

One afternoon, just before they began preparations for the evening meal, they sat together having a cup of tea. Pearl gave Margaret a quizzical look.

'Some times, Cookie, I dunno if you're a convict or a lady.'

Margaret laughed, surprised and delighted at the remark. 'Why on earth do you say that?'

'Well. ya always dress neat, ya don't drink or swear and ya talk real swell.'

'Do you really think so?' Margaret was flattered. She thought for a moment, then said. 'When I was your age, Pearl, I had a Suffolk accent so thick you could spread it on bread. It was working in the houses of good gentlewomen that changed me. I was nursemaid to some of their children and spent time in the schoolroom with them. Some of it must have rubbed off. But most of all I wanted to be like my mistresses, especially Mistress Cobbold. She was the greatest lady I have ever known and she took an interest in all her servants. If it had not been for her I could not have endured the disgrace of my imprisonment and, if I had only trusted her, a good man would still be alive and I would never have come to this place.'

The memory of all that might have been overwhelmed her and she was close to tears.

Pearl had never seen her lose her composure and strove to cheer her up. 'Never mind, Cookie. If ya hadn't a come 'ere I'd never 'av met ya and I'd be as wild as I used ta be. I certainly wouldn't 'ave lasted this long.'

She stood up and gave Margaret a little hug. 'When I grow up I'm gunna be just like you.'

To cover her embarrassment she began cleaning up the big table ready to spread out the bread for making sandwiches, but Margaret sat awhile, thinking of what the girl said. Could she really pass herself off as a lady? Here maybe, but in England, never. The name Margaret Catchpole was too well known. Even if she changed it some one was sure to find it out eventually. Her exploits, much exaggerated, had reached even this corner of the globe. Her father had said that people forgot when some new piece of scandal happened, but not with her.

And how could she live in England and not see her family and friends? If only she had been just Mary Jones no one would bother about her, but she was too well known to slip into oblivion.

In April, Philip Crawley came to see Margaret before setting out on his second expedition. He was excited about returning to the mountains, which held such fascination for him.

'I will be able to achieve so much more this time. Margaret. Much of the equipment I took last time was unnecessary. I will be able to travel lighter and should be able to find my old marks, which will speed my progress. It will all be much more familiar to me this time. I am accustomed to the strangeness of the land now; the nights so still that you can hear a leaf drop, as if the earth were holding its breath, the stars so close that you feel you could reach out and pluck one from the sky.

'Morning is heralded by the most amazing laughter from the kingfisher. You should hear it Margaret. If I had not seen and heard it for myself I would not have believed that such a noise could come from a bird. It's as if he has a private joke but has no intention of sharing it. Then the sun comes out so brightly. You can feel its heat on your skin, even that early, and the lorikeets, so brilliantly coloured, flash through the trees screeching and squabbling.

'Night and day, so different they could be from two different planets; one soft and warm and intimate, the other harsh and dry and remote; and the smells from the trees and the undergrowth so strong and heady you could lose your mind to them. People are starting to call it the 'bush', and that is what it is, for it is no English wood.'

'You speak in riddles, Philip. One minute you seem to love it, then the next you are repelled.'

'That's true, but I wouldn't say repelled, rather bewitched. The more I fear it, the more it attracts me. It challenges me and I feel it is changing me. I do not know who I will become but I do know that I will no longer be the conceited, elitist person I was. I know now that England is not the crown jewel of God's creation, and that all she stands for must not be accepted without question. When I return, I will ask my question again and this time there will be no reason for you to hesitate.'

Margaret resolved, in her heart, that when the time came her answer would be yes.

Philip Crawley began his second expedition at the beginning of September. The first days were easy as he followed his earlier marks, avoiding the detours that had wasted so much of his time before. Soon he reached the extremity of his earlier journey and a heightened sense of expectation began. He now had another reason to succeed in his endeavours. Whatever he found would be offered to Margaret as a betrothal gift and should he, by some chance, discover a route over the mountains, then his triumph would be for her.

He loved the darkness, silent except for the occasional scuffle of night creatures. This was the time he spent with Margaret, talking to her about the day just gone, hearing her voice in the soft night wind, forming her shape from a nearby shrub until the outline was disturbed by a breeze.

By day he struggled up narrow gorges and tramped through flowing streams. Showers often caught him without shelter, but they no longer worried him. His clothes were constantly wet from rain or fevered sweat but he hardly noticed as he struggled along, proudly showing all the wonders he was discovering to Margaret who now walked beside him, speaking words of love and encouragement to him. Soon she ran ahead of him, calling him on and on into the wild places.

Philip Crawley did not return.

After some time the authorities sent out a search party. His markings were easy to follow, but then it was as if they disappeared. An extensive search yielded no clues. Neither Philip, nor his body, was ever found.

Margaret's grief for the loss of her second love was different to the desolation she had felt when Will died. Unlike the first death, Margaret had no sense of guilt. Philip chose to go on the expedition. He was doing the thing he loved best. She remembered his fascination for the wild interior.

'He must have finally answered the call of the bush.' she told Pearl. 'I only hope his going was peaceful. I would not like to think of him lying somewhere injured and unable to get help.'

Margaret became quieter, more thoughtful, as she carried on her duties as diligently as ever. Twice she had had the choice of marriage; twice she had delayed it. She was sure now that she would never marry. She would spend her life single, depending on herself alone for survival.

In September, while Gregory Humphris was away on government business in the newly founded colony of Van Diemans Land, Isobelle received a message from Richmond that her sister was dying. She had been suffering from consumption for some time and there was now no hope for her. Her husband,

Samuel Platt, wrote, begging Isobelle to come and spend time with her before the end.

Isobelle did not hesitate. She knew that Mrs Weatherstone was more than capable of taking over the day to day running of the orphanage and that Margaret could be relied on to care for the feeding of the girls. Her only regret was that she could not take Frederick with her, but she would not expose him to any infection. However, she knew he would be well cared for by Gracy.

The day before she left Pearl approached her. 'Please Mrs Humphris, take me wif ya.' I'd be ever so useful. I can do anythin' in a'ouse as well as cook. Please take me.'

'I don't think that would be a good idea, Pearl,' Mrs Humphris reasoned.

'Ya' gotta' take me Misses. I've tried that 'ard to be good for Gracy's sake but Mrs Weatherstone 'ates me. She's got it in for me proper and I know I'll do somefing I shouldn't if she's in charge. I'll blow me chances, I know. I promise I'll be ever so good and useful too. You'll see.'

Mrs Humphris consulted Margaret who assured her that she could manage. She thought it a good idea, as she knew how hard the girl had tried to stay out of trouble.

The party was farewelled by the staff and all the girls. As soon as they were out of sight Mrs Weatherstone turned to Margaret. 'I will have the keys to the storeroom.' She held out her hand.

'Why?' enquired a bewildered Margaret.

'It is inappropriate for the keys to the store room to be in the hands of a convict.' The tone was reasonable but the triumphant gleam in her eyes told Margaret that a very different Mistress was now in command.

'Of course,' she replied, unbuckling her belt to release the key which hung from it.

The Orphanage became an unhappy place. The girls were subdued but sullen, taking any opportunity they could to sabotage the draconian discipline imposed. Corporal punishment was handed out by Mrs Weatherstone for trifling misdemeanours and deprivation of meals and humiliations became commonplace

The Reverend Marsden and his long puritanical sermons became a regular feature of the institution. Little attention was given the to girls' formal education as they were drilled in the practical skills that would equip them to be servants of the rich or useful wives for the poor.

They were reminded, almost daily, of their inferior state. Though the storeroom was well stocked and the season had been good, rations were cut back to a bare minimum. Breakfast consisted of a thin porridge and the evening meal was two slices of bread and dripping. Even jams, made from the orchard's harvest, were forbidden. The midday meal, the main one for the day, consisted of a watery soup or stew. Apart from potatoes, the rest of the garden vegetables had run out but Mrs Weatherstone refused to buy any of the produce from the Hawkesbury.

'Potatoes will see them through until the new season,' she reasoned. 'The Irish live on them and I don't see them dying out.'

Two sheep a week was all the meat allowed. To eke out so little to provide sustenance for sixty or so people took all Margaret's ingenuity. She knew that the girls would not starve, that there were probably many worse off than them, but they were used to good wholesome food and there seemed to be no reason for this stringent economy.

Meanwhile, Mrs Weatherstone herself ate as before. In fact, she indulged in little delicacies, particularly when entertaining her good friend, the Reverend. She ordered the cook to prepare these dishes, often spending time in the kitchen supervising. Her invasion of Margaret's domain was obviously meant to antagonize her, but there was no reaction. Margaret quickly realised that the woman, envious of her special relationship with Mrs Humphris, was setting traps, hoping she would violate some rule so that she could be reported and, hopefully, removed from her position.

Being aware of the game afoot, Margaret began to find amusement in bypassing these snares. She took some pride in playing her part of docility and subservience, being careful not to retaliate. The Margaret of old would have revolted against such treatment but life had taught her wisdom. She would carry out her duties, knowing that Isobelle was relying on her.

Her heart went out to the girls so suddenly thrown into this new conflict. They became listless and servile. The atmosphere of camaraderie that had existed in the establishment gave way to a grovelling toadyism. The survival instinct was strong in these young creatures and if it was at the expense of others, so be it. Margaret often wished that she could intervene when unjust punishment was handed out, but she was fighting for her survival too, so she held her peace. It was not as if it would go on forever and she was determined to still be there when her mistress returned.

The only person that Mrs Weatherstone had no power over was Gracy who, quickly realising her privileged position, made the most of it. She was needed for Frederick's well being, and even Mrs Weatherstone had neither the desire nor the courage to jeopardize his welfare.

The girl was Margaret's solace. She was free, at any time, to enter the kitchen and spend as long as she liked talking to Margaret and keeping her abreast of all the happenings in the rest of the house.

'It's a absolute disgrace, Cookie, the way she's behavin'. Lady of the Manor, she finks 'erself. It's a wonder she ain't moved into Mrs Humphris' rooms. She would, only she's scared that Mr H might turn up unexpected.

'It's the poor kids I feel sorry for. They're scared t' open their mouths for fear of a beltin'. I have t'keep well away otherwise I'd give 'er the back of me tongue and then, Frederick or no Frederick she'd find a way t'git rid of me.'

The change in the girl buoyed Margaret's spirits and reinforced her belief that her presence was needed here to give the girls a sense that they could contribute usefully to the life in the colony.

'I'm that glad that Pearl went wif Mrs Humphris. I reckon she would 'ave killed 'old Weatherstone by now and been 'appy t'swing for it,' Gracy confided to Margaret. 'I'm that glad I 'ad Frederick otherways I'd 'ave gorn by now too.'

Isobelle Humphris was impatient to return home. Her sister had lingered for a month and her passing had been a tragic affair. Samuel Platt and all six children stood around the bed sobbing as their mother struggled for her final breaths.

Isobelle's grief was tempered by anger as she looked at the young brood. Six children in ten years would have put a strain on any woman, but to one as delicate as her sister, it was a death sentence. She was sure that, had there been fewer children, her sister would have lived longer to enjoy them.

Isobelle looked at Samuel, bereft in his grief. Only good manners stopped her from accusing him of being responsible for her sister's death.

With the help of Pearl, she had managed the establishment, remaining for another fortnight after her sister's death, but she was determined to return to Sydney as soon as possible. She was missing the inhabitants of the orphanage, particularly Frederick. She longed for the gossip and social intercourse of the town, but most of all she knew that Dear Humphris would be returning soon. She was determined to be there when he arrived. She had been so brave, holding the household together throughout the final illness and death when everyone around her was falling apart. The household had been poorly run for some time. With no mistress to take control, the servants, convicts all, had done the minimum required, usually for their own convenience. They had resented Isobelle's interference but quickly realised that she was made of sterner stuff than her sister.

Though his wife had been seriously ill for more than a year, Samuel did not seem to have come to terms with the fact that she was dying. It was as if he believed that some merciful angel would come to save her at the last minute. He had made no plans for the inevitable. Isobelle shuddered at the thought of what would have happened if she had not been there to bring some normality to their lives.

But now she was tired. She longed to rest her head on Humphris manly chest, be enveloped in his capable arms and have all responsibility taken from her. She longed to make no decision more important than what dress to wear.

Pearl had been her one consolation. The girl had proved to be invaluable in the kitchen as well as possessing a natural ability with the younger children. Isobelle sounded her out about continuing in her brother-in-law's employ but Pearl was honest in her refusal.

'It'd be no good Mrs Humphris. I'd go crazy in this place in a week. It's aright wif you 'ere but I'm that lonely for the sounds of Sydney. I can't stand the silence here, and when there's noise, it's them birds. cawin' away in the trees. The sound of 'em drives me crazy, same as the lot what works 'ere. They drive me crazy too. They're that igorant. All they do is argue and gossip. I'd run away if ya left me. I wouldn't be able t'help meself.'

Isobelle looked at Pearl and marvelled at the change the time at the Orphanage had made to the girl. Whenever she doubted the wisdom of that establishment she had only to look at Pearl to know they were doing good work. Though the girl had lost none of her rebellious spirit she had learnt to channel it for her advancement. She realised that the girl was speaking the truth. Wherever her release was to come from, it was not from Pearl.

So she turned to her brother-in-law. 'Samuel, you can't look after the children by yourself. I can take the four girls back with me and you can get someone to look after the boys. They should be getting regular tuition. They are growing up as ignorant as savages.'

But Samuel was not ready to part with any of his children. 'I can't let them go yet, Isobelle. Not so soon after parting from their mother. Their little faces remind me of her and bring me comfort. Give me more time, Isobelle. For love of your sister, give me time. I made a promise to her that I would not split up the family. I can't break that promise so soon. Please stay a little longer.'

Isobelle felt like stamping her foot at him. She retired to her room to contemplate her future. She was not going to be blackmailed into staying, but how could she leave him and the children. They needed someone strong and reliable to take control. Someone kind, but sensible. Someone like . . . of course; someone like Margaret Catchpole!

Who would be more suitable? Margaret was capable and wise. Morally she was above reproach and she had serenity about her that Isobelle envied. Her cooking skills were excellent and she was kindly but firm with children. The more she thought about it the better the idea seemed. Pearl had proved that she had become an able pupil. She would be able to take over the kitchen at the Orphanage. That would surely please the Reverend Marsden. Margaret would also be able to take over the work of educating the younger children, something that had been neglected of late.

She could hardly wait to put her plan into action.

'Samuel, I have in my employ a convict, one Margaret Catchpole. She is indeed an exceptional woman. Not only is she the best cook in Sydney Town, she is also a steady, reliable person whose advice I have always found to be sound. La, I don't know how I can part with her. It is only for love of my dear, dead sister that I make the sacrifice.

'Do not take her convict status into account, Samuel. Treat her with the respect to which she is entitled and you will have the most loyal of servants.

'Now you must also do something about the education of your children. Margaret will be able to take care of the little ones as well as her other duties, but you must employ someone for the older children. They have reached the age where they need a full time tutor, not the haphazard learning you have been able to give them. Joseph, in particular, will soon have to be sent home for a proper education suitable to his state. You have a fine property here and one day he will take his place among the first in this society. He must be trained for the job. I will find a suitable person for you as soon as I get back to Sydney.

'My Darling Humphris will be home shortly and I am sure he will be able to find someone with the right credentials. Dear Samuel, please forgive my blunt speech, but you must know that

I have your best interests at heart, as well as that of the children. I will leave immediately so that I can put my plans into place.

'Take heart, dear brother. She will never be able to replace my sister, but Margaret will make your house a happier place for all who live in it. She is a treasure, Samuel. Accept her as the greatest gift that I can give.'

CHAPTER EIGHT

Margaret was hurt that she had been handed over to another master without consultation. She knew that there was no malice in Isobelle's action, in fact the trust placed in her was a compliment. Nevertheless, it confirmed her opinion that, among the ruling class, little thought was given to the feelings of the lower order. It strengthened her desire to be in control of her own life.

Waterview itself, while not as grand as the Orphanage was a pleasant enough, wooden house of eight rooms with a wide veranda on three sides. There were several outbuildings including a large kitchen and storeroom. The house had been well designed but an overall neglect gave it an untidy, unloved appearance. A once pretty cottage garden was now overgrown and full of weeds. There had been an attempt at painting but the work had not been finished.

The children, ranging in age from fourteen to three, seemed similarly dispirited and Margaret's motherly feelings were aroused, especially for the three youngest. They were handsome children but lacked the sparkle usually found in the young. They seemed to wait patiently for whatever fate had in store for them, asking few questions. The two eldest, both boys, seemed to dominate their sisters, but, apart from riding their horses, did little else to fill their days. Samuel Platt was a devoted father but, still grieving for his wife, seemed unaware of his children's needs. He spent much of his time alone in his study or riding around the property.

The household staff consisted of three convict women and a ticket-of-leave man, Peter, whose job could be loosely described as handy man. There were several men, all convicts, who worked on the property and were housed elsewhere. They had no contact with the house. An overseer who reported once a day to Mr Platt conveyed instructions. He seemed to be worried about something called smut, which was affecting the growing wheat crop.

This was the only topic that seemed to rouse Samuel Platt from his despondency. The little energy he could spare from his grieving seemed to be spent worrying about what would happen to the harvest. He had none left for his children or for the order in his household.

Margaret quickly realised that if anything were to be done it would be up to her. Convict she might be, but she seemed to be the only person capable of co-coordinating the various duties of the house.

Just as she had with Isobelle, she now approached her new employer to give her the necessary power. 'Sir, Mrs Humphris sent me to be of use to you, following your sad loss. As there is no longer a mistress in charge, you need someone to supervise all the duties needed for the smooth running of the house. You already have a Cook so I see no reason to take over her duties. It would only make her resentful. If you will appoint me as House Keeper, I will be able to see that the food is well prepared and served. At the same time I can carry out other duties.'

'Do as you like Miss Catchpole. My sister-in-law places great store by you so I'm sure you know what you are doing. '

'But I will need your help,' Margaret persisted. 'I am the outsider. You must give me the authority I need, yourself.'

Samuel would have preferred to have been left to his reverie but Margaret's steady gaze made him realise that he would get no peace until he complied with her wishes. He called the household staff together.

'As you all know, my sister, Mrs Humphris, has sent her servant to help us in our hour of need. Miss Catchpole will be my House Keeper and you must follow her orders as you would my own.'

Armed with this authority, Margaret began to organise the

running of the house. She got Molly, the cook onside by complimenting her on the few good things she did, and tactfully suggested ways to improve the meals. One of the women was made responsible for general duties in the house while the other was given charge of the laundry. She tried to make each woman feel that hers was the most important role in the house.

Peter was immediately put to work planting a decent vegetable and herb garden and then redeveloping the cottage garden. He, at first took umbrage at being ordered around by a convict when he had his ticket, but complaining to Samuel proved useless and the woman, herself, seemed to know what she was talking about so he decided to comply. Soon he found he was taking pride in his little patch, as he called it. There were initial grumbles by the three women but soon everybody began to appreciate the routine she had brought to the house.

When the house was in order she turned her attention to the education of the children. Isobelle had written to say that Humphris had found a suitable tutor who would join them as soon as his present charge left for England to continue his education there. Once again Margaret sought the authority before she began implementing her plan.

'Mr Platt, could I speak to you about the education of the children?'

'Mrs Humphris has already procured a tutor. I thought I told you that,' replied Samuel, wondering how often this woman was going to disturb him.

'Yes, Sir. But we need a proper classroom. I'm sure you do not want us to use your study. If we covered in one side of the veranda we could have a large room. I could take over the education of the girls at one end and the boy's tutor could work at the other. That way there will be supervision of my charges if I have to be absent performing my other duties.'

Samuel was shocked at the thought of having a schoolroom invading his personal space so was pleased to have the problem solved without interfering with his privacy. The thought of losing his retreat filled him with horror.

'I see no difficulty in that. Talk it over with Peter.'

Margaret set about not only the organising of the veranda, but also the planning of the curriculum she would teach. The three 'R's' of course, though she was worried that her knowledge of accepted spelling was not great, and she also intended including those skills she felt necessary for a colonial wife to know. Sewing would be of the practical kind rather than the decorative, and cooking and the running of a kitchen was another priority.

She was also determined to inculcate in her charges, a love of botany. She planned that her girls would soon be making journals, similar to the ones her charges had made at 'home', but the specimens and information would be those taught to her by Philip Crawley. This activity required walks outside the immediate precincts.

Because their tutor had not yet arrived she included the boys in her walks. She was amazed to find that the girls had hardly left the small area around the house and even the boys were not very adventurous, especially near the river.

'You've got to be careful there, Miss Margaret. The river is a dangerous place.' Joseph, the eldest informed her solemnly.

'But not if you take care, surely.' Margaret remembered how the children at Cliff enjoyed the tributary that had run through their place, but she had not forgotten the tragedy that had nearly befallen Roland Cobbold.

'We was nearly all drowned once,' David explained, reinforcing his brother's warning. 'Leastwise me and Joseph and Annie and Rebecca. The others weren't born then.'

'I was nearly born,' corrected Katherine.

'Whatever happened?' Margaret enquired in surprise.

Joseph, as the eldest, felt it his responsibility to relay the family history. 'It was when we lived in the old house. It had been built near the river so it was easy to get water. But one night the river rose suddenly. There had been almost no rain. It just rose overnight and overflowed its banks. Luckily Father heard the sound of the water and woke us all. We had to grab our bedclothes and run. It was very hard for Mother because she could hardly run for being so big with Katherine.'

'She couldn't help us at all and I nearly got drowned,' David interrupted. 'Father was carrying Annie and helping Mother and I had to do it all by myself even though I was only six.'

Margaret smiled approvingly. 'You must have been very brave.'

'But I saved him.' Joseph wanted recognition too.

'You were all very brave,' Margaret agreed, 'but why did the river rise so suddenly if there was no rain?'

'It's bewitched,' Annie assured her. 'Sometime it's all right and then it just rises.'

'Father says it's because there is rain up in the mountains and it all runs down to the Hawkesbury,' Joseph instructed. 'We keep an eye on the mountains now. We're quite safe. The house is on the highest ground, but you have to watch it for the animals.'

'During the big flood all the food was washed away and most of the animals. We didn't have much to eat after that.' Annie just remembered the event. Most of all she remembered the hunger afterwards. 'Mother used to say that's why Katherine's always sick 'cause she didn't get enough to eat when she was born.'

'But there is plenty of food now, so we'll soon get her well.' Margaret decided to change the subject. It was obvious that they all took a morbid fascination in reliving this momentous event. She had never known them so animated on any subject before. She decided that walks along the river would be out for a while, but when she suggested a walk among the trees she found they were also taboo.

'You're not allowed to walk in the woods. It's too dangerous.' Rebecca assured her.

'Whatever is dangerous in the woods?' Margaret enquired.

'You can get lost in them, of course,' Joseph said in a disdaining manner. Miss Margaret obviously didn't know much about living in the bush.

'And there's run away convicts and Indians,' David assured her. 'You can't go out there.'

Poor frightened little mites Margaret thought. No wonder

they have no adventurous spirit. She was determined to lighten their fears. They would take small walks at first but gradually she would get them used to the world in which they lived. She would teach them how to mark their way in the bush the way that Philip had told her. But Philip had become lost? She would have to be careful. She would make further enquires about escaped convicts and the blacks. She had seen neither in the time she had been there.

The festive season passed quietly, in deference to the recent death, but Margaret marked it with special food, new pinafores for the girls and shirts for the boys. She also made simple rag dolls for the three youngest.

Early in the New Year an incident was to occur that proved that some of the children's fears were well founded. Margaret and the girls were sitting on the veranda when the sound of galloping hooves brought them to their feet.

A red-faced settler dismounted hastily, doffed his cabbage tree hat and demanded, 'Where's Samuel Platt?'

The girls moved closer to Margaret and little Ruth hid in her skirts. 'Mr Platt has gone down to the landing.' Margaret boldly looked the man in the eye, hoping to give confidence to the children. 'I am the housekeeper. May I be of any help?'

'No. Just gather the children, go inside and lock the doors.'

'Why? What is happening?'

'The Croppies are coming.'

'The who?'

'The Croppies, the Irish. They've broken out at Castle Hill and they plan to take over the colony. They're roaming the countryside, pillaging and burning and killing settlers. All the convicts are joining them and some of the small farmers also.

'One army is heading for Sydney and another group is heading for the Hawkesbury. There's so many Irish here they'll join them for sure.'

Margaret was terrified but she tried not to show it. Like most of the English she held a very low regard for the Irish, although the two maids at the Orphanage had seemed quite normal.

'But what can we do? Where can we go?'

'That's up to Mr Platt. The best thing to do is lock yourselves up and hope that the soldiers get here before the rebels.'

Just then the two boys rode up to the house. They had seen the visitor and had come up to see who it was.

'Joseph, do you know where your father is?'

'Yes, Miss Margaret, he's just ridden over to the convict hut. '

'You boys go inside and look after your sisters. I'll go and tell your father,' the man commanded, and, mounting his horse, galloped off in the direction that the boys had pointed.

'What's up?' David's eyes were like saucers.

'Put your horses in the yard and come inside at once,' Margaret instructed. 'We must wait for your father.'

The girls tried to give their brothers a garbled account of what they had heard, but Margaret hustled them into the house. When the children were inside she called everyone together.

'What's happening?' the frightened Cook demanded.

Margaret, remembering that they were also convicts, wondered about their loyalties. How much should she tell them?

'There is an emergency. I don't know much about it but we have been instructed to lock ourselves up in the house and wait for Mr Platt.'

'Is it the natives?' Peter asked. 'Can't be the river. There's been no rain for ages.'

'I reckon I knows what it is,' Doris, one of the women, remarked. 'I reckon it's them Irish. I've heard rumours that they was goin 'to break out. Lot of good it'll do 'em. They'll all be whipped or hung.'

Margaret marvelled that this woman could have known anything about these rumours. Where would she have had a chance to hear about them?

'Well, whatever the emergency, we had best do as we were asked. Peter, put up the shutters on all the windows, Doris, go and get a good supply of wood, Maud fill up all the containers with water. Cook and I will go and get some supplies from the storeroom then see that it is properly locked.'

'What can we do?' Joseph demanded.

'For the present you can take care of your sisters for me. When your father arrives he will tell you what to do.'

Samuel and the overseer arrived about half an hour later. From what Margaret could gather, all the convicts had been rounded up and locked into their long, low hut.

There seemed to be a disagreement between the two men.

'They're happy enough to be gettin' out of work,' the overseer was saying, 'but they know somethin's up, bein' locked up so early in the day. You'll have to giv 'em some sort of explanation, somethin' to distract 'em.'

'Would it be good to give them a special meal?' Margaret suggested.

'Couldn't hurt,' the overseer agreed. 'They're fond of their grub and a variety would help, but you've still got to tell 'em something.'

'Right' Platt agreed. 'You provide the food Miss Catchpole and Brown can take it to them. Tell them that we have heard rumours of an emergency and we've taken them in so that we know they are all safe. We will let them out in plenty of time if there is any real danger. Say we don't know what the trouble is yet.'

'There will be some wild guesses, but I reckon that a few of 'e will have a fair idea. Nobody keeps secrets around here.'

'Why have they been locked up?' Margaret ventured to enquire.

'They are convicts,' Samuel stated, 'and we don't know where their loyalties lie. We can't question every one of them so it is best to lock them all up for now. Can we provide some food quickly, Miss Catchpole?'

'Yes, I could have it all ready within half an hour, as long as they don't mind cold meat.

'Damned if I care whether they mind or not. Get it ready at once.'

While the food was being prepared Samuel and Brown got out guns, checked the ammunition and brought the horses closer to the house in case they would have to make a quick getaway. Margaret knew that there were only five of them and wondered who would be chosen in the event of an evacuation. She had never seen Platt so animated, so decisive. The emergency seemed to have brought out the best in him.

The original alarm had been given about two in the afternoon. They whiled away the afternoon but, by evening, everybody was restless. They had geared themselves up for action but all they had done was sit around and wait. Slowly Samuel seemed to sink back into his habitual lethargy. Nobody knew what was going on in the outside world. Brown suggested that he ride in the direction of Castle Hill and see what he could find out but Samuel forbade him.

'I will need you here if anything happens. I can't be left alone with a houseful of women and children. We must just wait and see.'

They waited all night. It took some time but eventually all the children slept. One by one the servants also succumbed to sleep, only Samuel Platt sat, alone in his study, staring at his wedding photo.

Margaret, rising in the early hours, found him there. He had not moved all night. Was he sad that his wife was not here to share his vigil, Margaret thought, or was he happy that she was not here to be exposed to the danger?

'Would you like some tea, Mr Platt?' she enquired but he shook his head. 'Later.' and returned to his private thoughts.

The night seemed interminable but eventually the early morning light began to filter through the shutters. The children were still sleeping so Margaret roused Cook and they began to prepare breakfast for everybody. She was happy to have something to do.

When she took a pot of tea into the study Brown was there arguing again with Platt.

'We cant keep 'em locked up all day. They don't know what's going on but there'll be plenty of speculation. They're not a bad lot, as convicts go, but if you don't give 'em somethin' to do they'll have too much time to think and then we'll have a rebellion of our own to deal with. Them locks won't hold 'em five minutes if they really want to break out.'

'I don't want them roaming around the property, joining up with the rebels. I want to know where they are all the time.'

'But Mr Platt, we could give 'em work close to the house and keep close supervision on them.'

'Excuse me,' interrupted Margaret, 'there is a deal of work to do close at hand. We could do with wood being cut and you promised some time ago that we could have an enclosed area for a proper vegetable garden. The job's too big for Peter alone.'

'Don't be stupid woman. That would mean arming them with axes and spades!' Samuel was horrified.

'That wouldn't matter if we kept an eye on them and we'd have them all together.' Brown argued.

'But what will we do if they decide to attack us?'

'Then we shoot 'em,' replied Brown in a matter of fact tone. Margaret knew he meant it.

So it was decided. All the women and the children were to remain inside the house while Samuel and Brown patrolled the area with loaded guns. Peter was appointed overseer for the day.

As the day advanced tensions eased. Surely, if the Croppies were coming this way they would have arrived by now. The convicts, still unsure of what was going on, were nevertheless happy with their changed occupation, especially as they were being fed large quantities of good food instead of the fare they usually cooked for themselves.

About three in the afternoon two scarlet clad figures appeared, riding towards the homestead. There was no urgency in their approach. Platt and Brown relaxed for the first time in twenty-four hours. Samuel walked towards the two men as they reined in their horses.

'You have news for us?' he enquired.

'Yes, Sir. The emergency's over. The rebels have been routed. We have captured the leaders. Cunningham has been hung and the rest are being transported to Sydney. About three hundred have already surrendered but some are still hiding out. We'll get them if the blacks don't first.'

'That is indeed great news.' The relief in Samuel's voice expressed his feelings. 'Would you come inside and share a glass to celebrate?'

'Thank you but no, Sir. We have other properties who will be waiting for the news. I would just ask that you keep a sharp look out for a day or two in case any of the escapees should try to steal food.'

The doors were unlocked, the shutters removed from the windows and everybody in the house came out onto the veranda to breath the fresh air, but they were warned not to leave the house.

Margaret was relieved that her first ordeal in the Australian bush was over, and chastened that she had scoffed at the dangers foretold by the children. It was not like Sydney Town and she would treat it with more respect in future. But she was still determined to help the children get over their timidity

By the time the tutor arrived she was quite proud of what she had achieved. The girls were having daily instructions, from little Ruth, who now knew the words to several nursery rhymes and simple prayers, to Annie who could read her primmer and also make damper. Margaret could do little to help the boys with their studies apart from insuring that they join the daily walks, observing and learning.

Soon they were even venturing further afield by themselves on their horses. This worried Margaret a little, but she knew that they would have to take risks if they were going to grow into useful men.

CHAPTER NINE

Dafydd Lloyd, having escaped from the slate quarries of North West Wales by way of education, had a great respect for learning. He was a teacher, not for gain, but to spread the love of learning to the young. He had ambitions to run his own school but, in the meantime, earned his living tutoring colonial sons, sufficiently well for them to be able to take their places in the great learning establishments in England. He was gaining a reputation as an excellent teacher and hoped that soon, with the help of a patron, his dream would become a reality.

His other abiding passion was the equality of all men. He had studied the revolutions in America and France and had attended meetings in England of the London Corresponding Society, where men were striving to gain the rights bequeathed to them in Magna Carta. He was a disciple of Thomas Paine and treated his battered copy of The Rights of Man with the same reverence as he did his John Wesley's English New Testament.

Samuel Platt, locked away in his study, had no idea of the political beliefs of his tutor, and would have been surprised, if not horrified, by the republican undertones of what Dafydd was teaching his sons.

Margaret, busy with her many duties, at first took little notice of the new tutor. Short, solid and swarthy in appearance he had little to commend him but soon, listening from her end of the veranda, she became enthralled with his history lessons.

Though she had grown up during some of the most momentous times in Europe, she had almost no idea of what had been going on outside her little corner of England. She had heard about the big events, the conquest of India, the French

Revolution and the dreaded Bonaparte, but had no idea of the causes of these events or the effect they were having on old thinking and old ways. She had never heard of the American War of Independence. If she had thought about it at all she would have believed that America was still an English colony.

Dafydd was a natural storyteller and, with his passion for the subject, even the boys were interested. Margaret found herself distracted from her own work and spent much of her spare time pondering the things she had heard. She longed to discuss them further.

Botany had opened a new world for her. Now her world began to fill with such wonders that she could hardly sleep at night, so active was her brain, thinking of what she had learnt and wanting to find out so much more.

At last she found a reason to speak with Dafydd. 'Mr Lloyd, I could not help overhearing your lesson today. You seemed to approve of those terrible French executing their King and Queen.'

'No, Miss Catchpole, you misunderstand me. The guillotining of Their Majesties and so many others is a black mark on what was a glorious revolution. Yet one who studies the facts can understand the passion of hate that overwhelmed the peasants. They were human beings, not animals, but they were being treated as if the sole reason for their existence was to serve wicked men who thought no more of them than they did of flies.'

'But surely, Mr Lloyd, it is the job of a servant to serve his master?'

'But the servant has rights too? Is he not owed the dignity of his manhood?'

'Of course.'

'And what gives one person the right to be master over another just by accident of birth?'

'Mr Lloyd, I find your questions disconcerting.'

'As well you might, Miss Catchpole. As well you might. Men have given their lives for the pursuit of such thoughts. But the desire for freedom is so strong that they will gladly suffer death to obtain it.'

'And women too.'

'Yes, women too. History recounts the struggles of men, but of course women have struggled beside them, though their struggle is seldom recorded.' He smiled. He had seen the excitement in her eyes. He recognised another disciple. Here was yet another mind he could open to the world.

Another time she asked his opinion on the recent uprising of the Irish convicts that had occurred before he came.

'Surely you do not approve of their actions. They were out to murder us all in our beds.'

'Why do you think they had planned to do that?' Dafydd enquired.

'Why, everybody knows. Everybody says ... '

'Ah! The famous everybody. And did everybody tell you that, apart from one revenge killing, no lives were taken? That instead of the mayhem reported there were few properties destroyed? Most of what you heard was racist rumour. All they wanted was a chance to return to Ireland. Many of them are political prisoners, transported here for protesting about English rule at home.'

'But Ireland belongs to England.'

'Why?'

'Because,' Margaret stopped. She could guess where the discussion was going.

'Like Scotland and my own unfortunate country Wales, England has conquered and plundered Ireland for its own ends. The people have no say in their own government. You would think that Britannia should have learnt from her American colonies, but no, she goes around the world subjugating countries for her own profit without thought for the people in them. Mark my words, freedom will not be denied, and one day all these peoples will rise up and throw off the imperial yoke, and where will all that English wealth be then?'

'Mr Lloyd, your words fill me with confusion. I have been proud to be part of the British Empire and yet I can see that there is much to be said against it.'

'It is not just the English, Margaret. It is the inequality between the wealthy and the common people. Owning land and wealth does not give one the right to own the body, nay the very soul, of another.'

Margaret had no answer to this. She knew that what he said was right but still she wondered what kind of world it would be if the things he hinted at came to pass.

From such discussions they soon became good friends. Often, after the children were asleep they would sit on the veranda, Margaret with her sewing and Dafydd smoking his pipe, and discuss the books he lent her to feed her growing curiosity. He would explain difficult passages, seeking her opinion on the views expressed by the author.

Such a respect did Margaret have for the written word, that she had never thought to question it. To find that two prominent scholars could hold differing philosophies was a revelation to her.

'Why, they're no different to two old men talking over a pint of ale.'

'And they are nothing more than that,' Dafydd instructed her. 'Everyone has an opinion, but the man to listen to is the one who has studied both sides at first hand and knows what he is talking about. Sometimes there is merit in both opinions, but often the evidence is so strong that any decent person can see the validity of the argument.'

'Then why do things not change?' Margaret asked, perplexed.

'Often because of self-interest, but mostly through ignorance. Unless you know the whole picture it is hard to change a set belief.'

'I know what you mean,' Margaret cried excitedly. 'Before I was imprisoned I thought all prisoners were wicked people. Now I know that most of them are there through misfortune that could happen to anyone. I also know that there are evil people who will never see a prison.'

Their discussions were not always serious or pertinent to world events. They gossiped about their present state and personalities in the colony.

Dafydd held a strong belief that, in this new colony, despite its convict origins, the common man would evolve and create a country free from privilege and prejudice. Margaret, remembering the Orphanage, felt that while there were more Mrs Weatherstones than Mrs Humphrises in the community, things would not change.

Yet Dafydd's vision thrilled her. She began to believe that living in New South Wales might not be such a dreadful punishment after all, if only she were free to live her own life.

She began to plan for life after she had gained her ticket-of-leave. She would not remain at the Orphanage. She most wanted to own her own land, but that would be impossible unless she could gain a full pardon. Convicts were only allowed to lease land from others.

Her thoughts turned to her old neighbour, Bella Cracknell, who had run a little business from her own house. Though it had been the goods she sold in her shop that had helped cause the downfall of the Catchpoles, still the woman had been canny and made a good living to add to her husband's wages. She had seen a need and exploited it. A similar need existed here. Little things like needles and thread, small quantities of tea, sugar and pepper were desperately needed by those who could not afford to buy in large quantities or wait for a ship to come in.

Most of the goods in her wicker basket still lay, unopened, at the Orphanage. They could form the nucleus of her stocks. By now yet another basket could well be waiting for her. She had written regularly to her former Mistress and to her Uncle, giving them a comprehensive picture of life in New South Wales and explaining the difficulty of buying items found everywhere in England.

She was sure that they would supply her with these goods. If her shop prospered she would be able to get a regular supply of such items cheaply and sell them at a profit.

The more she thought about it the more excited she became. What with Dafydd's philosophies of the equality of all men, and her own plans for the future, Margaret felt more alive than she had ever believed possible.

Apart from Katherine, all the children were thriving. Healthier and happier, they became like normal children, sometimes to the annoyance of their father who preferred children to be seen but not heard. But even Samuel would have been happy to see pale, small boned Katherine as jolly as her sisters. She reminded him so much of his dear, dead wife. He feared she had the same delicate constitution. She caught colds easily and often spent days at a time in bed.

Margaret, too, worried about the tiny, wide-eyed child, tried hard to fatten her up and strengthen her bones, but even her skill could not make up for the deprivation she had suffered as a baby. It seemed that her father's premonitions would prove correct.

As the heat of the summer gave way to a mellow autumn, Margaret felt herself being bound more closely to Waterview and the people living there.

She fought against it, particularly the attachment developing between herself and the children. If she were to be in control of her own life she would soon have to leave them. She began to develop a sense of independence and self-reliance in them, particularly Annie.

'You are the eldest girl, Annie, and you must take over the role of your dear Mama. I will not always be with you, so you must learn to care for your Papa and your brothers and sisters.'

'But will Papa not find us another mother?' the girl enquired.

'I'm sure he will, but it may take some time. Your sisters will need you, even then, and think what a help you will be to your new Mama if you know how to run a house. One day you too will be a wife and mother. What a treasure you will be to your husband if you can run an efficient household.'

Even as she said these things, Margaret realised the contradiction of what she was saying. She wanted her own freedom yet she was encouraging the girl to dedicate her life to others. Still, it is almost certain that she will marry, Margaret reasoned, and the better equipped she is, the easier will be her life.

Margaret was now firm in her desire to remain single. At thirty years of age she was past the emotional passion of youth. She now believed that no relationship could compensate for the loss of freedom. Her relationship with Dafydd was one of minds, not hearts. She would never have believed that such a relationship could exist between a man and a woman. She felt so comfortable in his presence that she discussed her feelings with him.

'Are you shocked, Mr Lloyd, that I have decided never to give up my independence to marry?'

'It is an unusual decision, Miss Catchpole. Few women would be brave enough to make it. In fact I have known several women who have made less than satisfactory marriages rather than face life as an old maid. But tell me, do you think that wives are so put upon?'

'I'm sure there is a great variety in marriage, and it must have its compensations, but you must admit, Mr Lloyd, that it is a man's right to make the decisions in a family. Why, I doubt there is one free woman in the whole colony who has not come here only because it was her husband's wish, and they will leave when he decides, whether they wish it or not.'

'I believe you are right.' Dafydd paused, drawing on his pipe. 'But tell me honestly, will you not miss the great desire of every woman, to be a mother?'

'Ah, Sir, that is true. It is the one sacrifice I will always regret. But, as you yourself have taught me, one must be prepared to make sacrifices for freedom.'

'Oh, Miss Catchpole,' he laughed. 'You have indeed become an able pupil. I fear I have created a monster. If every woman felt as you do then the human race would cease to exist.'

'Or maybe it might cause men to change their attitude to their wives,' Margaret parried.

'My goodness! I have created a revolutionary.'

'Do not take all the credit, sir. I have a mind of my own.'

'Indeed you have, Miss Catchpole. Indeed you have.

It was with such spirited discussions as these that they spent most of their evenings. Sometimes Samuel Platt left his study and sat with them, even joining in the conversation. He was slowly coming back to life and taking notice of the world around him.

The students had been dismissed to have an hour of play before preparations for the evening meal. Dafydd was busy correcting exercises and preparing for the following day's lessons and Margaret was hurrying towards the kitchen to check that preparations for the evening meal had begun. Samuel stepped out of his study and called to her.

'Miss Catchpole.'

'Yes Sir.' Margaret turned and walked back towards her employer.

'I have decided to marry you and make you mistress of Waterview. You need not trouble yourself to make any preparations. The Reverend Johnson is planning to visit in a few days so then we will be wed.'

Margaret stood stupefied. She shook her head, wondering if her hearing had become defective. Samuel thought it was a negative response.

'I said, you will be mistress of this house.'

Margaret tried to compose herself. 'Mr Platt, I have no intention of marrying at all. But if I was so inclined it would not be because you say so.'

'What do you mean, woman?' Samuel demanded, turning very red.

Margaret smiled to herself. Here was a perfect example of a man assuming his domination over a woman. She drew herself up to her full height.

'I was sent here as servant by your sister-in-law and I am still her responsibility. I would need her consent, should I wish to marry. But I must tell you, sir, that, even if I had the will to marry, which I haven't, I would never accept a proposal couched in such abrupt terms.'

'Damn it, woman,' Samuel exploded, 'I am a man with a man's needs. I have no time for mincing words. You are a convict and I could have taken you to bed and no one would condemn me, but I have taken the honourable course of offering you my name and my property. The children are fond of you and I find you not unpleasant in appearance. Let us hear no more of this maidenly nonsense.'

Margaret could feel the heat rise in her but she was determined not to lose her composure.

'Sir, what you offer me is nothing more than an insult. Convict I may be, but I am not a chattel to be used without consultation. I can no longer stay in this establishment. I will return to my Mistress immediately, and I would add one piece of advice. If you have the desire to take a wife, polish up your courting skills, for no decent woman would countenance such a proposal.'

Margaret went straight to her room and packed her bag. She had been collecting a number of curiosities, seeds of plants, shells, fossils, feathers and mineral rocks, intending to send them back to England. She would have to leave these behind as she intended to go at once and so must make the journey on foot.

She took a tearful farewell of the children and said goodbye to Dafydd.

'I am leaving to pursue my quest for freedom. Thank you, dear friend, for opening up the world to me.'

Dafydd stood at the door, a sad smile in his eyes. 'Go safely, Margaret. I will miss our little talks.'

'We did have had some good times together, didn't we?' she replied, regretfully.

'And may do once again. Keep in touch and when you feel that you are your own person I will come and visit you.' Dafydd took her hand and held it, giving it a squeeze, to offer her strength for her journey.

Margaret, resolute, took a firm grip of her carpetbag and with the setting sun behind her, straightened her back and began her long trek.

A little way down the track she saw the boys' horses peacefully grazing. She stood still watching them, then, picking up a tuft of long grass held out her hand to them. One trotted over and bent to eat her offering. She felt the hot breath and velvet mouth. She patted his nose gently and he responded. They were old friends.

It would be easy to capture such a docile creature. Her journey was long and night was coming on. The temptation was there. Who would ever know that she had taken the animal?

But it would still be stealing, even if she had no intention of keeping the horse, and if she were caught she would lose all hope of ever being free. She gave the nose a parting pat and set off on her long journey.

CHAPTER TEN

'Oh, my Gaud! It's Cookie!' Pearl, who had risen early to prepare breakfast, had answered the early morning bell. She left Margaret on the doorstep and ran down the passage, shouting, 'Mrs Humphris! Mrs Humpris! Come quickly! It's Cookie!'

Her shout aroused everybody in the Orphanage. Girls crept from their beds and peered from the landing. Mrs Weatherstone stood at her door, unwilling to be seen in public with curling rags in her hair, but Gregory Humphris, quickly adjusting the cord of his dressing gown, hurried towards the door.

Margaret was slumped against the wall, wet and exhausted. She had journeyed through the night, fearful of running into convicts or blacks, frightened that she might be arrested for leaving her place of employment and terrified of losing her way. She had stepped off the track to sleep, but a light mist turned into a steady rain, so eventually she began walking again to keep warm. It was only her determination that had kept her going but now that she had reached her destination she could hardly remain upright.

'Go back to your rooms,' Mr Humphris ordered. 'There is nothing to be alarmed about.' Then he led the exhausted Margaret towards his own apartments.

There, seated, with Isobelle's arm comforting her, she told her story.

'Dear Mrs Humphris, do not be angry with me for leaving my position but I could no longer stay. Mr Platt, without any warning, informed me that I was to become his wife. Truly Mistress, I did nothing to encourage him. I have no intention of marrying anyone but, when I informed him of this, he became quite abusive and said things that no decent woman could abide, so I left.'

Isobelle was shocked. 'My dear Margaret, do not fret yourself. I would never have sent you there had I known you were going to be abused. No one is going to punish you. Now you must get out of those wet clothes before you catch a chill.'

But it was already too late. The cold and exhaustion had taken their toll. For several days she ran frighteningly high temperatures and they feared for her life. In her delirium her mind wandered back to the banks of the Orwell, there to be tormented by Robinson Crusoe's demons. Time and again they tried to drag her down into the depths of the river; time and again she was rescued by people from her past, Jonathan Catchpole, Dr Stebbins, Mr Cobbold and a shadowy figure she could not quite place.

In her troubled state she was sure that, could she reach that person, she would be safe. Eventually the fever broke, her mind became calm, and she fell into a peaceful sleep. When she awoke she was smiling. Of course, she thought, now I know who it was, it was my good friend Jack. Of course he would be the one to rescue me.

When Margaret was fully recovered she discovered that the kitchen was running very well without her. She was proud that Pearl had become so competent but worried about her own future in the Orphanage.

'Mrs Humphris, you must be aware that I am no longer needed in the kitchen. It was all right while I was still delicate but now there is not enough work to keep me occupied. With Gracy's assistance, Pearl can run the kitchen without me. What shall be my future?'

'La, Margaret. Do you think that I would part with you again?' Mrs Humphris sounded shocked, but actually she was glad the topic had been raised. Margaret was due for her ticket-of- leave, after which she would need to be paid wages. She knew there would not be enough money in the Government grant to provide for this. The Reverend Marsden would see to that. He guarded the grants as if they were his own money.

'While I was away,' Margaret continued, 'I made a decision

that as soon as I got my ticket I would like to become self-employed. There is a great need for a small village shop among the Hawkesbury farmers. I have a fancy to run such an establishment.'

Isobelle was delighted. 'What a wonderful notion, and how brave you are. I'm sure Humphris will be able to get your ticket-of-leave immediately, and I think he may have just the place for you. He has bought several properties from unfortunates who got themselves into debt during Governor Hunter's time. Among them is a tiny shop with just a little land, at Richmond Hill. Goodness knows what it was used for, making rum I suppose. He has, for some time, wanted to do something with it. He hates waste. I'm sure that, if it is suitable, he will let you have it for a very low rental. Does that sound what you might be after? Also, I have a little money, which I have been putting away for a good cause. You could use that to help you start your business and repay me when you are successful.'

'Dear Mistress,' Margaret's eyes filled with tears. 'You must surely be an angel sent from God to protect me.'

'Oh, tosh,' Isobelle replied, but she was rather flattered by the idea.

It was hard to tell who was the more excited over the next few weeks, Margaret or Isobelle. Gregory Humphris had advanced a small loan, at no interest, and the two women set about buying stock for the enterprise. Along with the contents of her basket Margaret bought essential goods such as salt, sugar, tea, tobacco and matches in larger quantities, to be broken up into small amounts that the poor farmers could afford. She also bought more cloth for she planned to make garments as well as candles and soap.

With a cart loaded high, the Humphries and Margaret left Sydney to set up the shop.

The house had been built on a mound and had a wall, made of logs, all around it. The building was of strange design, one large room and a loft for storage. The front of the room had an earthen floor but at the back two steps gave access to a raised area tiled with slate. There was a large, open fireplace there. Margaret decided that this would be her kitchen and living area. A screen made from plaited reeds would give privacy yet let her supervise the shop in front. She would use half the loft for storage and the rest for a sleeping area.

Rough shelves and a counter were constructed, a small window cut into the front wall and the whole building white-washed. By the time it was ready to open everyone in the district knew that there were small quantities of most essential items to be had at Margaret Catchpole's village shop.

Gregory Humphris gave her some parting advice. 'Margaret, these are good people, on the whole, but some are poor managers. Until you know them well, do not give credit to anyone, and even when you do always try to get something on account. You have a generous spirit but, if you are to succeed, you must be firm, not hard, but firm. Start as you mean to go. State your terms and stick to them.'

Margaret took these words to heart, for she knew they were wise. She tried very hard to live by them.

The inhabitants of the area known as the Hawkesbury, after the river that cut its bed through fertile plains, consisted of some large land holders such as Samuel Platt, but most were poor settlers on small holdings which they worked themselves, usually with the help of one or two convicts. If they were lucky enough to have a wife and children they were added to the work force. They had few tools and all the work was manual.

Some were free settlers, lured by the promise of cheap land. Others were emancipists who, having been granted pardons or served their sentence, had opted to stay and take up land in what had formerly been their prison.

Theirs was a precarious existence, at the mercy of the capricious weather of this alien land. In good years they produced most of the food, to be transported down river, to feed the colony, but drought and flood were ever present enemies and there was nothing they could do to protect themselves. In 1799, without any warning, the river had begun to rise, bursting its banks and flooding the surrounding plains.

Crops, stock and even houses were destroyed. Fortunately, only one life was lost but most settlers, with greater respect for the river, rebuilt their houses further back from its banks.

Most were hard workers, grateful to be given a chance to own land, but few had formerly been farmers so learnt their trade by trial and error. These were Margaret's customers. She learnt to recognize their good points and they, in term, respected her and appreciated the service she was providing. Her shop was popular with the inhabitants of the tiny settlement at Richmond Hill and with the surrounding settlers but the profits were not great. Goods were often paid for in kind.

The pennies had to be put aside to pay back the loan and buy future stock. Still, she had a roof over her head, food to eat and work to keep her occupied. Best of all she was her own mistress. She could rise and retire when she wished, work as little or as hard as it suited her and everything she did was for herself.

Margaret's shop was on the outskirts of Richmond Hill, a small village with storehouses, on the banks of the river. It was convenient for those coming and going, as well as the settlers who lived on the surrounding farms. The variety of her goods was much appreciated, especially by the women, as simple goods such as sewing and knitting needles were hard to come by. One commodity in constant demand was tea. They were happy that they could buy those precious leaves in small quantities as they lacked the funds to buy in bulk from the Government Stores. It was the one item that Margaret would always sell on credit because she knew the comfort it could bring, and it was one debt that she knew her customers would honour. She gained quite a reputation and many called at her shop on the off chance of finding something of interest to them.

At Miss Catchpole's shop it was possible to get much more than produce. Margaret gave advice on cooking, sewing and other household chores. Their lives were such that some of the women had never learnt these skills. Many of the settlers were illiterate so she was often called on to read or write letters. They knew that she was discreet and none of their personal matters would be spoken of afterwards.

She blessed again Mistress Wade who had given her the opportunity to learn to read and write. She deplored the lack of education among the inhabitants of the area.

If this country is ever to progress, she thought, they must do something about providing education for everybody, not just for a privileged few. She began to see how the lower orders were kept in place by their ignorance. She looked at things differently since her eyes had been opened by Dafydd Lloyd.

Women were still a minority in the colony and Margaret, as a capable, single woman, was seen as a prize. She received a number of proposals, some from men who were well on their way to becoming wealthy, but she clung to her single status.

She became the friend and confidant of most of the women in the district. Listening to their stories she felt fortunate that she had the means to support herself and did not feel the need for a male protector. She was never molested, but had acquired a large, cross-breed dog and a musket. She would have defended herself if the need arose, even if it meant punishment for possessing a weapon, seeing she was still a convict.

Her life was such that she often forgot her status but a visit from an official or the periodic need to present herself for muster soon reminded her.

She began to be called on to act as midwife. The women liked her because she was clean, sober and she did not bully them.

One evening, as she was preparing for bed, she heard an urgent pounding on her shutters. She stilled the barking dog then, holding a lamp in one hand and her musket in the other, she went to the front of the shop.

'Who is there?' she called in a tone braver than she felt.

'It's Bert, Miss Catchpole, Bert Cooper. Nancy wants you. Her time has come.'

'But it can't be. She can't be more than six months.'

'Well, I don't know. She says it is. She's raising hell. Told me to come and get you straight away.'

'All right. Give me a minute to put on some clothes.'

She dressed hurriedly, unbarred the door, instructed the dog to stay and guard the shop, and followed Ben into the night. The Cooper's house was about twenty minutes away. The walls were of slab construction, the roof made from bark shingles. Inside, it was sparsely furnished, the two most prominent features being a long table in the middle of the room and a large, hammock style bed against one wall.

Cowering in the corner of the bed was a terrified woman. Margaret turned up the lamp on the table and went to her.

'Nancy, what's the problem, dear?'

'I think the baby's coming, Miss Catchpole. There's blood running down me legs and I've got a terrible pain in my back. I feared I'd bleed to death. Is it the baby?'

As Margaret peered closer she saw three little children, the eldest not yet four shrinking back behind their mother.

'Bert,' she called, 'come and take these children away. Take them outside, or to a neighbour, but take them away from here. And take yourself too. This is no place for a man.'

Turning back to the frightened woman, little more than a child herself, she tried to take away some of the fear.

'Nancy, dear, I think the baby is dead, but now's not the time to grieve. We must remove it to stop the bleeding. If you do as I say it will be all right.'

She stoked up the fire and filled an iron pot hanging over it to produce plenty of hot water, the stand-by for all deliveries. She filled another tin dish and put it outside in case she needed cold water later. Then, exhorting Nancy to be brave, she began to press down on the lower part of Nancy's stomach in a kneading motion. She could feel the tiny sack and worked it gently towards the vagina.

Slowly, with the help of Mother Nature it moved until, with a rush, the tiny creature, complete with its placenta, was expelled in a rush of blood and water. It was perfectly formed but showed no sign of life, for which Margaret was grateful, but she knew that this would not lessen the mother's grieving.

Many paid no heed to premature deliveries, but Margaret

knew that the women often grieved as much for them as for a full term baby.

'See Nancy,' she said softly, showing the dead child to its mother. 'It would have been a little boy, but God has seen fit to take him before his time. Do not mourn him, dear. He would never have survived in this harsh place. Better we concentrate on getting you well so that you can care for your other wee ones.'

Margaret allowed Nancy to hold the tiny form while she went outside to collect the cold water. As yet there had been no contractions. She began to pour cold water on the abdomen. Soon the contractions began and she knew that the danger of haemorrhaging had passed.

She washed Nancy, took off the blood stained covering, dressed the young woman in a clean nightdress and settled her down to sleep. She found an empty cigar box and gently laid the foetus inside.

She went outside to confront the husband who was hovering around near the door.

'Is Nancy all right Miss Catchpole?' he enquired as soon as she appeared.

'For the moment, she is well.'

'And the baby?'

'The child is dead. It would have been a boy. It was too tiny to survive.'

Margaret was angry but she kept her emotions under control. She presented Ben with the box. 'However, it was advanced enough to deserve a proper burial. It will be a consolation to Nancy when she is better.'

'Can I see her?' There was concern in his voice.

'No, she's sleeping now. She will need a good deal of rest in the next two weeks. In the meantime I would like to ask your advice on a matter. You have a reputation for knowing a lot about sheep.'

Bert thought this a strange topic in the circumstances, but he was proud of his reputation. 'They do say that I know more than most.'

'Then you will be the one to advise me. I have a sheep, a very good ewe. She had just lambed. How long must I wait before putting ram on her again?'

'Why, bless me Miss.' The man was embarrassed to be discussing such a topic with an unmarried woman. 'Everyone knows it would be a waste of time until the lamb is weaned. Even then it's best to give her the best part of a year to get back her strength.'

'And yet, Mr Cooper,' Margaret continued, giving full range to her anger, 'you went back to your wife, time and again, before she was fully recovered from her births.'

'Now look here Missus,' Bert was indignant, but Margaret hadn't finished.

'Your eldest child is not yet four and the next two were born within a year of each other. Why your youngest couldn't have been more than three months when this one began. You wouldn't do that to a sheep but you do it to your own wife!'

'But she was still feeding. I thought it would be safe.'

'That's as maybe. You know the only safe way is to abstain.'

'What would an old maid like you know?'

'More than you think.' Her anger had cooled and she began reasoning with him. 'You're a good farmer, Bert. You husband your flock well, but do you husband your wife and children as carefully? If you look after them you will have a healthy wife and strong children. But if you do not husband them well, you will have a weak, even a dead wife, and a string of sickly or motherless children. How old is your wife?'

'About nineteen,' he replied sulkily.

'Then she has many years ahead of her to give you a large family. Only give her time to regain her strength.'

'By God Miss, you've got a cheek, but what you say is probably true. I love my Nancy and it'd break my heart if anything happened to her. Since you claim to be such an authority, how long do you think she needs between bairns?'

'About two years,' she counselled him

'Two years! That's a powerful long time. And what am I supposed to do in the meantime?'

'The same as the ram does.' Margaret smiled, a vision of a

sad old ram, penned up in a little paddock, came to mind. No doubt Bert Cooper, being wiser that the animal would find another way, but at least she had given him some food for thought.

Just before Christmas in 1805 Margaret had a pleasant surprise. Dafydd Lloyd arrived at her shop.

'The cart was coming to Richmond to collect some seed so I hitched a ride. I thought I would come and see how your venture was progressing. Your name has spread to Waterview. Mr Platt deliberately ignores your presence, but the children send their love and would visit you if they were permitted'

'I have longed to hear news of them. I feel that I deserted them. How are they?'

'All, except Kathleen, are well. Annie has proved an apt pupil and runs the establishment as well as a grown woman. Her father is immensely proud of her. I have taken over the education of the girls, as well as the boys so you need not worry that they will grow up ignorant.'

'That news pleases me. Since I have come here I have developed an even greater respect for learning. I wish you could set up a school here.'

'I'm afraid there would not be enough paying customers for me to earn a living at present. But for the future, who knows?'

Dafydd managed to visit her several times over the years. She was always overjoyed to see him, especially if he arrived late in the day for then she could shut her shop and they could have a meal and conversation without interruption.

Of course his presence was noted and caused talk, but she replied, to anyone who bothered to enquire, that they were no more than friends, They would leave, shaking their heads, and Margaret would smile, knowing that they could never understand the relationship between herself and Dafydd. In a way she did not understand it herself but she was grateful for it.

She would always be indebted to him for opening up the world to her. He had made her see things in a different light and he had asked nothing from her in return. They were so comfortable with each other that she was not embarrassed to ask, 'Dafydd, have you no interest in women?'

'Don't be deceived, I find great pleasure in the presence of some women, yourself included, but I do not have any great desire to become intimate with any of them. My passion is for humanity as a whole. There is no room for one individual. I'm afraid any woman would find me an unsatisfactory lover. You perhaps can understand that.'

'But I, at least, have known love.'

'And what makes you think that I have not known it also,' Dafydd replied, drawing on his pipe and gazing into the fire. 'I was not always the zealot you see today.' Then he gave a little laugh. 'Speaking of romance, you will be interested to know that Mr Platt is courting a young lady. He must have taken notice of your parting instruction for he is the most honourable and romantic of suitors.'

'That is great news,' Margaret replied. 'The children need a mother. It would be unfair to saddle Annie with the job of bringing them up. She should be permitted to have a life of her own'

Another time they spoke of the native population. They were less numerous now and Margaret had lost her fear of them.

'They are now much more manageable and a lot less uncivilised than they were. They are disinclined to work, but I am able to obtain the rarest of skins from them. They are fond of sweet things so are happy to trade. Some of them can make themselves well understood in English and I enjoy speaking with them. They brought me a mountain pheasant that I have stuffed and intend sending to my former mistress as soon as I can find a suitable box. It is a magnificent specimen and in very good condition. Let me show it to you.'

As she displayed her treasure she continued. 'They were most amused to find that I was not going to eat it. You will be surprised to know that they hold some common beliefs with you about freedom. They find our way of life strange. They cannot understand why we labour so hard to build and farm when we could roam through the woods finding food where we can.'

'They certainly have an understanding of freedom, but it could never work in a civilised society.'

'Yet Dafydd, much of what they do reminds me of activities you used to speak about to the boys. Remember how you told them about the knights and their tournaments and that sometimes a knight would be killed? Well, what people call their barbaric public fights are just the same. They form a circle and follow a ritual. They have fixed rules and fight as fairly and gallantly as any knight. However they do not show the same chivalry towards their women. Still the women seem to take no pleasure in these displays any way. There are no Fair Maidens cheering on their champions, so perhaps they are the more civilised.'

'I fear for their future,' Dafydd said. 'Their values are so different from ours that I feel they will never be able to find a place in the society we are building here. It is a pity as I am sure they have much to teach us.'

'Philip had a similar belief,' Margaret remembered. 'You have great faith in this land, Dafydd.'

'Oh yes. If only the governor can break the strangle hold of Macarthur and his cronies this will become a land of freedom. I hope I may play my small part in it.'

Margaret sat back, looking at this man burning with passion for his new society. 'You will be willing to spend your life here? For myself, though I am content, my one desire is to walk again the fields of Sussex.'

Thus these two spent many a pleasant evening discussing matters great and small, while poor Governor King, fighting continuing poor health, little by little lost the enthusiasm that had been his in earlier years. He was worn out from the constant undermining of his authority. He had written, time and again, about the abuses of power among the officers of the New South Wales Corp, recommending their removal. But the government at home had more pressing matters to occupy its time, rather than those in a distant colony.

To add to his worries, John Macarthur had returned as a private citizen. He had a commission from Lord Camden to establish a new wool industry and a grant for 10,000 acres of land. Defeated, King begged again to be relieved and was happy when informed that his replacement, Captain William Bligh, would soon be arriving.

The day could not come soon enough for King, but fate had one more crisis for him to cope with before he could hand over to his successor.

1806 had promised to be a good year. There had been good rain towards the end of the preceding year and the summer had not been so fierce. There was plenty of pasture, and crops were ripe for harvest. There had been some rain in February but nothing like the summer storms of 1805.

Away from the worries of Sydney Town, the Hawkesbury farmers were looking forward to a good year. Some had heard rumours from the natives that big floods were coming but few believed them. But at the end of March, just as the Platt children had described, the river swelled. There had been no rain, and the water rose so suddenly that Margaret, like most of the settlers, was taken unawares.

Daylight showed her the extent of the devastation. A muddy, swirling mass of water rushed past her door. She could now appreciate the strange wall that surrounded her shop. It had obviously been built after the 1779 floods. Within her walls she was quite safe, but many were not so lucky. As well as the loss of livestock and grain, seven people were drowned.

The floods brought out the best in the settlers. As soon as people realised they were safe, they set about looking to the safety of others. Margaret, like most of the settlers, shared her house and food with those who had lost everything. There was a wonderful feeling of comradeship among them, coupled with a determination not to be beaten by this strange land. They would suffer, but they would start again, wiser and more resilient than before.

CHAPTER ELEVEN

As a good servant of the Crown, Gregory Humphris accompanied his Governor when he went to survey the disaster caused by the flood. He found time to inspect his own properties. One of these was that of his former servant

'It is good to see you safe and well, Margaret. Isobelle was very worried about you. I see the building stood up well to the flood.'

'Thanks to the levee. Whoever built it knew what he was doing. He must have been a boat builder before he came to the colony.' Margaret laughed. 'My home felt like the ark, with water all around.'

'I must mention the design to the other settlers. They would do well to copy it.' Humphris was inspecting the structure as he spoke. The river had retreated towards its banks. Much of the water had sunk into the ground leaving miles of soggy silt that would, in the coming year, produce a bountiful harvest if only the settlers could get the seed to plant a crop. At present their immediate thoughts were how to find enough grain to stay alive from day to day.

'Do you have enough food, Margaret?' Gregory enquired.

'I have enough flour and potatoes to get by for a while, but I must share them with those who have nothing, so it will not last for long. What will happen to us then, Mr Humphris?'

'The Governor is doing all he can. He has sent the *Tellicherry* to China for rice and the *Sydney* has gone to Calcutta for seed wheat. We need that more than anything. We must start planting as soon as possible.'

'It's all very well for people in Sydney to talk about planting, but what about the farmers here? What are they going to live on in the meantime?'

'There is still food in the Colony', he explained.

'And most of it belongs to the merchants and wealthy land owners who see this,' she spread her arms to indicate the sodden ground, 'not as a disaster, but as a means of acquiring more land.'

Margaret now knew all about the dealings that went on and had such confidence in herself that she thought nothing of stating her opinion in front of a man.

'The farmers have nothing, so they must go into debt. The prices will rise and soon it will be beyond them to pay back that debt, so their land will be sold to cover it. Thus the land-hungry rich grow richer and the poor go to the wall.'

The passion in her voice made Humphris pause. He had bought a number of small farms at rock bottom prices, over the years, but at least he had done nothing to contribute to the situation.

'You have become quite the politician I see.' His tone was patronising but Margaret ignored it.

'I know many people claim that these people are lazy drunkards, and I'll grant there are some that are, but even they are trying, to the best of their ability. When you know what they have been through, and the continuing battles they fight just to survive, you can understand why they prefer to exist in a haze of alcohol.'

'Well, this time at least, they need not go into debt. The Governor is going to let them borrow food and tools from the Government Stores and to pay back later in grain.'

'That will be good news,' she agreed, 'but it won't please Mr Macarthur and the Officers of the Corps.'

Humphris looked anew at this woman, his late servant, present tenant, and still a convict. His wife had maintained that she was an exceptional woman and he was inclined to believe her. Still, he thought, I'm glad Isobelle does not harbour such political ideas.

As Gregory had predicted, Governor King permitted farmers to borrow on the Stores and put a ceiling on the price at which grain could be sold and, as Margaret had predicted, it did not go down well with those who saw themselves as the new aristocrats of New South Wales. If poor Philip King had thought that his final days in the colony would be peaceful he was disappointed. He would be hounded right to the end.

By the time Captain William Bligh took up his position as Governor General of New South Wales, the colony was bubbling like a simmering porridge pot, only waiting for the heat to be raised to cause total eruption. The new Governor was not known for his diplomacy. It would only be a matter of time before a small incident would grow into the insurrection, known as The Rum Rebellion.

Along the Hawkesbury things were getting back to normal. Some farmers had gone under, sold their land and gone back to England or joined the work force where good wages could be obtained for hard work. But many stayed, tougher and wiser. The deep soaking had produced a carpet of green to feed animals and the new harvest promised to be bountiful. One good season and they would be on their feet again. Margaret was proud of these people who would not be denied their independence.

Dafydd remarked, 'They are the type of farmers this country needs. It's no place for the faint hearted. It proves what I have always believed. Back home they would have been defeated because of the hopelessness of their situation but here they feel they have a chance and they are grasping it with both hands. They may have been the dregs of society, but they are men still. Now they see that here is a place for them to run their own lives. Mark my words, one day these common nobodies will make a great nation and they will understand what freedom really means.'

The river returned to its bed, the crops were sown and life got back to normal. The farmers coming into Margaret's shop had a smile on their faces and a spring in their step, especially after a visit from the new Governor to the region.

Bligh was brisk and business-like and he enquired into everything. Stopping at farms along his way he would bombard farmers with questions, criticising their methods and giving advice.

Far from antagonising them, he inspired them. No matter how humble, they knew he was interested in them, he appreciated their struggles, he told them they were the backbone of the colony. He listened to their complaints against the monopolies. They became his staunchest supporters.

When Hunter and King were Governors, Gregory had gone about his work, proud to be their servant but he found William Bligh a hard master to like. Not only was the man a demanding autocrat, his crude shipboard speech and uncontrolled tempers made it impossible to respect the man. He was totally lacking in diplomacy and quickly managed to alienate every person of importance in the colony.

When John Ingham visited the Orphanage he confided his fears to his old friend. 'I don't know where it will end, John. You know I am no friend of Macarthur, especially after the way he treated King, but even I would never antagonize him. When the man first met the Governor and moved the conversation to his dreams for a wool empire, Bligh exploded. 'Sheep Sir? What have I to do with sheep? What this country needs is food, wheat and corn to feed the growing population. Exports, you say. We could grow enough grain here to feed the whole world. That's where the future lies for this country, industrious farmers, not vagabond shepherds wandering the wilderness following sheep. You wish to have flocks Sir, such as no man has ever had before. You already have 50000 acres of the best land in the colony, but by God man I will see that you do not keep them.'

John was appalled. 'Never! And what was Macarthur's reaction?'

'He never said a word. He just stood there, utterly silent. You know, that special silence that he does, his face pale, his eyes piercing the Governor. I tell you it was frightening. The Governor seemed unaware, but we all knew that swords had been drawn and Macarthur will not sheath his until he has the Governor, one way or another.'

'I'm afraid for my future. There will be no way not to be sucked into this vortex unless I can get an appointment away from Sydney. I envy you, your isolation. You can stand aside from all this.'

'Why don't you resign and become a farmer too?' John enquired.' You own several farms.'

'Yes, but they are all small holdings. What I want is a large property, like yours, but I doubt Isobelle could stand the discomfort of developing virgin land and I, myself, have had no experience at it. No, what I need is an established property complete with home and amenities.'

John had greater confidence in Isobelle. 'Don't underestimate your wife. She has run the Orphanage well in spite of much opposition.'

'She quite amazes me,' Gregory confessed. 'Such a scatterbrain and yet she has stood up to the pressure well and I have often not been here to help her. At least she won't have to worry about the Reverend for a while. He has tested the wind and decided to go and convert the Maoris, to get himself out of the crossfire. I wish I could find as good an excuse.'

Gregory decided to pay a visit to his brother-in-law to see how he was recovering from the floods. The family had been quite safe, but his crops and pastures had been inundated. Fences and outbuildings had been washed away and he had lost over one hundred sheep.

He found Samuel in a despondent mood. 'I wish I had never listened to you, Gregory. This is an accursed place. If it's not drought or fire, it's flood. It must be the most cantankerous place in Christendom.'

'But surely, Samuel,' Gregory protested, 'you have done well in this country?'

'That's as maybe. But the place is so unpredictable. It was all an adventure when I first came but now that I am comfortably off, I don't want to gamble it all on the vagrancies of the weather. Also my lady wife finds it very isolated here.'

'Ah, our new sister Amelia is not enamoured with

Waterview? Surely she does not hanker after what passes for society in Sydney?'

'You know what women are,' Samuel confided. 'Poor, sweet Lillian was content with my company and that of the children, but then she was often sick. Amelia is young, healthy and longs for the company of other women of her class. She wants me to buy a house in Sydney for herself and the children, but I wish to have my family around me.'

Gregory decided to change the conversation to happier topics.

'And how are the children? Joseph must be of an age where you will be sending him to England for his education.'

'Yes, that's another thing.' Samuel sighed. 'First it will be Joseph and then David.'

'And the girls too,' Gregory reminded him. 'It won't be long before you will be having to look for suitable husbands for them.'

'I know. It's all so distressing. I don't know how I'll part with them. You're a lucky man, Gregory. Not to have the worry of children. Not that I would willingly part with one of mine, but they are a worry.'

Gregory stayed the night and pleased Amelia with snippets of the latest gossip. In the morning he inspected the property with a more discerning eye. Before he rode away he felt he had planted a seed in his brother-in-law's mind that might be to his own advantage in the future.

Beyond the settlements of Sydney and Parramatta, life ebbed and flowed to the moods of nature rather than those of the Governor. Still his decrees had improved their lot. He had insisted that wages must be paid in cash. This stopped the practice by the officers, of drawing large amounts of goods from the stores then asking common soldiers and settlers to pay for them at inflated prices, or else insisting they take goods that often they did not want. In this way the officers had goods aplenty, to sell to the settlers at anything up to 200% profit. Should the settlers pay in kind, at the inflated rate, the officers could then sell the grain back to the stores, thus making yet more profit on the original transaction.

Most of the settlers welcomed the outlawing of exchange of liquor as payment for labour and goods, and the extension of credit whereby, armed with an order upon the Government Stores, they could receive articles and pay for them at the next harvest at a fixed price. This not only tided them over during the lean months but broke the power of the traders who formerly adjusted prices, often creating a dearth by withholding goods to do so.

Dafydd was one of the Governor's greatest supporters. 'He's just what the country needs. He has no regard for the Exclusives who would have him treat them as aristocracy.'

'But they say he has a very bad temper and uses such dreadful language, no better than the convicts.' Margaret was puzzled by the things she had heard.

'A good deal worse,' Dafydd laughed, 'but you must realise that he is used to commanding a ship, where many of the men were the scum of England. He spoke to them in a language they could understand. '

'They say he was very cruel.'

'Maybe, but he is just. He sees the whole colony of New South Wales as his ship that he must steer through the seas of famine and isolation. He has a vison for this colony, a diligent band of small farmers working in harmony to become the breadbasket for the motherland, hard working, contented, and easy to control. He has no time for big estates. Vast tracts of land, stocked with thousands of sheep and a few itinerant shepherds, is not his idea of a well run colony. They are too hard to govern. A few individuals can become so powerful that they can even threaten a governor and the sovereign he represents. Bligh knows the harm monopolies can do and is determined to break them. '

'If they don't break him first.' Margaret retorted.

Dafydd's political beliefs had become known to his employer. Since his marriage, Samuel had begun to take a greater interest in his children and their welfare. He had no argument about the education his sons were receiving but he did not approve the democratic philosophies that were being imparted to them. Joseph and David were of an age to be sent 'home' to be educated to their station and Annie had advanced to a stage where she could tutor her sisters, so he saw this as a good time to get rid of someone who might prove to be an embarrassment.

The termination of his employment proved to be the opportunity Dafydd had been looking for. A school of sorts had been started in Richmond in 1807. He applied for and was granted the position of Head Master. At last he had his own school where he could develop his education theories. He planned to make it the best school in the colony. It came at the best of times, he believed. The Colony was on the cusp of change and he would train young minds to take their place in this new society.

But it was not only children's minds that he wished to change. He was soon holding political meetings in the evenings. Some of the settlers had been sent to the colony for their political beliefs and others knew at first hand the injustices that existed in English law, so he found many like-minded men. The little schoolhouse often rang with the sounds of heated political argument.

Political meetings should not have been taking place in the school building, but Dafydd did not see that what he preached was against the law so they continued. Without meaning to, he became the spokesman for the Hawkesbury settlers and soon had links with like-minded people in the other settlements.

Among the Exclusives he was marked as a Governor's man and as such he was an enemy of landowners and traders. He had become the leader and spokesman for the Hawkesbury settlers. They presented the new Governor with a 'bill of rights,' aimed at restoring free trade and preventing powerful monopolies from distorting prices. They had high hopes that, with a man like Bligh, they would get the justice they sought.

But trouble had been brewing ever since Bligh had set foot in the colony and in January he struck the match that ignited it. He ordered the arrest of John Macarthur.

The speed of events caught the settlers on the Hawkesbury by surprise. While they were celebrating the anniversary of the foundation of the colony, Macarthur was bailed and, with the overwhelming support of the New South Wales Corps, persuaded Major Johnstone to arrest the Governor. It seemed a spontaneous act but Gregory Humphris, now fearful for his own future, saw the web that Macarthur had so cleverly spun, capture any who had tried to stand in his way.

As soon as the news reached him, Dafydd called a meeting. There were those who were for marching on Sydney to free the Governor, but cooler heads prevailed. They were not strong enough to take on the New South Wales Corps, which was, after all, the army of the Crown. Better to wait until Colonel Paterson returned from Port Dalrymple.

In the meantime they must show their solidarity with Bligh. Dafydd, forsaking his school, travelled all over the County of Cumberland, collecting signatures to a petition, denouncing the rebellion, and declaring Macarthur the scourge of the colony and the creator of a system of monopoly and extortion.

As soon as the Colonel arrived the petition was presented, but Paterson proved a weak leader, putty in the hands of a master conspirator like Macarthur and his clique. He confirmed the house arrest that Major Johnson had imposed on Bligh.

For his pains Dafydd was dismissed, arrested for desertion of duty and sentenced to twelve months imprisonment.

The settlers on the Hawkesbury were horrified but knew there was nothing they could do. They had no power and any action would result in similar arrests. Pressure was being put on anyone who had supported Bligh. It was a time to keep ones head down and hope that English justice would eventually prevail.

CHAPTER ELEVEN

Margaret could do nothing for her old friend. He was one of many who were punished by the new regime for their support of the Governor. Knowing how loyal he had been to previous Governors, she also worried about the fate of Gregory Humphris. She wrote to Isobelle, asking after their welfare and also inquiring whether it was possible for Mr Humphris to find out anything about the fate of Dafydd.

She was relieved when an answer arrived.

My dear Margaret,

It was good of you to enquire about our situation in these dangerous times. Thanks to Dear Humphris' diplomacy we have not been tarnished by these present events. Of course we have our secret plans should things turn nasty but we must wait and see how the drama unfolds.

Sydney Town, at present, is a sad place. With no Governor in charge there are no social events, not that there has been for some time, what with the sickness and death of poor Mrs Putland's husband. I do admire her so, even though she is so forthright. Of course the Exclusives entertain lavishly, but honest folk try not to attend. They never know what they may be asked to do in return, favours being bought and sold with impunity. Former friends now avert their eyes while passing in the street.

The women are in a worse position. They must, of course, be loyal to their husbands, which often means cutting old friends. I keep myself apart, attending only to Orphanage business and spending time being mother to my Darling Frederick. La, if I didn't have the wee lad to cheer me I would be sad from morning till night.

As to your request about your friend, I am sad to say that he has been sent to Norfolk Island. Humphris says it is a pleasant, healthy place but one hears rumours about dreadful goings on there.

What a dreary letter this is, but there is little good news to write. One consolation is that I have Humphris with me all the time, but he worries so, about the future of the colony. All I can do is hope that I am of some comfort and support to him in these uncertain times, and hopefully we will both live to see happier days.

Till then we are in God's hands.

Margaret was distressed by the sad tone of the letter. It was so unlike Isobelle who could always find a cheerful side to any event. She was also upset at Dafydd's fate. She went about her days as before, helping where she could. She knew that many of the settlers were struggling to overcome their losses from the flood. They hardly needed this upheaval among those who were supposed to be ruling the colony.

Thanks to Dafydd's tuition, she was much more aware about the shortcomings of those in control but she kept her thoughts to herself while keeping an ear tuned for any snippets of gossip among her customers. Isobelle was not the only one worried about her future.

A few months later she had a visit from a man who had lately come back from Norfolk Island. He had with him a letter from Dafydd. It was in fact two letters, one inside the other. Written on the outside of the larger one was the instruction, Read This First.

Puzzled, Margaret dutifully obeyed these directions.

Dear Margaret,

I hope you have followed my instruction otherwise you will think I have lost my reason as well as my freedom. I am, at present on Norfolk Island, a place blessed by the creator but besmirched by man, but enough of that. First the reason for the two letters. Because I am a man of learning, I am looked on with suspicion both by authority, and by the poor devils who are incarcerated here. Because I am not an ex-convict and because my crime was minor, Dereliction of Duty. (they could not pin the charge of sedition on me) I am not subject to the punishments of other poor creatures. I will say no more of that, except to say that all reformers should spend a time among the poor wretches who are the victims of a corrupt society. This has been a great school for me. I will see things differently when I gain my freedom. Back to the letters. When I asked for material to write a letter I was immediately suspect. They thought I would write some inflammatory epistle and would only give pen and paper to me when I insisted that I only wished to write to my sweetheart. They also censored the letter and had some fun at my expense. How I rave on, and I have so little paper to pen my thoughts. If you see any if my friends assure them that I am in good health and let them know that all is not lost. Those in command here are already trying to distance themselves from the present regime. The more knowledgeable among the common soldiers do not expect things to last. England must send out another governor who will punish those who have defied the king's representative. Take good care of yourself and do not make too much fun at my attempt at love writing.

Margaret sat back and looked at the familiar hand, then eagerly opened the second letter.

Darling Girl,

I miss you so and long to have you near me, to see your wonderful eyes and kiss your soft, sweet lips.

The time hangs heavy on my hands here and I count each day away from you a year.

I will serve my time quietly hoping to return at the first possible moment.

My only fear is that you too may find the time too long and find another to take my place to warm your bed.

Do not desert me, my love.

Be faithful and we will yet spend happy years together, but should you leave me I will surely die.

From your devoted lover – Dafydd.

Margaret read the letter over and over. She marvelled that a man who seemed so unaffected by women could write such an emotional letter, one that any woman would be happy to receive. How funny, she thought. This is the only love letter I have ever received and it was written in jest and as a subterfuge. She thought about her feelings for Dafydd. They were devoid of sexual emotions but they were nonetheless comforting. Many marriages had been based on less, but she had resolved to remain single and she doubted that he would ever offer marriage anyway.

In spite of the trouble in the colony the gods seemed to be smiling on the settlers on the Hawkesbury. The devastating floods of '05 had left a layer of fertile silt that made the already fecund plains reach a fecundity never known before.

Unfortunately, the lack of rain had spoilt any hope of good crops in '07 but in '08 the rain and sun came in season, pastures flourished, vegetables grew in profusion and the grain silos were full to overflowing. This made it difficult for the merchants, now in power, to plead shortages as an excuse to raise prices.

1809 began favourably enough Both rain and sun were sufficient to give promise of another bumper year. Then, in May, the first floods came. The level of the Hawkesbury rose and soon water was flowing over its banks, spreading out over the plains, inundating crops and dashing the hopes of the farmers. There was a lull for the next two months and the more optimistic began to hope. Perhaps it was not too late to plant and reap a crop, and the silt from the river would make the land more fertile than ever.

But in the middle of July a sudden, strong wind began to roar down from the mountains. It whipped up the muddy water so that brown waves formed and crashed against the levee banks. Bushes, shrubs and even large trees washed down the river causing snags and eddies. Navigation on the river became difficult. The rain began falling again. 29th, 30th, 31st. Rain, lashed by howling winds, fell night and day, a rain of biblical proportions. Some saw it as divine retribution for the things that had been done in Sydney.

One by one the levee banks broke, the muddy water escaped from its barriers and spread across the land for miles, taking all before it, fences, trees and houses. Barns where grain had been stored were washed away. Bags of precious wheat and barley went hurtling down the river. Sheep, goats and even cattle were seen struggling in the water, or their lifeless bodies bobbing up and down in the muddy cascade.

Families, caught unprepared, were swept into the swirling mass and owed their lives to the bravery of those who, at the risk of their own, rowed furiously to their rescue. Once again Margaret threw open her dwelling to those who had lost their homes. She spent her days helping where she could.

On the 1st of August she joined a small crowd on high ground and was horrified to hear the cries of a poor family who were being swept down the river, clinging desperately to the roof of their house. As she watched, its swift movement was arrested when it flowed into the path of a large tree that had been brought down, roots and all. A quantity of earth had gathered around it forming a little bank.

Turbulent water surged around it. Soon it too would be washed away.

'Help us,' the desperate people cried. 'For God's sake help us.'

Margaret noticed two men standing by a rowing boat moored by the side of the water.

'Why aren't you saving them?' she demanded, as she slid down the bank to where they were standing, helplessly looking on.

'We can't, Missus,' one of the men replied, ashamed. 'We've tried but its hopeless. The current's too strong.'

'We'd only drown ourselves,' the other assured her, belligerently. He was no coward, but he was no fool either.

Margaret looked at the family. There was a man, his wife and three children, one of them no more than a babe in arms. They were not far out on the river. They could be reached easily enough. It was getting them back that was the trouble.

'There must be some way of helping them,' she pleaded. 'We can't just stand here and watch them be swept away. Once the earth gives way they will be swept to their death. Now is their only chance.'

The men shook their heads and pointed to the swirling river.

Inspiration came. 'I think I can see a way of helping.' She shouted up to the people on the rise. 'Has anyone got a rope, a long, strong rope?'

One was found and thrown down to her. She tied it to the mooring loop then jumped into the boat.

'What do you think you're doin'?' one of the men shouted. 'Ya can't row out there on your own.'

'If you don't help me, I'll have to,' she answered, grabbing an oar.

'Hang on lass,' the other said, getting into the boat, followed by his reluctant mate. 'No need for you to go.'

'Yes there is. You will need all your strength to control the boat when we get there. You'll need me to assist the people into it. Tell the people up there to come down and hold the rope.'

Some of the onlookers had already guessed what her plan was and had come sliding down the bank and took up the slack.

The intrepid party set out. They struggled to avoid the eddies and reached the people on the roof. The men kept the boat steady by pushing it into the trunk of the tree. Margaret stood upright in the rocking vessel.

'Give me the baby then you can help the other children into the boat.'

The mother eagerly handed over the little bundle. The child was shivering with fright.

'Now, you first,' Margaret said to the little boy. 'You can help your sister. Make her move down the boat and sit in the centre.' The children, fearful of leaving the relative safety of the roof for the rocking boat, had to be encourager by their parents. Margaret spoke calmly, giving confidence. She deliberately slowed down the pace of the rescue. She knew there was little time, but was more worried that someone might fall overboard. There would be no chance of rescuing them from the river.

The wife, then the husband stepped in. The combined weight

meant they were seriously overloaded, but the distance to the shore was not long. Their offer of thanks was quickly cut short by one of the men. He could see that the earth holding the roots was breaking up. Unless they could get away before this happened they would all drown.

'Just sit still and hang on t'sides,' he shouted. 'No matter what happens don't let go. The return journey's goin' to be pretty rough. Just hang on.'

He gave a signal to those on shore and, on command, they began to pull. As soon as they left the comparative safety of the tree roots the boat began to spin, threatening to pitch them all into the river. Those in the boat screamed, terrified of being thrown into the muddy water, but hung onto the sides as they had been instructed.

Margaret, who had handed the baby back to its mother, sat between the two children, soothing their fears. For what seemed like an eternity the boat rocked and spun out of control but gradually those on the bank began to win the struggle. There were so many people in the boat that there was no room to row. The men used the oars to fend off floating trees and livestock.

As soon as the boat was near enough some of the men waded into the water and helped to bring it to shore and assist the rescued and rescuers. Cheers went up from the bank, where a large crown had now assembled. Hands were extended to help them to safety.

The mother, exhausted, sank to the ground, rocking her baby and thanking God, her rescuers and all who had helped. The children were subdued and clung to their parents. When the men had secured their boat they joined the happy crowd. The crowd parted for them, cheering them and patting them on the back.

The owner of the boat came up to Margaret. 'Lass, let me shake your hand. You're the bravest woman I've ever met.'

'That's Margaret Catchpole,' someone shouted.

'Yeah, it's Miss Catchpole from the shop,' informed another. Soon everyone was around her, congratulating her.

A voice in the crowd cried, 'Three cheers for Margaret Catchpole.'

Margaret stood, eyes downcast, while she was being cheered. She remembered other times when this had happened. It seemed to be a recurring event in her life. Once again she had made herself noticeable. Though she had sought anonymity she was never meant to be a nobody. Once more people would be talking about her.

CHAPTER THIRTEEN

'John, it is so good to see you.' Isobelle Humpris was delighted to see her old friend and benefactor. She had so much to tell him. 'We were worried about you during the floods. We did not know if you were safe.'

'My dear Isobelle, thank you for your concern. I have just been too busy to communicate with anyone. We were not too badly troubled on the Neapean, though we did have our fair share of water. I lost most of my stored grain, but I had already sent some of the harvest to market. My crops were all washed out, but thanks to the high ground, I lost little stock. Now that the ground has dried out there is plenty of feed for the rest of the year. I came to see Gregory to offer what assistance I can to the poor souls along the Hawkesbury.'

'Oh John, poor Humphris has been so depressed with all the sad news, not just the loss of life, which is tragic, but the devastation of those who have lost everything.' Isobelle sighed. 'It seems that the whole world is conspiring against them. With no Governor to protect them, those horrible Exclusives will grind them into the ground. Humphris says that they will be punished for supporting Governor Bligh. What will happen to them, John? Will they lose heart altogether?'

'Some will, but it is up to honest men like Humphris and myself to protect them until the new governor arrives.'

'Please God it will be soon and may he be a compassionate man. But I must tell you, Humphris is no longer a government man. He resigned in June. He never felt he owed allegiance to Bligh as he did to dear King.

'You must understand that he does not approve of the Governor's arrest, in fact Humphris refers to it privately as a 'rebellion' but he feels, under the circumstances, he must think of himself first. Did you hear they have arrested Mr Robert Campbell? A kinder, more honest man you cannot find. So, what else could Humphris do? He resigned and is now a private citizen. And I will be happy to resign too. The only sad aspect is that there will be no one to champion my poor orphans. The Reverend, whatever else you can say about him, was a tireless worker for my poor charges. I know he was more interested in their souls than in their bodies, but he did help dear King procure the taxes from entrances and clearances to provide us with a steady income. It is impossible to run an establishment like this relying only on subscriptions. Now that he has gone to New Zealand I am afraid those greedy men who run the colony now will cast their eyes on this source of money. Goodness knows what will happen to the children then.'

'I must admit that the floods gave me a good excuse to absent myself from all the goings on down here,' John explained. 'I was totally on the Governor's side in all this, though one would have wished that Bligh could have been a bit more temperate in his actions. Still, once Macarthur had set his mind against the man, the colony was not big enough for both of them.'

'And now they are both on the high seas, although Governor Bligh only occupies the waters of the Derwent. Humphris says that he has made a big mistake allowing Mr Macarthur to reach England before him.'

'But what else could he do? To leave the country before he had been relieved would have been a dereliction of duty. Whatever else they say, no one can accuse him of that.'

'Well, the new Governor cannot come soon enough for most of the colony, even the convicts. Humphris says there are quite a few of the Exclusive's clique quaking in their shoes. Colonel Paterson spends most of his time at Government House in Parramatta. Humphris says he now realises that he has backed the wrong horse and is trying not to make his position worse. He leaves the day to day running of the colony to Colonel Foveaux.'

She leant forward to whisper, even though they were the only ones in the room. 'They say that he is much addicted to drink, these days. La, I feel so sorry for his wife. She is such a gentle lady.'

'Do you think Gregory might change his mind once the new governor arrives?'

'Oh, no! You know what kind of a man he is. He does not make decisions lightly but once his mind is made up, nothing will change it.'

'But what will he do, Isobelle? Surely he is not going to desert us just when we need people like him? When last I spoke to him he felt he could not resign until he had acquired a substantial property.'

Isobelle clapped her hand, her eyes sparkling. She could never remain sad for long. 'That is the amazing thing. It was as if the Great Provider had had us in mind, not that He sent the floods just for our benefit. But they do say that all things work for good for those who serve Him.

'My brother-in-law was relatively unscathed by the floods but he says he has had enough. The boys were overdue to be sent to England anyway so he decided to sell up and take the whole family back home and,' she bent closer, 'this is a secret. Humphris is to buy his property.'

John laughed heartily. 'So, he will become a farmer at last. But I must say I am sad to hear that you will no longer be in charge of the orphanage. You have been so good for the girls. Still, I will not withdraw my patronage.' He looked around the room. 'Will you not miss all this?'

'Yes and no. We intend buying a small house in Sydney Town of course, but I am determined to become a woman of the land. If my dear sister, God rest her soul, could do it, I'm sure I can, too. Best of all I will have my beloved Humphris with me all the time. No more going all over the world on government business. He and Darling Frederick and I will be one little family. I will be the happiest woman in the world.'

John could sense her excitement. She was already looking forward to her future. 'And now I have some other news to tell you. Do you remember that excellent cook you found for me a few years ago?'

'I do indeed,' John replied. 'She proved to be an excellent

choice, you said. But didn't you tell me that she had gained her ticket-of-leave and had left your service some time ago?'

'Yes, but now she is famous' Isobelle beamed. 'I have just finished reading about her in the Sydney Gazette. See, My Margaret is a heroine.' She handed John the paper.

He took it, a smile on his face. He loved the way Isobelle adopted those she liked, but one glance at the headlines and he turned pale and gasped. The sudden change in his appearance alarmed Isobelle. She placed a hand on his arm and gazed into his face.

'Dear John, what ails you? Are you suddenly taken ill?'

John patted her hand and shook his head, trying to regain his composure. It was some time before he could find his voice.

'Isobelle, do you mean to tell me that your cook was Margaret Catchpole?'

'Yes,' she replied. She was mystified that this news should cause him such distress.

'She has been here all the time and I never knew?'

'Yes John. Did you know her?'

'Know her? Oh yes, my dear, I knew her. I knew her once, very well.' He passed a hand across his eyes, shaking his head. 'Been here all the time, and I never knew.' Then he pulled himself together.

'Isobelle, I must sit down. Could I trouble you for a glass of sherry? I have a story to tell you, such an amazing, wonderful story.'

He sat in a chair, still shaking his head and muttering, 'Margaret here. I cannot believe it,' while Isobelle poured two sherries, gave one to him, and took a seat opposite.

'I am ready, and oh so anxious to hear what you have to say.'

'Do you remember,' he began, 'how once you asked me why I had never married? I told you then that I had given my heart once and I felt I could never give it again. Well the object of my affection was Margaret Catchpole.'

'My own darling Margaret.' Isobelle clasped her hands in amazement. 'But how, when?'

'Oh, it was along time ago, when we were both quite young.

It was because of her that I left England. I couldn't bear to see her throw herself away on the man of her choice. But how did she get here? Was it Will Laud's fault?'

'I don't know. She was sent out here for horse stealing, but there must have been some mistake, for a more honest person I have never known.'

'Horse stealing, eh? She always did have a way with horses.' He smiled. 'And no one from home ever thought to tell me. They probably thought I would go looking for her, and they were right. But I still can't believe that we have been in the same building, that I have even eaten her cakes, and yet never met her or heard her name. Did you never mention me to her?'

'La, it is all my fault. I do so like to give special people special names. You are not often here and I probably referred to you as Our Benefactor. She would have had no idea of whom I was speaking.'

'Never mind,' he reassured her, 'I know now. Tell me all about her, what she is like, what she is doing. I want to know everything.'

They spent the next half hour sharing their stories of Margaret. Eventually Isobelle suggested that John should go to Richmond to see her.

'I don't know. I really don't know. I wish, with all my heart, to go, but how will she receive me? Remember, she is a proud woman.' He pondered the situation for some time.

'No. I have a better idea. As soon as the new Governor arrives I will petition for her pardon. It was such a brave thing that she did. Why, the Gazette calls her a heroine. Surely she will be granted a pardon for such a courageous act. I'm sure it will please a new governor to grant a full pardon for such bravery, and, if half of what you say is true, she has led an exemplary life since she came here. But you must not say a word to her until it is accomplished. It would be too cruel if it didn't come to pass. But it will. I know it will.'

'Oh yes, yes,' Isobelle replied fervently.

'You and Gregory will speak for her, I'm sure.'

'Of course. When Humphris hears all about it . . . '

'No. You must not tell anyone, not even Gregory about my former association with her. I must seem to be an impartial witness. I will admit to knowing the family, but I must not seem to have an ulterior motive in petitioning for her pardon.'

'I see,' Isobelle was disappointed. 'I suppose it will have to be our little secret, but how I will keep it from Humphris I do not know. It is all so romantic.'

It took until the middle of 1810 before the pardon was granted but, at last, Isobelle could write to Margaret.

'My dearest Margaret, Isobelle's letter began,

It is some time since we have had any communication with you. Knowing you as I do, I am sure you have been busy doing good works. You must indeed be a blessing to those unfortunate settlers who have lost so much. But while you are helping others you must not forget those who love you here in Sydney Town. We long to see you so, to that end, I am entreating you to come to us next Friday.

The enclosed money is to make sure that this time you travel in style; we do not want you walking as you once did. If you cannot find someone to take care of your shop, then close it, for I have such exciting news that I can only contain myself from writing because I want to see your dear face when I tell you.'

Margaret read the letter through a second time, smiling to herself. What could the exciting news be? Was it possible that Isobelle had at last conceived? Was her Humphris going to receive some great honour? Were they returning to England? No, it could not be that. Margaret knew Isobelle well enough to believe that returning to England was something she dreaded.

When Margaret arrived at the Orphanage she found several changes. Gracy was now in charge of the kitchen. Pearl had fulfilled her ambition. She had found an acceptable husband, graduated and was now the mistress of her own home and one hundred acres.

Frederick was a handsome eight year old, unspoilt in spite of the attention of so many females. Isobelle was immensely proud of him and enjoyed showing off his talents.

Having always had a propensity to chubbiness, Isobelle was now quite plump, contrasting with Margaret who was thinner than she had been when she was living at the Orphanage.

Having dispensed with greetings and small talk Isobelle, hardly able to contain herself, began.

'My dear friend, I have a paper here that will gladden your heart.' and, with a flourish she presented an official piece of paper.

Margaret read that 'Margaret Catchpole, spinster, of Richmond Hill' is hereby granted a full pardon.' She read the words, but their meaning hardly registered. 'Mistress this says . . . Could this be true?'

'Yes, yes, Margaret. It's true. You are a free woman! To come and go as you please.'

'Oh Mistress! Mrs Humphris . . . ' Margaret tried to speak but her eyes filled with tears. They ran unchecked as she shook her head in disbelief.

Isobelle waited impatiently till she had gained some control. 'Is this not the grandest of surprises?'

'I still can't believe it. It is so unexpected. It has always been my dream, but I hardly hoped it would come for many years. To be free to return to my home, to see all my beloved family and friends in England again.'

Isobelle frowned. This was not part of her plan. 'Are you so ready to leave us then?'

'Oh no! No. Of all the kindly people who have come my way you are surely the best, the most beloved. You have done so much for me and now you have given me the greatest gift of all.'

'I cannot take the credit of gaining your pardon. It was a gentleman who pleaded your cause.'

'A gentleman? Would that I could thank him.'

'But you can, Margaret. He is here in my parlour waiting to see you. Close your eyes and take my hand,' and she led her into the room. 'Now open them,' Isobelle commanded, stepping back and leaving the room.

When Margaret did, she looked around, nonplussed, not knowing what to expect. Near the window stood a man of average height, his back to her. As she looked he turned and spoke.

'Margaret!'

Her eyes were still focusing on the face seeking recognition, but her ears immediately knew the owner of the voice.

'Jack,' she managed to cry, before sinking to her knees, covering her face with her hands.

'Margaret,' John repeated, hurrying forward to take her hands, but Margaret would not uncover her face.

'What is it, Margaret?' Jack knelt on one knee before her. 'Will you not look at me?'

'How can I? How can I look at you, who knew me when I was an honest maid, and now I am a convict?'

'But you are not a convict any more. You hold your pardon in your hands.'

'Yet I did commit a crime. I am so ashamed. It was my consolation that you would never know of my disgrace.'

'Margaret, my dearest friend,' Jack spoke softly, taking her hand and drawing her to her feet, 'I have known and loved you since we both were young. Why do you think that I would judge you? I'm sure you had your reasons for doing what you did, but I also know that you would not have done it for personal gain. Please look at me and let me see you smile.'

Margaret dared to look at him and read in his eyes that he held her just as dear as he ever had. Jack gave her his handkerchief and she wiped her tears, composing herself then, taking his hand, permitted him to lead her to the little settle.

They spent some time filling each other in on their histories since they had last met, and the quirks of fate that had brought them both to New South Wales.

'When last I heard from you, Jack, you were going to join your brother in Canada.'

'Blame the weather. If you remember, 1792 was a particularly miserable winter. Then I got a letter from my brother telling me of the depth of snow on his farm. It was at this time that I met Gregory Humphris, singing the praises of this new country he was going to. It was a land where the sun shone all the time. The thought of so much sunshine captured my imagination so I bought a ticket on the first available boat. I never regretted my decision. I am now a man of substance and well respected in the colony. I have no wish to go home, except for a holiday. But your story! It is truly amazing. I have heard many strange tales in this country but I doubt there is another who has been condemned to death twice and lived to tell the tale.'

'I have been blessed, Jack, though at first I thought my commuted sentence was worse than death.'

'But you have changed your mind?'

'Yes. I had become content to spend my life here, but now I am so happy that I can return to England.'

This news was not what Jack had been hoping to hear but he did not show it. He looked earnestly into Margaret's face. 'I understand your elation but, before you make your decision, Margret, compare your situation here and what it will be like in England. Here you are respected, you have good friends and you are your own mistress. If you go home you will always be Margaret Catchpole – Convict. Though your friends will never judge you, most people will look on you, at the least, as a curiosity and possibly with suspicion. As for work, you will have to go back into service and be subservient to others. '

Jack's words gave pause to Margaret's thoughts. She had been so overwhelmed with the possibility of returning home that she had not thought beyond the going. Now she recognised the enormity of what it would mean. All that Jack said would be true. He father was dead and Edward, now grown to manhood, was a stranger to her. She had heard that he that he had a good position in a law house so would he be happy to have his convict sister return to remind everyone of the family shame? She had become so used to controlling her own life, could she ever go back to being at the beck and call of others? She felt not.

'Oh Jack, I was so overjoyed with my pardon that I did not think beyond the moment. Now that you have pointed it out to me I must weigh up the pros and cons.'

'Before you received your pardon, what was your greatest

wish?' John asked.

Margaret smiled, 'I have longed to own my own land and to farm it.'

'Then you will be able to do that now,' he assured her. 'Whatever you decide I will be happy for you, but may I add one other option?' He took her hand in his and began seriously.

'When you refused my proposal, all those years ago, I vowed that I would never love another woman. I have kept that vow, and it has not been difficult, for I have never felt for another as I felt for you. I still love you, Margaret. You are the love of my life and if you would say yes, I will spend the rest of my life doing my best to make you happy.'

Margaret did not answer immediately, letting his words sink in. Then she spoke carefully. 'Often you have come into my mind, Jack, and I have wished that I had met you before I knew Will. You are very dear to me and I know that you would always have my welfare at heart. However, we cannot deny the years between.

'Though I now have a full pardon, I have been a convict. I know that this will never matter to you, but it will to others. Your family will not be pleased if you should marry me. When I was but a servant girl your father thought me unfit to be your wife. He would never accept me now.'

'I don't care what my father, or the rest of my family thinks. Their opinion means nothing to me,' John protested indignantly.

'But it does to me. Even if I should never see them I would always know what they thought. If I should marry I hope that I would be blessed with children. They would never be accepted by your family. They would inherit my convict stain. Even here I am sure that, as society becomes more particular, people will try to hide their convict origins, particularly that of their mother, for you must know that women, even the best of women, have been branded as prostitutes here. I could not bear to think that any child of mine would suffer or have to hide their relationship to Margaret Catchpole.

John tried every argument he could, but Margaret was adamant. 'It seems that there will never be a right time for me,' he commented. 'First it was Will and now it is your reputation. I begin to think that you do not like me.' He was only half joking.

'Jack, never think that. If things were different I would willingly become your wife, but I cannot change the things that I have done.'

'Then, if you will not be my bride, at least become my neighbour. I have an extensive holding on the Nepean with an abundance of fertile soil. I would give it all to you but, knowing your independence of mind, please let me sell you as many acres as you feel you can manage.'

Margaret had to think seriously about this offer. Her own farm had been her dream but could she accept his offer. She knew that Jack had only suggested it because of his feelings for her, but to refuse would be a terrible insult to one who had always shown her kindness.

'I will be honoured to purchase land from you and will be happy to live near you where I can see you often. You are the truest friend anyone could ever have and I do not want to lose you again.'

Mrs Humphris, hovering outside the parlour door, held her breath in anticipation as they emerged.

'Isobelle, I know you are nearly as anxious as I was to know Margaret's decision. Well, she is not going to leave us and return to England, but no, she is not going to become my wife. Instead she is going to become my neighbour. She is going to come to the Nepean and take up land.'

Isobelle's reactions were mixed. She was glad that Margaret was not going to return to England, but she was disappointed that there was not going to be a wedding. She couldn't understand why Margaret would give up the chance to have such an eligible husband. At lest, they would be living close and perhaps things could change.

While making arrangements to hand over her shop Margaret had another pleasant surprise.

Governor Macquarie had overturned most of the prison

sentences, which had been imposed during the rebellion. Among those released was Dafydd Lloyd. He arrived one morning as she was explaining her method of book keeping to the young girl who was to take over.

'Good morning, Margaret. I see you prosper still.'

'Dafydd!' Margaret was so pleasantly surprised that, forgetting her usual reserve, she threw her arms around her old friend.

'Dafydd, how good it is to see you again. You are well?' She had felt how thin he had become.

'Yes, I am well, a little lighter I must say. Nobody goes to Norfolk Island to get fat. Thanks to Governor Macquarie I am now a free man and thought to come and beg a kiss from those ruby lips I wrote about, but to my surprise I have no need to beg.' He laughed and Margaret blushed, then took his hand and led him to small bench.

'Oh, Dafydd, so many good things have happened lately and your return is the best of them.'

'So, you have blossomed without me. Tell me your news.'

Margaret spent time relating all the events, from the flood to her pardon and her proposed new life as a farmer.

'I have good news too,' he told her. ' Not only am I a free man but regarded as something of a hero among the settlers. So much so that Mr Fulman, a landowner on the Hawkesbury, has promised to build me a school house in the settlement and grant me a small pension so that I will be my own master. Instead of tutoring the sons of rich settlers I can educate the children of convicts and poor farmers to become good citizens of this great country.'

'You believe that ordinary people can prosper after what has happened?'

'With all my heart. Poor they may be, but they are free and that freedom will not be taken from them easily. That is why I must instruct the young so that they can be masters of their own destiny.'

Margaret looked at her friend, proud that he had lost nothing of his former spirit. In fact he was more dedicated than ever. Her own dreams were small beside his.

'And in this wonderful school will there be a place for girls too?'

'Perhaps, not at first. But when people see the advantages of education some of them will want it for their daughters also. And my school will welcome them.'

It was 1811 before Margaret could dispose of her property at Richmond and take up residence in the tiny house that John had lived in when he first took up his land. She became the owner of fifty acres and began her life as a farmer.

CHAPTER FOURTEEN

The new owner of Margaret's shop was Lucy Maher, the daughter of one of the families she had sheltered during the 1805 floods. She had become a constant visitor to the shop and loved working there. She was becoming a canny business woman and Margaret was often amused to hear Lucy repeating to a customer, instructions that she herself had given. When Margaret went to Sydney she had left the girl in charge of the shop.

Lucy was distressed to hear that Margaret would be leaving, but her tears turned to joy when her father suggested that he could buy the business and she and her mother could run it. He had never gone back to farming after the flood but had made a good living ever since, hiring himself out as a day labourer. He was never without work though sometimes he was away from home for days at a time.

The plan pleased Margaret. She knew how much the small farmers relied on her stock. Mr Humphris was happy to have them as tenants and Margaret accepted an agreed amount for the sale of the goods she had in store.

After a tearful farewell to all her friends in Richmond, Margaret set out for her new home with her belongings piled high on Jack's cart and her goat tied on behind. Lucy was very fond of the dog so Margaret gave her faithful guardian to the girl. She would miss him, but he was growing old and she felt it would be unfair to uproot him at his age.

It was early Spring and the grey-green of the bush was changed. The rosy tips of the gum leaves, catching the sun's rays, flickered and shone in the breeze and the wattle was bursting with fluffy golden blooms. Bird sounds and flashes of colour added to the brilliance and over it all was the honey-scented smell of new beginnings.

Margaret prayed that this new beginning would bring fulfilment at last. Though, late at night, she sometimes thought of the gentle fields of her childhood, she was now wedded to this strange country and was discovering, to her surprise, that she was falling in love with it.

The journey was long. There were few roads in the country. They could not drive directly to Jack's property but had to take the road to Prospect Hill then a lesser one to South Creek. They followed the Creek for some distance then, crossing over a ford, headed along a track defined only by wheel ruts.

As they neared Jack's property, Margaret saw no signs of human habitation either white or black. She was now in the wilderess but somehow she did not feel afraid. With Jack beside her, chattering about everyday things, they could have been taking a ride along the road to Parramatta.

'Are there many natives in this area, Jack?'

'No. Not a great number. You will see them sometimes in their fragile canoes fishing or skimming along the river. They seem to treat it as a highway. So far they have made little contact with us, but they are friendly when they do. They are living as they always have done here, not like in the degrading way they do in Sydney Town. I hope that things can remain that way as long as possible. We exchange food and tools for fish, but I will not allow any of my men to offer them tobacco or alcohol. I have seen how these things lead to dependence.'

'You do not employ any of them on your land?'

'No. Not that I doubt their ability, but they seem disinterested. Anyway, why would they want to work for me? What would be in it for them? They seem to live happily doing only what they want. They sometimes sit in their canoes, watching us toil under the hot sun and I think they are laughing at us.'

'My friend, Dayfdd said something similar. He felt sad about their future, though. He did not think they would survive as the colony grew.'

'I fear that he is right.' John turned in his seat to look at her. 'And who is this Dafydd? Is he someone I should regard as a rival?'

Margaret laughed. 'Oh no, Jack. He is just a dear friend who loves people so much that he hasn't room for one woman.'

'That's all right then. I can accept losing you to your principals but I refuse to lose you to another man.'

They laughed and continued their conversation, Margaret entertaining John with stories of the little Welshman.

The land John had chosen was south west of South Creek and bordered on one side by the Neapean River. It sloped gently towards the water. On the higher elevation John had built his home. He had built it over a period of years using rock cut from his own land. He had been in no great hurry and took every care to make it a building of grace and substance. He had a dream that one day there would be properties all along the river and Orwell House, for that is what he had named it, would be the centre of a thriving community.

It was almost evening when they arrived and the last rays of the sinking sun were colouring the pillars that supported the wide verandah. Standing alone with a backdrop of the dark, forbidding mountains it seemed a magical place.

'Jack, it's unbelievable. It's like something from a fairy story,'

'And you could be mistress of all this.' He stood and spread his arms out, encompassing all that they could see, 'if you would only say yes to me.'

He said it, half jokingly, but Margaret grew grave, surveying all that she was rejecting. It would have been so easy to agree. Yet, in the dark recesses of her mind she knew there would always be the fear that her reputation could harm Jack or their children. Being Margaret Catchpole was a curse she would not inflict on another.

'Dearest Jack, do not tempt me. One day I may be too weak to resist, but I know it would be wrong. I lost your friendship once because you asked me to be your wife. Please do not let it happen again.'

John sat down, chastened. 'All right, my dear, I will not speak of it again but remember, the offer is always there.'

For the first time since she had met Laud, Margaret felt secure. She had her own house and fifty acres of land. They were hers and nobody could take them from her. What did it matter if her home consisted of a one room, wattle and daub hut? It was cosy, with a bed behind a curtain at one end and a wide fireplace at the other. Though there was only one small window, the door was mostly open and she had an oil lamp to light the interior at night.

Most of the many trees on her land had been cleared so, with the help of two of John's servants, she had cultivated about half an acre and planted vegetables and corn. She had a goat, a dozen hens and was planning to get a cow.

Her most prised possession was Lady, a beautiful chestnut that John gave her as a birthday present. She worked the farm alone only asking for help when heavy work was needed to be done. John's men had been with him for some years and were all ticket-of-leave or free men. They were mostly shepherds and had their own huts scattered throughout the property. They were no threat to Margaret as she seldom saw them. The farm kept her busy but she found time to ride around the countryside and visit the Whiteheads, the only other settlers within a day's ride.

She no longer hungered for the soft greens of the English glades. She had grown to see beauty in the dull, olive greens, and the shining, red tips of the trees of this new land. She now saw and appreciated the infinite shades of green that existed in what she once saw as a mono-coloured landscape.

When the corn was ripening she could imagine the fields of her childhood but the burnt, dry grass of summer was a sight she had now become accustomed to.

She shaded her eyes against the setting sun and gazed at the misty, blue- green barrier that boarded her world. There was one spot, not far from her hut, which was especially precious to her. Jack said that it was why he had built his first home where he had. The river was not very wide at this point and had a slight bend in it, where the water had been pushed against the red rocks. It was always cool and, in hot weather, after a hard day's work, she would walk down there and sit, gazing at the trees which grew layer upon layer up to the horizon.

She knew the names of many of the trees, thanks to Philip, but there were those he would never have seen. The misty-blue mountains looked as if they had been there since time began. There was a peace about them that calmed her. She felt that, at last, she had reached the point towards which destiny had pushed her so relentlessly for most of her life.

This was her world. At last her mind was at peace. This really was home. She had survived death sentences, flood, fire and rebellion. Her relationship with Jack was satisfactory. There were times when she wished she could weaken and give herself to him, but Mr Ingham's words, spoken so long ago, still haunted her. She had promised that she would never retard his advantage and she meant to keep her word.

'But I have no ambition for high office,' he had argued. 'I am content as I am. Anyway, with more than half the population ex-convict, how could it be such a disadvantage?'

'Can't you see Jack, those without taint consider themselves above anyone who was transported, be they ever so lowly themselves. Do you think they will gladly give up their superior position? Mark my words there will be many an alteration of documents and changing of names as the colony grows.'

'Then why can't you just change your name?'

'If I was just Mary Jones, unknown convict, I could perhaps get away with it, but Margaret Catchpole is too notable to disappear. My notoriety will go with me to the grave, I feel'

Jack had persisted for some time, but now he, too accepted the situation. He was just as caring and kind as ever. Better to have her as a friend and neighbour than to lose her altogether, he consoled himself.

Standing one day at the door of her cottage she surveyed the produce of her labour. Her spring planting of potatoes, carrots and onions were all ready for harvest. The corn had already been harvested and now she was preparing beds for winter potatoes, turnips and beans. The produce gave her a feeling of achievement and independence that more than compensated for the aching back, the soiled hands and the dark tan of her skin. She always wore a bonnet but it seemed to spend most of its time hanging down her back.

Black curls had escaped from the bun at the nape of her neck and blew across her face causing her to smear her cheeks with dirt as she tried to push them away. She looked at her hands and decided it was time to wash and change her soil stained dress. I'm a real farmer now, she laughed to herself She picked up the bucket near the door and began to pump water from the well in the yard.

A whinny from Lady caused her to look up. There were horses approaching through the trees. She felt rather annoyed. Although visitors were always welcome she preferred not to meet them in her work-stained clothes. Still there was no time to do anything about it now. She picked up the bucket and hurried back to her cottage, making sure that her gun was near at hand, then turned to greet her visitors. A flash of red through the trees had informed her that they were men from the New South Wales Corps.

She felt a moment of fear but forced herself to remain calm. She was a free woman now and it was their job to protect her. She watched as they dismounted and come towards her. The officer, resplendent in his uniform looked efficient, but the two soldiers did not inspire confidence. One, large, brutish looking, carried a pistol in one hand and a lash hung lazily over his shoulder. His companion was short and furtive looking. Margaret had seen his type many times in Newgate and among the convict work gangs.

The officer extracted a paper from his breast pocket. 'Are you Margaret Catchpole?'

'Yes, I am. How can I help you?'

'Are you alone here?'

Margaret noted the eager look in the eyes of the shorter soldier. She was glad there was an officer present.

She was worried, but she didn't intend showing it. 'Yes. Why do you want to know?'

'Escaped convicts have been reported in this area. They will be looking for food. Have you lost anything lately?'

'No, nothing is missing.' Even as she said this she remembered that there had only been eleven hens when she locked them up yesterday. She was not unduly worried then. The odd fowl often missed her curfew. They usually turned up next day. There was nothing in the bush to harm them. Not like in England where foxes were always on the prowl. She had not thought much about it then. But now?

She didn't give this information to the officer. She had been a convict herself and understood the desperate need for freedom that drove people to take great risks. How could she begrudge them one of her hens?

'You shouldn't be here on your own,' advised the short soldier, raking her body with his eyes. He took a step towards her but Margaret reached for the gun and held it loosely in her hands .

'I can take care of myself,' she informed them, planting her feet firmly in her doorway, defying anyone to enter.

The officer gave the man an angry look. 'I do not think it is a good idea that you should remain alone while these desperate men are around.' He would liked to have left one of his men to guard her but he had none to spare. He also pondered whether they would be any more trustworthy than the convicts they sought. He had no illusions about the men he led.

While he was debating what to do they all became aware of a horseman riding at break neck speed towards them. The soldiers turned expectantly but Margaret quickly recognised Jack.

'It is my neighbour, John Ingham,' Margaret informed them.

Nodding briefly to the soldiers John spoke to Margaret. 'You have already heard that there are convicts around, I see. You can't stay here alone. I've come to take you back to Hillcrest.'

'Jack, we have heard these rumours before. If I ran away every time I would never get my work done. I am quite safe here.'

The officer was pleased that his problem had been solved. 'I think you should listen to your neighbour, Miss Catchpole. This is much more than a rumour. There have been positive sightings.'

'All right. If you really think it is necessary I will leave but I can get myself to Orwell on Lady. It's more important that you take care of the Whiteheads, Jack. Their property is more remote than this and Nellie is near her time. Ted will need your help in getting them to your place.'

John was about to protest but the officer interrupted. 'If you could do that sir, it would be of great assistance. We were on our way to warn them but you can save us the trouble and we can join the main search party. Try and persuade them to accompany you back to your place. It will make our job easier. Protecting one property will leave us more men to continue the search.'

'Very well then,' John agreed. 'But Margaret, you must promise me that you will go straight to the house.'

'Of course I will. Just let me clean up and I'll go.'

She watched as John and the soldiers left, then went into the house to wash and change before riding to Orwell House. She emptied the water from the bucket into a basin. She threw off her soiled dress and sponged herself clean. She would liked to have taken the tin tub down from the wall for a full immersion but she had no intention of being caught naked by convicts or soldiers.

She put on a pale pink, muslin dress and her favourite shawl. She brushed out her hair and let it hang loose. She had no mirror to check but felt sure there must be a big improvement.

Taking the bridle from behind the door she called softly to Lady who trotted up obediently. Margaret had never bothered with a saddle, preferring to ride as she had when a girl. It was a matter of minutes before she was on her way to Orwell House. She arrived long before John and the Whiteheads and went straight to the kitchen to help Lottie prepare a meal for them all.

CHAPTER FIFTEEN

After a satisfying dinner they sat around a dwindling fire, the men enjoying a fine port and the ladies relaxing with a brew of tea.

'It's good of you to put us up Mr Ingham,' Nellie said. 'Are you sure it is not too much trouble?'

'John please, Nellie. We are too few to stand on ceremony.' John was happy to break the ice with his neighbours. They were new migrants and still expected old world social structures. He was sure they saw him as the local squire and hoped that these unusual circumstances might introduce them to the sense of equality growing in the colony.

'When I built this house I hoped it would become a place where anyone might call. Mark my words, it won't be long before all this land will be taken up and we will be having all manner of entertainments here.'

'Just like the old country, with all the nobs arriving in their grand coaches to stay at the grand house.' Ted's remarks were made in jest, but there was an edge of cynicism to them.

'Hardly a grand house, Ted, rather a place of hospitality. And there won't be too many grand coaches. Most of the settlers will be working farmers just like us. There is no aristocracy here.'

'Yet there are those who would have it so.'

'You mean the Exclusives? Their power is waning. Governor Macquarie is even inviting emancipists to Government House.' John had given his full support to the Governor's plans for reform.

'The poor Governor,' Ted sighed. 'He has a mammoth task ahead of him. The Exclusives had so much power. They won't relinquish it easily. Macarthur may not be in the country but his influence is still strong. I think he may be more dangerous in

England than he was when he was here. He has had practice at destroying governors and even our feisty little Scot may not be a match for him.'

They sat quietly, each with their own thoughts. They had all lived through the tumultuous times of Bligh's governorship and the rebellion. Though they had not taken sides, they could not help being affected by the events.

To break the silence Ted broached the subject that had been occupying his mind. 'These constant reports of escaped convicts, how many do you think are real?'

'With so many convicts in the colony,' John replied. 'It is to be expected that there will be some escapes.'

'And do you think that they represent a threat to the colony?' Ted enquired.

'Since the Castle Hill rebellion some settlers see rebels behind every tree. I must admit that I would not employ an Irishman. Still I think many of the reports are exaggerated. Few of the poor devils who do escape are interested in anything but freedom. What do you think of this report? Do you think it is real?'

'Oh, it's real enough,' Ted informed him. 'I think they have been around for a couple of days. I've missed a few things.'

'Yet you didn't tell the soldiers?'

'I don't think they're very dangerous. They haven't got guns or anything. They only seem to have taken enough to stay alive. They'll be moving on soon. God alone knows what the poor devils have been through. They must be living in desperate conditions to take their chances with the bush.'

'It's freedom that drives them,' Margaret said passionately. 'It is worth any risk.'

The Whiteheads did not know Margaret's history so did not understand her outburst.

'You see, I was once a convict too, so I understand.'

This revelation brought a sudden end to the conversation. They sat in silence until Nellie, who had been stifling yawns for some time, rose awkwardly to her feet. 'I'm afraid I am not very good company at this time. Could I retire?'

'Oh goodness, yes,' replied their host. 'It's time we all retired. I must apologise but I was enjoying the company. You know the way to your room? I think Lottie has arranged everything. I'll just get you a . . . '

A shot rang out and then a scream, the scream of someone in agony. Everyone froze. John was galvanised into action. 'Stay here everyone. Ted, look to your wife,' for that good lady had sunk back into her chair, clutching her throat.

John grabbed his pistol, which was kept handy on the sideboard, and hurried to unbolt the front door. Margaret, in spite of his instructions, followed close behind. One of these days, she though, he will get used to the idea that I am used to danger.

Orwell House, though not yet a grand manor, had a magnificent drive, lined with young pines and ending in a wide circular driveway with a large garden bed in the middle. In the light of the moonlight, beside this garden bed, they could see a man in convict clothes lying on the gravel. Under his skinny arm was a dead fowl and beside him lay Margaret's musket.

As they watched, the soldiers began dragging him away. Where they intended taking him or what further punishment they intended inflicting on him was best known to themselves for it was obvious that he was near death.

'I suppose we had best go back inside,' John said lamely. He found the sight unnerving and worried about its effect on Margaret. He felt her grip his arm but, when he turned to comfort her, realised that it was not shock or fear that had prompted the action. She was pointing to another soldier who was walking towards a prone figure.

Margaret, who had seen the figure a moment before it had fallen, whispered, 'Jack, it's a woman!' The soldier was using his foot to turn the prostrate body over.

'Poor devil,' whispered John. 'One of the convicts I suppose.'

Something impelled them to move towards the couple.

The soldier pointed his musket at the body and yelled, 'Hey! Come here, Sir. It's a woman!'

Margaret reached her just as another soldier, the one who had come to her hut earlier in the day, held up a lantern while the other knelt on one knee and roughly turned the woman's head.

'Oh my Gaud. It's Margaret Catchpole!' he shouted.

Margaret, shocked to hear her name, looked and saw that the woman was wearing the dress she had discarded earlier. She was slim and dark haired, and, in the fitful light there was a resemblance.

Her mind racing, she summed up the situation and acted on impulse. 'Oh Margaret, what has happened to you? Why didn't you come up earlier?'

The woman stirred but, seeing the soldier seemed to faint again. The officer came up, bent close, and lifted the convict's head. 'The woman we saw at the cottage?' he asked. 'Yes, I believe it is.'

'It's her all right,' agreed the soldier who had upset Margaret earlier. 'She must have been trying to escape from them. Do you think they have molested her?'

'Either way, the danger seems to be past. Just as well we got this fellow. No decent woman would be safe with the likes of him.'

'I'll take her back to her place now if you like, Sir,' volunteered the ferrety looking soldier.

It passed through Margaret's mind that she'd rather be at the mercy of the dead convict than this lot. She would have to do something to see that the woman didn't fall into their hands.

'No, she can . . . ' Margaret started to say, but John intervened.

'I'm afraid, gentleman, she'll have no home to go to. Look,' and he pointed to flames that could be seen above the trees. 'They have fired her house. The woman is a neighbour and she is welcome to stay here until arrangements can be made.'

Margaret acted quickly. She knelt and turned the woman's head towards her, trying at the same time to keep her own out of the lantern's light. She smoothed the woman's hair and wiped her mouth with the end of her shawl, muffling any sound the woman might make.

'Bring her into the house, John. She's too weak to walk.'

'I would like to ask her a few questions about the other convicts first,' the officer interrupted.

'Good God, Sir!' John exploded, 'can you not see that she has been through a terrible ordeal? She won't be going anywhere. You can talk to her tomorrow.'

Not waiting for any argument he bent and picked her up. She opened her eyes and seemed about to speak.

'Shh, Margaret,' he soothed. 'It is all over now. You are among friends.' He stressed the last word, hoping that she was coherent enough to get the message.

'Right sir,' the officer replied. They had one body but still had other escapees to find. It now seemed obvious that the convicts had been at Margaret Catchpole's cottage, but would have left before or after they had burned it. That would be something else. He would have to check the ruins tomorrow, though he didn't expect to find anything there. Perhaps the main party would have some information. It was getting late so it would be best to regroup now and get an early start in the morning.

'I'm obliged to you, Mr Ingham. There's not much more we can do tonight and I have to remove this body. It will be a great help if I do not have to worry about this woman, but make sure she stays here. I will need to speak to her in a day or so.'

'She'll be here for some time, I should think.'

'If you and your wife could take responsibility for her I would be much obliged.'

'Yes, yes,' John said quickly. 'You look to the convict. His presence seems to be upsetting her. We will look after Margaret Catchpole.'

But the man was beyond help. His dead body was thrown across one of the horses and the men mounted. The officer gave John and Margaret a quick salute and they headed back into the night.

The woman slumped into a chair but revived a little when Margaret brought her a glass of milk, which she drank, but it was obvious that she was exhausted.

'Come on,' John said cheerfully, 'I think you need sleep more than anything else. Can you walk?'

'Yes,' she murmured, 'but what is . . . ?'

'Don't worry. We'll talk about it in the morning.'

Margaret led the woman towards the bedroom that had been prepared for herself. No sooner had she lifted the spread than the woman, having removed her clothing, sank into the comfort of the feather mattress and was instantly asleep.

John was still sitting before the dying fire when Margaret came back into the sitting room.

'Poor woman. She's completely exhausted.' Margaret sat on a hearthrug at his feet and leant against his knee He rested his hand lightly on her shoulder.

'Margaret, whatever made you suggest that she was you?'

'I didn't say it. I just went along with it. Oh Jack! Would you let those animals take her? I don't care what she's done I couldn't have handed her over to them. Yet if they had known that she was a convict we couldn't have stopped them.'

'You are right, of course. But what happens now?'

'I don't know,' she replied. 'I can't think about it now. We will talk about it in the morning and work something out then.'

John bent and kissed the top of her head. 'Same old Margaret, racing off to save someone and thinking about it later.'

'Well, this time I haven't hurt anyone and I haven't broken the law.'

'I'm afraid you have, my dear. But this time I've done it too. I think we should sleep on it and come up with a solution when our minds are refreshed, but whatever we do she will have to stay here until the soldiers are gone. And you will have to stay too until we make your house liveable.'

He ruffled her hair then stood up stretching. 'Sleeping arrangements?' he enquired, a hint of mischief in his eye.

'It's too late to make up another bed. I'll sleep on the couch.' Margaret jumped to her feet.

'No you won't. You sleep in my room and I'll doss down beside the fire. It's about time I slept rough like I used to. I'm getting too soft.' Margaret protested, but he was adamant.

'Did you hear what the officer said? 'Your wife.' Now if only you would marry me we'd have no problems with beds.'

Margaret blushed and he laughed. 'Don't worry. I'm much too tired to get into that debate tonight. We have a more immediate problem on our hands and we both need a clear head in the morning to tackle it.'

John spent a sleepless night, going over in his mind the mess they had got themselves into. He realised, more than Margaret, the serious nature of their actions. To harbour or assist an escaping convict was looked on as one of the worst crimes in the colony. The fact that he was a prominent citizen would be of no help. He would be declared a common criminal. But it was Margaret who was in real danger. Even though she had a full pardon, the fact that she had once been a convict would be held against her. She would, at least, have her pardon revoked and in the worst scenario she could even be condemned to death.

Yet how could they have let the woman be taken? It was more than possible that she would be abused by the brutish soldiers even before she was resentenced. She would then be whipped and possibly sent to Coal River or Norfolk Island. Nobody deserved a fate like that.

They could take a chance and keep her hidden until the military had left the area, but what then? Where could she go? Wouldn't it be better in the end to let her go, to take her chances? He tossed and turned, dismissing one plan after another. There was always a 'what if.'

Just before daylight he suddenly sat bolt upright. He had the solution but would it work? It depended on a lot of co-operation. But would they all go along with it? He got up, went into the kitchen and lit the fire that Lottie had set. Over a cup of strong, sweet, black tea he went over his plan looking for flaws.

Soon after a tousle-headed Ted appeared. 'Thought I heard someone. Hoped it would be you. What really happened last night? I need to know before Nellie wakes up.'

John told him all that had transpired and Ted gave his opinion that they had done the right thing.

'The problem is, what do we do now? I have a plan but it will mean involving others. At present Ted, you and Nellie have done nothing illegal, as you were not there. But if you help now you will be putting yourself in danger too.'

'What do you have in mind, John?'

'I can't tell you yet. I have to see Margaret first. All I need to know for now is your feeling about helping this woman.'

'I can tell you frankly that I will do anything to help her find freedom, however I must speak to Nellie first. She has to have a say in this too.'

'Quite right.' John agreed. 'What I'd like you to do now is speak with Nellie, tell her everything that happened and see how she feels about helping this woman. When I have spoken to Margaret we will have a meeting in the sitting room.'

Next to arrive on the scene was Lottie, John's cook and housekeeper.

'What are you doing in my kitchen? You should have called me.'

John gave a start. He hadn't given her a thought, but of course she would have to be in on it too.

'Lottie, do you know what happened last night?'

'No. As soon as I saw those soljers I knew it was none of me business. I didn't want to get mixed up in nothing so I went to bed and stayed there. Knowed I'd learn all about it in the mornin'.'

John explained to her all that had happened and asked the important question, 'Should we give her up?'

'Never,' Lottie declared forcefully. She folded her arms across her chest and stared defiantly at him. 'I've been a convict too, remember. Before I was lucky enough to come to this place me life was hell. I'd have absconded too, given 'alf a chance. The only thing that stopped me was fear of the blacks. I didn't mind dying but I wasn't goin' finish up dinner for some heathens.'

John smiled. 'To my knowledge there is no proof that they ever were cannibals, though rumours still persist. So, if I came up with a plan to help her, you would be willing to back me up?'

'Wouldn't be the first time I've bent the truth a little,' Lottie laughed. 'Cor, pretty kettle of fish we're in now if we've get found out. S'pose you'll keep 'er here till the heat dies down then send 'er off with a few provisions?'

'Not necessarily. I must speak with Margaret first, but I'm pleased to know that you are on my side.'

Lotty chuckled. 'It 'id be one in the eye for the redcoats. If you're looking for Margaret I heard 'er splashing away in the washhouse. She'll be lookin' for 'er breakfast soon. Why don't you go an' talk to 'er and leave me to get a Christian breakfast for everyone.'

John found Margaret on the front veranda surveying the scene of last night's encounter. She had not yet tied up her hair and he felt pleasure looking at the dark curly mass cascading over her shoulders. To him she was now so much more beautiful than the young girl he had first fallen in love with all those years ago. Surely, this time, he would win the prize he had sought for so long.

'Margaret you look lovely in the morning light.'

She turned and smiled at him. 'It all looks so peaceful. Did last night really happen or was it all a dream?'

'It was real enough. We still have the evidence in the house. I spent most of the night thinking about our problem and I believe I have come up with a solution. Come and sit here and I'll tell you. You will have to decide if it is a good plan.' They sat side by side on wrought iron chairs.

'You do realise how serious this situation is, especially for you?' She nodded. She was fully aware of what might happen to her now.

'As far as I can work out we have three options. Firstly we can turn her in.'

'Never!' cried Margaret, horrified.

John nodded in agreement. 'Second, we can keep her here for a few days. We will have to keep up the pretence when the officer calls. Then, when they are gone we can help her on her way.'

Margaret frowned. 'But what would happen to her then? She'll finish up being found, that's if she doesn't die of starvation or get killed by the blacks first. I've seen absconders when they return, more dead than alive. We have got to find a better solution.'

'Which brings me to my third idea. She can become Margaret Catchpole!'

'What do you mean?' Margaret stared at him as if he had lost his mind.

'The soldiers mistook her for you. It was not only the dress. There really is a resemblance. There are not many people around here who know you, apart from Ted and Nellie. She could live in your house and soon everybody will think she is you.'

'But what about me? Who will I be?'

John took a deep breath. 'You would become Mrs Ingram.'

John watched as Margaret tried to comprehend what he had said. He waited for her response but she was speechless. He took her hand and squeezed it gently. 'Don't you see. You can change your name. We can get married and Margaret Catchpole can go on living on her farm.'

He sat back watching the range of emotions passing across her face. She would begin to form a question, then frown and shake her head. He wanted to develop his argument but knew that she must come to her own conclusion.

Eventually she just looked directly at him, opened her hands and shrugged in surrender.

'This is not just another attempt to persuade you to marry me, though I'd try anything. You have said yourself that it was only your name that was stopping us from marrying. Now we can get rid of that impediment. Just think,' he went on earnestly. 'You will be saving some ones life, giving her a second chance. Say yes Margaret.' He leant forward. 'Please say yes.'

She regained a little of her composure. 'And if I give up my name what will I be called? I mean, if I should marry you, what name will I put on the marriage certificate?

'I've thought of that too. Do you have a second name?'

'Yes, Ellen. Why?'

Ignoring the question John went on. 'You told me that you believed the vows you and Will took were real. That would make you his widow, and entitled to his name. You would not be telling a lie if you signed yourself Ellen Laud.'

'Oh Jack!' Margaret was overcome with the enormity of his suggestion. 'You must be the most gracious and the most generous of all men. You would be willing to let me use Will's name on your wedding certificate!'

John laughed. 'Why not? It was Will who kept you from me for so long. I'm sure he wouldn't mind giving me to you now.' He bent over and kissd her long and lovingly.

Margaret enjoyed the moment then pushed him back gently. 'Jack, we are making all these plans but we haven't even spoken to the woman herself. Let's see what she has to say.'

Lottie made a pot of tea and Margaret, taking the tray, went to wake the convict woman but there was no need. She had been awake since dawn, but hadn't dared to move, first because she was afraid and secondly because she hadn't a stitch of clothing to put on.

She lay as still as death, the sheets pulled up to her chin.

'Are you awake?' Margaret whispered, placing the tray on a bedside table and pulled back the heavy drapes.

The woman sat up, keeping the sheet close to hide her nakedness. Margaret said nothing. She poured tea into the two cups, added milk and sugar, handed one to the woman then sat down on the side of the bed. The frightened brown eyes followed her every movement.

'Don't be frightened. You are among friends here,' Margaret informed her.

The woman thought she had heard those words before, or did she dream them? She took a tentative sip of the hot, brown liquid.

'What happened?' she asked in a husky voice. 'Why didn't the soldiers take me?'

Margaret said. 'Ah, there you were very lucky. You see, in my dress they mistook you for me.'

'For you!' The woman gasped in astonishment.

'Yes. Do you not think we look alike?' Margaret made a pretty pirouette. It was a silly question to ask. Margaret, with her rosy cheeks and sun tanned face, the poor woman paled and emaciated.

'Oh mistress, I would never presume to be mistaken for you.' cried the poor creature.

'And yet you were.' Margaret put her head on one side and surveyed the other. 'Actually, I can see a resemblance. And don't call me Mistress. I was once a convict like you and before that a servant in a grand house.'

Margaret laughed at the look of surprise. 'Yes. These things do happen in this strange, new land. All you need is a bit of luck and a lot of effort. Now we've been trying to work out a scheme to help you, but first I must know a bit about you. When you escaped did you make any plans to go somewhere?'

'No. We had no plans. Life was so terrible and when the chance came we just grabbed it without thinking. We knew nothing about this place. We thought that if we could get over the mountains we would find a place where we could live. Some people even said there were white people living there who would welcome us. But it was all wrong. We couldn't even get to the mountains, let alone climb them. I don't think there is any way over them. There was no wild food to eat so we had to stay close to the settlements to get food and we couldn't even light a fire for fear of being seen. I have eaten raw fowl, even though it stuck in my throat. We couldn't build a proper shelter as we had to keep moving. As soon as we stole anything the soldiers knew where we were. Until last night I haven't slept for more than two hours at a time. I never thought I would, but sometimes I wished myself back in captivity. If it wasn't that I was so afraid of the lash I'd have surrendered days ago.'

She put her head in her hands and wept bitterly.

Margaret waited until she was calmer then said. 'You said we. How many were there?'

'Four. Poor little Paddy, the one who was shot, and two

others. They frightened me. I quickly realised that if ever we did succeed, my life with them would be even worse than it had been. They had had such terrible things happen to them that they are no more than animals. They have no humanity left in them. I would have been a beast of burden and someone to service them. It was only because we were always in imminent danger that they hadn't already used me.

'Paddy and I had decided to strike out on our own. We got to the cottage first. I thought I would have a better chance in your clothes. Paddy took your musket and we left before the others came. We hid until it was truly dark then headed in the direction you had gone.

'We knew that you had a horse. We decided that if we could catch it we could get a long way away fast. Paddy went to see if he could catch one of the hens, and you know the rest. I was a fool to abscond with them but the desire for freedom is so strong.'

'I know,' Margaret assured her. 'When you see a chance to be free, nothing else matters.'

The woman gazed at her. 'You too?'

'Oh yes. But that's another story for another day. Today I need to know yours. Tell me why you were sent to New South Wales. I don't mean what appears on your charge sheet. If I'm to help you I need much more than that. I was charged with Horse Stealing but that's just the facts. The real story is something different altogether. I would like to hear your story now.'

The woman nodded. 'Mine says Accomplice to Robbery but it should have said 'Transported for Stupidity,' for that's what it really was, stupidity and gullibility.'

CHAPTER SIXTEEN

My name is Martha Reynolds, seamstress of Norwich. I made a passable living making shirts for an old Jew. It was little enough but I had a room and enough food to keep me from starving. I worked from sun up to sun down seven days a week. Because he was a Jew he didn't observe Sunday and because I wasn't, I couldn't have a rest on the Sabbath.

It was hard but I should have been content, and I was until I met clever Jerry Porter. He was quite a charmer and I was flattered that he noticed me because I was past me prime. He wore flash clothes and seemed to have money to throw around.

'What's a pretty girl like you doing workin' for that old Jew?' he said. 'You can do better than that. I've been watching you for days.'

I was flattered, but I had a bit of spirit so I gave him a bit of cheek. 'I suppose you've got a better offer?'

'As a matter of fact I 'ave. Meet me tomorrow night at the Woolshed Arms. I may 'ave somefing to your advantage.' And with a wink and a tip of his hat he was off.

Of course I went. It wasn't often I was invited out, especially by a swell like him. When he arrived he had a lovely piece of Egyptian cotton.

'Could you make a shirt from this? A really fancy shirt with ruffles and all?'

'Course I could,' I said. I knew I could sew like the best of 'em. It was just that I had never been asked before.

'O.K.' he says. 'Meet me 'ere, same time next week and I'll see. If you do a good enough job you're the girl I need.'

How hard I worked on that shirt? I still had me day job so I had to do it by candlelight but I so wanted to impress Jerry, apart from the job he was offering.

When he saw the shirt he gave a whistle. 'Good, very good, I think we can do business. I'll just put it in this fancy box and tomorrow night you can take it to this address. The geezer will give you an envelope. Bring it straight 'ere to me at the Woolshed and I'll pay you. You'll see I pay better than that Jew.' And he did. He also had some more material, this time silk.'

'It's going to be a bit harder with this,' I said. 'It's hard to work on silk by candle light.'

'Then do it in the day,' he says.

'I can't. I've got to sew for the Jew.'

'Sew for that old scoundrel? Not for my girl.' He gave me a hug. 'Toss your job. You're working for me now.'

So I gave up me job. Jerry and I moved into two rooms, one of which had a large window so that I had plenty of light. I was sewing fancy shirts all the daylight hours there was, and sometimes into the night. Jerry often had to go away on work for a few days and then he would come back with more cloth.

Sometimes he was grumpy and hit me around a bit but most times he was loving. He even took me out sometimes and he bought me some lovely things. You know, after that first time, he didn't give me any of the money but I didn't care. I was that happy.

As he explained, he had to buy the cloth to fill the orders, and anything I wanted I just had to ask. I always took the shirts to one of three places and I always knew that Jerry would be there on delivery day.

This must have gone on for about three months and there wasn't a more contented woman in Norwich. I never changed the style of the shirts, just used different materials. He always packed them in these fancy boxes. When I asked where the shirts went to he just tapped me on the nose and told me not to worry my pretty head about it.

What a fool I was, but he could always charm me.

Then, one day, it was a Wednesday, I was on my way to deliver a silk shirt when a constable stopped me and asked me what I was doing. I knew I hadn't done nothing wrong so I told 'im all about the shirt. He asked me a lot of questions, about where I was going, who I delivered the shirts to and who did I work for.

I didn't suspect anythin' because the places I went to were all respectable. I even opened the box and showed 'im the shirt. He admired it and asked how much it was worth. I told him I didn't know and explained about the envelope. Finally he told me I was a lucky girl to have such a good job. Then he went on his way.

I collected the envelope and hurried back. I was looking forward to seeing Jerry and telling him all about my meeting. Jerry was in a good mood when I arrived. He took the envelope then gave me a little cuddle and told me I was his treasure. I remember thinking I must be the luckiest girl in the world.

Suddenly there was a knock at the door and three constables, including the one I had spoken to, burst into the room. Jerry reacted like a trapped rat. He darted this way and that, knocking over things. Two of the constables grabbed him and the third tore the envelope from his hand.

'It's all right,' I screamed. 'That's the payment for the shirt.'

'Is it now?' smiled my constable tearing open the envelope and taking out more money than I had ever seen in my life. He waved it in front of my face. 'Mighty expensive shirts you make.'

I couldn't say a word. I was looking at all that money and thinking of all the shirts I had made. Where was the money I should have got?

'You stupid whore!' Jerry shouted. 'You stupid, bloody whore! I knew I should have dumped you weeks ago.'

'Now, now,' said the constable 'We don't want to know your domestic problems. You just come along and tell us all about these hundred pound shirts.'

They started to drag him out. 'What about her?' he cried.

'She's just been helping us with our enquiries.'

'Helping ya?' Jerry replied mockingly 'Helping ya. That's a good one. You don't think she wasn't in on it? You don't think she wasn't part of the chain? Well, I'm not taking all the blame. You can't believe she was so stupid that she didn't know what was going on?'

My constable eyed me suspiciously. 'And what do you have to say for yourself?'

In my shock I couldn't say a word. Half me mind was still on the money and the other half was trying to accept that Jerry had been planning to leave me. I still didn't even understand what the crime was.

'Better take her along too,' my constable nodded to the others and I was unceremoniously bundled into a cab. After that it was all a blur. When the Magistrate charged me for being an accessory to robbery I still hadn't worked out what had been going on. I thought Jerry had been stealing the cloth. It wasn't until we were being tried that I found out that Jerry was a jewel thief and the customers were go betweens who passed the jewels on to a smuggling gang who used them to buy goods.

The fancy boxes that me shirts was in had false bottoms. That's where the jewellery was, and I was the stupid fool that delivered them. If I'd have been caught with them I'd have got all the blame, for you can be sure that Jerry would have scarpered. But instead, in me innocence I had betrayed them all. All four men tried to say that I had set the whole thing up but the judge was clever enough to see that I didn't have the brains to think up such a plan.

But even he couldn't believe I was so stupid that I didn't know what was going on. They were all sentenced to hang but I was given seven years transportation.

To tell the truth I still don't know that, if I had been told what they were doing, I wouldn't have gone along with the plan. So I suppose, in a way, I was guilty anyway.' Martha hung her head. 'But I often think they got the lighter sentence.'

Margaret looked at the sad brown eyes, so like her own. 'Never think that, Martha. While you live there's always a chance that things will get better. I believe every word you said and I swear, before God, that I will do everything in my power to see that you are given your chance to make a better life. We have an idea, but we have to work on it. Rest now.' Margaret laughed. 'In fact you have to, as all your clothes are being washed.'

She gave the bewildered woman a hug, drew the drapes again, collected the cups and left quietly.

Martha sank back on the pillows, a lethargy creeping over her. She didn't have to run any more, she didn't even have to think. She had handed her life over to other hands and she was sure that it would be safe.

Margaret walked slowly back to the others. She had a lot to think about. She was determined that Martha should never be handed back to the authorities. If that meant giving up her own name then she was willing to make the sacrifice. But where would it leave her? If she gave her life to someone else, who would she become? She gave herself a little shake. Time enough to think of that later. First they would have to make sure that the subterfuge would work.

All the others were in the sitting room. Nellie had been informed of what had gone on the night before. She expressed support for the convict woman, but not as forcefully as Ted had. She tended to believe, like most in the colony at that time, that all woman convicts were prostitutes. Having met Margaret, she was willing to concede that there were perhaps some who were virtuous, but as an absconder, this woman was probably a bad lot.

'Ah, here's Margaret,' John announced. 'She will be able to tell you more about the woman. Then we can make our plans.'

Margaret told the story, stressing the point that Martha was not a criminal but rather an unfortunate woman who had been duped and betrayed by the man she thought had loved her.

'Do you really believe all she says?' Nellie enquired.

'Oh yes,' Margaret assured her. 'During the time I was in prison I heard many similar stories. I doubt half the women sent out here deserve their punishment.'

'But what about the way they behave in Sydney? They aren't penitent at all, drinking and carousing.'

'Nellie,' John interrupted, 'most of those women have no homes and no other means of support. They have to pay for their food and lodgings with their bodies. As to the drinking, if my life was as hopeless as theirs I'd probably become a drunkard too.'

'Drunkenness is not confined to the lower order, Dear,' Ted informed her. 'Even the Judge Advocate is often so drunk he can hardly perform his duties. They all do it, but society does it behind closed doors. This is not England. Those who should, give no good example. Until we get a strong but fair governor things won't change.'

'There's a great deal of injustice here,' Margaret instructed her. 'If I can help one person redeem her life then I will.' She looked knowingly at John. 'I am prepared to do anything to keep that woman from those soldiers.'

John nodded in return. He understood her message.

'Very well,' her neighbour agreed. 'I can always pretend that I know nothing about it till she's gone.'

'But where will she go?' Margaret asked them.

The Whiteheads looked at each other. Where indeed? The settlement lay on a narrow shelf between the sea and the mountains. No one had yet succeeded in penetrating those mountains. Explorers who had tried reported that trying to journey over those broken, immense, sheer, towering platforms was like trying to walk over the steep rooftops of an unplanned town. One remarked that there was such a tangled mass of mountains and craggy chasm and precipices that even the crows lost their way.

'If she leaves here she will eventually be captured, die of starvation or run into the blacks,' John explained. 'If they could live off the land most of the escapees wouldn't rob us. Their one desire is to get as far away as possible from us. If they don't die they all come back in the end.

'As for hiding her in Sydney, that's not possible. There are not enough people to hide her. Apart from that, the people who might be expected to hide her are themselves assigned.'

'And an extra body would be noticed. I see.' Ted stood up and looked over the cleared ground to the mountains beyond. 'It's really one great prison.'

'Until they find a way over the mountains,' John agreed.

'There's really only one way. She must get a new identity.'

'A new identity!' Ted cried. 'What do you mean?'

'Martha Reynolds must become Margaret Catchpole.'

'What!' Husband and wife were amazed now.

'It's logical really,' explained John sitting back, relaxed as if he were discussing the weather. 'The soldiers made the first mistake so, if we confirm it, she can become Margaret.'

Nellie's eyes were round as saucers. She turned to Margaret who nodded in agreement.

'But what about you? Who will you become?'

'We'll speak about that later. What we must do now is to make sure there is nobody or nothing to connect Martha Reynolds with Margaret Catchpole.'

Margaret, having made her decision, felt calm. It could be done. The plan would work out as long as they thought it through thoroughly.

Martha Reynolds, much refreshed by a good night's sleep and a warm breakfast, could not believe, at first, the plan Margaret put before her. Finally convinced she began, with Margaret's help, to concoct a story to tell the Captain, for she would not be able to get out of giving him an account of her movements before she reached Orwell House.

Nellie, without meaning to, played her part, for about ten o'clock she went into labour. It was still early stages but it gave Margaret the perfect excuse for being out of sight during the interview.

Martha, dressed in Margaret's newly washed dress, was set up in a dimmed sitting room. John showed the Captain in and took up a position behind her, ready to come to her aid should she falter, but she knew that her freedom, and that of those who were helping her, depended on a convincing performance.

'After you all left, I thought I would do one or two chores before I left too. I was down by the hen house, checking their water when I heard Lady, my horse, making a great fuss. I peered around the hen house and was horrified to see three men trying to catch her. They did not know much about horses because she easily escaped them and galloped off towards Orwell.

'They were so intent on catching her that they had not noticed me. I fell to my stomach and crawled slowly backwards, hoping the grasses would hide me. Eventually I fell into a little ditch. Lady was gone so there was nothing I could do but stay there till night and observe them.

'They found my musket and must have decided to rest. They must have lit a fire, for I saw smoke coming from the chimney. They took it in turns to stand guard and must have raided my larder and ate and drunk the cider there. I suppose they also slept. They were probably planning to stay till night then move on, but I was planning to get to Orwell House and raise the alarm.

'When it was really dark I started towards this house but I was terrified that they might discover me, so travelled slowly. I had just reached the edge of the drive when I saw movement. I stood stock still, hardly daring to breathe. When the shot rang out I thought it was one of the convicts shooting at me. When I realised that the shot had instead come from a soldier's gun and saw the fugitive fall to the ground I was so overcome with relief that I just fainted from exhaustion and relief. The rest you know.'

The captain rose from his chair.

'Thank you, Miss Catchpole. You have been very brave and you have saved us the need for further searching. You have confirmed that there were only three men. There were four escaped, one a woman, but she must have died long before this. I wouldn't have put it past them to have disposed of her themselves for she would not have been able to keep up.

'When we examined the ruins of your house we found two charred bodies. They must have been sleeping and were caught in the blaze. They probably didn't even wake up. The smoke would have got them.' Then speaking to John, 'We will be leaving the area now, Mr Ingham. May I leave Miss Catchpole in your care?'

'Of course Sir,' John assured him. 'She can stay as long as it takes to rebuild her home. My future wife will be glad of the company. Mrs Laud and I are to be married soon. I'm glad that this danger has past.'

'Congratulations.' The soldier shook John's hand. 'I do hope I did not embarrass the lady by assuming that she was your wife.'

'No. Not at all. In fact she was quite amused. We are but waiting for friends to arrive before the ceremony will be held. It is a pity you will be leaving the area. You could have joined in the festivities.'

'One of the sacrifices we must make for duty,' the captain replied.

John saw his visitor off the premises, excusing his lack of hospitality on the imminent arrival of Nellie's baby, then called them all together to rejoice that their plan had succeeded.

There was one more person who would need to know of the subterfuge, Isobelle Humphris. To this end John wrote a letter.

Dear Isobelle,

You have no doubt heard of the incident that happened here recently. Unfortunately, for our mutual friend, her house was burnt to the ground. Margaret is living at Orwell House until it can be rebuilt. I am sure it would cheer her greatly if she could see you. She would also welcome some cloth as she has only one dress, all the rest having been burnt in the fire. I would also like to show you my house. It is almost finished and the garden is superb.

You have often expressed a wish to see it. Now would be a most opportune time. I have one more piece of information that I hope will please you. I know you have never approved of my single status. I have met a young widow of whom I have become particularly fond. She returns my affection so we intend to get married. Because I value your opinion I would like you to meet her before the big occasion. If you approve of her we would be honoured if you and Humphris would be our witnesses.

If Humphris cannot join you on this visit, do not fear that you will be compromised as there are three ladies here to chaperone you, and keep you company. Do come as soon as it is convenient.

He sent one of his workers with the letter, instructing him to wait until the lady had read it and given an answer as to when she might visit.

Orwell House became a centre of activity. Everyone went over their role, again and again. The futures of John, Margaret and Martha depended on Isabelle's reaction. Would she be deceived, if only for a short time?

Nellie had got over any reservations she had and before she and Ted went back to their own property they made John promise that, if the plan succeeded, they would get an invitation to the wedding.

CHAPTER SEVENTEEN

Isobelle frowned as she read the letter. She was happy to read that John was, at last, going to change his bachelor status, but what he had written did not suit the romantic story she had woven around him and Margaret. Who could this widow be, who had captured his heart? He had always asserted that he would remain faithful to Margaret even though he expected never to see her again.

Now, when she was living so close, he had rejected her for some hussy who was surely after his wealth and had no real affection for him. And how would Margaret feel to be rejected after all this time?

'Oh, yes, I'll visit him,' she told the birds flitting among the trees. 'I'll visit him, look over this floozy, and make him see reason.'

She expressed similar sentiments to Humphris, who took her to task. 'My Dear, you are condemning the woman without having seen her and without any evidence against her.'

'But Margaret,' she protested.

'Oh yes, Margaret. You have become too closely connected with Margaret Catchpole and her virtues. She had her chances and rejected him. He has every right to change his mind. Give John some credence for discernment. If we are to visit them you must suspend judgement until you have met the woman.'

'You are right, as usual, my Dear.' Isobelle demurred to his superior judgment, but secretly was more determined than ever to press Margaret's case.

Isobelle had been living at Waterview for some time. She found she enjoyed being mistress of her own property. She hardly missed Sydney at all. There were several large holdings not too distant from her so she had quite a social life.

She enjoyed visiting and entertaining. She was popular with the ladies of the area. When she did become tired of country life she would take up residence for a week or so at their house in Sydney. Though Humphris was no longer a government employee, his years of service and knowledge of colony affairs made him useful to Governor Macquarie, particularly as he had been in no way associated with the Exclusives during their time of administration. He was sometimes called on for advice.

Consequently they were sometimes guests at Government House. Isobelle transferred her affection from Anna King to Elizabeth Macquarie. She admired the woman's quiet efficiency, her generosity and her devotion to her, sometimes, imperious spouse. She was an island of calm.

Isobelle decided to model herself on the Governor's lady. She had brought a little of the Orphanage with her to Waterview. Gracy refused to be separated from Frederick, so took over the running of the kitchen there. She insisted on being referred to as Cook.

Joseph Rankin, fearing that life would not be so pleasant when management changed at the Orphanage, asked Mr Humphris if he could find a position for him. As Gregory had plans of turning Waterview into a grand house, he employed Joseph as gardener and groom and his wife was put in charge of the small dairy he was planning to establish.

There was no place for Jimmy, now twenty-two years of age, but that young man had ideas of his own. He obtained work on one of the boats that plied the river and hoped that, in time, he would own his own boat.

Gregory was interested to see his old friend and compare notes. He checked his appointments and found that he had business at Toongabbi. He would travel with Isobelle that far then join them at Orwell House when it was finished. He was sure Joseph would be protection enough for his wife and son.

Isobelle replied, stating a date. She made no mention of John's desire to marry, hoping that he would recognize her displeasure. She was excited about the trip and conveyed her pleasure to Frederick.

'Darling, do you remember Cookie from the Orphanage?'

He thought a moment. 'I think I do. I can certainly remember Gracy speaking about her.'

'Well, recently her house was burnt down. Remember she sent us that pretty sketch of it?'

'Oh, that one. I didn't think much of the house. More like a hut I'd say.'

'That's as may be, but it was Margaret's home and she was very proud of it. She must be very sad. How would you like to go and visit her?'

'Can I ride my horse?' he asked happily.

'Oh no Darling. It's a long, long way away. We will have to go by carriage. Now put your horse away and I will tell you all about Margaret while we eat. As I remember, Margaret was an excellent horsewoman. You and she will have a lot to talk about.' Isobelle was proud of Frederick's horsemanship, even though it caused her great fear that he might fall and injure himself.

Her, so called carriage, was really a converted four-wheeled cart. It was not as elegant as the name bestowed on it but it was eminently suited for the rough roads it had to travel. It was built for safety not for style or comfort, but Elizabeth was willing to put up with the hardship to see her special friend. She also wanted to learn, at first hand, all the goings on at Orwell House.

From the time she knew of the visit, Margaret began schooling Martha how to impersonate her. If she were going to take over her new persona then she would have to learn everything about Margaret Catchpole. It was John who had come up with the idea that if they could fool Isobelle, even for a short time, then the plan would work. Fortunately, coming from Norfolk, Martha's accent was not dissimilar to Margaret's so their voices would be similar.

'You must call her Mrs Humphris, not Ma'am. You can do a little bob, but don't hang your head. Our relationship was more that of friendship than mistress and servant and she knows I would never be subservient. Look directly at her. Your eyes are so like mine they will help the deception.'

They practised every day, perfecting their act and asking John for a critical assessment. Margaret made Martha conversant with the names of relevant persons and also thought of a number of topics they should talk about.

'But you probably won't have a chance to say much,' John assured her. 'Isobelle usually likes to monopolize the conversation.'

John was waiting on the veranda when the carriage arrived. He walked down the steps to greet them.

'How lovely to see you again. Young Frederick, how you have grown! He is growing into a fine young man, Isobelle.'

The boy jumped down and shook John's hand. He was eager to explore a new place. John helped a very stiff Isobelle down from the carriage.

'La' John, you live too far away. In future you will have to visit us. I do believe it will take me a week to get the stiffness out of the bones.'

'Then you must stay at least two weeks before you make the return journey.'

'Do you have horses, Uncle John?' Frederick asked hopefully.

'Yes, I do. Perhaps you would like to go around to the stables with your groom and after he has seen to your horses I will arrange for you to see mine. There is one special one called Lady. She belongs to a friend of mine.' He turned to Isobelle. 'That is, of course, if your mother will let you.'

'Yes, yes. Run along Darling, but be careful.' She turned to John. 'He's such a fearless boy, particularly where horses are concerned. Gregory thinks he will make a great horseman.'

She watched him proudly as he moved away then turned eagerly to John. 'Now, tell me everything that happened on that dreadful night. I want to hear everything, but I was afraid the details might be too horrendous for his young ears.'

Though she was even more curious about his plans to marry

she was determined not to bring up the topic.

Knowing that she would enjoy the drama, he told her, in graphic detail, most of the events of that night but left out any reference to Martha.

'To think,' she said dramatically, 'that I am standing on the very spot where that convict was shot.' She looked at the ground, hoping, perhaps, to see a sign of blood.

'But Margaret! What a terrible experience for her. And to have her little house burnt to the ground with those villains inside. She sent me a sketch of it, you know. Is she terribly upset?'

'Come and see for yourself.' John suggested. 'She is inside waiting for you. She is anxious to hear all the news about the Orphanage and your new life at Waterview.'

Martha, in a dress Isobelle knew well, lowered her eyes and made a slight bob. Then, following Margaret's instructions, looked Isobelle full in the eye. 'It's good to see you again, Mrs Humphris.'

Isobelle hurried forward and drew her former servant to her ample bossom.

'My dearest Margaret, what a dreadful time you have had. And your dear little house that you sketched for me, all gone. I should have come sooner to see you.'

Martha began to reply, but Isobelle went on. 'I shuddered with fear when I read John's letter. Dear Humphris has reassured me that such incidents are rare, for you know that I, too, have become a country lady at Waterview.

'That scoundrel my brother-in-law has lately left for England with his new wife and his children. I hope he does not inflict as many children on her as he did on my dear sister. We also have a small cottage in Sydney, but spend most of our time in the country. Darling Frederick can't wait to become a country gentleman but we are determined that he will be educated here, not in England. Your good friend, Mr Lloyd, has opened his own school at Richmond so, when he is a little older, Frederick can attend.

'Gracy is with us. She came as cook. She says she will never marry, just wants to stay with me and Frederick. She is so devoted to him. You must come and visit us. You could come back with us and stay until your house is ready. You will find Waterview much changed. Clever Humphris sold all his little farms and we are quite wealthy now so I can indulge myself in little luxuries. I love playing the lady of the manor.'

She prattled on, so that Martha had little to do but nod and smile in agreement. Eventually John interrupted.

'We have another visitor I wish you to meet, Isobelle.' Then turning to Martha. 'Margaret, would you please go and ask Mrs Laud to join us?' John noticed the tightening of Isobelle's mouth and smiled to himself. She had made it obvious, by omission that she did not approve of his desire to wed. What a shock she was in for!

'Well. How do you think she looks?'

'John,' she replied, 'she is so thin, and she seems to have aged. Have the recent events caused this or is all this farming aging her? Is she well?'

'Do not fear, she is perfectly well, but I agree, she has changed.' He turned as the two women entered.

'Ah, there you are ladies. Isobelle, allow me to introduce Ellen Laud, my bride to be.'

Isobelle turned; ready to dislike this woman on sight. What she saw completely unnerved her. She was so astonished that she had to grab the back of a chair for support.

She took a step back the better to make sure that her eyes were not deceiving her. Totally nonplussed she looked from servant in her workaday dress and severe hairstyle to the other, in soft pink, her curls becomingly arranged on her head.

They all burst out laughing at her bewilderment.

Eventually John explained. 'Isobelle, forgive us? But we had to see your reaction to Martha. Only then would we know our subterfuge would succeed.' He began to tell her the full story of the night when the convicts came.

It took some time for her to take it all in but she was happy that at last John and Margaret would be together. It was so much more exciting than she had ever dreamed of and she was thrilled to be a part of it. Her happiness at knowing that her two favourite people were, at last, together, overcame any scruples she had about the deception.

'It's all so romantic. Better than anything written by Clara Reeve or Fanny Burney. Of course I will keep your secret and when I explain it to him I know that Dear Humphris will feel the same. He will be as delighted as I am at your happiness.'

'We have one more request to make, Isobelle. Our wedding is to take place this Saturday. Will you and Humphris be our witnesses?'

'John, dear John,' she gushed 'and my dearest Margaret, no Ellen, oh what am I to call you?'

'Yes Jack,' Margaret asked, 'what are people to call me, among friends, I mean?'

'I don't know about anyone else,' he replied, drawing her close, 'but from this moment on, I am always going to call you Darling.'

THE END

JOHN INGHAM: lived a happy married life for twelve years until he died suddenly from appendicitis.

ELLEN INGHAM: (Margaret Catchpole) had two children.
After her husband died she ran Orwell House until her son, Jonathan was married.
She retired to a cottage in Sydney Town.
Although she did not mix in society she became well known for her charitable works, especially for convict women and their children.

MARGARET CATCHPOLE: (Martha Reynolds) spent the rest of her life keeping a small store at Richmond. She was well known in the district for her work as midwife and nurse.
She died from influenza, which she contracted while nursing a shepherd.